The Girl in the Tree

The Girl in the Tree

ŞEBNEM İŞİGÜZEL

Translated by **MARK DAVID WYERS**

amazoncrossing

Text copyright © 2016 by Şebnem İşigüzel
Translation copyright © 2020 by Mark David Wyers
All rights reserved.

Previously published as *Ağaçtaki kız* by Can Yayınları in Turkey in 2016. Translated from Turkish by Mark David Wyers. First published in English by Amazon Crossing in 2020.

Published by AmazonCrossing, Seattle

www.apub.com

Amazon, the Amazon logo, and AmazonCrossing are trademarks of Amazon.com, Inc., or its affiliates.

ISBN-13: 9781542041461 (hardcover)
ISBN-10: 1542041465 (hardcover)
ISBN-13: 9781542041485 (paperback)
ISBN-10: 1542041481 (paperback)

Cover design by Philip Pascuzzo

Printed in the United States of America

First edition

*Dedicated to all the children and youth who have lost
their lives.*

A walnut-shell, elegantly polished, served her for a cradle. Her bed was formed of blue violet-leaves, with a rose-leaf for a counterpane. And here she slept at night.

"Thumbelina," H. C. Andersen

1

IN YOUR ABSENCE

This is a story of freedom and love. The story of two young people ailing in heart and soul. I was one of them.

That night I climbed with effortless ease the tree where I was going to live. You might say it was a bit of a miracle. When I say "miracle," I don't mean that living in a tree is miraculous. I mean how swiftly I clambered up its trunk. It was as if a powerful wind whisked me right to the top, throwing off my pursuers. Indeed, I was being pursued, and I was trying to run away. But from whom? I was going to say that I was fleeing from life itself. But I fear that you would mock me for the little experience I have of life.

I was about to turn eighteen years old. That night when I found myself perched high in the branches of a tree, I had run all the way from Cihangir to Gülhane Park. My backpack, which contained only a few personal belongings, hadn't slowed me down in the least. Who knows why I even bothered to bring it. In any case, I hadn't planned on climbing a tree and staying there. It just happened. I was racked by despair, at a loss as to what I should do next. I'm tempted to say that I'd lost my mind, but if that had been the case, I would've at least found some solace in madness. And, as you will see, not once did I lose my grip on reality.

People are nothing more than the accumulated stories of others. In particular, the stories of their mothers and fathers. I'm not talking about genetics—this is purely a matter of the spirit. Try with all your might to resist, but in the end, you turn out to be no different from them, in your very essence and being. While my thoughts may be as scattered as my breathing is labored, what I want to tell you is nothing like that. It is a singular whole, complete. Well, in my mind that's how it is.

Perhaps knowing that I am the girl in the tree will leave you feeling confused. Not a problem. In fact, all the better. You too should be a little confused because that is my constant state of being. Life itself is confused. Even Robert Pattinson, the vampire, said, "I'm definitely very confused." So be it. I have a poster of him in my room. As I was leaving, we exchanged glances.

He didn't look at me as if to say, "Wait! Where are you running off to?" To the contrary, he seemed to be saying, "Well, fuck off already!"

This is the story of a seventeen-year-old girl who wound up high in the branches of a tree one night. But there's more to the story than that. You have to step back if you want to see a picture more clearly. You have to start with the good times. For instance, the night of July 23 in 2011. Actually, that wasn't the best of nights, as that was when Amy Winehouse died. I had a picture of her troubled, tragic face as the wallpaper on my phone. The background on my laptop was a photo of Robert and Kristen, who became a vampire later on. But don't try to draw any connections between how I ended up in that tree to vampire lit because there aren't any. In fact, I'd lost all interest in both Robert and teenage vampire stories. An act of rebellion is what led me to where I am now. Those posters, which needless to say are so out of fashion now, are only there because I didn't bother to take them down. Vampires don't rebel, they suck blood.

But Amy is different, and she always will be. That's because she rebelled and then she died.

I'm here for only one reason, and that is to die before death comes to get me. I may have said this already, but I'm going to say it again for the simple reason that I'm definitely very confused: It's a miracle that I got all the way up to the top of this towering tree. The trees here have been here for centuries. They say that the park used to be part of the palace grounds. Do you know how smooth the trunks of plane trees are? It was as if my hands and feet stuck right to its beautiful, bare trunk. There's no other way I could've climbed it. I know Gülhane Park well because for years my father worked at the Archaeology Museum, which is right behind it.

I'd taken off my red Toms sneakers at the bottom of the tree, and now they were sitting there like a tiny stain on the grass. There's this tired old story that they always make us read in our literature classes at school: driven by its love for a rose, a nightingale impales its heart on a thorn of the rosebush and the blood runs down, becoming the deep red found at the base of such thorns. If Amy had heard that story, maybe she would've written a song about it because her love always went unrequited and she sang her laments like a nightingale. In the end, however, the pain broke her heart and she died. In a way, she rose up in revolt against life and all the callous ignoramuses around her. Admittedly, that was a pointless comparison. I mean, the one before, the one about the nightingale, the rose and the red Toms shoes. But you see, it's not easy to write. Thinking is the hardest part of all. Put crudely, I guess what I was really trying to say was this: Lying under the tree, my red canvas shoes looked like two drops of blood that had started seeping into the ground. A stain.

After seeing my shoes so far down below me, I felt certain that no one would find me so long as they didn't look up. And even if they saw the shoes, it would never occur to anyone that whoever had left them behind would now be nestled in the upper branches of the tree, hurled up there by the violence of life. The world below, the streets and sidewalks, struck me as being particularly dangerous once I found myself high up in the tree, and the thought of getting lost down there filled me with fear. If I'd stayed down below, I would've struggled to stay alive, and in the process I might have lost all sense of humanity.

I thought about how practically difficult it was going to be to live in the tree. I wondered how I'd come up with the idea. Books, perhaps? If I'd found a deserted island, would I have chosen to live out my life there? Or spend the rest of my days in the belly of a whale, like a prophet? No, I'd grown out of my copycat days long before. So why had I clambered up a tree like a cat fleeing for its life, a snarling dog nipping at its heels? Never mind that. The important thing is that I was able to climb it, all because my friends died. But I can't tell you about what happened. Not yet. After all, I don't know what kind of person you are. On that note, I once saw a tweet that I liked:

"Maybe you're one of those people who have a prickly pine cone for a heart."

I don't want to cry now. When I think of my friends, I break down in tears.

Let me tell you about something else: No one can climb a tree in a blink of an eye. But ever since Amy Winehouse died four summers ago, I've been learning how to slackline, which may have helped me in my miraculous ascent. While you've most likely heard of Amy Winehouse, I'm not so sure you know much about slackline, so let me briefly describe it. Slackline involves tying a strap between two trees a little ways off the ground and then balancing on it, not unlike a tightrope walker. I first saw it on YouTube. My father, who is adept at making such contraptions because of the work he does as an archaeologist, helped me put together my first setup with some ratchets and a strap we picked up in Karaköy. I started practicing, rain and shine, and I signed up for a mountain-climbing class as well, which required that we do slackline as preparation. You might be thinking, "Well then why are you talking about miracles? You were better trained than anyone else to climb up it." That's a logical point. But still, climbing a tree, and a very tall one at that, poses its own unique challenges, and even if I had gone through some training, it couldn't have prepared me for shimmying up a tree trunk like a sheer cliff without a rope, carabiners, or spikes. Also, I'd had to quit the mountain-climbing club because it turned out to be far beyond my "modest means," as they say. Those were the days my family plunged from being middle class to hitting rock bottom. You have to admit that to a certain extent, happiness is related to whether or not you have any money. We were a bit better off the summer that Amy Winehouse died; at the very least, we were able to pay our bills. If we'd known that we were heading for darker days and that our last free and easy summer was slipping away, we would've enjoyed it as best we could.

An Amy Winehouse concert was scheduled for early that summer in Istanbul, and I already had my ticket. Truth be told, my aunt, who was a journalist at the time—or to put it another way, she was still allowed to practice journalism in those days—had said to me, "I'll find you a ticket." Things were always like that. We sponged our way through the world of the arts and culture. Sometimes she'd send me along with a photographer. Handing me a flash card for his camera, he'd gesture toward me and say, "She's my intern," and even though I looked rather young, they'd let me into the events. Because they were good people. Because good people worked in the industry. Because even the name of the publishing company was good: Pozitive. Mehmet Ağabey worked there. He laughed and smiled as innocently as a child, and when he laughed, his eyes lit up. He ended up dying too. But it was cancer that got him.

"Living in this damn country is enough to give you cancer."

That's what my aunt said at his funeral.

Suffering is like a jammed lock that gives you no end of trouble. But when you do finally get it to click open and for the briefest of moments you feel a sense of relief, suddenly you fall to pieces, just like me. Not to ramble on like some geezer, but the fact of the matter is that I was raised by one—my grandma, to be precise—so sometimes I do tend to babble. The others my age, like my best friend Pembe, would put things differently, using a younger idiom. They wouldn't even use the word "idiom" in the first place. Only a geezer like me would say such a thing. Oh, Pembe!

"Pembe . . . What a lovely name." If you ask me, Pembe—meaning "pink"—isn't really so special. But everyone said it was a fine name. Our teachers from France called her "Mademoiselle Rose."

She liked it, so we called her Rose too. We were the only ones who knew why her name was Pembe.

When Pembe's mother went into labor, it was their housekeeper who took her to the hospital and looked after her for two whole days, all because that's how long it took for her closest relatives to show up, including her husband. You see, Pembe's father, who was known in the tabloids as a bit of a player before he got married, was off scuba diving at the time. After she gave birth, Pembe's mother said to him over the phone, "Mehmet Bey, it's another girl." I guess she addressed her husband as "Bey" because he was eighteen years her senior. Mehmet Bey couldn't hide his displeasure when he found out that he was now the father of yet another daughter. He said that he didn't want his wife, who had graduated from the Austrian High School and worked for a while as a flight attendant, to have more children because, in his words, he loved her so much and three children was more than enough. At the same time, however, he said with male douchebag finesse that before all was said and done, he'd need to have a son. She asked him, "So, what do you think we should name her?" By asking that question, she was trying to win his forgiveness for having given birth to another girl. Curtly he replied, "Whatever you want." Afterward, she was so upset that her milk dried up. Day and night she murmured, "What are we going to name this child? What on earth are we going to name her?" The housekeeper, whose name was Pembe, settled the matter once and for all:

"Names don't get worn out, now do they? Name her Pembe. She'll be my namesake."

And so that's how Pembe's mother got revenge on her husband for breaking her heart. By way of explanation, she said, "If it hadn't been for Pembe Hanım, I would've had to give birth at home, and both my daughter and I probably would have died. I forever owe her a debt of gratitude." That's how Pembe got her name and that's what it has been ever since.

But then there was the matter of her husband's wealthy family. "You mustn't," they said, "sully our family heritage like this. We will not tolerate our grandchild being given such a lowborn name." This all happened in 1998, meaning that this particular father, who above all wanted a son after having sired two daughters, is alive and kicking. And when I say "father," allow me to refine the term by saying that this jackass of a womanizer broke a pool cue over his girlfriend's head at the turn of the previous decade. This is a man who was once a confirmed bachelor, as modern as the Mercedes he drove. He pestered his wife, hoping to break her determination, by saying, "At the very least, we should give her a middle name as an alternative."

"How about Rosy Pembe?" his wife offered. "Or Pembe Pink?"

Pembe had told us the story of how she got her name one day after school as we dug into a basket of fried potato wedges at the Star Beerhall in Beyoğlu. At first she chuckled from time to time, but by the end of the tale, tears were pouring down her cheeks. That was the first time we'd ever seen our Pembe—our Rose—break down like that.

The world is made up of stories. If it wasn't, life would be insufferable. Who knows why I was drawn to Pembe's story or why I felt a need to share it with you. Perhaps it dovetailed with something inside of me? Dovetail . . . That word is an heirloom passed down to me by my grandma. Maybe it rings hollow, signifying nothing. Pembe's story,

I mean. The story of Amy Winehouse's life is nothing like that. It filled to overflowing—and I'm sure that by now you've picked up on the irony of her last name. I was counting down the days to when I would watch her onstage and take in that story with my own ears. As usual, the ticket had been arranged through Freebie Flights. (It sounds forced when I say that, doesn't it? "Freebie Flights." But it rolled right off the tongues of my best friends Derin and Pembe.) Before coming to Istanbul, Amy was going to perform in Belgrade. She stepped onto the stage there and looked at the audience as if she'd recently risen from her grave. After that night, the rest of her tour was canceled. I wasn't one of those people who cursed her name for canceling her other shows. Quite the opposite. I was angry at the people who'd let her go onstage in that condition. Sure, I'm wise beyond my years. People call that "maturity." But I swear, it's not. It's anything but maturity. A mature girl my age would not find herself perched high up in one of Gülhane Park's stately plane trees in the middle of the night. No, she would settle her accounts with life while her feet were planted firmly on the ground.

For now, I'm not thinking about what I'll do next. Still, I feel like I've promised you something. Everything I've been through has happened because of my nature, because of my sense of responsibility. My mother would disagree, saying that if I were more responsible, I wouldn't have lost my scholarship. In her mind, responsibility meant working like a mule and studying harder. Slaving like a damn mule . . .

I was a student at the Hunchback of Notre Dame High School. That's what I called the place. And that's part of the reason why I lost my scholarship. You see, one day my thoughts were wandering and I wrote the name of the school on one of my homework assignments like that: the Hunchback of Notre Dame High School. With a guffaw that was reminiscent of a braying mule, Pembe said, "Well, just be glad you didn't write what I call it: Our Virgin Merry Cunt High School."

What do you expect from a ninth grader? Sharp, witty, highbrow humor? Not going to happen. Pembe and Derin were laughing. I was sitting there in silence. My grandma could swear up a storm, so I was used to it even if I didn't indulge much in profanity myself. The sole reason I chose the two foulest-mouthed girls at school to be my friends was because I trusted them in the same way that I trusted my grandma.

On the very first day of class, Pembe's and Derin's paths crossed when they got into trouble for swearing. They were both being punished in front of the headmaster's office, and from that day on they were inseparable.

Pembe said, "Okay, but what kind of name is 'Derin'? In the sense of 'deep,' right? So what's so deep about you?"

"My intellect."

"You sure about that? Try this: Take the last letter of 'intellect' and use it to start a word that rhymes with 'swat.' That'll give you the answer you're looking for."

"Ahahahaaaa."

As they stood there in front of the headmaster's office balanced on one leg—what a ridiculous form of punishment!—whispering to each other, Pembe found her soul mate. She'd gone through life trying to find ways to exact revenge on the universe for the name she'd been given, and now she was one step closer to achieving that goal.

The two of them posted a video of themselves on YouTube that, from beginning to end, showed them bantering back and forth with the vilest swear words they could dredge up from the depths of their minds. Actually, "showed" may not actually be the best word, as they were wearing paper bags over their heads in the clip. They even managed to make a bit of money when a shampoo ad was cut into the video, which also included Derin's explanation of how she got her name.

It all starts with Derin's family living in a basement apartment in ritzy Nişantaşı as the caretakers of the apartment building. Fade in music now, as this cheesy number is Derin's go-to story. You know how it is: there's always a tenant who takes it upon themselves to look after such caretakers and their children. This particular tenant, a lonely woman living in apartment 9 who didn't have children of her own, helped Derin and her siblings with their homework, took them to the doctor when they got sick, and gave them presents on the holidays. She was the one who named Derin when she was born. Since the woman had helped them out so much, the family couldn't bring themselves to object when she came up with the "perfect" name for their newborn baby. When Derin's father went to get his daughter's birth certificate, he slipped in an additional name. "Let me see that document," the woman from apartment 9 snapped when he came home with the paperwork. As soon as she saw what was written there, she exclaimed, "Get rid of that name! I told you what you should call her." Being told to bow down to someone else's wishes is a guaranteed recipe for exasperation, and revolt is the natural response. So, all because of that woman, they moved out of the apartment building. Sometimes kindness can bring about more harm than the most malevolent acts. That's a good demonstration of how, at heart, goodwill can be the greatest of evils. As they were moving out, the woman cried out after them, "Ingrates! As if I didn't give you everything you wanted!" Most likely she was sick in the head.

"Well, there you have it. The road to hell is paved with good deeds and names." That's how Pembe responded between hiccups as she stabbed a potato wedge into the glob of mayonnaise at the bottom of the basket.

After that, Derin's father was hired on as a janitor at the school, and when she passed the entrance exam, the board of trustees awarded her a scholarship. Once in a while he'd call out to her at school, using the name he'd given her: "Emine, Emine! Hey, Emine!" But his efforts were in vain. Thanks to her high-society appellation, Derin was able to hide the fact that she was in fact the daughter of the janitor.

Derin said, "Don't be fooled into thinking that the school is all about generosity and being good-hearted." We were still at the Star Beerhall; the waiter brought out a second plate of potato wedges, and we had moved on to our third round of beers. The mugs were so heavy that our hands trembled when we picked them up. Pembe and I glanced up when Derin said, "You know why they let me stay? Because my father has got dirt on someone there. A real sex scandal."

"Who?"

"I don't know. But it must be a big deal because I'm on a full scholarship and they'll let me keep studying no matter how many classes I fail."

We didn't fit in at the school one bit, always drifting through campus as if we were planets that had been knocked out of orbit. We were misfits, outcasts bound ever closer together by the punishments the system unleashed on us.

Blackmail wasn't in the cards for me. When I put it like that, it sounded funny. And how we laughed! We laughed far more than any situation called for. In a last-ditch effort to keep my scholarship, I signed up for the school's writing competition. I signed up but lost. Not only did I lose, but my novel was subjected to the harshest review of all. Before taking part, we'd been asked, "Once the competition is over, do you give permission for your work to be subjected to critical review, whether positive or negative?"

Naturally, people have no idea what may befall them in sickness and in health, or on their best or worst of days. But I remember that day. My hand shot up so fast that it seemed to be in danger of snapping off my wrist. Not once did it occur to me that I might lose the competition; even more unthinkable was the possibility that I'd write the worst submission of them all. As a rule, whenever people start something new, they're incapable of thinking straight. Everything starts with an amorphous cloud of dust and gas, nothing more. I glanced around at the other students, grinning like a grilled sheep's head as I waved my hand, enthusiastically yet blindly showing my support for the idea of critical reviews. At this point I should note that cooked sheep's heads do, in fact, grin. Our biology teacher, who was French and had first seen sheep's heads in the windows of the butcher shops in Istanbul, explained the neurological reasons underlying the phenomenon of the dead sheep grin. Later someone showed him the red carnations that butchers stick into the buttholes of the slaughtered lambs hanging in their storefronts.

"Turkey," he said, "is a very interesting country."

"Like we've never heard that line before," Derin muttered as she drew a picture of a skull in her notebook.

The teacher said, "Mademoiselle, what was that you said?" He was a prime example of a fascist who paints himself as a conservative.

She replied, "You heard what I said. So why are you asking?"

That's how *mon amie* Derin ended up in the headmaster's office for the second time.

Still, I wasn't uncouth like Derin and Pembe. My father was fond of that word: "uncouth." Whenever I said it, he'd laugh. "Oh, sweetie," he'd say, "the old mothballed trunk is chattering again . . . You've got to keep up with the times."

"How about if I lick up the times instead?"

"Lick them up and swallow them down?"

I was always baffled by the inscrutability of time. Something else I found incomprehensible was why I hadn't won the writing competition. My entire being was shaken to its core. That was the end of my scholarship. Even now as I remember those days, I can feel the disappointment deep down in my bones in a way that can best be described as uber, ultra, mega . . . I think you get what I'm saying.

Her lips curled into a sneer, our literature teacher said, "When you were cranking out that novel of yours . . ." But when she said "cranking out," I could've sworn it sounded more like—let me put this delicately—"crapping out." A few moments later, she added, "I don't know what you were thinking when you were working on it, but . . ."

I thought, *Ha! I was thinking of my mother's privates!*

After class, as Pembe and Derin tried to console me, they also completed the teacher's sentence with a sexist slur that often rolled off their tongues. I don't refer to Pembe as "Rose" here because after all she went through she came to appreciate her name and, in fact, truly came to embody it—in all its pinkness. In those fine days, we used to laugh and say things like that. Those fine bedraggled days. Those bittersweet days when we were on the verge of outright rebellion.

If I'd been able to articulate my hurt and anger "in proper terms," I would've written the best novel and won that scholarship.

In the end, the most pretentious girl at school won it. The saying goes that even lies express some truth. Her? None at all. First of all, she didn't even need the scholarship, while I was worrying about how I was going to pay the following year's tuition. I know that I may have caused some consternation because I wrote the book for the sake of a scholarship. But please don't confuse me for those people who dream of what they're going to become through writing rather than what they're going to put to paper. True enough, I wrote to win a scholarship instead of studying harder to improve my grades. But the reason is simple: I wanted to write, to express something.

For me, the world was full of injustices.

"It's the downtrodden who will create the world anew!"

I saw that scrawled on a wall. Why am I telling you this? Because I get the feeling that you think I write whatever comes to mind. No, that's not quite true. I mentioned it because our literature teacher said about my book, "This is not how novels are written!"

We should write about our thoughts, not our feelings—right? By thinking things out. At least, at present that notion has taken hold of my thoughts. Sentences, words, letters, even those pinched commas and anal full stops—they can all pick up on your hesitation.

In my mind, I replaced the word "downtrodden" in that sentence: "It's the writers who will create the world anew!"

And that's how I answered the question "Why did you write this novel?" I should've known from the start that I'd lost the competition, in which a mere fourteen students participated out of the hundreds at the school, when I saw the cynical look on the teacher's face as she read my answer.

We should all agree that it was such heartbreak and injustice that killed Amy. And in the end I found myself where I was because I was running from that pain, the world, my "fucked up life," as my two more verbally graphic friends would've said. All these things happened long after that half-assed writing competition and the summer that Amy died. We hadn't rebelled yet. After the rebellion, a new world built upon tear gas and clouds of dust started to come into being. But that world didn't exist yet. That's why I'm in this tree. In other words, you're not listening to the ramblings of some teen. Instead of the term "ramblings," I'd rather use a sexist swear word. I'm here because I don't feel at ease as a woman on the face of the earth and I'm a feminist through and through, even though I may not know about the meaning of this or that, or devour books and pamphlets. That's the way it should be. My friends swore because they didn't know how else to deal with the world either. But I'm going to get my thoughts straightened out here. They never got the chance.

To throw another mothballed word at you: I'm *sequestering* myself!

Or, to use the modern idiom: I'm going to *reset* myself!

I laughed to myself when I said that. When we laugh, it helps us pull ourselves together, like how the wind carries something from one place to another. Laughter is the wind of the mind and soul—it picks you up and whisks you far away. Laughter signals that the place where you are now is no longer a good place to be. The wiring is fried. A belt has snapped. The brakes are overheating and you can't stop.

My poor mother, who was one of the biggest losers in life, used to say to her patients, "Laughter is the cheapest medicine." When I say patients, I mean overweight people. You see, she was a dietician. People with a weight problem shouldn't take offense. If I were in their shoes, I'd resist the fascism of body size. Don't fall into that trap. I'd push back against the idea that people can use your body as a source of employment and make a living by forcing you to adhere to a certain standard. Take Pilates, for example. It was used in World War II for bedridden soldiers. Are you bedridden? You can do the same exercises on your own without having to pay into the industry. As you may have noticed, I've got something to say about everything. It's just that today's day and age hasn't been able to hook and reel me in.

I'm also surprised that I've suddenly opened up so much. It must have something to do with being at the top of this tree. An astronaut I follow on Twitter said something similar. Once in space and seeing the earth so far away, the astronaut suddenly became a chatterbox, saying everything that came to mind and eventually describing the condition in one tweet as "diarrhea of the mouth." The astronaut's husband—by the way, the astronaut is a woman—is an agriculturalist.

The tweet clarified, "In fact, he's a farmer!"

@Travis, one of Twitter's most vicious users, replied with more than a hint of sarcasm, "Ooo realy!"

To which @ticarisagacek, a Twitter user I also follow, replied, "He's an agriculturalist with a university degree who decided to do his own thing, so what's it to you if his wife said he's a farmer?"

So there you have it, a woman astronaut who looks out at the world from space and asks, "Hey, I wonder where my husband's fields are?" and there's her husband the farmer. I say everything for a reason: My father, who studied archaeology, and my mother, who graduated from the Health Sciences Faculty's Department of Nutrition and Dietetics, were brought together by the fact that they were born and grew up in Cihangir. That particular neighborhood of Istanbul, which is now quite posh, was the brothel quarter in Ottoman times. The apartment building in which we live was apparently built over what was once the area's most extravagant whorehouse. I'll pick up that discussion later, as it'll be a long one. For now, how about: What am I doing at the top of this tree? Why are people born into the world? That's easy. So they'll have a story to tell. Some of us die before the story ends, some of us die long after the story has ended, and some of us die right at the very start.

I don't know if you remember me saying this, or if I said it at all, but you see—and I'm not trying to be evasive here—it's just that I've reached a point where I can't remember much at all, so I might be repeating myself when I say: The tree I climbed was a plane tree. Its branches forked out at the top of the towering trunk, creating a deep curved hollow. I settled in quite comfortably but still felt uneasy about leaning back against one of the tree's branches. Feeling uneasy and going through life constantly hounded by concerns are terrible things. I learned that from my mom. And from my aunt as well. Unease weighs you down, like melancholy or grief. It is an emotion, and an unpleasant one at that. And that is exactly how I felt. Uneasy.

I looked down, which made me feel dizzy, but quickly enough I realized that I could find some peace of mind by just keeping my head up. That, however, was a passing feeling. If I fell, I knew I'd die, and I was perched there for the precise reason that I didn't want to die. Still, I have to ask: What was threatening my life? What was it that had threatened Amy's? Unease, depression, melancholy, sorrow, anxiety, unhappiness, and fear are far more harmful than drugs. At the very least, drugs numb you. Yes, I've tried them. I never had the desire to go too far because I didn't like the feeling of being out of control. Still, I'd probably go for some weed if I came across it. As if I say no to anything at all. There was this one time I tried to commit suicide in the most ridiculous way. I didn't even know if I really wanted to die or not. Here's what I did: I took a bunch of my mom's sertraline, drank a bottle of Efes Dark Beer, and then I puked. For a whole week my mom tried to find her bottle of pills but gave up in the end, deciding that she must've misplaced it somewhere. Not once did she consider the possibility that her daughter had taken them in an attempt to end her own life. I'll talk more about my mom, but later, because I haven't even got to the night that Amy died! As Pembe and Derin would say, "Whoa, ho, no!" I miss

16

them so much. "Aw, seriously?" The way that Derin would say, "Done deal," and, "Sherioushly"?

When I wrote my novel, I tried not to say things like that. And I still didn't win. It was all for nothing. Let me put it like this: "At first, I was writing it for the scholarship but then it turned out to be a salve for my soul . . ." I'm pulling that description out of my ass, but I couldn't think of anything else, sorry. Then I could continue with: ". . . and to heal my wounds." But the thing is, the girl who wrote the winning book spoke of her adventure with writing in precisely such "assburg" terms. Everyone listened in dead silence to her speech. But do you know how it seemed to me? It seemed like everyone else was asleep while I was the one who was awake. Yet I still lost. Why? Because the ignorant hordes flock to that which is vapid and spiritless. Literature can't be that way. I don't want it to be that way. But those are the times for you. The times change. Time speeds up. But if you ask me, literature shouldn't keep up with the times. It should linger in the fields and pastures where Jane Austen walked with her skirts trailing behind her in the grass and in Ahmet Hamdi's rooming house, Dostoyevsky's gambling halls, and Tolstoy's farms, tearooms, and the train station to which he fled. That train station was his treetop.

Maybe I was exhausted. Maybe I was afraid. Well, I *was* afraid—why am I being such a sissy about that when I already admitted it? *Sissy*—I dislike such masculine language. It has seeped into every aspect of our lives. That's why my aunt took me to meetings at a women's NGO, so that I could break free of it. And I did a bit. Pembe and Derin came a few times too. Our awakening that summer when we were fifteen years old came about because instead of going to the shoddy Star Beerhall we spent time with those splendid women.

As I was saying, I was afraid, and I puked. Whatever went askew in my body, that's what happened, I puked. In any case, I know that I write like I'm puking up everything inside of me. I never would've imagined that it could be so easy to pour out my thoughts and feelings, that it could be so easy to start explaining this all. Did I mention that already? So be it, life is but a series of repetitions. Like repeating a year at school. It's not good to be stable. If you ask me, the best way is to be weak and then break away and fall apart, letting yourself go to pieces. Because then you're exempt from life. Exempt, excluded. Like the insane. I suppose they're the only ones who are truly exempt. That might also hold true for writers because they create whatever worlds they damn well please in their writing and then live in them as they flesh them out. Let's include actors and artists as well. And girls in trees, like me. Yes, I climbed up here so that I could be exempt from life. Not that anyone was going to come along and ask why, but still.

If someone passed by the bottom of the tree, they might think that some bird up above was making the mess. A stork, for example, upset over all the empty nests. My poor stomach was heaving up the remains of last night's dinner. Actually this new life is nothing but the remains of what was left of the life down on the ground. I was going to have a new life there, high up in that tree. I hated puking. It's disgusting when people disgorge what's inside them.

I almost fell to the ground but managed to grab hold of a branch at the last second. I wrapped my arms around it, wishing I'd had someone in life I could hug like that. Even my passion for balancing on a rope—the slacklining I mentioned—was something to which I could have held. Writing was like that as well, but I lost the competition. If it had been a passion for me, maybe I could've gone on, but it didn't turn out that way. Perhaps I felt insulted. That's what happens when you lose, when you're disappointed and defeated. I was in no condition to pick myself back up and forge ahead, ax held high. In terms of writing, I mean. And when I say writing, I imagine it to involve dangers similar to those obviously involved in the act of running with an ax. Well, so be it. Everyone writes now. On Facebook, on Twitter, in emails, in their aspirations, whatever they set their sights on. We're writing the story of our lives. I was cramping up. I was cramping up like my puking stomach.

Amy puked as well. Before she died. After she had a heart attack, when death was certain. I mean, she didn't choke on her puke. The puke that her stomach heaved up in its final struggle didn't even escape her mouth but remained trapped there within the cage of her teeth, which were clamped shut. It couldn't even trickle out as a nasty-looking line of drool. When they found Amy, she was lying there as if asleep, her large lower jaw pressed tightly against her upper jaw. Her eyes were half-closed, like they always were when she was enjoying herself. Like the moments when she took flight. Her thin legs were clad in a pair of blue jeans, and she was wearing a sleeveless blue top, and her tattooed arms were spread out. She was lying on her back, and her hair, which looked like it had been tousled by the darkest of storms, was draped over her shoulders. That's how Amy was lying there. As though fast asleep. As though she had found peace. As though she had, at long last, found everything she'd sought in life. There was a certain peacefulness in her expression. Or nothing at all. That's how I had imagined it to be like, because when I first searched for pictures on Google, I was just thirteen years old. Much later I came across a photograph showing her gaunt body being carried out of her house. She was covered in a dusty pink sheet, looking like a tiny, empty package. And then an even thinner version of her being carried down a London street on a clattering stretcher to an ambulance. Farewell, Amy. I was so sorry to see you go. You sang beautiful songs for us. Maybe if this world had given you some peace, you would've kept singing, but it was good that you were saved from the troubles of this place. I hope you didn't suffer when you died. And I hope that the life after this one is better. Maybe this world, this life, is hell. Maybe this world is the hell of another world. A writer once wrote something similar to that, a writer also imbued with that English culture that infused in you the blood to write those songs filled with emotion, a writer from the empire on which the sun never sets. To tell the truth, I'm just copy-pasting what that writer said, because somewhere someone is making a living by copy-pasting, staying alive because of it.

Perhaps the way to heaven really is death. Of course, we're afraid when taking that first step toward the unknown, it's quite natural and logical.

That's why I puke. Because I'm afraid.

The things I wrote above, the parts about Amy . . . I wrote them on my Facebook page. I got replies like:

"That was wonderful. You're such a great writer. You're amazing . . ."

I'm not at a complete loss when it comes to writing. To tell the truth, I hadn't taken part in the writing competition only for the sake of securing a scholarship for my final year. I wanted to write. But the jury, which included many of my classmates and teachers, didn't find my novel worthy of an award. So was there anything special about the novel that won? There was. It was the kind of shit people liked. I don't know exactly what that was, but something. Something shitty. Don't expect too much of me. If I were stronger, I wouldn't be the girl in the tree. I would be down there, among you.

My head hurts.

The night is cool and quiet.

The night that Amy died wasn't like that. London was probably cool, but Istanbul was quite the opposite. I know that I'm a bit off in how I say things at times. It's because of my grandma. If you said to her, "Women's speech should be like poetry," she'd reply, "Screw that!" Followed by, "Why, so that the boys'll like it?" I told the women at my aunt's NGO about my grandma's approach to the matter. They laughed, saying, "Speak for your own self, not for anyone else, especially not for a man."

When I got home, I told my grandma what the women had told me. "Well, they're right," she said.

I was confused. Everything that came out of my grandma's mouth was a swear word. A levelheaded friend of my aunt who would drop by our place made the following diagnosis: It was a sickness. I mean, what my grandma had. An invisible sickness. And invisible illnesses exist either in our heads or buried deep within our souls, what we could term "the ghost." My grandma's mind was fine. Which meant that perhaps her soul really was afflicted. I wished that it were possible to take X-rays or MRIs of such sicknesses so we could see them.

Like, "Look, you can see it here. You have a neurosis. That dark area there . . ."

My grandma was stricken with an invisible illness that flowed with pus when she swore. Once she said to my aunt's ex-husband, "Why do you go around acting like some big shot with his cock slung over his shoulder?"

That sentence was even included in the divorce proceedings. And that was why my aunt lost their house when they split up, even though they'd bought it together. While the law, per EU regulations, states "properties bought during marriage are common properties," he got the whole place. The law always takes sides. They brought me to the trial because no one was free to look after me at the time. My other grandma and aunt, the ones on my mother's side, couldn't look after me because they had gotten involved in some strange secret women's meetings—goddamn my politically minded uncle, may he rot in hell—but I'll talk about that later. So in the end, they weren't at home. As if they ever were at all, in any sense.

The judge asked, "And what about this child?"

Meaning me. While I wasn't the daughter of the couple getting divorced at the time, I would be that child when my parents got divorced later. But there was more. There was so much more to come—everything, you might say. There was the start of those fine days and Amy's songs.

"We've got no time," my uncle said, "for a kid. My wife's too busy with work for womanly things. I'm lucky to get a plate of food once in a while."

At which point my grandma caused a stir in the courtroom by snorting in disgust.

The judge asked, "What does this woman do for work?" Meaning, my aunt.

My grandma cut in: "Did you say 'this woman'? First of all, you should learn how to speak respectfully to the people who come to you for justice."

As a result of this interruption, my aunt was unable to reply, "I'm a journalist." True, my uncle was also a journalist. But not like my aunt. Eventually it would come to light just what kind of journalist he was. Pro-government. A sellout. At the time, the lines hadn't been drawn yet. Still, the judge was a representative of the political will that was on the horizon.

My uncle had listed my grandma as one of the reasons he wanted to get divorced. The judge ate it up.

"What can I do?" my grandma said. "My mouth's a hotbed of cussing—that's just the way it is."

Afterward, we got on the underground in Şişli near the courthouse and started heading toward Taksim. The underground was new at the time. For us, being in the depths of the earth was like a blessing. But in those days everyone was talking about whether transportation should be aboveground, saying that life in the city could be worked around it. At school they made us read an article in *Le Monde* about it, which is why it stuck in my mind.

Shaking her head, my grandma was saying, "I'm the reason that prick of a judge gave him the house . . ."

"No, Mom," my aunt said, "he knew whose side I'm on. That's why he made that decision. It was all political."

My grandma was incapable of holding back the torrent of swearing inside her. On the way to Taksim, she told us about how her mouth came to be a "hotbed of cussing," as she described it:

She was born in Cihangir and grew up there in the same house as her mother, her mother's mother, her mother's mother's mother, and maybe even her mother's mother's mother's mother—who knows how far the list goes back. In 1987, they made a deal with a developer to have their rickety wooden two-story house torn down and replaced with an apartment building, in exchange for which they would get three apartments. Actually, no one knew why at the time, but first my grandma traded the plot of land for another on the same street. We were living in one of the sixty-five-square-meter apartments that came out of the deal. The ones on the upper floors had views, so before the roof was installed, we would go up to the top of the building with our picnic stove and teapot, and take in the views of the historic peninsula. My grandma hadn't chosen any of the apartments with views because that would've meant that she could only get two of them, and she wanted to make sure that her children would have places of their own. That's what she said. But if she hadn't traded the plot of land because of the injustices carried out on Kumrulu Street, each of the three kids would've ended up with an apartment with a view. Streets, like life, are full of injustice. My father and aunt asked my grandma again and again, "Why did you trade the land?" They even asked the neighbor: "Why did she trade land with you? Was she in debt to you?" As the story goes, the neighbor was as forthcoming as a tight rosebud. Secrets are bombs that slam into homes. I'm saying this—not my father, not my mother, not my aunt, and certainly not my grandma. Secrets, as I said, are bombs that crash into homes. But that's all for now on that.

My grandma's innate stubbornness drove her to negotiate with the developer—in her words, she haggled "cheek by jowl"—to get at least one apartment with a view, but she couldn't get him to budge. The reason that her mouth was a hotbed of cussing, of course, had nothing to do with her altercation with the developer. The neighborhood of Cihangir got its name when Süleyman the Magnificent's hunchbacked son died of grief and the sultan built a mosque there in his memory, as well as in an attempt to bring order to the area, which was renowned for being a den of vice. But his efforts were in vain, and the neighborhood plunged even deeper into debauchery, its rows of houses populated by the city's prostitutes who lived and died there.

Once the developers had set their sights on our house and started digging up the foundation, they found a gravestone with an inscription. Some things are inescapable—they came and told us about it. My father cleaned up the gravestone and, after having a thick piece of glass cut for it, turned it into a coffee table for the living room. My grandma would say, "If it wasn't the gravestone of a whore, he'd be hexed for sure." It's strange how all that can remain of a person's life is a slab of stone.

All her life my grandma looked after the neighborhood cats, and as soon as she stepped outside, they would follow her around. Perhaps some of you are thinking that I can't bring myself to explain why she swore all the time. That may be true. In her words, "That's just how I express myself." She even cussed out the cats, and when she stroked the heads of her own cats, she swore at them too. But as a timid eighteen-year-old girl playing the oud and singing in Beyoğlu's tavernas, swearing had been a way of defending herself. Everyone was afraid of that girl who swore up a storm. Maybe that's one reason why I started swearing as soon as I clambered up the tree. Fear me! And love me because you fear me. Love against your will. Love grudgingly. Because if you love something, it thrives. If you hate something, it dies. That was the story of my grandma's life. A bonding force, eccentric. Raw, unexplained, lacking . . . I don't know if I've been able to get across what I mean, so I hope I'll have enough time to relate everything. When I first got here, I was so disoriented I thought this was a dream. Maybe that's why.

I climbed up the plane tree closest to the wall separating the old palace from the park.

It was as if there was nowhere left for me to go in the world. Not a single place. I was overcome by a feeling of uneasiness. Actually, since I was a child, maybe since I was born, I've never really been able to find any peace of mind. About an hour ago I had a nervous breakdown and rushed out into the street, barely aware of what I was doing. And then I found myself here. A feeling of victory surged through me. I hadn't been defeated, meaning it was still possible for me to win, to survive. So, you should understand why I have so much to say. You see, being able to speak is proof that you're still alive. To put it a better way, as I mentioned before: it was as if I'd found a way to die before actually dying. You wouldn't believe how easy it was to climb this giant plane tree. It was as easy as walking down the street . . .

I was at the top of the tree, panting for breath. When I reached my perch, I felt like the trees embraced and protected me, taking me into their arms with an open heart in a way that my mother had never been able to do. The night was beautiful. The city lights, the sounds . . . When I say "sounds," I mean the thrumming coming from deep down below.

The park was silent.

I hadn't brought my phone with me. If I had, what difference would it have made? I hadn't known that I was going to live in the top of a tree. The thought had never occurred to me. In fact, I hadn't planned anything. It all just happened, like letting yourself be swept away by a current. I don't mean to keep saying the same things, but that's how it is, and in any case, nothing else comes to mind. Can't the mind repeat itself again and again, like day turns into night which turns into day? Being alone and turned inward all my life matured me. But being overly mature is like what happens to a fruit that has over-ripened on the branch and starts to rot. I was rotting. My spirit was rotting. I was dying. Forgive me—I can't quite put into words exactly what happened to me. My thoughts wander. You know how it is sometimes, stringing words together is such an exacting and difficult task. Isn't that true for all of us?

If parents mistreat their children, all of life will conspire to mistreat them too. That includes other people, the world, and, if there is one,

God. But don't take that to mean my parents treated me badly. They did the best they could. They tried. I feel worse for them than for myself because life battered them a thousand times worse than me.

It was dark. There was a hotel on the other side of the wall, and at one point its air conditioner turned on, filling the night with its roar. In the distance I could see the silky deep blue of the calm sea. The leaves of the trees fluttered occasionally in such a way that you couldn't help but think they were living creatures in their own right, as if it wasn't the breeze setting them into motion. There weren't any people in that part of the park. The automatic sprinklers for the grass would come on and go off, sending plumes of vapor into the air. I felt like a strange dampness, a humidity of sorts, was clinging to me. The air was neither cool nor hot.

Time passed so quickly high up in the trees . . . I closed my eyes and yet again found myself being carried off to a place between dream and reality. Either I fell asleep and dreamt or I was awake as all those things were happening.

I imagined trying to find a suitable branch I could use for peeing. Because, obviously, I would have to pull down my pants and then my underwear. I didn't want to soil myself, you see. As if that wasn't enough, I realized that I was starting to smell sweaty, meaning I would have to find a place to wash up. Who knows, maybe I could've licked myself clean like a cat, but I didn't want things to reach that point. Next, I found myself feeling as though I was accustomed to being up in the trees, moving fearlessly from tree to tree as if I'd been born up there—I surprised even myself. Like a bird flitting to another branch to perch. Like flying. Like smoke. Like something carried upward by the wind. I surmised that what was weighing me down like a stone was the unease I carried inside. But when I bounded fearlessly from tree to tree as if I had wings, I felt light. That feeling of lightness was wonderful. Everything was wonderful, so long as I couldn't tell if it was real or imaginary. When I found myself back in the hollow at the top of the tree, I didn't have to pee anymore. I wondered if I'd really peed down onto the thick canopy of the laurel tree below, or if I'd always been in the hollow of the tree and imagined it.

My red Toms were lying forlornly on the grass below like a symbol of all I'd loved and abandoned. At one point a small pack of street dogs came along and, snatching up the shoes in their jaws, ran off with them. Not a single trace was left of me.

2

SOME PEOPLE YOU MIGHT KNOW

On the night that Amy died, I ran down to my aunt's place, apartment number 2 on the floor right below ours. She opened the door, cigarette in hand. The way her face emerged from the smoke was part of the melancholy of that night. Tears in my eyes, I threw my arms around her neck.

"Is something wrong?" she asked, emphasizing each syllable like swinging the knocker of a door.

She had a friend over, a woman who was a journalist like herself. Covering my face with my hands, I brushed past my aunt into the living room, sobbing uncontrollably. At first they thought that I'd had an argument with my mother, but then it all came to light. All night long they listened to Amy's songs, and eventually I dozed off on the sofa.

"How old is she?"

"Thirteen," my aunt replied.

I was thirteen years old the summer that Amy died.

Now that they knew what was wrong, my aunt and her friend put on "Back to Black" and sat there drinking their wine and smoking cigarettes. The windows were open. The sheer curtains slowly billowed in and out with the evening breeze. At that moment, there in my aunt's place, I was happy and felt at peace. As I sat there on the sofa, I listened in on their conversation, but occasionally I drifted off to sleep. My aunt was telling a funny little love story about the developer who had built the place. At one point she brought out an old photograph. I was dying to lean over and take a look at it myself.

"Which one is he?"

"This one."

"He looks just like Kadir İnanır!"

Their laughter filled the small living room, seeping into every crevice and corner, just like the smoke of their cigarettes.

"So you sacrificed a sheep before laying the foundation?"

"Well, my mother had made a vow, you see . . ."

"How old were you at the time?"

I heard my aunt exhale a puff of smoke. "Seventeen."

"Was it your first time?"

"More or less."

"How did it happen?"

"It was the developer's first time."

"And for you?"

"This isn't about me! I'm talking about the apartment buildings on this street."

I wanted to turn around, pry open my eyes, and watch those two young women as they sat there across from each other, laughing and chatting, their thighs shifting under them as they crossed and recrossed their long legs. Every time they took a sip of wine, I could hear it. But then I decided it was better to imagine what they were talking about, conjuring it up in my mind's eye, as they leaned back on the threadbare mustard-yellow sofa. When she paused for a second, I could sense that my aunt was peering at me to see if I was really asleep or not. The world stopped, time stopped, and not even a VPN could get around that frozen moment.

Her friend asked, "Is she asleep?"

The poor woman would end up getting shot at the Syrian border. It would happen on the pretext that she had ignored a warning to "stop" as she was reporting about people crossing the border to the other side. What a wretched thing, not knowing how you're going to die.

My aunt pursed her lips—I even heard that. I think those were the days when I started being able to see things I couldn't see and hear things I couldn't hear.

"Is what you're going to tell me so private?"

"No, not at all!"

They opened another bottle of wine. The cork released its stubborn, passionate grip on the mouth of the bottle with a satisfying pop. Years later, when I saw my aunt twirling a bottle of wine in her hand, I would remember that night when she opened bottle after bottle of wine for her friend without a second thought. It stuck in my mind because my aunt said, "Wine is so expensive now—it costs a small fortune! It took me hours to decide whether or not to buy a bottle." Because she was unemployed. Because she couldn't find work. Because she had no way to make a living. She couldn't work as a journalist—they wouldn't let her.

But back then, she had a job. That wasn't long ago. Just four years, to be precise, and yet so much has changed. How can life change so quickly? Or rather, how can it go to shit so fast?

Wait, let me get back to the point. My aunt was telling a love story:

"So he built our place. They agreed that my mom would get three apartments in return for the plot of land. The developer had just taken over the business from his father, who was starting to run an even bigger operation. They were from a town on the Black Sea coast."

Occupational disinformation, digression . . . My aunt always starts off with the past, by delving into the background. Because you can't live today without the past. Especially childhood and youth—they are like the sky above us, always there.

She went on:

"He had this sweet, crooked smile. I think that's what hooked me first. And he had an amazing car. I saw it for the first time parked in front of our old wood house. My mom pulled out a chair for him and he sat down, placed his hands on his knees, and bowed his head. He was wearing a well-cut summer suit and his hair was immaculate. You know, the classic look. He smelled nice, not like strong aftershave or cheap cologne. Something softer. He asked for a glass of water, so I brought him one. He looked me up and down, and I melted on the spot."

"How old was he?"

"Around twenty-seven."

"Was he single?"

"Of course he was. His family married him off in a hurry when they found out that he and I were spending time together."

"And that's how you parted ways."

"That's exactly how we parted ways. But who cares—everyone splits up sooner or later. Who's ever heard of love ending happily?"

"Sure, so let's say that there's no such thing as happy love—the kids'll hear it and post it on their Facebook pages."

"Right. 'As my aunt says . . .'"

Laughter and more laughter . . . Such a fine means of shaking off gloomy memories. My aunt laughed and laughed some more, and then she broke down in tears. This time it was her friend who asked, "Is something wrong?" emphasizing each syllable like swinging the knocker of a door.

I could hear my aunt sobbing. By that point I may have forgotten to pretend to be asleep, or at the very least not bothered to put on a show of breathing gently like someone in the depths of slumber. In any case, my aunt was in no condition to be checking to see if I was asleep or not.

"Were you madly in love with him?"

My aunt nodded sadly. I could now clearly see without opening my eyes. She was nodding, trying to hold back her tears.

She'd been deeply in love with him.

And she'd been worse off than if she'd died from love.

After that night, I understood when I heard my grandmother yelling at my aunt.

"If only that love of yours had done us some good! You gave yourself away to that guy, so why didn't you at least get him to throw an apartment with a view into the deal?"

"Is that the kind of thing you do in a car on the Bosporus? Okay, so you did it. Of your own will. That's what you wanted. But, you stupid girl, you should've convinced him to give you an apartment with a view!"

My other grandma and my mother's sister used to have conversations like that as well. Talking about the past is like chewing gum. Or maybe it would be more apt to say that it's like chewing the cud.

My mother would defend my father's sister, complaining, "You still haven't had your fill of gossiping about our in-laws after all these years . . ."

In the end, my mother solved the problem by threatening her sister when she caught her alone once:

"Now look here, she saved herself by becoming a journalist. What have *you* done with yourself?"

"What's wrong with what I've become?"

"You've had your hands in the pants of just about every guy in your department. Traditional handicrafts, ha!"

"Watch your mouth!"

"At least my sister-in-law has stuck with one guy the whole time. But you? If you let our mother egg you on to say one more bad thing about that woman, I swear I'll—"

"Are you threatening me?"

"Yes. The whole school's talking about you, saying that you're unbeatable in the art of handicrafts."

My mother punctuated that last sentence with a gesture I later understood to mean a hand job. Her sister's jaw dropped.

"How dare you! And for your information, your mother-in-law is quite the slut herself."

"You're the one people call a slut."

My mother and my aunt—her sister, I mean—would get into spats like that. But quietly, so I wouldn't hear. I was around ten years old at the time.

"Don't talk like that in front of her."

My aunt decided to drop out of university, and dropping her habit as a serial dater as well, she got married to a guy from the neighborhood. He in turn dropped his ambitions in the field of engineering so he could work at his father's appliance-shop in Tophane. His political aspirations, which began with membership in the youth branch of a party, were undeterred by the fact that he never managed to become a member of parliament.

I know that I've been talking about everyone except for myself. But that's the only way we can exist—by talking about others, by seeing ourselves in their darkest moments and being afraid. We are secreted away not so much in the stories about the things we like, but the things we dislike. And that is precisely why we dislike them, because we know that, by shifting our position ever so slightly, we could be the protagonist of such stories.

So my father's sister had fallen head over heels in love with that developer with the crooked smile who wore pristine suits and stepped out of his Mercedes with a swagger. But a Mercedes wasn't enough for him—he wanted a BMW. His father said, "Well, do some business and you'll get one!" That's why our handsome developer was driving around in his father's old Mercedes. But my aunt didn't pay any attention to that. As they say, love is blind.

"He had such a wonderful laugh," my aunt told her friend that night, the night that Amy died. "I've never met another man with such a wonderful laugh."

Personally, I would have asked more questions about him, but my aunt's friend asked, "So, you never saw him again?" That's a journalist for you—always so technical.

My aunt shook her head sadly. As I lay curled up on that mustard-yellow sofa, I watched everything unfold as if I was watching a movie. In my mind's eye, I could see that excited young woman in love and the old wooden house, which I had seen in photographs. I could see it all: how she dashed down the stairs when she heard his Mercedes turn onto the street at the top of the hill; how she stepped out the door nonchalantly as if she was just going for a walk and strode past the Mercedes with a swish of her skirt, only to lock eyes with the developer in the rearview mirror as he pretended to be checking on the progress of the construction of the new buildings; how the construction workers looked at her in profound quietnes—yes, I intentionally left off the final *s* because I want the quietness to be even more quiet, but let's get back to the story—and the developer cocked an eyebrow when he saw their glances and how they quickly looked away; how she reached the bottom of the hill and turned in the direction of Tophane, looking back once in a while; how he caught up with her in Fındıklı and honked the Mercedes's horn; how she leapt into the car with a laugh; how the lovers gazed into each other's eyes but didn't kiss out of fear that someone they knew would see them; and how they set off down the road together.

That's how I described it to the girls.

We stopped hanging out at the Star Beerhall after school. Because we didn't have a car, we walked everywhere, our uniform skirts rolled all the way up to our asses, cigarettes in hand. Hoping to be more like them, I'd started smoking as well. We tried to be as rude as we could be. When we were crossing the street in Şişhane, we bumped into a woman. She snapped, "You call yourself students of Dame de Sion?! What a disgrace!"

"Disgrace? You and your mother—that's the disgrace!"

Derin blew smoke in the woman's face.

"What's the world coming to? Girls from *my* high school acting like this . . . Shocking, simply shocking! It's enough to give you a heart attack."

But even that wasn't enough.

So, why had it happened?

That dour, doughy-faced woman had pushed a young boy who tried to sell her a packet of tissues. Not just pushed, but *shoved*—so hard that the poor kid fell down and his packets of tissues flew into the street. Clutching his arm in pain, he got to his feet. Just then a car went by, nearly hitting him, and he started gathering up the packets in a panic. We helped him. So yes, we bickered with that hag for the sake of getting revenge on her for how she treated that kid.

Still, why were we so rude, so vulgar?

Who were we trying to fool by acting like that, while we spoke French fluently and were even learning Latin? We were even fooling ourselves. It was as if we'd murdered the real Dame de Sion students and pulled their uniforms onto our corpses, like freakish attire slipped over the life and culture of Istanbul.

Laughing, we made our way down to Unkapanı Bridge. That was the first time I told them the story about my aunt's love affair, and I even remember flicking my cigarette butt into the water as I talked.

The night that Amy died still hadn't come to an end. But it was ending, as my aunt pulled a blanket over me and turned the music down. Her friend had just left. There was still some time before she'd be shot and killed while reporting on the border. Syria hadn't been dragged into chaos yet, and as people contentedly went about their lives, war was the last thing on their minds. Sadly, life is like that: shaped by things that are the furthest from our minds, things that we don't imagine could ever happen. I think that Amy found peace. If she hadn't died, life would've taught her what she needed to do to go on living. But she's gone. And I'm still here because I don't want to go.

3

What's Going On?

Finally I took off my backpack, which involved a rather frightening balancing act, and then I settled comfortably into the hollow at the top of the tree. As I leaned against a stout branch, I wondered how I would go on staying there. Sure, I had imagined how I'd handle the matter of pissing and all that business, but then what? Then again, perhaps imagining was the flip side of reality.

I was like a child who had wept and wept, becoming cleansed on the inside and rejuvenated in the process. Carefully, I opened the zipper of my backpack, making sure I didn't drop it. Since I didn't have my phone, I could only guess about the time, but I don't think that more than an hour had passed. And while I knew it was September, I didn't know what day it was. If the world was filled with emoticons—and I wish it was—I'd put one here; that way, we could understand each other more easily and with much more sincerity.

In order for me to come to the conclusion that it was September 14, my mind had to make certain leaps like a nightingale hopping from branch to branch, all the while fearing the fact of my own existence. On September 11, I'd visited Pembe's grave. I'd planned on paying a visit to Derin's on the next day, but it didn't happen, I was too exhausted to get out of bed. I called her mother—or maybe she called me, I'm not sure—and she said to me, "I go every Friday, as that's the day of prayers.

Come with me if you'd like." Friday was the eighteenth of the month. As of that morning of the call, two days had passed.

If she were still alive, Amy would turn thirty-one today.

Shit!

So there I was at the top of a tree on Amy Winehouse's birthday. Ugh!

This is very strange. But I'd better not get hung up on such details. Obsessing is dangerous; it'll give you cancer in the end. The best approach is to forget everything right away, because if you start thinking about things too much, you'll get screwed twice over, and then what? Get well soon! What else can you say?

The contents of my backpack proved to be anything but useful. If I were to get thirsty, for example, what would I do? And if I fell asleep, would I roll out of my perch? I decided to lash myself to the tree with the turnbuckles and straps I found in my backpack. So my hobby of slacklining turned out to be useful. But where I really needed such acrobatics was in real life, down on the ground.

I wonder if the dead can see us. I mean, when the people we love depart from this world, do they come back sometimes, watching us as we go through this adventure we call life?

At last I could close my eyes, free from the anxiety that had been haunting me. Before, I'd been thinking about what time it might be. Midnight, perhaps. Maybe later. Then I told myself to stop thinking about such matters and cut myself off from the world. But just as I was saying that to myself, I heard a voice: "Hey, you. Yes, you, up in that tree . . ."

4

FOLLOW

I haven't said much about my mother, who as I may have said was a dietician. She'd go from door to door in search of work. Telling you more about her would be the proper course of action, but I know if I should do that now, you might get upset, as you're probably wondering about that person who called out to me in the darkness of night. It's true that I see others my age as being younger than me. That's because I've been through so much more than them.

Yes, you're curious about that person. Admit it. Go on being curious.

It wasn't for nothing that I said this was a story of love and freedom. A story of two youths stricken by illness. That person was looking up at me from below. In order for a story to be a story, two people have to be involved in the plot.

I felt like Gulliver in the land of midgets. Allow me to apologize for repeating myself, but I don't want you to overlook an important point—I myself have a habit of overlooking things—and that point is this: I climbed a tree that was at the farthest end of the park. There was a high wall that separated the palace grounds from the park, and the tree that I climbed was next to that wall. In the past, the gardens of Topkapı Palace extended all the way to the sea, with pavilions and mansions scattered here and there. One of those was later turned into a boutique hotel. I think I told you that I heard the sound of the hotel's air conditioner. The person who called out to me—a young man—was standing in the garden of the hotel, which was glimmering in the night like a lantern. Later I'd say to him, "You've got some sharp eyes!"

And he'd say, "At first, I thought you were a monkey of some kind. Or a really big bird."

But at that moment, when I wasn't swinging between the past and the future like a pendulum, I wanted to shout at him, "Leave me alone!"

You see, I was afraid that he would alert others to my presence in the tree. I was also mad at him for spoiling my peace of mind. For a while we just looked at each other. It was clear that he was more excited about this turn of events than I was; in the glow of the lamps in the garden, I could see the curiosity in his expression, but he also seemed unsure of what he should do—even though I was the one up in the tree, not him. It occurred to me that he might be afraid I'd fall. Hoping the gesture would stop him from doing anything rash, I pressed my finger against my lips. Much later, he told me that it worked.

When I saw him go back into the hotel, I immediately set about unstrapping myself from the tree, as I was more afraid of being caught there than falling to the ground. After putting the straps into my backpack, I got to my feet for the first time—that is, if we don't count the imaginary scenarios I played out in my mind. My feet were numb. As I stood there barefoot on one of the plane tree's thick branches, I kept thinking that I needed to find a more secluded tree. I also thought that, since I didn't fall out of the tree as I stood there, barely able to feel my feet, there was little chance I would actually fall to the ground after all. Just then, I realized that the park wasn't so dark. It was strange; I could even see the grime between my toes. In the city, there are always lights. High up in the tree, the light made its way among the branches, bathing me in its dim glow. That dirty light that made the stars invisible was like the never-ending cycle of good and evil in life.

I had an impulse to start walking along the branch as if I was just a foot or two off the ground, like I'd done in the past when I was slacklining. Closing my eyes in the hope that it would allay my fears, I almost took a step, but then I changed my mind. I didn't feel prepared for such balancing acts yet. The only way I could bring myself to move around at that height was on all fours, my arms wrapped around the branch and with a strap lashing me to the tree like a mountain climber. As I started slithering along the gnarled branch like a snake, thinking that I'd be less visible that way, I heard the same voice call out, "Do you need any help?"

I couldn't understand it. I mean, I'd seen him go inside, so why did he come back out?

Later he would tell me that they'd called him inside to do something. He was wearing a funny-looking red jacket with silvery epaulets and matching trousers with a stripe down the side, and on his head was a squat, pointed hat, the most laughable part of his getup. His outfit reminded me of what you'd see monkeys wearing at a circus. As a bellboy, he sometimes had to lug around suitcases that were almost as big as him and certainly heavier. To move them, he used a wheeled cart that he nicknamed Tayyo, but he still struggled to load the massive bags onto it. As he later said, he often thought to himself, "What the hell are these people carrying around in their luggage?"

One time he saw what was in one of those suitcases: a person. But dead. In other words, a corpse. The suitcase belonged to an English couple. Perhaps I'll tell you that strange story at some point.

I started to get the feeling that he wouldn't bring me any harm.

That night, he didn't have to deal with much luggage. All he did was put a rather fancy-looking small suitcase into the trunk of a taxi that was bound for the airport. Then he ran back so he could go on watching me.

Much later, he would say, "I thought I was dreaming. You just don't expect to see a girl sitting high up in the branches of a tree."

No, it wasn't a dream. It was real. During our first encounter, I didn't say a word to him—I just vanished into the darkness of night like a wild animal. I crept and crawled along the branch of that huge plane tree until it started bending under my weight, and then I leapt into the arms of an old eucalyptus. From there, I made my way to a laurel, where I found an abandoned stork's nest. Tucked away deep in the branches, the nest looked for all the world like a cradle. I felt around inside it, deciding in the end that its tightly woven frame could bear my weight.

That was the second miracle of the night: among the branches of that tree, a bed for the night.

Yunus would ask, "And what about me?"

That was his name: Yunus. There wasn't a trace of sarcasm, wickedness, or greed in the way he looked at me. When he laughed or grinned, he was as adorable as a monkey. He was like an angel. Over time, I would come to love him and feel a deep compassion for him. I'd never seen such a glimmer in someone's eyes. His teeth and mouth were beautiful, even if I did compare him to a monkey when I said that he was cute when he laughed . . . If my aunt could have seen him, she would've conceded that here was a man who had a lovelier smile than her handsome developer. He had short hair and a charmingly soft red beard, which I must admit was a bit sparse. The hotel had asked him to grow a beard as part of his job. It was about image, they said. The manager was a Scottish man who had his own particular sexual preferences. Love of all kinds is a fine thing, but one day the manager pinched Yunus's cheek and said, "Come to my place tonight." It turned out that he did that to a lot of the employees. When the manager quit—rather, when he was forced to quit—Yunus shaved off his slight beard. The owner of the hotel said to him, "What have you done?" Yunus replied, "He made a laughingstock of us all for his idea of an image. I made tons of money for that queer!"

People can be so unsympathetic in the face of difference.

Yunus would say, "I didn't like it when he stroked my cheek, that's all."

"Well, maybe he couldn't stop himself. You should take that into consideration."

"He tried to kiss one of the guys working in the kitchen!"

"So he was full of love! Why are you making such a big deal about it?"

I didn't mean to start off by describing Yunus like that, but that's just the way it happened. He was handsome. He told me that a Belgian tourist had tried to get him into bed. And she succeeded, literally climbing on top of him.

"I suppose you didn't resist much."

"You don't understand. It wasn't like that at all."

I wonder if Yunus made it possible for me to live in that tree. If it weren't for him, I know it would've been much more difficult.

One time, as we spoke of that night when we first saw each other, barely visible in the gloom, he would ask, "Well, wasn't I one of the miracles that happened to you?" Some other time, I'll tell you about that at length. But now I'm exhausted. All that excitement and fear wore me out. I just want to curl up in that stork's nest and go to sleep. Still, I should finish telling the story that I started:

Yunus would ask again, "Wasn't seeing me that night a miracle?" Not because he was being spoiled or insistent, but out of sheer naivete and the goodness of his heart. And I would look into his eyes as if I was trying to remember a dream. Then those mysterious words fell from my lips: "I had seen you before."

But where had I seen Yunus?

Time is a key, not a remedy. With it, you can delve into the past and unlock doors that open onto rooms filled with things you couldn't otherwise remember.

At the time, however, as I spent my first night in the tree, I was more excited about settling into the stork's nest than making the acquaintance of a young bellboy whose name I didn't yet know.

"Maybe this is all a dream," I said to myself, resting my head on my backpack. I was feeling uneasy. How many of you have slept in a stork's nest? One by one, the twigs were crackling beneath me as the nest gauged my weight, the sound quietly echoing in the silence of the park. I was afraid. I had already felt enough fear that night, so much that I needn't be afraid of falling. That's what I told myself, saying that, even if I did fall, I'd held out for as long as I could.

I was 159 centimeters tall, but I always said that I was 160. In the nest, I curled up as tightly as I could: 79 centimeters. Small enough to fit into a suitcase. If I tucked my head down a bit more, 75 centimeters. Maybe 70 centimeters, if I really tried. My knees were pulled up to my chest. My mother once read "Thumbelina" to me. That tiny girl had a crib made of a polished walnut shell. Her mattress was woven violets, and for a blanket, she had a rose petal. "Just like me," I said, my heart aching. As my eyes filled with tears, the sprinklers down below suddenly stopped and the lights in the park went off. At last I was shrouded in the darkness I had so desired. I heard a few birds as they flitted from tree to tree, probably watching me. Slowly I let myself drift off. I had been so tense, so very, very tense . . . But now I was as supple as water flowing into an earthenware bowl. I thought of my mother. If I remember correctly, I was going to tell you about her, right? As you may have noticed, what I really want is for people to like me. That's why I've always tried to satisfy your curiosity. Sure, I mentioned my mother and then told you about Yunus. But you see, I was filled with such pity. For her, I mean. My mother. Because, like everyone else, I loved my mother more than anyone.

5

BLOCK

I don't know if I slept through the night or not.

Time and time again I have asked myself that question.

Am I dreaming, or am I really curled up in a stork's nest?

I thought of my mother. Naturally she'd be worried about me.

"Let her worry," I muttered, my voice laced with a bitterness and vengefulness unbecoming a daughter who loves her mother. The thing is, she was so preoccupied with herself it made me wonder if she had ever really been a mother to me at all.

My grandma would say, "What do you expect her to do? She's got enough problems to deal with."

"And just what problems are those?" my aunt would ask.

As a journalist, she always asked the right questions.

Indeed, what problems did she have? I started to ask myself that quite often. When my mother and father got married, they were in love. But that's not what I want to tell you about. I'm thinking more about the days when she went from door to door, trying to find work. In those times—I guess I was around six years old—just about everyone was out of a job, including my aunt and my father. He had quit working at the Archaeology Museum, and later he picked up work as a tour guide. Then he was taken on by a publisher that put out books about archaeology, and at one point he organized someone's personal collection, for which he made a small fortune, enough to last him two years. Around that time, my mother landed a job. In terms of their working lives, both of my parents were pretty unstable. Eventually, my mother was let go, as a result of which my family really hit rock bottom. My grandma died in March of 2013, which meant that she was spared having to see her children sink into poverty. Of course, Amy's death had nothing to do with the problems my family was facing. At the end of December in 2013—well, let's say the start of 2014—my aunt got fired as well. My mother had been out of work for a while by that time, and it pained me to see her struggling to find a place that would hire her. She'd take the underground to the district of Levent, where she'd go from clinic to clinic, walking streets she came to know like the back of her hand as she trod up and down their length, streets that for the most part were named after flowers. The neighborhood was desolate—it was as if no one actually lived or worked in those fancy villas surrounded by manicured gardens and high walls. There wasn't a trace of life. My mother was feeling dejected and beaten down in those days, but when she had the chance at an interview, her heart would fill with hope again, one last hope, and she'd be excited as she walked through the office door, feeling—as they're so fond of saying in interview lingo—"motivated." There is nothing more humiliating, degrading, and dehumanizing than trying, without success, to find work.

It's difficult to talk about my mother. Writing about her is even harder.

When I was signing up for the writing competition, in response to that ludicrous question "How would you go about writing a novel?" I'd said, "Well, you have to start off with your deepest feelings. The characters don't have to be anything like yourself as the writer. And as for the story, it doesn't really have to be based on anything you yourself have experienced. What the characters really do is give voice to our emotions, to the things that have had a profound impact on us. Writing is like looking in a mirror, but the face we see there isn't our own. What we write doesn't actually belong to us as the author. Rather, it comes from the depths of our being."

Cocking an eyebrow, our literature teacher asked, "Tell me, is that really what you think?"

Meaning, "Moron! You couldn't be more wrong!"

Trying to shift my approach, I hoped to offer up a stronger line of thinking: "I'm just saying that our feelings and experiences do provide us with material that we can use, but . . ."

For the most part, I had zero self-confidence—that is, except when I was writing. As I think always happens to writers, I became another person as I wrote. It gave me courage. And now, here I am at the top of a tree, bolstered by my newfound bravery. But in life, I was nothing. I don't know how I'm going to tell you about my mother; it's as if her story is my own. However, I am her daughter, and I was aware of what was happening when she set out on those tragic adventures to find work. Like everyone, she'd had better years, years that seemed to glimmer like a star, but those weren't the times when she married my father and brought me into the world. No, they came later, much later. When she fell in love. The winds of that passion stirred her to life.

Things happened when I was around five or six years old that marked a turning point in her life. Before, she'd been a stay-at-home mom who was subjected to my father's constant verbal abuse. I know that isn't a very elegant way of putting it, but it's the truth. How can I dress up the pain of a hurt heart? I want to tell it like it really was: for years, my father had been treating her with the bitterest contempt for some unknown reason, which is precisely why I used that rather unpleasant term to describe the situation: verbal abuse. So let's make do with it and move on. Those years, many of the details of which have slipped through the cracks of my memory, were terrible. That's all I know for sure. I've tried time and time again to recall them, but I can't. I think that when we're one, two years old, there are only emotions, scents, and sounds—nothing more.

As for the times that I can remember from my childhood: My mother was irritable, always on edge, and she made me suffer for the frustration she felt in her unhappy marriage. I'm pretty sure that she felt bad for doing so, but I don't think she knew what else to do. Instead of talking to me, she shouted, her body shaking like she was on the verge of a nervous breakdown, and she hit me whenever she got the urge. I may not have bled or gotten bruised, but those blows rained down, usually landing on my head and back. Her hands were like the hands of a diligent housewife fluffing up a pillow with dogged determination. What frightened me the most was when she'd clench her teeth in anger, because I knew what I was in for next: her tiny fists pounding on my head as if it were a door that refused to open. One time I snapped, "There's no one in there!" Out of confusion, she stopped hitting me for a moment. I calmly went on: "There's no one in my head." I never cried or shouted. When my mother beat me, I'd let myself sink into a ponderous quietness; like I said, I think that's why I sometimes forget to write the two *s*'s in the word. I'd try to convince myself in the depths of that silence that my mother wasn't actually beating me but making a cry for help. She was, in fact, a proud, strong woman who found herself in an unbearable situation. It wouldn't be an exaggeration to say that she, in fact, suffered far worse than me. She loved my father very much. Sure, he may not have physically beat her—if that can be any kind of consolation—but the way he treated her was even more abusive than that. He ignored her. He was glum. He insulted her and jeered at her. He always did just what he wanted, spending all his time with his friends. He was stingy with his money. He acted like a man who has never grown out of adolescence and cannot let go of his mother. And do you know the worst thing about it? Everyone loved him. It's always like that: men feel that it is their right to be loved just because they're men. That will never change. My mother was unhappy and worn out by it all. I've been told that, when I started going to nursery school, she went back to work, but even that didn't bring her out of her depression. She wouldn't even cook for me, so she fed me with a baby bottle—even though I was three years old at the time. I lost a lot of weight that summer. At the time, my aunt and grandma were living on one of Istanbul's islands, so they weren't around to look out for me.

My father was still working at the Archaeology Museum at the time, and while he didn't make much, at least he had a regular salary. He was the one who paid for my kindergarten. Well, that's what he thought. Whenever the day came for him to make the payment, he'd get irritated, and once he said that he wasn't going to pay it anymore. My mother started crying, covering her face with her hands like a child. The truth of the matter was that my mother's sister was secretly paying the tuition, and the amount that he'd give my mother wasn't actually very much. Still, it made it possible for her to go to her favorite café to have a cup of fresh-brewed coffee and a dessert, and after that get a manicure and a pedicure. If she had any money left over, she'd ask the cleaning woman to come over to our place.

In the morning, she'd drop me off at school without preparing breakfast for me first, and while they offered breakfast there, we couldn't afford it, so I'd sit and watch my teacher and some of the children eat. The other kids—the ones who'd eaten at home—would already be playing. Out of pity, my teacher would slip me a slice of toast with jam, which I'd devour. I don't know why my mother sent me to school hungry. Maybe she just couldn't get herself out of bed at that hour of the morning. One time, my feet got eaten up by mosquitoes and I scratched the bites so much they started bleeding. After cleaning the wounds, my teachers bandaged them up.

"Her parents don't take very good care of her."

"Where's her grandma?"

"Living on the islands now."

"She'll take care of her when she comes back."

"The least they could do is brush the poor girl's hair."

One of the teachers leaned in close to me. The one with the olive skin and the beautiful face I couldn't get enough of looking at because I imagined that her thin-plucked eyebrows were the wings of birds arching across on her smooth, broad forehead. She was the one who said to me, "Tell your mother that you need a haircut."

I didn't tell her.

But when my grandma got back and saw the state of my hair, she went after the tangles with a pair of scissors. My mother didn't even notice.

The next day my grandma said, "Your hair looks like hell!"

She took me to the barber to get it fixed.

As we were sitting there, an old woman walked in. So old she looked even older than my grandma. She said something in a strange language. Greek, perhaps? And she was from a different city. Athens? The old woman and my grandma hugged. Maybe they were neighbors once upon a time?

"This is my granddaughter," my grandma said, pointing to me.

I swung my feet as I sat on the barber's chair. Now that the haircut was done, the barber started running a horsehair brush through my hair, which tickled the back of my neck. I could smell something like powder.

Squinting at my grandma, the old woman said, "Efrosa and I cut your hair once. Remember? You had a case of lice." Her glasses, which had gleaming thin chains hanging down from each side, were quite thick and made her eyes look larger than they actually were. I noticed that she walked with a cane, which seemed to be the only thing keeping her on her feet. As she leaned on the cane with all her weight, it looked like a nail that had been driven into the earth.

That was the first time I saw my grandma in a new light. What I'm trying to say is that, when you're a child, sometimes you can tell that something is amiss but it doesn't really make sense to you, and then years later as you think over it—like I'm doing now—you pick up on something. That is, of course, if you believe that intuition is more important than logic. Otherwise, logic will have driven it from your thoughts long ago.

I got the impression that my grandma wanted to avoid that old woman, as if she stirred up bad memories. If so, what were those memories? My grandma looked defeated, even overwhelmed. Taking me by the arm, she started pulling me out of the shop, and I remember bumping against a few things on the way out because my little legs couldn't keep up. As we walked away, the old woman said, "Efrosa couldn't get through it like you. She hung herself. Did you hear about that?"

She must have heard about it. The look in my grandma's eyes said, "Yes, I heard about it. I know what happened."

If the old woman wasn't a bad person, why did she look so angry?

"Forty-eight years after it happened, I went back to the place. I'm eighty-eight years old now, and I wanted to see it one last time before I die."

"What could be left to see, madam?"

My grandma was a changed person. Beaten. Hurt. Frail. Her question—so cordial, courteous, and innocent—wasn't even peppered with swear words.

"I think, madam, that you are overtaxing your strength."

"What strength? I have none left. This city took what strength I had. And my daughter."

"Why are you so angry with me?"

"Because you got over it. You're still alive. My Efrosa is gone forever."

"Would it have been better if I'd killed myself too?"

I couldn't understand why my grandma was talking so bizarrely.

"Peri, how did you manage to live with that pain? How could you get through life?"

At that point, Barber Ali said to her, "Ah, Perihan Hanım, is that what people call you for short? Peri?"

My grandma promptly swung her alligator-skin purse at his head.

Ha! My grandma was herself again!

Barber Ali threw up his hands to ward off the unexpected blow. He had a tattoo of a girl on his arm that looked like one of Amy's tattoos. I suppose he hadn't been able to come up with anything else to get tattooed there, and I also wonder why Amy got the sort of tattoo a guy would choose. As Barber Ali tried to dodge the purse, the round hairbrush in his back pocket fell to the ground, and the can of hair spray that he used to fix his handiwork in place toppled down as well. A container of combs took part in the chaos too when Barber Ali's big ass swung around, knocking it over along with a tuft of hair which, dutifully following the rules of nature, drifted to the floor.

Everyone in the barbershop, and everything as well, was thrown into bewilderment: the manicurist, the real estate agent getting a manicure, the assistant sweeping the floor, the models in the framed photographs with immaculate hair, the hair dye catalog, the smell of ammonia in the air, the old hair curlers that Barber Ali couldn't bring himself to throw out, the blow-dryers with diffusers, the glinting scissors, the towels washed without fabric softener, the blue light of the sterilizer used for the manicure set, and the moth flittering around above our heads.

At the time, I couldn't figure out why my grandma had acted that way with the old woman.

Upon our return to the building, she sent me home, watching from behind as I reached up to ring our doorbell and then making sure my mother opened the door before she turned to go into her own place. I heard my grandma close her door, not slamming it out of anger but something else, something strange. I even saw it. Those were the days when I started getting the feeling that I could see things that I couldn't actually see with my eyes—meaning that this ability of mine hadn't really begun as I sat on that mustard-yellow sofa the night Amy died.

"It's all just a figment of your imagination . . ." That's what Pembe would say to me.

That day when I came home from the barber, my mother was happier than I'd ever seen her. She even greeted me with a smile and noticed that I'd had my hair cut. Needless to say, she was like a completely new woman. She had fallen in love.

"To hell with that—everyone falls in love!"

That's what Derin said. We'd crossed over Unkapanı Bridge, and seeing as we drank some bosa at Vefa Café, it must have been winter.

We wandered the streets of that run-down neighborhood, sometimes in silence.

"You know what you should do? Write a novel about our girls' gang."

"Maybe you should," Pembe added.

"To hell with writing!"

"Language, please."

"Fuck writing. Is that better?"

That's how I swore for the first time, the words taking flight from my lips.

"As easy as unraveling a sock, right? As if!" I said.

"They asked what that expression meant on the end-of-year exam. I didn't know the answer."

"Pathetic!"

So, what were we doing there? Now I can see that we were in the grips of tedium. But the future was going to bring something entirely different to our lives, so different that we wouldn't even be able to recognize ourselves anymore. In those days, when we didn't know what fate had in store for us, we were preoccupied with winding up the springs of our souls. Perhaps it would be better to say that we weren't doing that to ourselves but the world around us was doing it. In short, the system. It did whatever it wanted, and it did it for us. Supposedly.

Love exploded into my mother's life like a bomb, bringing with it all sorts of new wonders. For example, she'd cook up diced beef for dinner along with something she threw together, like a pot of mushy rice or a salad of tomatoes and cucumbers. And I, looking as adorable and well behaved as a five- or six-year-old girl can be, gobbled it all down with a grin. No one could outdo me in putting on acts, and there was a reason for everything.

Mother, love me.

She would look at me and smile. The truth of the matter, however, is that she was smiling at the thoughts of love swirling through her mind, at the feeling of being filled with love. Allow me to go on: Around six months earlier, she'd started working for a well-known dietician. The weight-loss clinic was in the neighborhood of Nişantaşı, and according to the company's website, their office was "right across the street from the Toothsome Diner." Everyone in Istanbul who loves gorging themselves knows the place, and the location was ideal for anyone ready to break their diet. My mother was feeling better because she was finally working again. This all happened before the days when she couldn't land a job no matter how hard she tried, back when she didn't truly appreciate the value of the work she had. But now, making money brought back her self-confidence, and at the very least she was able to toss out her broken-down Adidas sneakers and buy a new pair of flats. After putting on a pair of black trousers and one of three blouses—all the same cut but different colors—she'd stride off to work, her old deerskin purse slung over her shoulder and her hair pulled into a swinging ponytail. That alone was a miracle for my mother because it meant she'd been saved from those dreary days of not being able to afford to go to the salon for a manicure. There was an odd new elegance about her, a glow you might say. Regardless of how dispirited, disappointed, and worn out my mother may have been, cut off from her own femininity to the extent that she would use scented pads instead of going to the trouble to change her panties when she was having her period, there was a glimmer inside her. The look in her eye was that of a woman harried by years of unhappiness but still hopeful, and soon enough, love would transform her life.

One day, the famous dietician she worked for called her into her office.

"How about getting a cup of coffee after work?"

At first my mother had thought she was going to get fired. That was her greatest fear, and for good reason: all the other places where she'd worked had let her go. I think the problem was this: my mother was rebellious at heart. I've never understood why she was so passive with my father, when without exception she got fired from or quit all the jobs she'd had in her younger days. And there was something else about my mother as well, an innate resistance to the work involved in food service. She had worked for a number of companies as a food engineer and dietitian for their cafeterias. When her employers wanted her to come up with the cheapest solutions, she'd say things like, "We'd be better off serving motor oil than the stuff you've given me, and those rotten vegetables aren't fit for human consumption." Needless to say, they wouldn't keep her for long. Rumor has it that some of those shameless bosses and their co-conspirators have tried to find ways to feed their workers seagull meat instead of chicken. Such dishonesty has worked its way into their DNA. And each and every time my mother was confronted with it, she'd end up losing her job and coming home with tears in her eyes.

One time my father said to her, "It's because of *you*. You keep getting yourself fired."

Before I was born, while she was working at the cafeteria of a publishing house, she managed to get a book of poems published. Yes, my mother wrote a book of poetry. She was a poet. Her book even did quite well, selling so many copies that in 1994 she had the means to buy a leather jacket and knee-length boots, as well as countless other things from the fashion outlet Beymen. That's considerable for a book of poetry.

Enchantress of the Kitchen.

That was the title of her book.

My mother was interviewed time and time again about pieces with titles like "The Kitchen Poetess." With her flowing hair, piercing gaze, and striking beauty, she proved to be a fascinating young woman in the world of literature.

"She could've gone on with it."

That's what my aunt—my father's sister—would say when she was talking about my mother or critiquing her choices.

But she married my father, and I came along.

One of her poems was put to music. It may come as a surprise, but every time the song played, a few *kuruş* would be deposited in her account thanks to the copyright laws of the day. But I'm not sure if I'll be able to do the next part justice as it always breaks my heart when women's lives are brought to ruin.

So, how had she started working as a dietician?

Okay, here goes. Both of them were interested in the arts. I mean, my mother and her sister. My aunt studied at Mimar Sinan Fine Arts University's Department of Traditional Turkish Art. Her real interests, however, lay in graphic design, painting, sculpture, and photography, so even though she got the highest score on the entrance exam, which required that the students submit drawings of the handrail designs on the burned-out Galata Bridge, everyone was surprised when she enrolled in the program for Turkish arts. The reason turned out to be simple: my grandfather had asked a friend of his for advice and that friend said, "If she studies traditional arts, we can get her a job at the Paşabahçe glassworks." So young women are dependent on the guidance of others despite the fires of creativity burning within them. In other words, they are poor passive creatures despite the fact that they carry within them a gem of artistic skill. Pathetic. Right? Of course, those girls are intelligent and realize what's going on—that's why my aunt went on to become a number one floozy at her school. Blow jobs under desks, flickings of the tongue while tracing the finest calligraphic sweeps, swallowing, sucking, and who knows what else. My aunt ended up getting pregnant by a finely sculpted, strapping young man—let's say a student from the sculpture department. She wound up having a miscarriage, her mother fainted when she heard, her father never found out, my aunt was terrified, the young man ran off, and posthaste she married the son of the owner of an appliance store.

"I said to myself, 'Save yourself, girl: get married.'" That's what my aunt said as she was telling the story, but naturally she didn't describe everything in such graphic detail.

They got her husband smashed the night of the wedding.

Later, they said to him, "I'm telling you! You shouldn't have had that last glass!"

The hapless groom passed out, and after stripping him, the women of the bride's family put him into the nuptial bed, the satin sheets of which my aunt had dyed to look bloodied. Her finest work. Because I was so young, the women spoke of it in whispers. The sound of their voices, like a breath of wind, had frightened me.

"I'd always imagined what it would be like the first time. Of course there'd be some rubbing, so the blood wouldn't really flow but would be more of a smear akin to a paintbrush stroke. Like the art of paper marbling, that's how I imagined it."

My aunt's name was Hülya, meaning "dream" or "fantasy." They couldn't have picked a better name for the woman she'd become: imaginative, cheerful, filled with exuberance, sharp witted in the face of life's unexpected twists. Sadly, she was unaware of the fact that she could've become a famous artist with those sheets she'd dyed. That was her story. So that's how my mother and aunt just missed the boat of art, that second life after death, and the chance for Hülya to become an artist, a new Tracey Emin. If you don't know who Tracey Emin is, you can Google it. Those women never really came into their own, partly because of their families and partly because of their tendency to bow under pressure, as well as their proclivity for giving up at the drop of a hat. It's a tragedy that a woman could be held back like that when she carries within herself all those feelings of rebellion, freedom, and the strength to stand on her own two feet. Rise up against everything, resist, shout . . . And just when you have the chance to be a poet or an artist in your grasp, cave to the pressure! Self-betrayal at its finest.

My aunt's marriage, established on bedsheets dyed with "virginal blood" as a symbol of her supposed virginity, was all she had to cling to in life. But my mother's book of poetry, written so many years earlier, was about to transform her world.

So, where were we in my mother's story? In the office of her boss, the high-society dietician, and now that they had finished work for the day, it was time to have that cup of coffee together. The dietician was famous for her candidness with her patients as well as her employees, and she displayed it now: "For the love of God, what've you come to?"

My mother later confessed to a friend that she was embarrassed when she heard those words. In those days, she always had her phone at hand, and she had just finished another free yet useless telephone therapy session with a woman in desperate need of help. My mother's three friends, to whom she would bare her heart, sat there looking at her expectantly. And bare her heart she did.

"I just love listening to you," one of them said. "It's like listening to radio drama."

Unruffled by the comment, my mother went on, speaking as if she was reading a fairy tale for adults, throwing in a dash of humor at times and breaking into a dramatic flourish at others. One thing is certain, however: her dramatic flourishes fell flat. What her friends wanted to hear were stories of love, passion, and sex steeped in hope.

When my mother's boss said, "You need to pull yourself together," something changed.

My mother started to change, all because of the personal attentions that queen of dieticians lavished on her, such as taking her shopping—and then withholding what she spent from my mother's paychecks. But the thing is, she had no need for such "pampering." She could clean up quite nicely, when she wanted to. But it was the prospect of love that set off a spark within her.

So, who did my mother fall in love with?

Yes, we're coming to that blazing point. She heard the footsteps of love, as soft and gentle as a fairy's.

The path of that doctor who had once caught my mother's eye, inspired admiration in her heart, and made her swoon at first sight led directly toward the clinic where she worked. He was a cardiologist, you see, and he was going into business with them.

Love never loses its way.

The first time my mother saw the doctor, she'd been so taken by him that she couldn't sleep a wink that night.

And where had she seen him? At a hotel where we, as a family, were vacationing.

She met him through some friends, and they had dinner together once. This all happened at a time when her unhappiness was at its peak. She was weary of life, fed up with my father's moods, and tired of looking after her three-year-old daughter, who was always tugging at her skirt. But to get back to the story: As I said, my mother was smitten. And he didn't seem averse to falling in love either. After that sleepless night, she and I went down to the children's pool in the morning. I don't remember all this per se—after all, I was just three years old—but there is one image that somehow remained lodged in the depths of my mind, only to surface much later. I was playing in the pool, the water of which came up to my waist, in a pink swimming suit. My mother was there with me. Who knows where my father was—he never spent much time with us. We bored him. He wouldn't talk to my mother or listen to anything she said. In a journal she kept when she was pregnant, she wrote that sometimes the only person she talked to for days on end was her obstetrician. As the woman went through her routine checkups, she would chat with my mother for a minute or two, which lifted her spirits for a while. My mother was a terribly lonely woman, buried in the wreckage of her life. And then I came along, and she was saddled with the burden of taking care of me. What I mean to say is that someone in her position could see a mere twig as a proposal of sorts and then fall head over heels in love with the tree.

That morning, my mother had fallen asleep by the pool. She was lying on a lounge chair in her red bikini with a faded towel tucked beneath her, a shapeless lump weary of promises of love, mouth open, drool running down her chin. Standing in the water, I looked at her. There she was, asleep, not paying any attention to me. No one was. When she awoke, my mother could have been confronted with the sight of her three-year-old daughter floating dead in the water. If I just stuck my head beneath the surface, I could've drowned on the spot.

At one point, my father came and woke her up.

I heard the end of the story as she was talking on the phone. In her mind, psychoanalysis was something you could do over the telephone, so with her friend listening silently on the other end of the line, she would talk and talk, which I also like to do. But there's a difference: she would only talk about herself. People are different that way; some can tell the story of their own lives by talking about others.

So there you have it, the path of that doctor who had swept my mother off her feet led directly to the door of the clinic where she worked, for he showed potential as the hero of a tale of adventurous love that had yet to unfold but very well could. His first day of work at the clinic happened to be his birthday, so they held a party for him. My mother gave him a copy of her book of poems as a present, which not only surprised him but secured his interest, which was precisely what she longed for.

The doctor was scheduled to work at the clinic three days a week, and my mother would anxiously await the arrival of each and every one, her excitement burning as brightly as a star. In turn, he would come to enjoy the attraction that this woman, who was eighteen years his junior, felt for him. So each week they had three days of flirtation that made my mother's heart flutter in her chest.

If something drives you from yourself, cast it from your life.

Even renounce the world if that is what you must do.

"Those are my favorite lines from your book," the doctor said.

My mother had become the paragon of a woman in love, and I had never seen her that way: blue spaghetti-strap dress, toenails painted red, a new hairstyle that suited her quite well, the graceful curve of her shoulders. She was talking on the phone, explaining and explaining. Explaining it all! As she held the phone, she seemed to be dancing, and I sat there watching her, wide-eyed. At last she hung up, which meant that it was time for us to be alone with that love story of hers:

"Have you finished eating your lunch?"

I nodded my head obediently, savoring the feeling of being loved by my mother.

"Would you like to go down to Grandma's place?"

No one could outdo me in the art of agreeing to anything.

How could I possibly bring myself to say, "But I just got home and I want to play with my toys"? After my mother turned on the stairwell light, I made my way down the two flights, clutching the handrail all the way. I knocked on my grandma's door, and before she even opened it, I heard my mother close our door upstairs. She trusted me so much! Or she didn't worry about me. My grandma opened the door.

"What are you doing here? Go home."

As I silently turned around, she sighed and took me by the arm to pull me inside. I had just gone up three flights of stairs to go home only to be sent down two, and now I was in my grandma's apartment, which was much darker than ours because its windows faced the apartment buildings on the side street.

She turned on the television for me and sat down by the window, which was her usual habit. But ever since that encounter in the barbershop, she'd been plunged into thought—I'd never seen her so quiet before. She just sat there as if she was taking in the view, though there wasn't much to see. While the living rooms on the upper floors looked out over the city, on this floor all you could see were the apartments across the way with their balconies shrouded in gloom, along with a few scraggly fig trees and some shrubs, the branches of which made me think of giant ferns. Most of the rear balconies were filled with a jumble of old furniture, while on the inside the houses were neat and tidy. It occurs to me that maybe our minds and thoughts are like that too. Just one of the balconies, a single one, had any semblance of order. There was a rope attached to the wall for beating carpets, a folding ladder draped with a piece of cloth, and some old newspapers meticulously stacked in the corner. Sometimes an old woman would sit there with her daughter, who looked almost as old as the woman.

My grandma could've looked at that balcony and said, "I wish your aunt lived with me. That way, we could rent out her place. It would be for her own good. Once in a while she has people over and I don't say anything because she's single, but still, they make such a racket! It gets so bad sometimes that I have to sleep in the living room. You know, I wish my bedroom wasn't under hers because that girl takes home any cock she can get her hands on. I'd move my bedroom to another room, but I just can't be bothered. The damn tramp. Hussy. Whore."

But that day, she couldn't even bring herself to say such things.

Because of the steepness of the road, the apartment buildings have retaining walls that secure their foundations, and the gap between the retaining walls of some of the buildings is extremely deep in places. I've been told that, before I was born, a woman who'd been living in the building across the street killed herself by jumping into one of them. My other aunt wrote an article for the newspaper about the incident. But it wasn't just sensational news about a random suicide—the woman's body was never found. True story.

"Is the chasm really so deep?"

"Not in the least. I remember when there were no buildings here at all."

Some geophysicists showed up, and a few Byzantine historians too, because underground cisterns often have long tunnels that connect them to the surface. As they worked, hitherto unseen things were brought into the realm of the seen. But they still didn't find her body. Who knows how many women have disappeared into it? What it really makes you think about is the fact that every suicide is the death of a person.

My grandma was gazing down into the chasm.

She closed the window.

And then she turned and looked at me.

She noticed that I'd been watching her. Maybe for her that meant a return to the realm of the living. After all, Efrosa hadn't come back.

"Don't gawk with your mouth open like that. People will think you're a dingbat."

I closed my mouth. But I couldn't silence the thoughts racing through my mind. At the time, I was five or six years old, about yea tall. What am I really doing up in this tree? Trying to grow up all over again?

My mind refuses to fall silent. It is inevitable that people will one day break their silence, but you can't explain everything all at once. You must do it slowly, hearing your voice as you go along. And when you get started, it's the voice of your emotions that speaks, not logic. That's what this is all about. If logic gets the upper hand, things fall apart because it doesn't have the power to heal.

Who would believe that I would curl up and go to sleep in a stork's nest, or that Pembe and Derin would die? Who would believe that one day my aunt—the reporter—would disappear without a trace? Who would believe that my mother's days of glory when I was five or six years old would collapse in ruin, or that it would come to light that my grandma harbored a terrifying secret that tormented her?

I hadn't really gone through anything yet. As you've seen, I was but a child back then. When I was three years old, playing by myself in that pool, I could've died. But I didn't. I survived. I clung to life. And I still am.

Just like the lyrics of that unforgettable song they'd play at my aunt's parties: "I Will Survive."

Ah, everyone was so happy at those parties. The ones at my aunt's place. The people there were reporters, both men and women, and all so cheerful.

Reporters who were happy, who loved their work more than anything else, made enough money to get by, and felt secure in their jobs.
My aunt had won an award. Is that what they were celebrating? There
was an older professor who had taught my aunt and her colleagues
everything they knew about journalism. Ünsal was his name. He was
chuckling on the mustard-yellow sofa, a copy of *Don Quixote* in his bag.

"I've been rereading it. What an enjoyable book!"

When I got curious about what was happening at the party and
went downstairs to investigate, he gave me the book because I'd once
told him that I wanted to be a writer one day.

"Good for you!" he said with an encouraging smile.

"He's the best of teachers," my aunt said to me. "Listen to what he
has to say."

"Is there any need for that?" her teacher asked. "She looks like a
bright girl already."

My aunt had another piece of good news to share: "By the way, I
finished writing my book."

"That's great! Let me take a look at it."

"Would you really?"

"Of course. Were you going to publish it without letting me read
it first?"

"No, no, I'd never do that . . ."

Everyone was happy. We were all happy. They probably played
"I Will Survive" ten times back-to-back that night. Laughter echoed
through the flat. The woman who lived in the apartment with the tidy
balcony called out into the darkness. She wasn't rude at all, or even irritated: "Excuse me? Excuse me, please? I was wondering . . . My mother
can't sleep because of the music. Maybe you could—"

"Please forgive us. We're having a celebration. Is there any way you
could sleep in the living room? Can you hear the music in there?"

"It doesn't bother me, but I'm not sure about my mother."

"Why don't you join us? We've already kept you up. Join the party!"

And she did.

That old lady who lived with her mother in the apartment with the tidy balcony came to the party at my aunt's place. She had short gray hair, eyes so dark they looked black, and teeth that glimmered like pearls. While she may have had a slight hunchback, she turned out to be the best—and not to mention most active—dancer of the night. Pulling Ünsal to his feet, she danced with unexpected skill and elegance. Roaring with laughter, Ünsal clapped and deftly stepped along to the music. He was a man who loved life.

"This woman is the best thing that's happened to this party!" he said.

"Dance like no one is watching, love as if you've never been hurt, sing like no one is listening, live as if the world is heaven itself!" Those are the secrets to a good life and happiness.

A gathering of journalists. Such beautiful people, enjoying themselves. The next morning, they would shower and go to their desks, smelling of shampoo and lotion. Newspapers would be printed thanks to their passion, the meeting to discuss the day's news would cause tempers to flare, but so be it—it's better that way. "I'm going to get the scoop on that story." That was the life my aunt led. Later, they all lost their jobs. It was unbearable to see. Do you understand what I'm trying to say?

I'm here because I want to live.

Either that or I'm imagining some other kind of death.

I'm astonished that the stork's nest is holding up beneath me. Then again, they wove the twigs together so skillfully, placing the nest on a sturdy branch far from danger.

No one else has ever slept in a stork's nest. Tell me, have you? I felt like I was becoming lighter and lighter as I longed to cast off my ties to gravity. I slept just as lightly, and the night was cold. When the lights in the park went off, I was buried in a deep darkness. It covered me like a blanket. Nature knows how things should be done—it's people who spoil the game. I breathed in the soft scent of the laurel leaves above my head. Such a secluded, tucked-away place. As I pulled my knees up to my chest, I wrapped my arms around myself even tighter. Taking advantage of the cover of night, birds and butterflies flitted around me, and one even landed on my chest, giving me a fright.

When our night drifts off to sleep, the sounds of the other night awaken.

There was a nursery rhyme that went like that. It always scared me when I was a child. One day, as we were singing it at kindergarten, I burst into tears because it made me think of the enigmatic behavior of the people in my family. Just what were those things—let's recount them, like the lyrics of that nursery rhyme: my mother's unhappiness and the cold way she treated me; my father always so distant, lost in his own world; the things my grandma kept to herself, refusing to speak of them.

But then a feeling of relief washed over me as I knew that I was in a dark place where no one could touch or reach me. If I were to say that I was no longer afraid because I lay there so stiffly, not moving a muscle, that wouldn't quite be true. I was frightened of falling to the ground, and for that reason, I feared waking up as well. But I slept. A deep, wonderful sleep.

In the morning, I was awoken by the sound of the sprinklers and the chill in the air. But I was still in the embrace of sleep and I refused to open my eyes just yet. There you have it: I had spent the evening in the tree. I'd survived my first night in its highest branches. When I heard someone call out, "Hey, you, I know you're up there," I opened my eyes.

Hey, me, have I been up here?

6

Notifications

It was him again. Yunus. But I didn't know his name at the time. Only later would I find out. I leaned over to peer down because his voice had come from below. No longer was he on the other side of the wall in the hotel's garden. Indeed, he was standing right beneath the enormous, ancient tree with the stork's nest. The tree's leaves made it seem like a laurel, but the trunk was more like an oak. Yunus had probably spotted my hand, which was hanging over the nest's edge. He wasn't wearing a uniform now but a pair of jeans, a T-shirt, and a plaid shirt with the sleeves rolled up, and he had a backpack. If his face hadn't been burned into my memory, I wouldn't have realized it was the same person. It was like a dream, and looking down all that way to the ground just after waking up made my head spin.

"Be careful," he said. "Don't fall."

I wasn't sure what to say. For a moment I considered telling him to fuck off.

Instead I said, "Go away." The words simply fell from my lips, as if he was an old acquaintance of mine.

"Why are you up there?"

Sneering like Derin would in such a situation, I replied, "What's it to you? It's not like I have to get your permission to be here, do I?"

"That's not what I mean."

"What do you mean, then?"

"You were up in a tree last night too. A different one, but still a tree."

"It's none of your business."

"Well, I was curious."

"Don't poke your nose in other people's business."

"Here's the thing . . . You climbed up that tree, and if you're stuck there like a cat, I can help you."

"I don't need any help. Leave me alone, and pretend you never saw me. That would be best."

"Are you hiding up there?"

"Shut the hell up already, fuckface!"

Pembe would say that sometimes swearing was the only way to get out of certain situations. It was, she said, a good shortcut to screw everything up in a flash, as well as to explain and present yourself.

"Well, damn, no need to be like that. When I saw that you were still in the tree, I decided to bring you some water and crackers."

In fact, I was hungry and thirsty, but I wasn't about to get out of my tree just for some crackers and water. Truly, have you ever seen a corpse rise from the grave?

"Won't you come down?"

It suddenly occurred to me that he might be setting a trap to get me out of the tree.

"How did you sleep up there? In a stork's nest, as if it were a crib? You know that even stork chicks fall out sometimes, right? How is it you didn't fall?"

"Don't your damn questions ever end?"

I went on imitating Derin, which brought tears to my eyes. She and Pembe sent me a video and then a Snapchat clip of them laughing on a bus full of young people. I replied with a message loaded with emojis: "Go on, have your fun, bitches! But we'll see who has the last laugh."

"Well, girl, you should've come too! You're missing out." Toward the end of the exchange, they sent an emoji of a hand flipping me off. Who knows where they found that one.

"Look at you, sounding just like your grandma! Puahaha, 'whoever laughs last, laughs best.' Yeah, right!"

"Sooo, sticks and stones will break my bones, but words will never hurt me. Puahaha!"

"Hey, our bus is leaving now, gotta run. We'll call when we get there."

"You're blowing me off?"

"Fine, we'll send you a selfie."

"I want some pizzazz! Dance for me!"

I waited, but the selfie never came. All they sent was a text saying, Take care :X, so I didn't push our banter. To tell the truth, I wrote message after message, only to erase them all. I think I blabbed something like, "Right, so you're heading off on your big mission!"

And then, "You guys are a real pair of Florence Nightingales! Bring your toys, go play."

That message was the last thing that Pembe and Derin wrote to me: "Take care." As if they sensed they were going to die.

Derin had posted a tweet saying, "Almost there. Right around the corner!" with a picture of the bus and the other young people on the same trip. Pembe retweeted it, so of course I immediately liked and retweeted her message. I thought of adding a joke, something lame like, "Go driver, go!" but changed my mind. Then my father's sister called me, as we shared the same life on Twitter.

"Why didn't you go with your friends?"

"I didn't want to leave my mom alone for so long."

"What kind of an excuse is that?!"

That summer, my mother had slipped into a deep depression. It was so bad that she could barely drag herself out of bed. As for my aunt, she had been out of the city for a while. When she lost her job, she eventually found work as the director of human relations at a municipal office run by a political party she had some connections with, so she put her place in Istanbul up for rent. She'd called from the office landline.

I said, "There aren't always answers to the questions we have in life. Some of them should go unanswered . . ." It was actually a bit about Pembe and a bit about Derin. But that's not what I said to my aunt. I didn't say anything at all. I found a way to get her off the phone by saying that someone was at the door. "Might be the Realtor." But it wasn't. It was a guy from the electric company delivering a notice stating that our electricity was going to get shut off because we hadn't paid the bill. We were left in darkness before all the others.

When I'm sad, there's this thing inside me that physically aches, as if I breathed in the sadness and it stays there, throbbing. In a way, that's a description of how spiritual pain is transformed into a soreness in the body. Then your eyes fill with tears. And when that happens, the violence of the pain dies down, even if just a little, but then the aching in your heart shatters into more pieces, multiplying with each tear. I know that I haven't explained this very well. Or perhaps you're thinking that now only because I brought it up. People are like that—the words of one person become like the wind. Still, I was able to describe the pain because I experienced it myself. I don't ever want to lose a loved one, a close friend, ever again. That's why I didn't want to get to know Yunus or fall in love with him. All the same, such things are beyond your control. Yunus, whom I thought I could keep at a distance by sitting in my perch, looked hurt. Even if I didn't know him, I got the feeling that I'd broken his heart when he was only looking out for my well-being. That's why I called out to him as he started to walk away, not because I was really that thirsty or hungry.

"Stop!" I said.

He stopped.

"Hang on, I'll take what you've brought."

7

UNFOLLOW

It worked: I lowered my backpack down with my slackline strap and then pulled it back up with the crackers and water inside. Still, at the last moment, I panicked, thinking that Yunus could be some kind of lunatic and that he might try to pull me down by the strap, so I lashed it to a tree branch and said, "Put them in my bag."

Somehow, it was like an exchange. The excitement I felt was genuine, but still I was afraid of that young man who wanted to help me. I didn't trust him, and all those feelings nearly made me tumble from the tree. I lost my balance and scratched my arm on the nest as I tried to keep myself from falling. Even though he wasn't trying to make me fall, I almost lost my footing anyways.

As I was pulling up the backpack, I said, "Now scram—or else." The heft of the bag pleased me. Of course, I knew that my threat was empty. It was as if we were playing a game of sorts, and over time, that's how it would really become.

Looking up, Yunus squinted at me as the morning light streamed through the branches of the tree.

"What are you waiting for? Go on!"

"Nothing," he said, slinging his backpack onto his shoulder. As he walked away, I watched him and then glanced around to make sure no one had seen what had just transpired. My guess was that he'd worked the night shift and was on his way home. I liked the way he walked. There was something diffident about his gait.

I undid the zipper of my bag and then opened one of the packages of crackers. At first, I was stuffing them into my mouth, but then thought better of it. Wouldn't it be better to save some for later? After all, it might be my last meal. Then I took a drink of water, but stopped myself, wondering if it might be something else, laced with some kind of acid, perhaps. For a moment, my fears turned the water to acid in my mouth, and I spit it out. After pouring a little on my hand, I became convinced that it really was water, so I took a few more sips. Ha, so I'd convinced myself it was safe! As I drank, I realized that I was dying of thirst. Water was going to be a problem, because at some point I'd have to pee, though I had imagined a solution for that. So that's how matters stood. But how would I fill my belly? I came up with an idea:

There was a pine tree next to the laurel I'd slept in the night before, and that meant there would be pine nuts. I shimmied across and ate my fill of nuts till the sun was straight overhead, shelling them as well as a bird. Then I had to stop because some moron with his friends in the middle of the park yelled, "Hey, there's something in that tree! Is it some kind of monkey?"

I had no choice but to quickly make my way to another tree in the most secluded spot in the park and wait for them to leave. My arboreal life, which was just getting started, was under threat of being revealed and brought to ruin. The best option seemed to be to hide out amid some branches overhanging the wall, but one of them broke. If I hadn't regained my balance with the nimbleness of a tightrope walker, I would have plummeted to the ground. The branch itself did fall.

One of the young men said to his two friends, "I swear to you, I saw something."

"You sure it wasn't a bird?" lisped another.

"No way, man. I'd say it was a monkey, but monkeys don't wear jackets."

The three of them stopped to look up into the branches of the trees, expecting to see some movement or at least something more convincing than a falling branch. In the end, they got bored and started to leave.

I realized that, from then on, I'd have to be more careful, even when hiding out among the branches at the farthest end of the park. *Or maybe,* I thought, *I should only move around at night.*

"Ha ha, it was Batgirl!"

Slapping their friend on the back of the neck as they teased him for imagining things, they walked off. I watched them, thinking I was more mature than them. Still, the revolt that had happened two years earlier had taught me not to be too judgmental about people.

So what the hell, there I was, hiding from men, hiding because I had to! When I lived among the people on the ground, I was the one chasing after men. Well, some of them. Okay, just one. Yes, I have a shoddy love story too. Okay, *had* one. But what I had couldn't really be called true love.

I scraped my knee during my attempt to hide out above the palace wall, and now it was bleeding. I glanced down at the trickle of blood.

Then I heard Yunus call out to me from somewhere that seemed to be near the foot of the wall. I realized he was back on the other side of the wall in the garden of the hotel.

"Didn't you go home?" I asked.

"No, I only came to the park before to check on you. We're not allowed to leave the grounds in our uniforms, so I changed clothes first."

"What's the deal . . . are there two of you or what?"

He laughed. "You're right, in a way. I work a double shift, both day and night. Admittedly, it's not normal."

There was a fire escape that snaked between the wall and the hotel. A hideous construction, really; it was like a crutch that had been wedged under the eaves of that elegant, fine building.

When Yunus realized that I was actually on top of the wall now, he scampered up the steps, then frowned when he saw that I was bleeding.

"What did you do to your knee?"

"Some guys in the park saw me—or they saw something, so I decided to hide in the branches here, thinking they wouldn't be able to spot me. But then I slipped and scraped my knee. I almost fell when a branch broke under me."

"I don't know how you're going to live up there in those trees . . ."

I liked the way that he talked to me; he seemed to know me better than myself. And I liked that I'd decided to live up in the trees. But he'd made his statement and was already turning around to leave.

"What? You can't stand the sight of blood?"

As he was skipping down the stairs, Yunus didn't even bother to answer.

8

Then he returned with some hydrogen peroxide and bandages.

I said, "If you are trying to come on to me, don't waste your time."

"It's not like that at all. I just want to help. And I'm seeing someone, anyways."

I must confess that I was disappointed when he said that.

"You can use these to clean up that cut," he said.

I watched as the blood started to dry. For like the 187th time, I swatted away a fly that kept trying to land on my cut knee. As I shooed it away, I said, "You cheeky little bastard!" I saw Yunus's face fall and realized he thought I'd said it to him. Since he was standing on the top step of the stairs, with one big step he could've joined me on the top of the wall, but he refused to go any farther. At the time, I thought he was afraid of getting his uniform dirty, but I later found out he was afraid of heights.

The knees of my pants were pretty torn up, and I thought maybe I'd fractured my foot in the fall, but it was starting to feel better. The plastic bottle of peroxide was cold, but I poured lots onto the cut and cleaned it up. As Yunus made his way back down the stairs, I called out, "Thanks!"

He didn't turn around to say anything in return.

I wasn't sure if it was a good or bad thing that I'd met him that way. I often wondered how I would manage and what would happen to me if I was alone. Don't judge me; you too would think it over a million times if you were in my position.

We always have the strength to deal with whatever comes up in our lives. After bandaging my knee, I lashed the extra bandages and peroxide to my waist so that I could take them back to the nest, where my backpack was. I'm incapable of living in the moment because I constantly think one step ahead, meaning that my mind is never really at ease. I wish that I could express all these emotions in a better way to you, but this is the best I can do. Also, I have a tendency to try everything again and again.

Why am I here?

I know that was the question I should have been asking at the very beginning, but people aren't aware of the true scope of the situation they're in until much later.

"Just stop and take a look around," I said to myself.

So I sat there on the wall and gazed at my surroundings. The reason is simple: Everything starts with seeing. Watching. Looking. My father told me that the wall between the park and palace was as original as Hagia Sophia. "Nothing," he said, "has ever changed about it. More importantly, it was built by prisoners working to earn their freedom." The mortar, he told me, had been mixed with egg whites. And there I was, sitting on that ancient wall, gripping its stones, feeling as if all of time and the history of the city were right there under my hands. The place I've been referring to as the hotel was built on the palace grounds as a grand residence, but when? Maybe in the seventeenth century? A massive air conditioner had been installed at the corner of the fire escape, but most of the rooms' windows were open and some had curtains, which were a brown fabric, probably cotton, billowing out like hair tousled by the wind.

Along the top of the wall were dappled shadows, and the leaves of the laurel tree were glowing in the sunlight. And then there were the birds, singing ever so beautifully. It was warm up there on the top of the wall. I pressed my thighs against its warm stones. The branches of the laurel tree surrounded me on all sides, and I stroked their soft leaves, reveling in their scent. I turned my face up to the sun, stretching my neck out longer and longer like a tortoise peeking out of its shell, and just sat there for a while.

That day must have been September 15, my first full day spent in the treetops. My knee ached and I was suddenly afraid that someone would spot me. That is one of the "normal" emotional states from which I suffer, though I would like nothing more than to be easygoing and carefree. If I'd had my phone, I would've taken a selfie up there on the wall. Maybe it would've been easier for me to come to terms with and understand myself that way, as it was impossible for me to see the expression on my face, but I wasn't about to go in search of a pond to gaze at myself like Narcissus. True, I could have asked Yunus to bring me a mirror or a phone, but what need was there? The realization that I didn't need anything filled me with melancholy. I'd given up on everything, lost everything. So perhaps it would have been better for me just to be alone with myself. Everyone I'd loved had given up too and lost everything. And then what? They died. I glanced up at the roof of the hotel, the tiles of which were an unusually bright red. If anyone looked out the window of their room, they would've had to really crane their necks to see me. I decided that people should look up into the sky of Istanbul to see what's there. Was there anyone like that? Yunus, perhaps. For a moment, I felt divine, like I was up above everyone and everything, way up in the sky.

Like typical Turks, the owners of the hotel had turned the rear garden into a small dump. Sure, it wasn't filled with the kind of garbage that would stink and draw flies, but there was a pile of useless junk down there: a refrigerator, a rusty grill, chairs with broken legs. All useless! Let me confess: my grandma would read books to me. Her own books, outdated novels. Some of the words I learned from them are keepsakes for me. Yes, that's it! Keepsakes, the most precious kind.

I thought that Yunus would bring me anything I wanted.

But it seemed to me that someone up on that wall didn't need anything in life. Was I wrong? No, I wasn't. Not at all.

9

LIKE

Yunus brought something that made me double over in laughter: Calvino's book *The Baron in the Trees*. It had been tightly wrapped and was sheathed in a clear plastic bag, meaning that he'd bought it new for me. He stood under the stork's nest, calling up to me. Thinking that it might be the guy who thought he'd seen a monkey, I peered down through the twigs of the nest. When I saw that it was Yunus, I smiled. My grandma used to tell me about how they'd peek out through the lattice windows of their old wooden house to watch the handsome young men walking down the street. She was born in 1937. Her mother was thirty-seven years old when she gave birth to her, which in those years was considered quite late, and I'm told that she too would go on and on about the handsome men of Istanbul in 1915. You see, she grew up in the very same house. Then again, the war was raging at the time, so not many men were strolling about on the streets. Still, she would stare outside to find out what men really were like, even scrutinizing the tips of their mustaches. There was a mountain of difference between how I peered down at Yunus like my grandma looking out through the windows and how I said, "What, you again?" When Pembe wanted to emphasize a contrast, she'd say, "There are mountains of difference and then there are Uludağ Mountains of difference." That's because her family was from Bursa, near Uludağ. Even though they worked in textiles, they still objected to her name. Maybe because they wanted to be bourgeois or high society? I don't know.

I have no intention of going anywhere with this. I'd like to dwell on just two or three things, but just like I climbed the plane tree, clambered over to the eucalyptus tree, and then settled into the nest hidden in the laurel tree, it's not working.

I said to Yunus, "Well, at least you didn't bring me a copy of *Tarzan.*"

And then, unable to stop myself, I burst out laughing, which again hurt his feelings. That was his destiny. If Pembe and Derin were still around, I'd tell them all about it. I couldn't understand why he was being so persistent. After I lowered my backpack on the strap, he put the book inside and said, "Now pull it up." I felt like one of those women in Cihangir who still lower a basket on a rope down to one of the few neighborhood stores still left to do their shopping. Before going through the rope routine, they'd shout down to the shop to get the grocer's attention. One time my grandma laid into one of those women, pulling on her rope like an enraged bell ringer, saying, "Fuck your shopping! Enough already! Just call out once. Don't scream your damn head off!"

"You crazy woman! That's what you are. Crazy Perihan!"

My grandma yanked harder on the rope, nearly pulling the woman out of the window. Eventually, new tenants moved into those apartments, and when they want something from the grocer, they call him on the phone. He doesn't take orders online. The wannabe bourgeois character in a sappy Turkish comedy film—Derin would say, "Just like us!"—also yanked on the rope of a basket being lowered to a shop, but pulled so hard that she really did tug the woman out of the window. We'd gone to see the movie while skipping school one day.

"Why are you trying so hard to fit in at this school?"

Pembe, Derin, and I had a quick conversation while waiting to get punished in the headmaster's office. Back then, I'd already read the book that Yunus brought to me. Even if we plunged into the depths of snide girl chat, we still had a certain refinement.

I looked down at the cover.

"I've read this already. And in any case, I didn't come here to read."

I couldn't understand why Yunus was so interested in me. Sure, someone trying to live in the treetops is bound to arouse some interest, but the way that he persisted in his efforts to help me was unsettling. Admittedly, I liked the way that he looked up at me, the expression on his face. It made me feel like I was his master in a way—at last I'd found my own slave. Love enslaves others or it is a slave itself. Granted, it can happen when you're equals as well, but in such cases, outside powers step in to meddle. Breath is needed to stir it to flames.

"I thought you might get bored, so I wanted to bring you something to read. Of course, I could've brought you a book of mine, but then I thought of this one. It never occurred to me that you might've read it."

"That's poignant. But you see, I'm up here for two reasons: poignant things and the fact that I want nothing to do with this shit we call life."

"How's your knee?"

I wanted to tell Yunus to stop trying to change the subject, but I couldn't bring myself to say the words.

"Do you need the bandages and peroxide back?"

"No, you keep them."

We gazed at each other for a moment. He seemed childish and naive as he stood there, insisting on helping me, clearly unsure of what he should do next.

"What are you gawking at?" I asked.

The fact of the matter was that I was acting just like any other ordinary girl. No one could outdo me when it came to playing roles, and it pains me to think about that lousy side of my personality. I was nothing more than a despicable actor, the lowest of the low!

He said, "You surprise me, that's all."

"Go on being surprised. It's good for you. Helps you pull yourself together."

I could hear people talking in the depths of the park, which made me wonder how crowded it would get when summer rolled around. Now that it was September, not so many people came around except for the snuggling couples strolling along the paths farther up the way.

"If you keep looking up at me like that, someone's bound to notice and come over to see what's in the tree."

As I said that, I got to my feet as if I were going to suddenly take flight like Peter Pan, standing in the fork of the branches of that plane tree where, just the day before, I'd been too scared to lean back against a bough. Holding on with two hands, I was suspended there in those branches that thrust up into the sky. I felt something moving within the tree beneath my hands and the soles of my feet: the pulsing of veins, a gently stirring life, a shifting, a heart beating in the center of the trunk, lungs breathing in and out. Do not confuse what I just said for the rustling of the tree's leaves in the light breeze. It was something else—the tree truly was a living being. That's why the revolt broke out in the first place.

"Wait here," Yunus said, and then he dashed off.

I wanted him to stay a little longer. I liked his calm, complacent ways. If I was afraid of being seen, I could've gone back to the wall where Yunus and I could continue our light squabbles—which, I must admit, were a bit one-sided. I decided to hoist up my backpack, the zipper of which was open. When he'd put the book into my bag, I saw the title on the cover from my perch high up in the tree, maybe thirty meters up. I watched as Yunus sped away, and then I went back to my hiding place. At the very least, in a single day I'd come to know those three intertwined trees and the birds and insects that inhabited them. A plane tree, a eucalyptus, and a laurel. A laurel that was born of a laurel that was an oak and looked nothing like a laurel. And let's not forget about the pine that so graciously shared the bounty of its nuts with me. It was impossible to know how old they were or who had actually planted them—even their graves were most likely already long gone, ground to little more than pebbles over time. But the trees still stood. And the wall too. Humans were the frailest of all, but strangely, it was they who brought the most harm to nature. Because the weak tyrannize others. They are cowards.

"Tyrants are afraid."

That's what I had scrawled on walls and streets with spray paint during the days of the revolt.

"Girl, you are such an idiot."

"Didn't your mother feed you well when you were a kid?"

"No, I bet they dropped her on her head when she was a baby. That's why she's like this."

"Derin, this girl's not right, I'm telling you!"

"The moron . . . She thinks that she can be a writer!"

"What could this girl, who put such a stupid sentence on a wall, possibly write? She says it would be a novel if she explained it."

"Well, if I did write a book, wouldn't you read it out of curiosity? At least just to see what it was about?"

"What an imbecile! Now she's all riled up."

"Come on, Pembe!"

I'd shot some paint into both Pembe's and Derin's hair, and they'd spray-painted my sweatshirt in retaliation. During the course of our little spray-paint war, Derin's legs ended up getting painted black. I'd decided that I was going to take out my revenge on the wall, and I came up with some good lines. We even tweeted one of them, which read, "*Liberté Égalité* Beyoncé!"

It was retweeted 1,356 times, and I suddenly had 1,056 followers. Pembe didn't bother washing out the paint I'd sprayed on her hair. "It brings out the color in my cheeks," she said.

Two years later, they both had ombré highlights done before setting off on that journey from which they would never return.

"Why not?" they said. "We got excited about the idea."

"What exactly is ombré? Your readers may not be familiar with the term." The main character in my novel had ombré highlights, and Özlem Hanım, our bigoted, zealously patriotic literature teacher, had asked me that question in that piercing voice of hers with perfect diction. I'm telling you, that woman was off her rocker. Inspired by the character in my book, Pembe and Derin went to a beauty salon to get highlights. Honey blond for Pembe and platinum blond for Derin.

"We look like idiots, don't we . . ."

Derin kept saying that as she leaned down to look at her hair in the side mirrors of cars parked along the street.

"I don't know," Pembe said, pursing her lips. Tossing her hair with a titter, she added, "It's not bad. A change, at least."

"But it's weird that both of us got it done."

"Well, ladies, you can get ombré for free at the *coiffure d'état!*"

We laughed all the way down to the bus stops by the seaside in Kadıköy, where I saw them off. Still not quite comfortable with her hair, Derin had tied it into a bun, even though, back at the salon, she'd been the one who kept taking selfies of her hair pulled into tiny foil-wrapped bundles.

It was a pleasant summer day as they waved goodbye. As usual, the Kadıköy promenade was bustling with people, and the sea was glinting silvery in the sunlight. I was planning on taking a ferry to the other side of the city. Before leaving, we'd had a "farewell beer" at a place in the heart of Kadıköy. A beer to wish them a good trip.

"Yeah, but now we're going to have to pee like crazy."

Derin had my iPod with her, but we hadn't transferred over the songs that I had on my computer because there wasn't enough time. There was never enough time. "So many things to learn, so many songs to sing, so many men to make love with." Those were Pembe's clichés. As for me, I had Derin's iPod. "iPod" is such a great word; for some reason I like it even better than the word "seedpod," after which it was named. I came across the surprise they'd prepared for me when I was on the ferry. The saps had made a song for me. They knew I was upset that I couldn't go with them, but if I had gone, I'd be dead. Who knows, maybe I'm dead now.

What else can I do but think about the past? If you want to move forward in life, you can't dwell on the past, and that's precisely why I'm here—because I couldn't go on. If I was certain that I'd lose my memory if I fell from this tree, I'd let myself plummet to the earth in an instant.

"Hey, can you come over here? I brought you something to eat."

"I don't even know what your name is."

And that's how I found out that his name was Yunus.

I was back to my spot in the laurel, feeling so heavy in my heart after thinking about the last day I spent with Derin and Pembe that I couldn't even remember how I'd gotten there. It was as if I'd walked on air. In that state of melancholy, I was distracted, so when Yunus whispered his name, I thought it was the cooing of a bird. Or maybe it was because my grandma told me that, when doves cooed, they were saying, *"Yusufçuk, yusufçuk."* You see, I thought that he'd said his name was Yusuf.

"I love the sound of doves cooing," my grandma would say.

We used to sit in the backyard with its greenery shrouded in shadows.

"It's a good thing we didn't have a balcony built off of the living room. This way, we can come out here to get some fresh air. That developer was hung up on the idea of the place having a balcony . . . Still, he wouldn't give us an apartment with a view. If he had, we would've had a real balcony, one with a breeze. And Istanbul would've been spread out before us. Then again, we've got our Istanbul now. It screwed us in the ass. But if we had a view, we would've looked out over the palace of fairies. Watched the passenger ferries going back and forth."

We listened to the sounds of the sea, the most wondrous thing in the world. My grandma's voice was echoing in the depths of my mind as I lay with my head in her lap. "That developer was flirting like crazy with your father's sister, but in the end the bastard couldn't say no to his own father. You know, he'd go around acting like a real tough guy, but he was as cowardly as a baby at its mother's tit. So, what did he do? He married some girl his family thought was a better match, leaving your aunt in the lurch without her virginity. Of course, she fell into depression. It was so bad that, one morning, she was about to jump out the window upstairs. I was woken by the cooing of the doves and stopped her before she went through with it."

When she told me that story, I was too young to ask what else had happened, but there was the magical sound of doves cooing in the background as she spoke. Even when I was that age, she trusted me enough to open up to me. Still, she didn't tell me everything, so the rest was buried in darkness. What I'm getting at here is that the cooing of doves reminds me of my grandma. In the end, it was not so much my heart that convinced me to trust Yunus but the idea of the sound of doves. All the same, I couldn't stop being prickly with him.

"You got over your fear of heights pretty quick."

"What do you mean? I still haven't."

It was true. He was still afraid as he stood on the top step of the fire escape. He only had to take one more step to reach the wall, but he lingered there, like an adorable monkey in a cage, frozen in fear.

"If you tie yourself to the tree with that strap of yours and reach out to me, I can give you this."

He was holding out a plastic bag. Even from my perch, I could feel its warmth and pick up its scent.

"Hold it out to me, I can reach it."

"No way! You'll lose your balance and fall."

"Don't you have anything else to do with your life? You're always coming around here. Don't worry, I won't fall. Can't you see I've already been up in these trees for a whole day now?"

"Yes, but you need to be careful."

"Why do you think you can boss me around like you're my father or something?"

"I don't know. Guess I've always been that way."

"Well, it's nice that you're at least aware of it."

"I can't stay much longer. My lunch hour's about to end. So take this, but tie yourself to the tree first."

"Just give it to me!"

I reached out and grabbed the bag from his hand. And as I was doing so, I just about fell. Yunus screamed. To be honest, I screamed as well, though I managed to cling to the edge of the wall like a tendril of ivy or a spider. If I hadn't thrown my right leg over the other side, I would've fallen for sure. Whenever I actually believe in myself, every-thing goes to shit—that's just how it is. But by making the slightest of movements, I slowly pulled myself back up with the ease of a lizard. Yunus looked at me wide-eyed.

"This time you've hurt your chin," he said.

I reached up. Indeed, my chin was bleeding. I noticed that some of the food had spilled out of the bag, but I'd managed to keep hold of it as if it were the joy of my life.

"Is it a bad cut? Hopefully you won't need stitches."

When I pulled my hand from my chin, it was covered in blood. Yunus looked on with a frown.

"Are you kidding me? I've had four stitches in my head already. I think I'd know if I needed stitches for this."

Bowing my head, I tried to show him where the stitches had been, but my hair had grown over the scar. I know the gesture was ridiculous, as we were more than a meter apart.

"Make sure," I said, "that no one else from the hotel sees me. Those nutcases would call it in to the fire department or the cops."

"Don't worry. No one but me will see you."

"Why are you always looking up at things? Because you're afraid of heights?"

"That's another story altogether. And anyone standing where I am right now would be afraid. How did you crack your head open?"

"Are you trying to ask me why I'm up here?"

"No, not at all. That's none of my business. But there's got to be a story about how you ended up having to get stitches."

"Maybe that's none of your business either. Did you think of that?"

"Fair enough. I take back my question."

"It's hard to tell you anything when I don't know whose side you were on."

"Side?"

"We ran down the hill from Taksim. There was tear gas. The police, water cannons. A real tussle. The next thing I knew, I woke up in the mosque with all the other people who'd been hurt."

"Were you part of the protests?"

"Were *you*?"

"I got hurt that night too. They also carried me to the mosque."

"Don't mess with me."

"I'm serious. I was hit in the stomach with a tear gas canister."

Excitedly, Yunus pulled up the shirt of his uniform to show me his stomach. There was a weaving, winding scar with five or six stitch marks. It looked like a worm trying to crawl into his belly button.

"I've got another one on my calf. My friend's chin was busted by the cops too."

"Well, *I* got my head cracked open."

"When were you born?"

"Ninety-eight. You?"

"Ninety-seven."

"So, you were only sixteen at the time?!"

"Yep. But the people from our neighborhood are used to that kind of thing. When the riots broke out and we heard that people were dying, we rushed out."

"I was there before it all happened. When they started cutting down trees and burning people's tents. They burned mine too . . . My friend Pembe was inside at the time. The poor girl nearly burned up."

A walkie-talkie in Yunus's pocket suddenly crackled to life. "Yunus, where the hell are you? We've some bags to haul."

Pulling out the radio in a panic, he replied, "I'll be right there, sir." Then he turned to me and said, "I've got to go."

"But you haven't eaten anything."

"Your story filled me up. It's been nice meeting you."

He stood there waiting for me to tell him my name. But I had a new one.

"My name," I said, "is the Girl in the Tree."

Before turning to go, he dryly replied, "Very well, Girl in the Tree. We'll talk later."

His departure was nothing short of a racket. Feet booming on the stairs, he ran as quickly as he could, and even as he ran across the gardens, his footsteps echoed up to my perch. A man was waiting for him in front of the hotel. When Yunus rounded the corner, I heard the man say, "Yunus, where the fuck have you been?"

"I just went out for a little walk. To get some air, you know."

"Screw your walks. You're just slacking off. There's a whole busload of people waiting for you. Get going!"

I watched as his red uniform disappeared into the vibrant greens of the well-kept garden of the hotel. He looked like a tiny, bright stain that slowly shrinks until it's gone from sight. I was still on top of the wall at the time, my chin bleeding just as my knee had done, which made me think that the sole purpose of the wall's existence was to bring me harm. My battle was with the wall, not with the trees. They hadn't hurt me in the least.

I made my way back to the stork's nest, which I'd started to think of as home. It may as well have been, as I always left my backpack there. With a smile, I pulled out the copy of *The Baron in the Trees* and set it aside before pouring some peroxide on a bandage to clean the cut on my chin. Admittedly, it was strange that I'd been wounded twice in a single day, but what was stranger was that, even though I didn't yet have a mirror, it was like I was sitting across from myself, watching myself clean the wound, as if I were sitting there looking back at myself. The overwhelming oddness of it all was that the me who was wiping away the blood sensed what was happening and hesitated. Suddenly feeling scared and unnerved, I dropped the bottle of peroxide. I watched the bottle as it fell like a white pigeon doing flips in the air.

My wounds ached.

I sat cross-legged in the nest like a child sitting in a small round tub, waiting for a bath. The dark green leaves of the laurel tree hung above, reminding me of an umbrella. I looked inside the bag Yunus had brought. There was a shiny plastic container that had spilled its contents: some rice, meatballs, fried potatoes, and for dessert, pastry rolls in syrup with cream, but half of the food was now on the ground somewhere. After putting what was left back into the container, I was pleased to find that the *ayran* hadn't leaked out from its cup. My plastic fork was at the ready. Even though I was starving, I ate with slow deliberateness, thinking it best to treat the meal as a banquet of sorts. The wet wipes were another pleasant surprise, as I could use them to scrub down my armpits and ass, even if just a little—that was the best

I'd be able to do up in the treetops in terms of hygiene. My only other option was washing with leaves on the off chance it rained. I was a mess, but I knew I shouldn't care. Otherwise, what was I doing there in the first place? Why had I left home, where my mother had an enormous showerhead installed in the bathroom? I told myself that I'd get used to it in time. "Look," I said, "you've done the hardest part, which was climbing up the tree and staying here." I smiled.

My plan was to eat everything Yunus had brought. So, with my white napkin laid out before me, I went on with the feast, which I was pleased to find included a salad in a little plastic box that I discovered at the bottom of the bag. "This," I murmured, "is what happiness should be. This and nothing more." That's what I was feeling, along with the sting of my wounds.

Suddenly, I remembered where I'd seen Yunus before. Or maybe I just made up the memory, I'm not sure. All the same, I was thinking that I'd had a similar feeling during the days of the protests, so that was probably when I'd seen him. After I'd been wounded and taken to the mosque, the doctors circled around me like white-winged angels, saying things like:

"She's got a head wound." "She might have a concussion." "It was hard to get her here." "The police wouldn't let us through." "Is she conscious?"

Had I been conscious?

There was an enormous sparkling chandelier hanging above me. Like the Little Match Girl who gave herself over to reveries as she tried to get warm by the flames of matchsticks, my mind started to drift. I was ready to slip into the other world. Just one step remained. One small step.

I knew that because, when I turned my head to the left, I saw my grandma, who had died two months earlier.

"Don't be afraid. Death is a sweet slumber."

Just to my right was a young man who was also wounded. He was lying there with his shirt cut open. As the doctors worked away, doing something to his stomach, he smiled at me. Drawing on his last strength, he reached out and stroked my fingers. That touch was something of this world. As I was on the verge of crossing over, something of this world reached out to me, and I too remained here. On this side.

10

DELETE

I resisted my urge to lick the dessert bowl, as I wanted to show myself that I was still a "civilized" person. Though it was tempting, I didn't even wipe my mouth on my arm—I used the napkin. No, I hadn't yet descended into savagery. Instead of clinging to the notion that I'd live out the rest of my days in that tree, I said to myself, "I'll just take it day by day. Maybe I'll go on staying here like this, who knows." I cast off all hesitations. About staying put, I mean. Even though I'd only been there for a day, it felt right. I couldn't have been in a better place. Just like during the days of Gezi. Being there and protesting had felt so good. And now I was protesting in the treetops, as I knew that in the world below I'd be harassed and harried to no end.

As I was cleaning up and putting all my trash into the plastic bag the food had come in, I found a toothpick. Sticking it into the corner of my mouth, I wondered how I was going to brush my teeth, given that I didn't have a toothbrush. There was always the option of asking Yunus to bring me one. I knew that he'd bring me anything. A new life, if I wanted. Even a new name. It made me feel better to know that, like me, he had been among the protesters. I felt safe. And that was comforting, just like knowing that I had something to eat.

I'd decided that I would throw the plastic bag into a green trash can I'd spotted a ways up the path, but it seemed most logical for me to crap in it first. As the saying goes, I'd kill two birds with one stone.

Luckily for me, my digestive system seemed to have slowed down up in the trees. I opened the bag in the middle of that nest where I'd taken shelter and created a new life for myself. My aim was perfect: three turds the size of Ping-Pong balls dropped right into the bag. After wiping my rear with a few laurel leaves, I tied the bag up. In the meantime, I noticed that the nest was making ominous crackling sounds. If I hadn't clung to the trunk of the tree like it was my mother, I would've fallen to the ground as the nest wobbled beneath me.

The trees were starting to get fed up with my presence.

They were right to not trust people.

The stork's nest was, in fact, strong enough to bear my weight. You know those wicker patio chairs, the ones that IKEA sells? Well, it was like that—tightly woven, as sturdy as an IKEA chair, ha ha! The only problem with the nest was its tendency to slide, so I pulled it back until it was resting securely on the branch and lashed it down with one of my slackline straps. I was no longer in danger. Looking up, I whispered to the trees: "You can trust me. I would never do anything to bring harm to you. So please, do what you can to keep me safe. From here on out, I'm going to be living among your branches. Never again will I set foot on the ground. I know that, wherever you are, your home is your inner realm, and you'll go on living your inward life there. The world below is filled with danger and evil. That's why I am looking to you for solace and refuge."

The branches of the trees swayed in a gesture of comprehension. The wind whistled. When you're afraid, every sound is a sinister rustling. A shiver of fear ran through me. Day had not yet descended into night. The afternoon was heavy with lethargy, but I no longer feared the advance of dusk.

I clambered onto the wall, because I figured that would be the easiest way to reach the garbage can. As I walked, I felt as though I was slacklining on the Great Wall of China. The world lay spread out beneath my feet, a realm unto itself. For a moment I felt lofty and sublime; as they say, if a peril turns out to not be very perilous, it enthralls you. Despite the smarting of my wounds, I felt content, and the ancient wall seemed to spring back with every step I took, probably because I'd grown accustomed over the years to the bounciness of a slackline. When I got close to the trash can, I tossed down the plastic bag. It sailed right in. I'd played basketball from sixth to eighth grade, so I was a decent shot. As a matter of fact, I was fairly good at all the games that children play. I just failed at life.

When I returned to my perch, I wondered if what I'd eaten was going to be my last meal up in the treetops. I decided that I'd better get used to eating less and sever all ties with life as I'd known it. I had a new life to live, and I knew that should be my only focus. As my grandma was fond of saying, "Never give up on your dreams. People can put up with hunger, but seeing their hopes dashed is a torment worse than any other."

I was undaunted by the prospect of going hungry and determined to make my dreams a reality. The only problem was that I didn't know exactly what they were. For that matter, I wasn't sure if I even had any. The dreams of my friends had all come to nothing.

How despicable! What gave you the right to destroy the lives of those brilliant young people? How could you hurt them so? And for what? Take the whole country, if that's what you want. It's all yours. Tear it to pieces. You disgust me. And you become all the more disgusting by doing what you do. You killed my friends. You tore apart my family. Yes, you are responsible for that too. You created a flora that makes it impossible for people to live their lives. You heartless wretch, do you even know what "flora" means? Vegetation. Do you know what it means as a figure of speech? If you don't, try to figure it out. I'd like to see you try to use that mind of yours for something other than cunning and deception. Take my aunt, for example. She had to stop working as a journalist because of the environment you created. And then what happened? She slipped into despondency. What is "despondency"? Looking

95

at the world around you like a dead fish. And what of my friends? You bombed the hell out of them as if they were your worst enemies. Then again, good people *are* your enemies. Just like all those conscientious youths.

I took a deep breath. When we remember, we reinvigorate life. That's what I'm trying to do here. As I've mentioned before, I don't know you, dear reader. And although I may not know who you are, please listen to me: Did you know that my friends volunteered to take toys to kids suffering from the ravages of war? We found out about the initiative from a couple of people we met at the park. Volunteers all around the country were working together on the project. There was only one condition: the toys weren't supposed to have anything to do with weapons or violence. For two whole weeks, we worked to make the project a success.

Forgetting doesn't alleviate the pain we feel—remembering does. That thought just occurred to me, now that I am feeling calm and composed. There's only one thing I can do for them.

They were so excited to go that they got highlights on the day that they were going to leave. It was a spontaneous decision.

"I just don't want to stand out too much," I said.

"You idiot! Didn't you protest together with people like that at the park?"

"Sure, but—"

"But what? Stop being ridiculous."

"Even being ridiculous implies a 'but.'"

"If you ask me, this whole conversation is becoming word salad. Shepherd's salad, at that."

As we waited for the bus to leave, we smoked, the ends of our cigarettes crackling in the wind. Ferries came and went as we stood there. I was feeling sentimental, but maybe it was the beer we'd drunk. Derin went to the corner shop and bought another beer.

"You've had enough already," Pembe told her. "You're going to pass out on my shoulder."

"So what? I'm feeling a bit nervous."

"Why?"

Looking back now, I can't help but wonder if she'd somehow sensed that they were heading toward death.

We'd already gone once to the underground public bathroom across from the entrance to the subway. Afraid that she'd have to go again, Derin handed me the can of beer. "Here, you drink this. It's going to be a long trip."

Seagulls swooped and soared over the silvery ripples of the sea. It was such a beautiful summer day. At one point, four young men walked up to us, along with a sweet-looking girl with braces.

"Are you waiting for the bus too?"

Derin looked more relaxed now as she fell into conversation with the newcomers. The girl, who had wavy hair and was wearing orange Converse high tops, gestured toward a car that was parked behind one of the buses. "Looks like we've got an escort."

"You think they're going to follow us?"

"Seems that way."

There were two men in the car. One driving, the other in the passenger seat. Their faces were shrouded in shadow.

"Do you think they're going to arrest us?"

"Like, when we get on the bus?"

"All because we're donating toys to those Kurdish kids stuck in the war . . ."

"It's not impossible. They beat people to death, you know."

"Really, who are those guys?"

"Enough already, let's talk about happier things."

"I couldn't agree more. My mom says that her generation might not have a shot at it, but we might when we reach her age."

"A shot at what?"

"Happier things."

A ferry blew its horn as I waved goodbye to my friends. Saying farewell always makes me feel melancholic.

I got a text message when I was on the ferry.

So, did you start crying when we left or what?

In my reply, I used some emoji that perfectly expressed how much I missed them already. I was sitting on the long bench that ran along the side of the ferry, and the water was so close that I could've dipped my feet into the sea. Luckily for me, as I sat there feeling pleasantly woozy from the beer, that side of the boat was in shadow.

When the ferry pulled up to the dock in Karaköy, I got a Snapchat message of them dancing the *halay* at a gas station.

"Seems the bus didn't fill up before we left."

They were leading the others in the dance, and Pembe was shaking a handkerchief as she danced.

"It's in my genes as a Bursa girl!"

I laughed as I watched Derin missing all the steps.

"Even though I'm a villager, I dunno how to do this!"

By that point, Pembe had stopped dancing and was hopping up and down. That family from Bursa that had made a fortune from textiles had finally come into its own through her, even if her name was Pembe and she swore like a sailor.

Smiling, I watched the Snapchats to the end, laughing out loud once in a while. We're used to seeing that kind of thing now: people who look like they're talking to themselves as they walk down the street (they're actually talking on the phone through their headphones) and people who laugh, get angry, or burst into tears as they look at their phones. Of course, there are also things to which we haven't grown accustomed despite the passage of time, but let's not go into those here.

I went into the Starbucks in Karaköy, but realized that I didn't even have enough money to buy a Turkish coffee, much less a cup of real brew. A bottle of water seemed to be my only option.

"Just give me what you've got and the rest is on the house."

Yes, there were still some good people in the world.

I trudged up the hill from Tophane to Cihangir. When I got home, I went straight to bed and slept like a rock. When I woke up, I checked my messages to see if Derin and Pembe had sent me anything. I felt like I was on the road with them thanks to their videos. After reading for a while and downloading some music, I started getting hungry, but there wasn't much to eat at home, so I cooked up a few eggs and nibbled at a salad my mom had thrown together along with some boiled potatoes; to be honest, I was surprised that she'd made anything at all. Afterward, I went back to sleep.

Pembe and Derin had breakfast at a cultural center while I was sleeping in Istanbul. While they were there, they sent me a video. It was the last one I got from them. They said that they were going to hold a press conference of some sort as they stirred sugar into their glasses of tea, being as impish as always. But they were also as kind as people come. They didn't have a selfish bone in their bodies, nor were they marred by the curse of conceit. In short, they had hearts of gold. In the video, they introduced me to some of the others. Others who would die like them.

I awoke to what I thought was the sound of an exploding bomb.

My mother burst into my room.

"There was a bombing!"

A bomb went off in my mind. Perhaps it would be better to say that it went off in my heart, in the very center of my life. I sat up in bed. It was hot in my room. I waved my arms frantically, trying to drive away the disaster with the back of my hand, trying to keep it far from us.

As I walked toward the living room, bleary eyed and still half-asleep, it all started coming together. The television was on and I was holding my phone. The Twitter app was still open, playing the video Pembe and Derin had sent me.

A list of the dead:

Pembe P. Yılmaz. But as far as I knew, Pembe didn't have a middle name—her mother had insisted on that—or so I'd thought. There was no mysterious *P* in her name, right? So it wasn't her. That's what I told myself.

Emine D. Erdoğdu. I was certain that couldn't be Derin Erdoğdu. The *D* could have stood for anything.

No, their names weren't on the list. I tried to believe that.

And then I had the first of my nervous breakdowns. When my mother reached her wits' end, she called over my grandma and Aunt Hülya.

"The poor girl's been crying her eyes out."

Murmuring a prayer, my aunt handed me a glass of water. I remember thinking, *Miss Deep Throat sure became a believer on the quick!* Those sinful lips had sworn to uphold her husband's political future. "Shut up! You killed them. It was your people who did it."

Her lips, which had been quivering like a leaf in the wind, stopped in mid-prayer. I knocked the glass out of her hand, sending water flying through the chasm between us. As my aunt reared back to slap me, my mother caught hold of her arm.

"Don't you dare hit her!"

In doing so, my mother protected me from the evil of the powers that be.

Am I wrong? I had a sudden urge to ask her that question, as I felt emboldened by the fact that my aunt hadn't slapped me. And I knew I wasn't wrong.

The conscience may be blind, but it isn't mute. While it may not offer up elegant laments, it speaks of its own faults and sins in whispers: "We're not killers."

That's what my aunt Hülya said. Her Céline sunglasses, the cat-eye type, were pulled up onto her headscarf, which was a lilac purple that matched the chiffon and silk blouse she was wearing under her long jacket, and she had on a pair of name-brand trousers and Jimmy Choo sandals. Needless to say, even though she wore a headscarf, she always dressed to the nines. I noticed that she was wearing a new perfume—a light summery scent, probably Tom Ford's Jasmin Rouge—and that she had a French pedicure. Just like how some people feel the need to make nonsensical comments about how women dress, I couldn't help but think: *She just had to show some skin, huh?* A diamond brooch was pinned to her headscarf. My mother had said of the brooch, which my aunt's husband had bought her for their anniversary, "It's gorgeous!"

After pulling that nuptial bed number on the night of her wedding, my aunt Hülya had truly become the virginal woman her husband had desired, and she was quite adept at pretending to be a scrupulous, understanding person. She was the one who paid for my plane ticket. I saw her put two banknotes on the table—400 lira in total—but my mom later insisted there had only been one.

By the afternoon, I was there in that city that had been stained with the blood of thirty-four youths. A police siren seemed to be hanging above our heads, flashing blue high up in the sky. I went to the hospital.

"They were blown to pieces."

The mothers kept repeating that over and over as they sighed in grief. The fact that their children had been killed was bad enough, but the explosion had been so violent that the bodies were unrecognizable.

"My daughter was like a porcelain doll. I loved looking at her."

The mothers were in anguish.

"They have to run DNA tests to identify some of them."

I recognized Pembe and Derin by their hair.

"Don't pull the sheet back any further. I can tell it's them."

"They were thrown so far from the bus that their hair didn't get burned in the fire."

The body parts under the sheets were like the bloody pieces of a puzzle. The pieces were intact, but no one knew to whom they belonged.

"This is Derin."

"That name isn't on the list."

"Her first name is Emine."

"Emine D. Erdoğdu."

"Here. Pembe is the one with blond highlights. Derin has platinum highlights."

"Pembe Paris Yılmaz."

"Her middle name was Paris? How did she keep that a secret from us? There was never a P on the attendance sheet."

That was the last trick Pembe pulled on me. They were lying side by side on a metal table. Rivulets of blood coursed along the table's surface toward the drains at each end. The blood made a sound as it flowed along the table. Then again, maybe I was the only one who could hear it. That was the last sound that Pembe and Derin ever made, and it gave me the impression that they were somehow still alive. Questions raced through my mind: How could they die like that? How is it that our loved ones die? How can they leave us like that, how can they just be wrenched from the world? The people we love can't just die.

Thinking that we were related, the doctors showed me their faces. We were related in a way. Bound by blood. That much is true.

I will always remember the good moments.

As we sat there drinking beer, they shielded their eyes from the sun with their hands.

"So," I said, pointing at my lip, "what do you think of my piercing?"

"Do you think you're Amy Winehouse or something?"

We had wanted to bleach a lock of our hair like Amy had done. I wish I'd gone through with it. When Derin was worried about something, her expression would become inscrutable, as if a curtain of fog had descended over her face. Pembe had adorably small ears, and Derin's upper lip was upturned like a baby's. Pembe had a tattoo of an angel, which she was still rubbing every day with Bepanthol cream.

"It looks great!"

"You don't think it's too big, do you?"

"Not at all. If Amy saw it, she'd wish she had one just like it instead of that bimbo on her shoulder."

"My nose is nothing like the noses of people from Bursa. I got it from my mother's side of the family; they've all got nice noses. But I got my dad's broad face, which ruins the effect."

We would stand in front of the mirror in the bathroom at school and talk about the pros and cons of our features. That's how I want to remember their faces. Smiling, laughing.

Both of them had beautiful teeth.

"Come on, give me a smile . . . I want a pic I can put on Instagram."

They'd flash me a full-toothed grin.

"I have my mom's dentist to thank. Did you know that a lot of dentists are real charitable people? They'll fix up the teeth of anyone who comes along, just like they did for me. Those poor people with bad teeth have just never been to a dentist. That's a true story. Spread the word."

"Stop kidding around—we had to wear retainers for years."

"I swallowed mine once. When I shit it out, my mom washed it and boiled it in a pot of water. Then she gave it back to me to wear, saying that the dentist had sent her a new one. Ha ha!"

My friends were lying on a metal table, their bodies now stitched back together.

How could you do that to my friends?

"It never occurred to me that they'd die. Not once did I think that they'd die like this at such a young age."

Pembe's father was devastated. Over the years, that philanderer from Bursa had developed a liking for the party in power and voted accordingly. In his mind, the state should have protected him and his children, but his lovely daughter had been blown to pieces.

"What business did she have being with those people?"

His wife, who I think I mentioned had once been an attractive flight attendant, screamed, "Enough!" It was like a slap to his face. "Get the hell out of my sight! I don't ever want to see you again, you bastard!"

Their funerals were beautiful. We buried them on a nice summer's day. If it had been cold and rainy outside, I would've been tormented by the thought of them lying in all that muck and mud.

"They're gone, so it's time to mourn for them. You'll remember your friends for the rest of your life. Over time, the pain in your heart will quiet down, but that doesn't mean you've forgotten about them."

My mother had taken me to see a therapist. She had no choice. I was balling up my hands so tightly that my fingernails were cutting into my palms. One night I tried to jump into that pit behind our house, the one that nearly every woman in our family had thought of throwing themselves into. The thing is, I don't remember doing it. Later, they told me that my mother held me back by one of my arms while my aunt—the other one, the journalist—held on to the other. In a panic, they had asked her to come talk to me.

She said to my mother, "I've missed Istanbul so much. I don't like my job. I miss working for the newspaper."

The place where she'd been living was, in her own words, a dumpy little town, and she had a dumpy little flat that looked out over some farm fields. One day, she went to the one and only beer hall in town. When she sat down at a table, she realized that everyone in the place—they were all men—had fallen silent. The only sound was the chirping of a canary in a cage. One of the men said with a leer, "That bird's male. Starts singing whenever it sees a woman." My aunt got up and left.

"I'm fed up with everything."

I'd never heard my aunt complain before.

"Our lives have all gone to shit."

My mind was mush because of the medication I was taking. They made me sleep in the living room so they could keep an eye on me. I wasn't feeling tranquil like I'd felt on the night that Amy died. On the contrary, I was stuck in my grief. It was as if I were at the bottom of a pit and couldn't get out. I constantly felt like I was out of breath. My two best friends hadn't been buried that day, I had—and I was pounding my fists against the boards that had been placed over my body.

"Get me out of here!"

When I started having the nightmares, they put me on heavier sedatives but, of course, they didn't help because my waking life was even worse.

I'm here because I wanted to get away from that miserable life.

Once I screamed at a man while I was on a ferry. There was a television in the seating area. The man, who was watching the news on the TV, had said, "Look at that. Those kids are blowing themselves up."

"What the hell are you talking about?" I shouted. That day, I was on my way to Pembe's mother's place on Bağdat Street, which was on the other side of the city, for my friend's memorial service.

The man tensed up when I stormed toward him, one hand raised threateningly. "Who's blowing themselves up?"

Without an ounce of shame, he said, "Those young people. The terrorists."

"You prick, can you even hear what you're saying?"

I was shouting so loudly that the veins in my neck were bulging. Everyone on the ferry fell silent. The ferry itself seemed to have fallen silent. It was as if the engine had stalled and the hull was just gliding through the water with its own momentum. As one of the crew members stared at me through the window, the only sound I could hear was the cries of the seagulls, which also seemed to be watching me.

"My friends died in that explosion! My friends!"

I was pounding my chest as I yelled.

"They're anarchists, the whole lot of them," he said. "All they want is to destroy this country."

"Screw your country, fuckface!"

"You better watch your tongue. The state will come after you."

"Fuck you and your damn state!"

He snapped. "You anarchist bitch, shut your trap! You're probably just a damn Armenian, like all the others! A damn Kurd! I'll bet you support ASALA! You frigging PKK terrorist!"

Even though he was seething with hatred, I could tell that he was afraid of me. As he leaned back in his seat and crossed his legs, I wanted to strangle the life out of him. I was so enraged that I was grinding my teeth. Sometimes I wonder if it was the medication that made me speak out that day or if I was trying to be more like Derin and Pembe to keep their memory alive. Either way, it was the pills that got me off the hook.

"A young woman attacked her mother while she was on the same medication. Do you remember that incident? She was beautiful, just a university student at the time. She slit her mother's throat, killing her. Everyone was surprised when she was being taken to prison because she was all dolled up. The medication was the problem."

That's what my lawyer was saying in the public prosecutor's office. My father had even gone to the trouble of showing up for the hearing.

"It's your fault that I had to talk to that bastard!" he yelled at me afterward.

Indeed, he had talked to that piece of shit in an attempt to get him to retract his complaint, begging him for my sake. Muttering to himself, the man finally backed down.

"The public prosecutor is on their side. He would've thrown you in the slammer!"

Everyone in the world seemed to be on their side, and I couldn't help but wonder: *Do you have to be evil to win in the end?*

After I gave my statement, an older cop walked up to me and said, "Do you know what they do to girls like you? They throw you into the worst ward with the worst criminals. You won't get a wink of sleep because the women there will feel you up all night long. Those lezbos have got tongues bigger than the biggest cock you've ever seen, and they wouldn't be able to get enough of a green girl like you. Then the guards would send you over to the men's ward so they could have their fun with you, and you can be sure that one of the male guards would take a shine to you too. And you were involved in those protests . . . They'd screw you over just so they could get in good with the head guards. After a few weeks of getting fucked every way possible, you'd be shitting and pissing yourself."

I puked. As that pig of a cop was telling me those things, I puked right there in front of him.

"You filthy bitch!"

Some other cops ran over and held him back. I figured he'd been a torturer at the peak of his career.

"Chief, cut it out. You're going to retire soon, right? Enough already. You should be ashamed of yourself, trying to scare the poor girl like that."

I was on the verge of laying into him like I'd done to the guy on the ferry. If I had, I would've wound up in prison, not in the treetops. That day, I even had a scarf in my bag so I could cover my hair. I said that I was going to a memorial for my friends. I slapped the guy across the face. He wasn't expecting that. He started swinging at me.

"You Armenian slut! You Kurd whore!"

God give the Armenians patience. They always get the short end of the stick.

A few people ran up and tried to pull the guy off me.

By that point I was on the floor. He got in a few kicks, swearing up a storm as the other passengers tried to shove him away. Later, at the police station, I found out that six months earlier he'd beaten his wife so badly that she ended up in the hospital. Despite that, I was the guilty party while he was as pure as the driven snow.

I know I should try to forget about that day.

My grandma used to say, "Forgetting is the only way to get through life."

Or was it: "Forgetting is the only way to get through this screwed-up life." Is that better? "If we didn't forget, this fucking life would be unbearable." She'd roll over in her grave if I were to forget the curses with which she peppered her aphorisms. Here's the thing: we can't live our lives by forgetting. All we can do is transform our past experiences into something else. And that's what we should do, turning them into memories that won't weigh on our hearts or drag us down into misery. While it may be true that stories of suffering cannot be transformed into wondrous tales in the way that coal becomes diamonds, if we go on living in spite of them, we ourselves can become something else, like a treasure chest, or an oyster containing a huge pearl. My friends died. I lost two people whom I loved deeply. Tell me, whose heart can I break? Whom can I hurt? What harm could I bring to others?

I knew that the sun was about to set because the birds were returning to their roosts. I wished that I could speak their language so I could ask them, "How is the city that I left behind? How is life going without me?"

If I didn't know how to forget, who could? I found myself in the treetops because I was stuck with my memories. Because I longed to forget. Because I couldn't forget.

11

Encounters between lonely people only occur in solitary places. I saw Yunus on top of the wall looking like a frightened—yet adorable—cat. At the same time, he struck me as being more handsome than ever. I was surprised, and my first reaction was to say something the likes of which would've fallen from the lips of Derin or Pembe.

"Hang on a second, I thought you were afraid of heights! What are you doing up here on the wall?"

"Come over here."

Based on the brevity of his answer, I guessed that he was still afraid, and he seemed confused himself about how he'd managed to get up there, straddling the wall like a horse. I saw that he was sitting on what appeared to be a fur coat. When I first saw him after emerging from the seclusion of the laurel tree, for a moment I imagined that he'd arrived on the back of some mythical beast. In turn, that made me wonder if—or when—I was going to lose my mind. At the time, all I could hold on to was my obstinacy: I wasn't going to descend from the trees or set foot on the ground. Maybe fear as well: terrible things had happened to me, and I was incapable of dealing with the pain and loss I'd suffered. And there was a desire to seek refuge: if it was possible, I would've gone back to my mother's womb. I also longed for seclusion: I could have slept for a hundred years. Like I may have said before, I wanted to experience death before actually dying. Don't be surprised if I repeat that hundreds of thousands of times because that is the story of my existence. So let me live out my story however I see fit because our lives can so easily be taken from us. You know what happened to Derin and Pembe. Why should two young women be plucked from this world when they were so full of life? They wanted nothing more than to bring hope to a war-torn town in a desert; and then they were blown to pieces. If the sorrow and grief I felt were to sprout leaves, branches, and roots, it would've been as massive as the trees in the park. I had no idea how to console myself, and I wished that I'd been committed to an insane asylum, as at least there I would've been able to find some respite. My sole desire was to slip into the cool dark of unconsciousness. Yet I was fully conscious and sound of mind even if I was living in the treetops. That's what I was thinking as I looked at Yunus, who had somehow mustered the courage to clamber atop the wall: *I am of sound mind.*

"I thought you were afraid of heights."

"I was."

"How did you get over your fear?"

"Fears exist so we can overcome them."

"If you ask me, you're the one who's going to be overcome. Not your fears."

Yunus was like a knight waiting for me as he sat astride that strange creature. I couldn't understand how he'd made the leap from the fire escape to the top of the wall, as I knew that fears cannot be conquered so easily. My guess was that he'd tossed the fur coat onto the wall and then jumped atop it like a cavalryman mounting his horse.

The wall was very tall. I cannot emphasize that point enough. It was even taller than the stately three-story mansion that had been turned into a shoddy hotel. The red tiles of the hotel's roof were practically beneath us, seeming to float in the air like a flying carpet.

"Why were you crying?"

I surmised that he'd seen me weeping in my perch in the laurel tree. Meaning that he'd been watching me, even if for a few moments. We could even say that he was observing me.

"You kept wiping away your tears."

I got the point. He didn't have any bad intentions. Right?

"You were sobbing like a child."

That much was true. The urge to weep had risen from the furthest depths of my heart.

"What's wrong, Girl in the Tree?"

That question made the tears well up in my eyes again, but it also made me laugh. He'd said that to bring a smile to my lips: "Girl in the Tree."

"What's wrong?"

"The world is what's wrong."

"If you have a problem with the world, your problem is as big as the world."

"Yunus Emre said that."

"He was one of my father's favorite poets. He named me after him."

"I've never met a person whose name didn't have a story behind it."

"Maybe people who lead simple, ordinary lives don't have such stories."

"If your heart is beating in your chest, you have a story. Everything you feel, your life, hopes, dreams, and moments of darkness are all your stories."

"Aren't you going to tell me why you were crying?"

I'd already moved past his question. That wasn't so hard, because I was faced with something rather bizarre and magical. It was far more interesting than the fact that I'd been crying.

"What are you sitting on? Is it a fur coat? Or some creature that whisked you here?"

"It must be something like that. Otherwise, how else would I have made my way up here? Earlier today, I was at the top of the fire escape, feeling so scared that I was shaking from head to foot."

"How can you be so open about your weaknesses?"

"I don't know. Guess I've always been that way. Maybe from birth."

"I have to disagree. We learn things like that from the world around us."

Now he was the one trying to change the subject, as if he could make it vanish like a dolphin—which is what his name meant—disappearing beneath the waves. Pointing to the fur coat, he said, "I found this in the lost and found locker, so I decided to bring it to you."

Yunus was preparing to offer up his spoils. Pressing his feet tightly against each side of the wall, he managed to scoot his skinny frame forward, and then he spread open the arms of the coat.

"For two years, no one showed up to claim it, and none of the hotel workers took it home for themselves. It was just lying there, forgotten. I figured you might get cold at night, so I decided to bring it to you."

"Thanks, but how did you get up on the wall? I know you were scared."

"You're really stuck on that point, aren't you?"

"That's the reason why I'm here. Because I tend to be obsessive. Because there are certain things I can't seem to get out of my head or my heart."

"Some things settle into our thoughts and feelings because that is the very place they need to be. That's why you can't get rid of them. They exist to be remembered, as they are the bedrock of our stories and that which we call life."

"Are you going to tell me why you're afraid of heights?"

"Aren't you afraid of anything?"

"Yes, but I asked you first."

"Now you sound like a schoolgirl."

"Which school did you go to?"

"Just a regular high school. Those days are behind me now. And honestly, the girls there weren't anything like you. They'd come to this park just to make out with their boyfriends, not live up in the trees. Most of them are salesgirls now. Two of them even work at the hotel as chambermaids."

"Now you're dodging the question. Or maybe it would be better to say you're stalling for time."

"You really are obsessive."

It's always annoying when other people speak of your faults. Truths can be like clouds that pass in front of the sun, blocking out its warm rays. That's what happened to me. So I was obsessive. Was that his point?

"But it was fine when you made fun of my fear of heights. Right?"

We were sitting on the top of the wall, facing each other. The time had come for confessions:

"I was crying because two of my friends were killed. Don't ask me why or how it happened. At least not until I'm ready to talk about it. That's why I'm here, because I got tired of people asking me questions."

I liked the way that Yunus listened to me so attentively.

He also had a confession to make:

"I've been afraid of heights since I was a kid. One day, some plain-clothes cops took my older brother away. In my neighborhood, when the cops come for you, no one ever sees you again. I loved my brother more than anything else in the world. One of our neighbors told me that the cops had taken him toward the park. 'They took him over to the sports center. Go tell your parents.' Both my mom and dad worked at a textile plant, so they weren't around. I ran after my brother. I ran as fast as I could because I didn't want to lose him. When I got closer, I saw the cops taking him toward the sports center. To get there, I had to climb over the rear wall. I knew how because sometimes we'd sneak in to watch the games. That's also where the police would take people when they did sweeps of the neighborhood, arresting people left and right, and they'd interrogate them there. And once I started climbing the wall, I could see him. One of the cops hit my brother over the head with the butt of his pistol and then another got in his face, baring his teeth. I could tell that my brother was scared, as the color had drained from his face. The cop kept hitting my brother in the head but slowly, as if it was a play. When he pressed the barrel of his gun against my brother's temple, I shouted, 'Stop!' I saw that my brother was crying. 'Stop!' His eyes were squeezed shut as the tears ran down his cheeks. The cops looked up at me, and so did my brother. That's when I lost my grip. I fell from a height that was about the same as the roof of the sports center. It all happened in the blink of an eye. Even I didn't realize at first what had happened. It broke my heart to see my brother in such a state, and I panicked, thinking that the cops were going to kill him. I lost my grip and fell, face-first. As I fell, I was afraid. I was afraid of the pain that I was going to feel. And it did hurt. It hurt just as much as I thought it would, as I was sure that my body would be pulverized. When we imagine things, creating them in our minds, we feel the pain they have the potential to inflict ten times over. I felt my cheek and rib cage smack the ground, and then the pain washed over my body in odd convulsions. The feeling was more intense than anything I'd ever experienced. It's difficult to describe. Then I felt thick warm blood oozing out of my mouth and nose. My eyes were open, and I could hear the world around me. My brother was running toward me, calling out my name, the tears now pouring down his face. Just like you were crying a few minutes ago. You know how dry branches snap when you step on them? Well, when someone cries because they're overcome by a profound feeling of grief and sorrow, that same sound arises within them. My brother knelt beside me, and I saw the cops walking up as well with slow, spiderlike steps. My vision started going blurry. Not like a mist had descended over the world, but as if everything was suddenly damp, steamed up, covered in an oily, sticky film. I heard the police say to my brother, 'Don't move him.' And then it all started going dark. I remember thinking, 'They want to help me,' even though just moments earlier one of the cops had his gun to my brother's head. I heard a cop mutter, 'Great, now they're going to pin this on us!' I thought, *Pin what on them?* Another one said, 'How old can this kid be?' Much later, I saw that cop on a crowded street in Istanbul with a boy about my age, probably his son. I felt a needling pain run from my ear to the top of my head. When I opened my eyes again, I was in the hospital. That's when the real trouble started. That summer, my kidneys started acting up, and one of them stopped working altogether. My mom was crushed. She couldn't stop crying. It's always mothers who suffer the most. But I went on living, with one heart and one kidney."

"How old were you at the time?"

Yunus pursed his lips and thought for a few seconds. "Probably ten or so? My mom was still around, so I guess I must've been about that age."

The topic of his mother seemed to be an open wound, so I didn't push the issue. But I did wonder what happened to his brother. When I asked, he said, "He wound up joining a rebel group."

"Which one?"

Yunus looked around nervously, as if even the leaves of the trees were listening.

"Forget about it," I said. "You don't have to tell me."

"No, it's not that . . . I just don't know where you stand on things like this. I'm afraid you'll get upset and stop talking to me. That would be the end of our little meetings."

"You're right. That scares me too. Disagreeing with the people I like, finding out that they have hearts of stone. But don't misunderstand me. I'm not talking about love or anything. I mean ideals and politics. Matters of conscience."

"I know what you mean. My brother joined that group to get revenge for all the women, children, and young people like us who've been killed."

"It's a messy situation . . . Don't get me wrong when I say this, but sometimes the state has a longer reach when it comes to things like that. I mean, it can get others to do its dirty work, don't you think?"

"Sure, it's possible. That makes sense."

"The best way is to get organized, like we did, out of a sense of protesting and love. For the east of the country, for the west of the country, for life, for humanity . . . All in the name of equality, fraternity, freedom, and justice."

Stirred up by what I'd said, Yunus finished my sentence for me. Shaking his fist at the emptiness below, he clenched his teeth and jutted out his jaw. What he said next came out in a single breath, as if he was trying to purge it from his thoughts and heart. He practically spit the words: "Not too long ago, my brother had another brush with death. Some people from his group were going to stage an attack on the courthouse."

I couldn't believe what he'd said. "You mean your brother was going to be one of them? The ones who took the public prosecutor hostage and—"

Yunus pressed his finger to his lips. I felt like I was standing face-to-face with a sunken-cheeked Jesus, his face shrouded in flickering shadows as he sought to silence one of his apostles who was about to say, "I don't think I believe in God."

"They didn't kill the prosecutor. They all got killed at the same time."

"But is that really what happened?"

His face fell as if his worst fears had come true.

Quickly, I added, "I don't blame you in the least. Neither the kidnappers nor the prosecutor should've been killed. But like everything else, there's so much we don't know. The whole story is veiled in darkness."

"Are you sure you understood what I was trying to say?"

For some reason, his voice sounded dubbed when he spoke those words. Yet the glimmer in his eyes was indescribably beautiful as he said, syllable by syllable, "They did not shoot the public prosecutor."

"Yes, I know. They all got shot together. I feel bad for them, and for their families too. I feel bad for all of them. I saw on the news that the public prosecutor had a son. They'd taken him to a soccer game. Such a sad-looking boy . . ." Unable to stop myself, I started crying again. "The young people who died were like that. Everyone who died was. Very innocent, good people. The best people in the world died. They were all young, so very, very young."

I spoke as if I were as old as the trees, as old as the wall. Nothing on the face of the earth could've been as old as me. "They were just kids. Most of the people who died were just kids. I kept looking at their faces, thinking that being so innocent was a kind of valor in itself."

"How did your friends die?"

Sobs shook my body. Deep within me, I heard a sound like the one Yunus had described: the sound of a dry branch snapping under your foot. Grief, sorrow, and sadness gushed forth. I hadn't cried that much when I found out that my friends had been killed. I couldn't. All those tears had been pent up but were now set free.

"It was a suicide bomber. They were blown up on a beautiful morning. The last time I saw them, they were all smiles and laughter as they held up their fingers, flashing the victory sign."

"It's such a shame. Such a terrible, terrible shame."

"We were together when Gezi broke out. When I got hurt, they were the ones who carried me. What was the deal with that chandelier? Pembe was hilarious. She said, 'Just look at the damn chandelier—it's lighting up the whole frigging world.'"

Yunus smiled. I went on. It made me feel good to make people smile and laugh.

"When the doctors were stitching up the gash in my head, the girls kept on saying things like that to distract me. Derin said at one point,

'God, I'm not coming to your arms. I'm going toward the light . . . The light of the chandelier.'

"It was like a star, a planet, a sun. I couldn't take my eyes off it. I was filled with this gentle feeling. And then I saw you. Then again, maybe you didn't see me and I didn't see you."

"But the chandelier was there. It saw us."

Both of us laughed when he said that. If I'd had my phone, I would've posted it to my timeline. Being alive is actually a lot like being online. Take the case of Derin and Pembe. They're not online anymore.

"If they were still alive, they would've said something similar. We would've had so many things to laugh about together. You and the three of us."

"You can relive such moments thousands and thousands of times. You'll be with them until the end of your days, and they'll live on with you. You only really die when there isn't a single person left on the earth who remembers you."

We fell silent. It always made me feel uneasy when two people having a conversation stop talking. I was always the first one to break the silence.

"The light of the chandelier made me feel warm inside. I wish that I could've stayed in that moment forever, bathed in that light."

"It's not time that passes with love, but light. I just thought of that. It's from a poem."

Rays of light were showering down upon us. I'd like to add a "practically" to that statement to make it punchier. The branches of laurel, eucalyptus, and plane trees were intertwined above where we were sitting, but the beams of the sun found their way through. The light was the yellowest of yellows, caressing us with a gentle warmth. It was autumn.

I could tell that Yunus, who was wearing a simple shirt and trousers, had finished his shift and was going home by the way that he made a decisive move to get up, as graceful as the leaves rustling in the breeze.

His body was extraordinarily beautiful, as lithesome as the branch of a tree, and in my opinion, just as smooth and flawless. I'd never seen him naked, but I had no doubt that's how it was. His skin was as sleek and soft as the trunk of a plane tree, and I wondered if he too had a thin layer of bark that covered his rippling body.

How do people know when they're falling in love?

Fate had surprises in store for me, things that I'd never encountered in the world below but found high up in the treetops.

"I'm going to leave now, but I don't want you to see me fall."

"Meaning that you're leaving but don't know exactly how you're going to go, right? You found yourself on the top of the wall, but now you're not sure how you got here. You need all your courage, but it seems to have left you. Am I right?"

I know—I was acting like a child. I called out in the direction of our little forest: "Bravery, o where have you gone?"

"Now you're making fun of me again."

"Hang on, let me help you. Forget your fear and cross over this way."

"Actually, it's not that hard. I'm going to reach out as far as I can and then, like Spider-Man, grab hold of the railing and make a blind leap. In the worst-case scenario, I'll end up hanging from the fire escape."

Yunus and I were about a meter apart. As I stood up on the wall to help him, I could smell the body odor that had been stirred up by my sudden movement. I smelled like something rotten. At the very least, my clothes were getting ripe. I felt embarrassed. I could see how that scenario was going to play out: As I went on living in the trees, my fingernails were going to grow out, my hair was going to become unkempt, and I was possibly going to become infested with lice. At the same time, my eyebrows would grow bushy and my legs would get as hairy as a yeti's, and eventually I'd be a jungle girl, casting off all vestiges of humanity. I had to ask myself: Isn't that why I was there in the first place? To become something other than what I was? Maybe even part and parcel of the trees themselves? I realize that I've explained all this in the most naive and foolish of terms. That's another reason why I lost the writing competition: I just don't have a knack for spinning off elaborate sentences.

"Do you really think you're going to win the hearts of readers by saying things like that?"

The person directing that question to me was none other than Özlem Hanım. She'd read something I'd written out loud. "What do you think about the range of your vocabulary in your writing?"

Some of the students in the classroom tittered behind cupped hands. You can cry all you want, but laughter is forbidden. That's the first rule of a fascist education system. Cry, but don't laugh.

"You jump from one topic to another, and it's hard to tell what you're really talking about. You shouldn't pour out your thoughts or your inner world. There's one thing you have to always bear in mind: your readers."

"Maybe she's writing for skanks like us."

"Derin! Get out of my classroom this instant!"

"Sorry, Teacher, when we use 'skank,' it just means regular people. Sorry if I caused any offense."

"Derin, I told you to get out! Wait for me at the door of the headmaster's office."

Flicking the Faber 0.5 pen she'd been twirling over the rows of desks, Derin got to her feet. As if it had lost its bearings, the pen first flew forward and then, breaking all the rules of physics, it flew back, only to swing in the other direction. Whenever things like that happened, an abnormal hush would fall over the classroom. Silence is the hallmark of fascism, while boisterousness signals good cheer. Although silence can be an aspect of peace of mind, it has its own particular sounds. And that wasn't the sound of a tranquil silence—it was the silent sound of fear. The silence of cowards who wet themselves. The silence of those girls who'd say in the school bathroom, "I was so scared that she was going to send me to the headmaster's office!" The response: "Honey, if you hadn't done anything wrong, why didn't you stand up for yourself?" In fascism, everyone gets their turn. There's no escaping it. The purpose of fascism is to call you to account for your actions. Life is filled with things for which we can be called to account. Fascism functions by calling us to account for everything because that is what it was designed to do.

"You drag out the story too much. The dialogues are clichéd, overly simple, and devoid of meaning."

"Just like in real life?"

Özlem Hanım raised her long, thin eyebrows and adjusted her tone of voice. She'd been teaching the lower grades, but that wasn't necessarily an impediment to her being a decent person. Still, she slid into spitefulness, lashing out with viciousness whenever anyone challenged her. And now it was time for Pembe to be taken down a peg: "No. Completely tasteless and inappropriate."

She paused, realizing that she'd left herself open. Pembe played her role, as if it were all part of the discussion: "Do you mean the dialogues? That is, the ones in our classmate's novel . . ."

"No. I mean *you*."

Pembe bit her lip. She'd do that when she was trying not to laugh, as she knew that even the wrong facial expression could get her sent off to see the headmaster.

After class, we were talking in the school quad. "Did you hear what she said to me in class today?"

Derin reported on her punishment: "They're making me help the ninth graders with their study group."

As the two of them went on chatting and laughing, I stood off to the side, not saying a word. I couldn't understand why our teacher, who had actually come up with the idea of the writing competition and worked so hard to get the administration to agree to it, was trying so hard to hurt my feelings. The competition itself wasn't so important to me, but writing most certainly mattered, and that woman had left me feeling crushed.

The other girl—the one who ended up winning—put on airs, being overly considerate in her dealings with me to show that I didn't represent a threat to her. She wasn't a loser like me, so everything was a bed of roses, and since the world bowed before her because she was beautiful, she was happy. I, in contrast, was miserable. She was nice to me because I could've been in her position but I wasn't, and the only reason for that, I reasoned, was a small miscalculation, bad luck, a tough break, or some crap like that. She'd taken my place, and I'd been put in my place. Hadn't it always been like that?

"Lost in your thoughts?" Yunus's voice was like the breeze rustling the leaves.

"Does that ever happen to you?" I asked. "You're thinking about something and then suddenly your line of thought pulls you in like a whirlpool. If that happens, you only have two choices: either let yourself plunge into the thought or shut it down completely. Otherwise, you'll get stuck in the midst of life as if you were sleeping with your eyes wide open."

Yunus listened intently, his eyes fixed on my own. Me? I'd cut in all the time when people were talking. The reason was simple: loneliness. If I found someone who'd talk to me, I'd prattle on, hardly stopping to take a breath.

The conversations that Derin, Pembe, and I had were the best imaginable. It was as if the three of us were playing tennis. Of course, tennis isn't played with three people, but my point is this: it's nearly impossible to strike a balance when there are three of you and even harder to share time equally. I can't think of any other way to describe it. Our conversations would shuttle back and forth. Sometimes one of us would finish the other's sentence. Sometimes it was two of us, and sometimes all three. I dreamt about Derin and Pembe twice. Occasionally I go to sleep for the sole reason that I hope I'll dream of them, but when I open my eyes in the morning, I'm crushed by the realization that a new day is starting and that my dreams have come to an end. I wish that I could dream about my grandma and my aunt—the one who was a journalist—as well.

Yunus left.

When he managed to make the leap from the wall to the fire escape, he said, "I cast off all my fears during the protests." Granted, it would've been better if he hadn't made such a trite statement, but you have to admit, he had the right to after his demonstration of courage. Without asking for my help, he closed his eyes and reached out, grabbing hold of the railing, and he hung there for a moment before swinging his feet up onto the other side.

The other side.

Warm water, a bed, shampoo, breakfast, hot drinks—those were all opiates used in the name of civilization.

Yunus was proud of himself for having made the jump from the wall to the stairs. He'd been forthright by confessing that he was afraid of heights, and he'd gone a step further by telling me about the serious health issues that had plagued his youth. Life was precious for Yunus. Later, he'd say to me, "I've got one foot in the grave," just like an old-timer.

When his feet hit the stairs of the fire escape with a resounding boom, I caught a whiff of myself and summoned the courage to say, "Sorry I smell like a garbage dump!"

Now that the sun was going down, the doves stopped cooing as they roosted in the eaves of the buildings along the street. His voice was barely louder than a whisper, as though he was saying something of the utmost secrecy: "The rooms on this side of the hotel are going to be empty for a few days. You can use one of them if you'd like, so you can take a shower and get some rest."

Before I could answer, he turned around and started bounding down the steps. Picking up the fur coat, which for me was like a spoil of my own war, I headed back to my nest. I found a small bottle of water in the coat pocket along with a package of cookies, the kind they serve with coffee at hotels. It was now clear to me that Yunus intended to feed me like I was a bird living in the trees of the park, which may as well have been my cage.

Days later he'd say, "When I started thinking about why you decided to live out your days there, my first thought was, 'Her feelings have been hurt.'"

He was right. People had hurt me. The world below was a hurtful place indeed.

12

ME

I was determined to stay in the treetops, even if it meant smelling bad, going hungry, shivering in the cold, and getting soaked when rainstorms blew through. However, if we consider the fact that I kept repeating those words to myself like a mantra, it becomes obvious that I wasn't truly convinced of my commitment or, perhaps, I simply wasn't ready for such a life. Maybe it would've been truer to say that I'd get used to it over time.

"Do you think that characters in books should be so outspoken?"

Another piece of criticism. A silent classroom. And me, heaving a sigh.

"Hey, emo girl, maybe you shouldn't have written that novel."

My friends' attempts to console me were failing miserably. I'd learned my lesson: in both real life and fiction, tight-lipped people are the most beloved of all.

"No," I said, "they shouldn't. Characters should never speak their minds so openly." That was the signal flare indicating that I'd given up. Özlem Hanım's cocky ego was standing fully erect, but it soon softened into a greasy smile that spread across her face. She'd succeeded in quashing my hopes of becoming a writer.

But now she wasn't up in the treetops—I was. And while I was capable of being just as outspoken as that character of mine who had been riddled with the arrows of critique, there was something that made it impossible for me to descend into the world and pick up my life from where I'd left off, no matter how I'd failed to convince myself that life among the leaves and branches was my destiny. That something was so powerful that it nullified all thoughts of going back home, returning to school, or mingling with society at large. Regardless of the difficulties involved, I had to stay put and become a bird. My determination was as dogged as the kick that sends the stool flying out from under the feet of someone who has tied a noose around their neck. Have you never had such feelings? That you'd fight back tooth and nail, no matter the odds? There are things you feel in life, the causes of which are incomprehensible to everyone but you. Things that are illogical, seemingly empty, opaque to the outside world. Things that cannot be reduced to terms explainable to others. Things that are laden with a significance that no one else can see.

The sun had set.

I folded the fur coat in two and slipped inside. It was quite cozy. I savored the feeling of being in there. My mother was fond of using the word "savor." Even though she was born in 1973, she liked words that had an old-fashioned tinge to them. My mother . . . That sweet, pale, wan light of my life. When the sun set, it would bathe our home in its light. Our apartment was no bigger than a cardboard box. I take that back; your average cardboard box is probably bigger.

My grandma would say, "If an apartment has a big kitchen and bathroom, you get the impression that the whole place is large. But that's crap. It's just an illusion."

The setting sun would paint our place in every shade of red. An apartment no bigger than a cardboard box. My mother would come home in all those reds, stepping through the door into the crimson scene.

"I'm hoo-oome!"

She was so happy in the days when she was in love. During those years when my father was making her life miserable, she wouldn't say a word when she got home. Nor would we. All you'd hear was the creak of the hinges and the inelegant, earsplitting thud of the featherweight door swinging shut of its own accord.

My father would snarl, "You sluggards, you're going to break the door off its hinges! Close it yourselves."

At every opportunity he would hurl insults at my mother. "Sluggards"!

I never understood how they'd fallen in love, married, and brought me into the world.

If my mother was happy, I was happy. I'd look at her, all smiles. All I needed was her happiness, nothing more. My mother's internal-combustion love affair went on for a long time, coasting in neutral. I don't think she ever slept with the man with whom she was in love. The doctor, I mean. That's why their love story was of such epic proportions.

The doctor would show up for his shift at the clinic on certain days of the week. My mother would tell her friends about their affair over the phone and I'd listen, as entranced as if I was listening to a fairy tale. She never read to me or told me stories, so that was all I had. Well, one time she read "Thumbelina" to me when I was sick. In her days of misery, my mother had been a wreck, but love slowly brought her around. Afterward, she managed to show me a little attention.

For the most part, she only took care of my most basic needs. At the age of five I started taking baths by myself, and when it was time to eat, she'd set a plate of food in front of me, expecting me to handle the rest of the dining process. I got dressed and undressed on my own, putting my dirty clothes into the hamper. In a monotone tone of voice my mother would tell me what I needed to do, and then her job was done. She was never endearing at such moments. Just tired and irritable.

Don't get me wrong. She wasn't a bad mother, and the extent of her faults is open to debate. As she drowned in her sea of unhappiness, she simply was doing the best she could. When she was on the road to becoming a well-known poet, there was a sudden swerve and she found herself working as a dietician. I have always thought, however, that she remained a poet at heart, and she carried within herself the rage of the lines she couldn't put to paper. Clichéd as that may sound, I'm not going to erase it. She married a man whom she admired and then was subjected to his scorn. Although she had a family of her own now, she was lonely and had no one in her life. The situation with her sister and her mother was different; if there's time, I'll talk about that too.

My father's mother and sister helped her out, but only up to a point, and they never really accepted her as one of their own. My father's sister always gave her advice, which sometimes bordered on meddling. She would've called it "women's solidarity," but that wasn't the case at all, as was made clear by the way she'd criticize my mother behind her back. Her favorite piece of counsel ran along these lines: "I know you love your husband, but try not to love him so much. Be strong. Don't let him treat you that way."

It never occurred to my bewildered mother to say, "Why don't you tell him the same thing? He's your brother, after all."

Only once when the situation had gotten out of hand and she couldn't stop crying did she ask my aunt to talk to my father. The catalyst had been a book that my father threw at my mother as she was walking away. It hit her in the back.

My mother said, "It wouldn't have hurt so much if he'd stuck a knife into my back."

Then there was the problem of money: my father wouldn't give her any. She had a credit card that she used to buy things for our household, and when the bill came, my father would pore over every single item.

If he saw something that seemed suspicious, he'd get in her face and say, "What is this?"

It was a clinical case of psychological violence.

My mother quickly stopped buying things for herself with the card. That's how frightened she was of him. In fact, she stopped buying anything except for household things like coffee, rice, and laundry detergent, and whatever they needed for me. Without any money, she couldn't go to the salon or do her own shopping, or even go out to eat by herself. All because "we didn't have any money." The irony was that my father had plenty of cash in those days, as he was working for that rich art collector. There wasn't a single country in Europe that he hadn't visited, and with the exception of two short trips to Paris and London, he didn't take my mother on any of his travels, purportedly because they were solely focused on going to museums. Business matters. He'd go on and on about how he spent a small fortune on Armani suits, Tommy Hilfiger neckties, George Hogg shoes, a Seiko watch that cost $1,250, and a two-year membership to the Swissôtel fitness and spa center. During that period of luxury and worldly pleasures, which could be aptly termed my father's own personal Tulip Era, it seems that he never had an affair with another woman, or if he did, my mother hadn't intuited it.

I heard about all these things as my mother poured out her troubles over the phone in tears, tears, and more tears. My father's sister once told me about those trials and travails, saying, "Don't ever let anyone walk all over you like that."

My mother never realized the severity of the psychological abuse to which she was being subjected. But it wasn't physical. Not once did my father raise his voice or hit her; there was just that one incident with the throwing of the book. He would still, however, have his way with her, but without talking to her or even looking at her face. Male violence is like smoke—it seeps in everywhere. And society and the state make it possible for that violence to sink its roots into every home, slowly poisoning women to the point that they are reduced to little more than walking corpses.

As the two of us were walking down the road one day, a beautiful woman stopped my mother and asked, "I couldn't help but notice, is your little girl sick or something? What's wrong with her?" But that beauty was all in her outfit. The woman's high-heeled Campers made up for the squatness of her legs, her fancy dress concealed her shapeless ass, and her rings distracted your attention from the fact that she had sausage fingers. To top it all off, even through her sunglasses, which my mother didn't have because she'd lost hers and couldn't afford to buy a new pair, I could see that her eyes bulged like a toad's. I stood there staring at her, mouth agape. All the same, she seemed to be a happy woman who took pleasure in looking after herself, and she spoke with a confidence that hinted at a lust for life. My mother, on the other hand, was as silent as a mouse cowering in a corner. My mother was unhappy. And unhappy people wear their misery on their sleeves. Everyone sees it, but pretends that they don't. You can tell if a woman is unhappy by the look in her eyes.

That outspoken, well-dressed woman and my mother were about the same age. It was for the best that she said exactly what was on her mind without hiding behind social niceties: "I've seen your daughter walking around all hunched over, shuffling her feet. Look at her: she's got bags under her eyes. I remember when she was such a pretty little girl."

For the next few days my mother looked like she was in a trance. I know that she was thinking a lot about what the woman had said. And about her own situation. I think that was when she started to realize that she'd been deprived of so much in the latter years of her life. I've been told that, when I was a baby, she'd go around wearing ratty Adidas sneakers and canvas trousers with a busted zipper, even attending dinner parties dressed that way, and not once did my father say to her, "Where do you think you're going dressed like that?" Because he didn't really see her. It was as if he was taking a ghost wife out—a woman who'd risen from the grave, a wife whom he'd murdered through disinterest and a sharp tongue.

At one such dinner party, my mother had been enthralled by the female host's shoes, so much so that she couldn't take her eyes off them all night. But not once did she lament her own situation or ask, "Why have I been brought to this state? Why am I at this dinner wearing worn-out tennis shoes?"

An unhappy woman. A pale, drained, ignored woman. A bone-weary woman.

I still think, however, that despite everything, my mother was a strong person. She persevered and then slowly reinvented herself. Although she wanted to divorce my father, she couldn't because she had nowhere to go. Now, as she looks back on her past, she probably sees that she didn't really want to get divorced at the time. People create their own suffering. If a separation is what she'd really wanted, she would've found a way and started working again, like she'd end up doing a few years later. And while she and her family may have had different outlooks on life, her mother and sister would've helped her out.

Take, for example, the fact that she never even considered accepting child support from my father. It was a matter of pride for her. Not that it was unwarranted; my father was trying to break her heart and chisel away at her dignity. In the same way that she was incapable of standing up to his abuse, she was incapable of leaving him.

I have vague memories of my mother wearing tight red corduroy trousers and a black turtleneck sweater, oblivious to her own beauty and grace as she went through life mired in despondency. Then again, it is possible that my recollections are merely the product of what her friends told me when I got older, of what my father's sister explained to me about the days of my youth. I can't be sure. The only thing I know for certain is that I was a silent witness to her misery, which I saw through a child's eyes. That is the role that children play: they document the lives of their parents through what they remember about them.

As my mother was bringing me up, feeling miserable and beaten down in her marriage to an insensitive, crotchety husband, she became friends with some of the women who also took their children to the park, and they started getting together at their homes so that the kids could play. Spending more and more time talking with them as she bounced me on her knee, she began to see her own situation more clearly. Every week they'd meet up at a different friend's house, and that's how she came to realize that almost all the women had babysitters or nannies; I think that my mother and a half-Swiss, half-Turkish woman were the only ones looking after their kids alone. Over time, she noticed that her friends all had happy households, which she admired greatly. Admiration, after all, is nothing more than envy that has been defeated and reined in.

"What is depression? A state of self-resentment."

Someone said that at one of the women's gatherings my mother attended. She'd jotted it down in one of her many small red-leather-bound journals. When I was old enough to read, one of the few pleasures I had was poring over those confessional entries in which she bared her soul.

One day, my mother borrowed a dress and a pair of size 37 knee-high Isabel Marant boots from my father's sister. Raising an eyebrow, my aunt said, "I thought you were a size 36."

"I was. But after giving birth, I had to move up a size."

That was a lie. She just wanted to wear something nice. Before putting them on, she stuffed cotton balls into the toes of the boots.

"Perfect."

My mother looked beautiful. But her air of happiness was borrowed. Seeing the happiness and satisfaction of her friends, and listening enviously to their tales of joyful, cozy homes, only drove her deeper into depression. As we returned home from those visits, I felt like I was walking with a zombie by my side.

My mother could barely contain her excitement when it was her turn to host her friends at our place. Now hers was the compassionate hand spreading bread crumbs outside a window that looked out onto the wall of another apartment building. Now there were cheery, chirping birds in front of that window. The women and their children were at *our* home. I'd never seen so many people in our apartment or my mother so happy.

When a newly established publishing house rereleased my mother's book of poetry, which had gone out of print, she made a little money. She felt better than she had in years, and the first thing she did was go out to buy herself a pair of boots. There was an indescribable glimmer in her eyes as she watched the salesclerk wrap them up. Soon after, she got a job, which I think I already told you about. All the same, those early days at that swanky diet clinic in Nişantaşı were anything but easy. The others there had little patience for my mother's gloomy moods, and if they'd seen her when she'd been walking the streets in search of a job, looking like a tramp, they never would've let her in the door.

The doctor represented a promise of love. My mother's transformation shifted into second gear.

One day, my mother picked me up from kindergarten wearing a pink silk spaghetti-strap dress, stylish sandals, a silk scarf, and coral earrings with gold inlays, and her hair was shimmering in the sunlight. On the days when the doctor was expected at the office, she blossomed.

"Mom, you're just like the Little Prince's rose."

Normally, she wouldn't have asked about anything that concerned me.

"Who read that book to you? Did they read it at school? So you liked it . . ."

My mother would come home, illuminated by the red glow of the setting sun despite the fact that a new apartment building had been built in front of ours and we had no view of the city. That's what hope is like. It doesn't seep from our hearts, nor does it drain away like blood, for if it did, we'd die and that would be the end of us. I watched her through the eyes of a five-year-old child.

Sometimes my grandma would pick me up after school. She'd place a heaping plate of peeled, diced fruit on the table in front of me and turn on the television, and when my father showed up, she'd waste no time in heading out the door to go back to her own apartment.

One time, my mother was wearing a nice blue cotton dress, which meant that the doctor had been at the office. The next day, before my father got home, she called one of her friends and excitedly told her about everything that had happened, and I listened carefully.

Wide-eyed, I'd watch my mother as she came through the front door: she'd set down her cloth purse and, cringing in fear as my father snapped at her for making too much noise, pull her shoes from her graceful feet and gently place them in the shoe cabinet, even though she would've preferred to kick them off after yet another day filled with elation and joy. Then she'd go through her evening routine but smiling, smiling, smiling the whole time.

She'd found a new brand of perfume that she liked.

"Are you going to squander all your money on that stuff?"

My father was ruthless in his questioning of her spending habits, despite the fact that she now paid all the bills and did the shopping. Ever since she started making her own money, she'd stopped using his credit card, and she even cut it to pieces with a pair of scissors before his very eyes but without the slightest trace of anger or disdain, as if she was calmly snapping green beans in preparation for dinner.

In order to avoid having to listen to his tirades, she secreted away the things she bought. A new dress. Makeup. Shoes. Sunglasses. Creams. Fine shampoos. Everything she'd been denied over the years.

All the wonderful things she'd let herself be denied. Now, she bought those things with pleasure and wild abandon, bringing them home in nondescript brown bags to keep them hidden from her husband, whom she still feared.

My mother was happy when she was seeing the doctor. Once, she described how, on the days when the doctor was at the clinic, she'd wander around like a ghost looking for him.

She'd become a ghost of love. A ghost of that love that was her life-blood, pulling her back from the cusp of death and a life of groveling.

"I could hear his voice," she said, "but I didn't know where he was. I wanted so much to see him and for him to see me, so I wandered from room to room at the clinic. If anyone had asked me what I was doing, I wouldn't have said a word because I don't want anyone to know that I'm in love with him."

Ah, that naive mother of mine.

How long can we keep a secret before giving in to the temptation to whisper it to someone?

If my father had been more of a friend to my mother, she wouldn't have felt a desire to stray. It was terrible loneliness that drove her to that point, the same kind of loneliness that led me to ramble on to myself like I'm doing here. Ultimately, my mother—to use an expression my grandma loved to use—started "traipsing after" that doctor. As far as I could tell, the doctor had his hesitations, though it was obvious that he longed to pluck that blossoming rose with his teeth so he could breathe in its scent. But he was afraid. As we all know, however, love is not for the timid. It demands courage. Love *is* courage. That statement, which admittedly is as trite as can be, was written on the piece of paper that Derin drew from a fortune-teller's stand in front of Hayal Kahvesi in Beyoğlu. Here's how it works: as you stroke the rabbit on the fortune-teller's stand, you ask a question, and then you choose a slip of paper, which supposedly provides you with an answer.

I got: "He will find you."

Pembe got: "Don't lose hope."

Derin asked, "Why are these things so damn short?"

"That's the way of the world now, accept it. Everything's an SMS."

"You are aware, little lady, that we live in the age of text messages, right?"

Ah, those messages! How quickly you forgot about that day when those girls got into a hair-pulling brawl in the bathroom at school over a text message from a private number. "Snapchat whore!" one of them cried. Of course, everyone knows about Snapchat now. Still, allow me to offer a brief explanation in case you've never heard of it.

When you view a Snapchat video, it automatically deletes itself after a while. In that way, people can share the most intimate images of themselves. I should note that our most intimate moments cannot actually be seen, but that's a topic for another time. Getting back to the story, one girl sent another girl's boyfriend a Snapchat of herself wearing nothing but a G-string. The second girl recognized the first by the tattoo on her ass, which consisted of a rose, a heart, and the words "I love you" encircled by a ribbon with tattered ends. Scandal, scandal, scandal! In the end, both girls were expelled from school.

Shaking with rage, the headmaster snorted, "Never in the history of our school has anything so scandalous happened!" Then again, Snapchat hadn't existed before, but anyways.

Those fortune-tellers with rabbits had caught a glimpse of the future of the wiles of time: in the past, we'd get hung up for weeks on end about something we'd heard, but now we don't even remember it the next morning. As for my mother, she was hung up on the doctor's intentions, as she didn't understand what he was really after. She'd lost her self-confidence. She'd ask her friends, "Do you think he's in love with me?"

They'd listen to her syrupy love story, as engrossed as if it was *One Thousand and One Nights*, and then offer their interpretations. My mother wasn't listening to her heart. Even if she'd listened, she wouldn't have been able to hear what it was saying. Although one might have expected her to cheat on my father not just emotionally but physically as well, she couldn't bring herself to do it, and the doctor was too much of a coward to make a move.

But who knows, maybe she held back because she really loved my father.

Still, she was having a romantic love affair, and she was content with seeing the object of her love and talking with him, and later imagining what it would be like if they made love. It was the kind of romance Jane Austen wrote about two hundred years ago.

They became closer and closer, and just as the fuse of their fireworks of passion was about to be ignited, the doctor panicked and fled. Based on what I heard my mother say over the phone, they'd never even kissed. As you can tell, we're dealing here with a love story of the most archaic and innocent kind. Sometimes the two of them would leave the clinic together to have lunch or walk from Nişantaşı to Taksim on the pretext that the doctor had to be in Beyoğlu for business later in the day. While my mother was pleased that he was showing an interest in her, she was also waiting for him to make a decisive step forward, which he failed to do, perhaps because he knew of my father or they had common acquaintances. Needless to say, what existed between my mother and the doctor never developed to the point of becoming a relationship.

If there has ever been anything that ended abruptly before it even got started, it was my mother's love story.

As for the doctor's flight . . . He fled far. Across seas and oceans, in fact. All the way to America.

My mother found out that the doctor was going to move away by coincidence. At a flower shop she ran into a friend of hers—not a particularly close friend—who, during the course of their conversation, mentioned that the doctor was making a change in his life. That friend knew nothing about the love affair that had turned my mother's heart into a pile of smoldering ashes.

"He's moving to Houston. He said that he probably won't come back. He already had his furniture shipped over."

He already shipped off his furniture!

My mother was in a state of shock. That chaste love story, for which she had been prepared to cheat on my father and leave him without looking back, had been going on for quite a long time. She had interiorized that love, which for her, as the saying goes, had roots as deep as the crown of the tree was tall, and told her friends all its leafy details. It had been a cry of loneliness from a precipice, a persistent longing for an echo. Instead of poetry, she'd written her story of love.

The doctor never told my mother about his plans to move away, which meant, "You don't mean anything to me." At least, that was the interpretation offered up by her tele-friends. Only one person, an older male friend of hers, said, "It's clear to me that something happened and he's running away." If you ask me, all she needed to ask him was, "Do you love me back?" It would have been that simple!

And if he'd gawked at her like a moron, she could've said, "Don't be afraid. My love for you is more than enough for the two of us."

She could've written a poem starting with that line and left it on his desk, but she didn't. I think she was even more afraid than he was when it came to confessing her desires.

One time I said to her, "Mom, you're such a coward!"

She was caught off guard.

"Why do you say that?"

At the time, I was in the living room, drawing in my notepad on the coffee table I've mentioned already, the one made of the gravestone overlaid with glass—don't worry, I'll come back to that at some point. My mom had just concluded yet another one of her despairing phone calls. Looking up at her again, I said, "You're a scaredy-cat!"

I said it with anger in my voice. Most likely, she'd never considered the possibility that I fully understood what she was going through or was able to put all the pieces together. Nobody would've expected that of such a young child. It would've been inconceivable. What my mother didn't know, however, was that her love story constituted the only relationship she had with me because she and I never talked. Just as my father never talked to her.

In the days that followed, my mother hit rock bottom.

She cut herself off from everything. How wrong she'd been! Her grand tale of love had come crashing down. The doctor would no longer be there to console and nourish her with love. She'd lost him.

The creases at the corners of her lips reappeared as her face settled back into that expression of glumness. It pained me to see her lapse back into that impenetrable silence, but my father didn't even notice the change. Once again, the light in her eyes flickered out. The sun that illuminated her inner world had set one more time. Night had fallen. A night of infinity.

"I see you've used the word 'infinity' here in this sentence. It's out of place. Why do you even bother trying?"

Özlem Hanım went on slamming my work in the space allotted for such attacks: the depths of my mind, the outer space of thought.

"You may as well have used 'infirmity.' It wouldn't have made any difference."

Unable to bear it anymore, I started crying, which, I think, was her ultimate aim. She flashed a tiny smile of victory, which then curled ever upward, as if an invisible thread were slowly pulling her lips higher and higher.

"Please," she said in a mockingly consolatory tone of voice. "Don't get so upset."

I could hear Derin and Pembe whispering to me, "Stop crying." Helplessly I looked at them, noticing that their eyes were as moist as mine. "Infinity" was clearly something I'd never forget, as it came to mind even when I was far up in the treetops. The mind is the outer space we carry within. Nothing ever gets lost there.

The doctor really did go. And in the end, my mother was left with a series of disappointments, including my failed novel, the writing competition I failed to win, and the fact that as a result I wouldn't be getting a new scholarship.

For a while she considered having another child, as she wanted to throw herself into a different kind of misery. It was a masochistic desire born of a yearning to punish herself. But her fears prevailed and she gave up on the idea, which was for the best. However, she did wind up getting pregnant, which came as a surprise. At first, she thought of keeping the baby, but then decided against it and made an appointment so she could get an abortion. By chance the doctor turned out to be an antiabortionist. He lied: "Legally it's too late. You have no choice but to go through with the pregnancy." One morning, she woke up and said, "No, I'm not keeping this child," and even though we'd already told my aunt and grandma the good news, she got an appointment with another doctor who told her she was only ten weeks pregnant, and that was the end of my chance to have a brother or a sister.

After pulling herself together to a certain extent, she set her sights on becoming a famous dietician as a way to fill the void left behind by the doctor and her lost love. To achieve her ends, she did some things that might be deemed unscrupulous. You might be asking yourself, "What could she have possibly done?" For starters, she told a massive lie that proved to be irreversible. She did become famous for a short while, but that all collapsed, leaving her more frustrated than ever.

So, did I start living in the treetops so I could ponder all these things? Let's consider that.

Your life is inseparable from everyone else's and you are inextricably bound up with the lives of others. Let me put that another way: we are all other people's stories. Have I said that already? My mind is like a music box that plays the same melody over and over as I keep winding it up. I apologize for repeating myself, but that's just how it is. On second thought, there are no repetitions here. You only think that because I said so. You believe everything I say, including all that passes through my heart and the depths of my mind. Do you ever stop to mull over things in all their dimensions? While it is true that my determination to live up in the trees reflects a certain amount of creativity, I am also just as ordinary.

"Your writing is serious, but sometimes it is also quite irreverent. In the same way, it is creative but simultaneously droll. Through the use of familiar sentences, the simple narrative is subjected to a transformation via your interventions, becoming something new and uncanny in the process."

After reading my novel, Monsieur Pierre had offered that commentary, which I never really understood.

Pembe said, "You idiot, what is it you don't get? He's saying that you picked up on your own frequency and went with it. You wrote the story of that girl's life and became her, but we know that you're really not her, that the character you created is someone else."

"Like seriously, how did you write that? I mean, how can someone write such a book?"

"I just close myself off to everything and stumble upon a new world."

Ha ha ha ha haaaa!

True, they were making fun of me, and later I laughed about it too, but that's just the way it was.

Monsieur Pierre offered us a piece of advice: "If you're going to touch the hearts of others, it has to come from the heart." That shouldn't come as a surprise, because he was a big fan of Yunus Emre and Goethe. I immediately typed what he said into the notes file on my iPhone, because unlike Derin and Pembe, I didn't like using notebooks. When we were deciding what to take to the children in the war-torn east, we opted for more stationery than toys, and those gifts of ours all survived the explosion that tore apart the bus. What a deplorable state of affairs: Human lives can be cut short so easily, while the things they bring into the world survive. You can bury a plastic bottle in the earth and after two hundred years it'll still be there, but people are nothing like that. My grandma would say such things as she looked out at the houses along the streets: "The people who built these houses, even the carpenter who made those shutters and the needleworker who sewed those thick velvet curtains, are all dead now, but the things they made are still here among us in this life, and when we die, they'll go on existing. Sad, isn't it?"

"All things ephemeral are allegoric in their very nature." That was one of the big statements I made in my novel. The winner of the writing competition wasn't just going to win a scholarship but also get their novel published. Özlem Hanım had personally spoken with some publishers to make the arrangements. If my book had been published, that sentence was going to be its crowning jewel.

"Did you come up with that?"

Who else would ask such a question but cock-mouth Özlem Hanım? I don't think I need to say that she suffered from a complex.

That question was the straw that broke the camel's back. I stormed out of the classroom.

After all that had happened, I wanted my mother to go to my school and talk to everyone, starting with the administrators, and including Derin's father as she walked through the gate.

"They broke my daughter's heart. That's why I'm here, to give them hell for what they did to her. Did she do anything wrong? She sat down and wrote. She thought and she imagined. Is that such a crime?"

Derin's father might have replied, "It *is* a crime."

"Emine's father"—that's what he would've preferred to be called.

Things really had reached such a low: Thinking was a crime. Writing was an even worse crime, because it spread that infirmity known as thinking.

Then my mother would talk to the administrators and, lastly, Özlem Hanım.

"You can tell her that she writes badly, but make sure you phrase it kindly."

My sole desire was for my mother to bare her claws like a lion or a tiger and tear to pieces the people who dared hurt her one and only daughter, snarling like a wounded beast and frightening them. Even street cats do that for their kittens. Why shouldn't my mother?

She didn't say anything.

She didn't go to my school to explain how they'd broken her daughter's heart. Why? Because in those days she was mired in her feelings of humiliation. She had experienced in all their profundity the two feelings that are the foundation of life: love and humiliation. The source of that shame was a story far bigger than the one about love. We discover who we really are through others, which is why we are better at understanding other people than ourselves. It's just like being a doctor; no one can peer into themselves to diagnose their own illnesses, so we must leave that to someone else. And that is precisely why I said that we are all, in fact, other people's stories. Yet, while no one can tell their own story, if another tells it, it will be lacking in some way. So everyone must tell their own stories, staring into the mirror and talking to themselves if need be.

To my great surprise, I also found a mirror in the pocket of the fur coat. Naturally, I wondered if it might be a sign in support of my approach to storytelling. It was a miracle that the small mirror was still hidden away there because the pockets were so torn, so I took it to mean I was going to stay hidden as well.

The laurel tree swayed in the wind.

In the faint light of the park lamps that trickled through the leaves, I observed my shadowy face in the mirror for a while, unable to turn away my gaze. I marveled at how, not so long before, I'd been wanting a mirror; if God exists, he'd heard me for once. I drank some water, thinking that I'd be in a difficult position if I got ill up in the treetops. Do birds get sick? I was on the verge of falling asleep. When the tree swayed again, I realized that I was the cause, as I was tossing around in the warm fur coat like I'd done in my bed at home. No longer would I spend cold, sleepless nights, shivering high up in the branches, and that was enough to make me happy. But was it really enough?

Monsieur Pierre sent me a message on Facebook, saying that he was going back to France because of what had happened at Gezi Park.

"I cannot bear to see what's happening any longer. As a foreigner, I can't look on as if I don't care. So many young people are getting killed. The death of just one person is cause enough to revolt, and yet so many are dying. There's simply too much suffering."

He sent that message to me, Derin, and Pembe as he was leaving the country.

And in a subsequent message, he wrote to me, "Yesterday I was thinking about the time I've spent in Istanbul, and your book came to mind. In my opinion, your novel is a powerful manifestation of brutal anger, steely logic, and keen intellect. Please keep writing."

My reply was crisp and to the point: "Monsieur Pierre, I destroyed everything that I've ever written. I don't think I'll ever write again."

As though asking me to reconsider, he asked, *"Pourquoi?"*

Why, why, Grandpa's in the rye!

"My reasons for not wanting to write are very similar to why you decided to leave this place."

"Pourquoi?"

"Isn't that reason enough?"

"Pourquoi?"

Fed up, I thought of writing, "You and your *pourquoi* can fuck off back to France!"

"You don't have to be leading a crowd of protesters to be a hero. When there's a bloodbath going on in your country, the greatest form of heroism and rebellion is to sit down at your desk every morning and write."

I didn't have a ready answer for him. Little by little I was losing all that was dear to me. Rather, all those people and things were being taken from me. In light of that, I couldn't help but think: *Is giving up on writing really such a big deal?*

13

MESSAGES

On September 20—a Sunday—I found myself in a hotel room. Here's how it happened: Yunus called out to me from the top of the fire escape. No, he didn't exactly call out. It was more of a strange whistle, an excited chirping of sorts, summoning me. Peering over the top of the wall, I asked, "What is it?"

I knew I was in for a surprise. Ever since the day Yunus had so heroically appeared on the top of the wall with the fur coat, he made a habit of never showing up at the same place twice. But he kept bringing me food, which I hauled up into the trees, using my slacklining strap like a kind of primitive cable car. Sometimes we'd chat, he sitting atop the fire escape as I perched on the wall. He stopped by every day, except on the days when he wasn't working, announcing his arrival with a whistle that I immediately picked up among the incessant cries and caws of the birds. In those days, it seemed like there were more birds in the world than people. Or, perhaps, all the fowl of the city had suddenly decided to take up residence like me in the treetops of the park. A park filled with birds of all kinds, but devoid of people.

"It's seasonal," Yunus said. "People come in waves in the summertime."

The park still seemed to be the sultan's garden. In spirit, I mean. No one was around.

"They pack the trams to get here."

"Are you a public enemy or something?"

"I'm the enemy of wicked, selfish people."

He spoke those words while seated on the other side of the railing of the fire escape, looking like a man in a cage. People think that they are free. But that isn't really the case, because being free does not mean being able to do whatever you please. In my opinion, we don't really understand the concept of freedom. We don't have to be locked up to be imprisoned. In fact, we can be in a state of imprisonment even as we go around, visiting the places we want to see. It's all in our minds. The entire world is a figment of our imaginations.

Perhaps, in that world in my mind, people existed outside my isolated corner of the park, where I spent my days among the branches of three particular trees. One night, however, a young woman wearing a headscarf showed up with her lover and I watched as they passionately kissed. It was dark at that hour. I heard her say that she'd lied to her family, telling them that she had to work overtime. Her lover said, "Let's go to the hotel. The same one as last time." Which meant they'd done it before. Stayed at a hotel. And everything that suggested. I doubt, however, that they went to the expensive boutique hotel where Yunus worked. Everything she was wearing looked cheap, from her long overcoat to her shoes with buckles, and her purse as well. It was a deliberate kind of cheapness. Pembe knew a lot about such things. She'd been the person to ask about clothes, fashion trends, and being stylish even when wearing knockoffs. And, of course, there was my aunt Hülya as well. I couldn't help but wonder why that young woman in the park was wearing a headscarf. So that she could be free? She could go out and return home at any hour of the night, and she'd probably acquired other forms of freedom that few women enjoy, all because she covered her hair. But if she was wearing a headscarf out of religious conviction, I've done her a great injustice by pigeonholing her so. As we all know, however, the world is full of injustice, and everyone gets their share of it. It's inevitable.

"But," she said, "it's so embarrassing. I mean, the way that the guy at the front desk looks at me . . ."

"Why?" her lover asked disappointedly. Why, indeed? Are men ashamed of us?

He had a close-cropped mustache that seemed capable of movement completely independent of his upper lip. Every ounce of his attention was focused on her: one hand was stroking her breasts while the other was caressing her thighs, and he was trying to work his nose past the folds of her headscarf so he could kiss her neck.

"Girl, you turn me on so much. I just might give it to you right here and now."

"You're crazy! Someone could see us."

"Who? There's no one around."

"I came here so we could talk. And now you're at it again."

"I know you want it too."

"Enough already! You said that you were going to get divorced this summer. Well, summer's come and gone."

"I'm going to talk to my wife when she comes back from her hometown."

"She isn't back yet? School's already started."

"Well, she did come back . . . But if she hadn't, I would've taken you back to my place again . . ."

"I can only hope that your neighbors saw us and tell your wife."

"Who cares about the neighbors? But if I hadn't deleted those pics from your Facebook page, everyone would've known."

"As if anyone would've seen them! But I do wonder if your wife and I have any mutual friends . . ."

"If only Facebook knew how sneaky you women are!"

As the mustachioed lover leaned in, he murmured, "You sure put on a show, but you don't put out . . ."

Seen from above, the young woman's head looked like a delicious piece of fruit. Although she weakly protested, she turned her face to the side, letting the man kiss her neck. I could see that her eyes were closed. Lust, that lascivious nectar! With her pale oval face, tiny crimson mouth, thin eyebrows, and upturned nose, she looked like she'd stepped out of an Ottoman miniature. I wondered if she'd see me if she opened her eyes or if I'd concealed myself so masterfully in the darkness that I was completely hidden from sight. I heard the young woman moan with longing as her mustachioed lover buried his face in her neck like a vampire sucking every last drop of her blood. The expression on the young woman's face, which was framed by her light pink headscarf, betrayed all those instincts particular to human nature, but, as I mentioned, when I looked at her, all I could think of was a juicy piece of fruit.

Her lover pulled back from that corner of heaven, suddenly filled with suspicion. "So, are you saying the neighbors saw you? Did you leave something at my place to show that you'd been there? Or maybe you've been posting things about us on social media. Is that it?"

Gone was his romance, replaced by a desire to interrogate her. His mustache now looked like a long dash that was incapable of twitching despite the gravity of the situation.

"Why, are you scared?"

Her face disappeared from sight.

"No," he said, shrugging.

My guess was that his wife and children were waiting for him at home, and at the end of the night, he'd go back as if nothing had ever happened. When he stepped through the door of his immaculate apartment, his wife would hold out a pair of house slippers for him.

"Just a minute, kids, I need to wash up first. My hands are filthy."

Truly, what is the filth of the world? Not that forbidden love that dirtied his hands? Hands that smelled of his lover's crotch, fingers he sniffed while going home on the Metrobus, sinful hands. He couldn't stroke his children's hair with those hands. Seeing as he couldn't simply lop them off, it only seemed fitting that he should reassess the coordinates of his life as a devout man. In my opinion, at least. Not everything happens as God wills. Religion had escaped from the bottle. A bottle of water from the Well of Zamzam! You, sir, have very wicked intentions.

The two of them were still murmuring to each other, but I was losing interest. My mind now turned to thoughts of the video of a young woman wearing a headscarf who'd been attacked on the street. I'd watched the video on Twitter, where I lived my second life. The footage of her fainting out of fear had been recorded by a security camera. I was so upset about what happened that I even reposted the video with a hashtag. How can we better look out for our sisters who wear headscarves? Why is it that, in our society, such attacks on women are so common?

As the young woman down below went on playing coy with her lover, the greenery surrounding them glowed even greener in the fluorescent light of the park lamps. I kept thinking about something the man had said: "Who's going to see us?"

"I will!" I said to myself.

I wanted to prove that I still existed and that, even up in my perch, I was going on with my life despite the actions of our murderous state and all those worthless imbeciles, as well as the ravages inflicted upon us by our warped society and the injustices so prevalent in our day and age. At least, that's how I felt at the moment.

No longer was I troubled by the prospect of being condemned to a life of thinking about the past up there in that nest that I now called home, curled up in the warmth of my fur coat like a baby waiting to be born. I spent much of my time just looking around, and when I wanted to have some fun, I'd juggle a few pine cones or gaze into my mirror, letting my thoughts drift to the past. When the painful times in our lives are transformed into memories, they are beautified in the process, just like how coal becomes diamonds. I know that I've said something along those lines already. In fact, I'm quite aware of what I have and haven't said. In the course of that damn writing competition, I was told that my novel resembled a series of tweets, which led me to break down in tears and run out of the classroom. Cock-mouth Özlem Hanım had said, "You're probably going to get angry with me, but I'm telling you this for your own good. Of course, you're going to keep writing. That's how it is, like life. You go on with it. The act of writing is like giving up control and going with the flow."

"Teacher, how do you know that? Do you write too?"

"Have you ever had anything published?"

I was so lucky to have those friends of mine. But now they're gone. What we really wanted to ask was, "Have you ever taken hold of a cock?" The beer hall. Thick-cut, greasy fried potatoes. Evaluating the events of the day. Laughter. An old guy wearing a hand-knit sweater raising his mug to us, saying how wonderful it is to be surrounded by young and beautiful people.

"I've written quite a bit, but I've never thought of trying to get anything published."

"My mom keeps a diary too."

"Pembe, the things I write aren't like that."

I wish that Pembe's mother had published her journals. The memoirs of the Beauty of Bağdat Street would outsell everything else on the market. Everything that comes from the heart has an innate value that is both literary and long-lasting. At any rate, that's how it should be.

If anyone aside from your mother says to you, "I'm telling you this for your own good," you can be sure that whatever they're going to say is most certainly *not* in your best interests, so don't listen to a word of it. Parents lament the fact that their own lives are passing by as they look after their children or they try to take comfort in their successes. In the end, however, it doesn't really matter because either way it's a burden, a constant act of cruelty. But that's not the issue at hand here. What Özlem Hanım had told me "for my own good" put me in a difficult position vis-à-vis my rival.

At the risk of making myself look the fool, I blurted, "I don't think I'm going to keep writing." Of course, I couldn't bring myself to say, "I've been working my ass off trying to be a writer," because it actually came quite naturally.

Our teacher turned to the twit who won the competition and said, "As the winner of the competition, what would you like to say to your classmates who didn't win? What critiques can you offer?"

She replied, "In my humble opinion, real writing shouldn't come across like a bunch of tweets. Writing on your Facebook wall and writing a book are two completely different things."

"That's exactly what I was going to say."

Özlem Hanım was pleased. The class discussion had shifted from writing to me. To put it more correctly, it was about chewing me up and spitting me out, along with that damn book I wished I'd never written!

"What you wrote was a bunch of tweets, not a novel. In some places, it is meticulously written, but in others it goes way off topic. The narrative jumps around like a bird flitting from branch to branch. You shouldn't confuse your readers so much. It's exhausting. That's why your classmate's comment is so spot-on."

Then she turned back to the class, a murderer trying to exonerate herself for her crimes. That woman murdered my book. She murdered my dreams.

"The best approach is to focus more on the parts that don't work than the parts that came together well. That way, you can see what works and what doesn't."

Fuck your approach, I thought.

I didn't dare say, "I wrote that book so I could prove my existence to the world." Even up in the treetops, I still felt a need to show that I existed. That's why I decided to throw one of my pine cones at the head of the mustachioed lover down below. Afterward, I settled deeper into the nest and continued watching the couple at the foot of the tree.

"Where did this come from?"

"It must've fallen out of the tree. Why, did it scare you?"

"Of course not. Why should I be scared? But it seemed like someone threw it."

It should come as no surprise that the guy was able to juggle two relationships at the same time. Mr. Mustache was as sharp as a tack.

"It's creepy. They say that ghosts and ghouls live at the foot of old walls that stink like piss. Maybe we woke one of them up?"

"You're a big government man now. Don't tell me that you believe in stuff like that!"

Ha! The state that fired my father and made it impossible for my aunt to work as a reporter was now run by people who believed in ghosts and ghouls. I threw another pine cone at him, and then a third.

"*Bismillah*, I swear that something weird is going on here."

Muttering a prayer, the young woman started pulling her lover away, but he kept looking back at the tree and the nest. Even though he couldn't see anything, he said, "I know something's up in that tree."

Now fairly frightened, the young woman started running, stepping on the plastic bottle of peroxide that I'd sent tumbling to the ground the other day like a backflipping pigeon. I could hear the swishing of her long overcoat as she ran, so I wondered if they could also hear me giggling to myself. The man kept turning around to look back as he was pulled away.

It was childish fun.

I peed myself in the process. Let's say it was an accident. It happened by mistake. Involuntarily.

I took a few steps on the branch of the plane tree so that I could spread my legs more easily. I let myself swing down a few meters from the eucalyptus tree with the help of one of my slackline straps. Then I slept the rest of the day away. I wasn't very hungry anymore. When I noticed that my teeth were yellowing like leaves in autumn, I rubbed them with my index finger and rinsed out my mouth with a sip of water.

Would a person who wanted to experience death before dying actually do such things?

Despite my efforts to stay clean, by the fourth day I realized that my face was slowly starting to resemble that of a wild animal. I'd longed to be driven from society, but I was still a part of life, though my only journeys were explorations of the past. I'd go to the park and the days of the protests, and I'd think about that chandelier glowing like the sun above me as I lay wounded on the floor. Then there was the young man beside me who touched my hand and how I turned to look at him, smiling in pain, finding the strength to go on living. I'd like to go back to that moment. But not in my mind. For real. In reality.

I wondered if it actually had been Yunus who infused me with life through his fingertips.

People in love find each other.

I listened to the birds, hoping that one day I'd be able to hone my skills to the point that listening to them became an art. As soon as I heard that strange chirping, I raised myself in all my lightness from the nest, which truly was a wicker cradle, and made my rounds of the branches of the plane tree, eventually stepping out onto one of the stronger branches of the neighboring pine. When I placed my foot on the branch, I felt as if I'd stepped onto firm soil that crackled under my feet. My sense of balance up in the trees was now almost flawless, but I always tread carefully, just in case. I didn't want to fall to the ground below because then I'd never be able to climb back up. It occurred to me that I was playing a game that wouldn't start again after a flashing "Game over."

I made my way over to the wall. Yunus was there.

He whispered, "The room's ready for you."

He was looking as adorable as a monkey in a pen as he stood behind the railing of the fire escape. The other day he'd even done an imitation of a monkey, which made me double over in laughter. For the first time, I was about to step off the wall into his world.

"Watch your step," he said.

I felt like I was traveling to the moon, or stepping out of a spaceship into the unknown. Or it could also be described as going through a critical operation, in the course of which your internal organs are removed and placed on a surgical table. A moment of momentous import.

All the same, I made the leap without a moment of hesitation.

When I saw the look of horror on Yunus's face, for a second I thought I must be plunging into the chasm between us. Even if I wasn't falling, I felt like I was. But then I landed softly on the other side. Turning around, I realized that it was going to be quite difficult to get back—the landing of the fire escape was much lower than the top of the wall.

I asked Yunus, "How did you make it across the other day?"

Pointing to a branch of the plane tree that extended over the wall like a helping hand, he replied, "I grabbed on to that."

"Why were you so nervous? As if you weren't the same person who'd done that before, crossing over and then coming back?"

"I wasn't the same person."

He spoke those words with such earnestness that I stopped in my tracks. Yunus had a good heart. I knew that he didn't want to needlessly confuse me. And he was so innocent. He kept nothing hidden.

"That day, I was high."

"Do you get high a lot?"

"No. But I got high so I'd be able to jump to the wall. I'd never taken those pills before."

"Where did you get them?"

"The pills? From some of the guys who live in my neighborhood. They're part of a gang. They steal things. But don't worry, they don't steal from the poor. They only take from the rich, swiping money that hasn't been made through hard work."

"How can they tell the difference?"

"They know which apartment complexes to hit. Those are the hardest jobs. That's what they say, anyways."

"Have you ever thought of joining them?"

"Yes."

"Why didn't you?"

"Because, even if she's not around anymore, I knew it would upset my mom if she found out."

We were still going down the fire escape. It was a beautiful Sunday. My grandma would say, "You can always tell what day it is by looking at how the sun is shining." She was right. Sunday is always different. Even if it's cloudy and rainy, that day is unique to itself. Friday night always marked the start of the good times and Saturday only got better. Winter Sundays were my family's favorite. We'd sit around all day in our pajamas, not caring if we spilled anything on ourselves, feeling safe and secure in the coziness of our home. And we always had wonderful things to eat, even if it wasn't a fancy spread: cold cuts of chicken, pastries, pasta with ground meat. My grandma would turn up the heater, saying, "Being warm is happiness."

Yunus stopped.

I stopped.

There was a door in front of us.

The fire escape was swaying gently under our weight.

A dove cooed, fell silent, and cooed again.

Yunus's back was broad. A good, strong back. He wore his bellboy uniform with the dignity of a general. I swear, it could've walked off without him. When he was wearing that uniform, he looked more handsome than usual, nothing at all like a timid young man. He paused for a moment before reaching for the doorknob. Autumn is the best season. A few brazen tendrils of ivy had grown over the steps of the fire escape; it would only be a matter of time before they engulfed it completely.

There wasn't anyone in the corridor.

Yunus said, "I'm going to take you to the room now. It's empty. And clean. The air conditioner doesn't work, though. The repairmen are coming in about two hours to fix it. So that's how much time you have. Don't hesitate to use anything you want. The robe, towels, shampoo—you can use all of it. If you want, you can take everything from the minibar, except for the alcohol. Well, you can take a bottle of the cheap stuff. There's a video camera in the hallway, so I'm going to slip out in this blind spot here. The door is unlocked. Act like you're any other guest. Room 116. I left some clean clothes for you there, so leave your dirty ones and I'll have them washed."

I slowly made my way down the corridor.

My bare feet sank into the deep, soft carpet.

There were odd photographs on the wall.

The place was thoroughly Turkish in style. The building, which had originally been constructed toward the end of the sixteenth century, had been fully restored, and then a family started running it as a hotel. There were photos of the opening ceremony, which were fine, but there were also others depicting the disgraceful process through which the historical mansion had been transformed into a commercial enterprise. In the end, people can't resist the temptation to show off. Personally, I think it would've been better if they'd hung up cheap reproductions of Ottoman miniatures.

For a moment I was overcome by doubt. Perhaps it was a trap? The whole country had been transformed into a living hell. While that statement may seem trite, it was true, and you didn't know whom you could trust anymore. But the heart knows best. If you want to be duped, that's precisely what will happen. If you want to be tricked, you'll get tricked. If you don't want to see something, you won't. After thinking it over, I decided that I should have faith in Yunus's intentions. If I was wrong, I knew that I could look after myself. As my grandma was fond of saying, "If there's a hell that is better than this world, I'd rather be there."

I stopped in front of room 116.

Hell had found me. Right next to the door was a photograph of some of the corrupt politicians who'd taken part in the opening ceremony. How many politicians does it take to cut a ribbon? I spit on the face of the most well known of them, and my saliva started slowly dripping down the glass over the photo. Ah, what a wonderful feeling! Just what I needed!

I walked into the room.

It was shadowy inside and smelled clean.

The curtains were billowing in and out in the breeze. I could've sat and watched them for hours.

"Don't do that," my mother would say whenever I gazed at something, lost in my thoughts. "It's creepy."

There was a phone. If I'd wanted, I could've called her.

There was also a computer, which suggested that the room was for people with a long stay in mind. If I'd wanted, I could've peered into the happenings of the cyber world or sent out a message indicating that I was still alive.

"This," I said to myself, "is nothing like fleeing the creature comforts of home only to rush back into their arms." It was completely different. In life, there aren't always clear explanations for everything. I hadn't descended from the trees. On the contrary, I was continuing my life there—this was just a small break.

"Why does your main character do such senseless things?"

Özlem Hanım picked my novel to pieces. By the time she was finished, there was nothing left.

"Things like that don't happen in real life!"

For the love of God, when do we ever get our way? Özlem Hanım, leave me alone! Please, forget that I ever wrote anything! If I want, I'll write descriptions a hundred words long, or a thousand if that's what I feel like doing. If I want, I'll write about things that are mediocre and superficial, or I'll tell the most grandiose, saccharine tales. Things can't always be the way you want. They shouldn't.

Looking out the window, I saw the towering trees in which I'd taken refuge. Only a few days before, I'd summoned the courage to climb up to their highest points, driven on by a state of tedium. As I gazed at their distant branches, which seemed to reach up toward the heavens in supplication, I mused, "I'm not really here." The thought echoed in my mind: *I'm not really here.*

14

MENTION

I panicked as I confessed that to myself. It was as if I'd fallen from the tree. As if I'd never be able to climb back up. Trying to calm myself, I thought: *Your feet never touched the ground. By mere artifice you went into that fancy boutique hotel.* "Artifice." One of the words deboned of my grandma's curses, seeking to remind me of her. While looking at the photographs lining the desolate corridor, I thought of my grandma. There was a similar series of photos of the foundation being laid for our apartment building. The young developer from a town on the Black Sea. In the background, his Mercedes with its doors open, as though spreading its wings to take flight. My father. My aunt. And there was a funny picture of my grandma drawing the floor plans of the apartment with a long stick: this is where the kitchen will be, and here is the bathroom and the living room . . . Funny, isn't it?

I really should have been there. Especially for such a brief, critical moment.

Now, I told myself, *you're going to install a quick update to toughen yourself up.* I looked up again at the tops of the trees where I'd said, "I'm not here." That side of the high wall was completely covered in vines. Birds were flying around in the greenery, immersed in deep shadows. While the trees hadn't yet started shedding their leaves, a few gracefully plucked themselves from their branches and drifted down, coming together with the earth in a state of awe. The birds suddenly stopped chirping. Then I heard the mournful cooing of doves, and more leaves slowly cascaded down. I thought, *I'm going to cry.* Everyone else seemed to have disappeared, driven away like the leaves falling from the trees, and I was the only person left in the world. I felt so lonely and abandoned. Trying to console myself, I thought, *But there's Yunus.* Then I found a more worldly way of consoling myself: I opened the minibar. There was a packet of chocolates, the round ones with nuts. Ten of them in a clear package, plump globules of joy wrapped in foil. I popped them into my mouth, thinking, *You've got it rough. You can neither die nor stay where you are. You're too scared to be in the world below, and you're too bound to life down on the ground to be up in the trees. Sadly, there's no middle ground.* I watched a few more leaves slowly drift down. When you're in nature, you can't observe it. If you want to see nature's grace and power, you have to take a step back. But isn't that the case for everything?

I devoured the chocolates like a savage. A trickle of sticky brown saliva ran down my chin. Then I drank a bottle of mineral water and made myself a cup of espresso with the capsule coffee machine on the counter. At one point, I got the urge to put on some music, but I decided that I'd better stay as quiet as possible. I was an astronaut taking a break on a space station, satisfying my needs. At least, that's how I felt.

I'd learned how to use those capsule coffee machines at the diet clinics where my mother worked. There was always one in the waiting room. She stole one once and brought it home. For a while I think she became a kleptomaniac out of loneliness and frustration, stealing everything that caught her fancy. Then her greatest fear came true and she got caught. "This is the last thing we needed," my father groaned. She called me first to tell me she was at the police station, and I told him. She'd gotten caught stealing a knit dress, black leather boots, and a studded leather backpack at Zara. Before she got caught, however, there was no end to the things she'd steal. That little mouse had come up with a great scheme: she'd take whatever she wanted into the fitting room and cut out the alarm tag, which she then stuck to the bottom of the stool. For a while, she only stole things for me. But she never said that she was stealing. Rather, she'd say she got them on the cheap at a place that sold damaged goods. Most of the time, the alarm tags were easy to find, and she'd stitch up the slit afterward—you'd never even know it was there. Pants, sweaters, blouses, shirts, a cashmere jacket. I was ecstatic, jumping up and down like a child, because I hardly had anything to wear in those days. When my aunt came around, she'd take me shopping to buy a few things, usually a cheap pair of pants and an acrylic sweater from DeFacto. Just as I was thinking that I'd have to make do with those for the winter, my mother came home with her arms full of plunder several days in a row. "Where's this store?" I asked. "Derin and Pembe want to go there too. What store has these damaged clothes?" The answer I got was evasive, not even worth mentioning. "Do they have shoes, boots, bags—things like that?" I was the one who'd laid the groundwork for that disaster by asking for the impossible. At the police station, she was sitting sheepishly on a bench. When she saw me, she broke down in tears.

"And now this! Perfect. To crown it all, you've added stealing to your list of skills."

My father was shouting up a storm as we left the station. My mother didn't say a word. She couldn't. She didn't have the strength. Zara decided to press charges. They had figured out everything that she'd stolen, which didn't really matter because she confessed anyways. She paid for it all. Actually, that's not true. My father paid for it all. I was wearing a pair of pants and a sweater that my mother had stolen. And let's not forget the cashmere jacket. It felt like I was wearing the skins of carcasses. Or the clothes of a dead person. My mother was hunched over out of fear and regret, cowering. The only time my father was ever outside of the house with us was when there was trouble. I decided not to tell Pembe and Derin about what had happened. We'd left the police station and were walking down the street, so I guessed we were going to take the underground home. Just as we reached the corner of Valikonağı Street, we ran into Pembe and her mother. Speak of the devil. Let me tell you, friends: this is a fucked-up world! I stopped, but my parents walked right by without even saying hi. Then it was my turn to lie: "My mom wasn't feeling well, so we went to the American hospital, and they put her on an IV. She wanted to come out to get some fresh air." With her mascaraed eyelashes, Pembe's mother's eyes were like a doll's as they widened in surprise. "What's wrong?"

"Stress," I said. It was the shortest answer I could think of that would stop her from asking more questions. She looked at me sadly. Compassion, consolation, respect for our private lives: all three in one. And then a bonus! Stroking my cheek, she said, "Ah, you poor thing . . ." Her fingertips smelled of Chanel No. 5. They said that they were out exchanging some birthday presents. Arm in arm, the mother and daughter walked off, their hands full of bags from Max Mara, Prada, Beymen, and Mapa. I guessed that, with the exception of Beymen, the other brands didn't have stores on ritzy Bağdat Street. My mind full of such pointless thoughts, I'm sure I watched them walk off with a twinge of jealousy. Her mother walked as if she was still making her way between rows of airplane seats, ignoring the fact that all the passengers were gawking at her. But gawk they did. If a passenger asked for a blanket, a pillow, or some cold water, she'd stop if he had the right look. She always knew who was who. If the passenger asking for a pillow was some geezer from a village, she'd walk right past, but when the man wearing a Rolex who had been bumped up to business class asked for some tomato juice, she'd stop and ask, "Would you like some black pepper with that?"

And my mother? Unemployed and desperate. Defeated, despite all her skills. Two women of the same age, walking toward two different ends of the street. One of them had found what she was looking for, in some way or another. The other was programmed to fail. And me? I was exactly in the middle, but would most likely veer to my mother's side of the street. I was madly jealous of Pembe. She was lucky from birth. Derin wasn't like me. I mean, she wasn't jealous of Pembe. Even though she was from the lower classes, she'd sharpened her tongue with swearing and didn't give a damn about anything. Or maybe she did, but she didn't show it. I couldn't help but wonder: *Why was I like that?*

I pulled my cashmere jacket more tightly around me. When we were talking, Pembe had straightened my collar, trying to match her expression to my look of sadness. She pitied me. And that felt good. I thought I was playing my role well. There is so much that the people with whom we surround ourselves don't know about us. I'd even say that everyone hides themselves away in a mysterious cocoon. How could they have known that my mother had been taken into custody for stealing? They couldn't. It was cold that day. I wanted a North Face jacket like the one Pembe was wearing, a jacket that would keep you warm down to twenty-five degrees below zero. If I'd told my mother, maybe she would've swiped one for me. Using her own special technique, she'd cut out the alarm tag, leaving a hole from which the down feathers hiding inside could escape. Patch it up as much as you want, but the genie is out of the bottle. The voices, anger, and other emotions we keep trapped inside are like that too. When they find a hole through which they can slip out, you suddenly find yourself in the treetops like me. I'm here because I know myself; otherwise, I might've wound up in the loony bin or, perhaps, like Amy, in a dark grave, down in the pits of hell. They cremated her, right? What did they do with her ashes? Did they bury them? Or spread them over England's broad, misty meadows? Maybe her father keeps the ashes of his daughter in an urn at home? So he can turn them into a handsome profit as the legend steeps over time?

I followed after my mother and my father, who had to walk by her side that day, shuffling my worn-out UGG boots. Now there was no way I'd be able to replace them. The real ones cost a small fortune. I remember that I stopped at one point so that I could think more clearly, or perhaps to gather my thoughts. The street was quiet. Was it the first day of the New Year or something? I've said that I'm against consumerism, like in the days when we rose up in protest. But my needs are important. Was I thinking of love, of being loved, as warm feet? Was it really so important for me to crown that warmth with a pair of real UGGs? I remember saying that I was feeling confused, like I said at the beginning of this adventure. The voids of youth, the voids of my soul. Still shuffling, I sped up a little. Something happened then that had never occurred before. Like in a dream, the faster I went, the farther away they became. And yet they were walking ever so slowly. I knew that I was going faster than them. It was like I was in a nightmare, but it was all the more frightening because it was real. As if that wasn't enough, the shop window of the bookstore at the corner of Rumeli Street reminded me of my dreams, of that book I'd written in vain, because the writing competition had ended not long before: "You wrote everything that popped into your head. But all you've done is copy-paste the subject of a great novel in your attempt to write something like the books of today's famous writers. And do you think dialogue is just swearing?"

I wanted to scream "Enough already!" at my literature teacher, who was bent on beating what I'd written to death. But she was insistent: "I will teach you how to write a novel. If you had that knowledge, no book could get in your way. You'd stomp all over every book that's been written."

As Özlem Hanım ranted on, the rest of the class seemed to be asleep, drifting into dreams and flights of imagination. The girl who'd won the competition didn't object so as not to compromise her own position as the winner. What about Pembe and Derin? They were in a different world. If I were to ask, "Should we really fight about books?" or "Isn't it enough to read? Why should everyone learn how to write?" it would have stirred up indignation. I kept my mouth shut. Not saying anything either encourages the other person to talk more or it's a shortcut to getting them to shut up. It all depends on the person.

Özlem Hanım got more and more worked up. Admittedly, she was a good speaker. The struggle to get through life must have left her deeply wounded, because the people who have been hurt the most are the best at hurting others. In order to feel compassion for herself, in order to love herself, she needed to see how hurt she'd been through someone else. And she was the agent of that suffering.

Then, Özlem Hanım wanted to go one "tick" further. In the center of my mind, as I lay propped up on all fours on the sidewalk, she wanted to kick me one more time in the side before fucking off: "On the one hand, your writing is quite mediocre and sloppy . . ."

Per the rules of our wondrous Turkish language, it was impossible for that sentence to be "a stick with shit on both ends," as the saying goes for situations in which you're screwed either way. When our philosophy teacher asked, "So, how do you pick up a stick that's soiled on both ends?" I answered, "In the middle," thereby revealing the endless well of hope I carry inside. Özlem Hanım herself was screwed. She was scrambling to find something to place in opposition to mediocre and sloppy, but in vain! My dear Pembe came to the rescue, finishing off our teacher's awkward sentence: "On the other hand, it is profound." That monument to perniciousness protested, "No, it's not like that at all. What I was doing was giving an example of the carelessly written, incorrect sentences that your classmate used in her writing. On the one hand, your writing is quite mediocre and sloppy, and on the other hand, it is shallow."

A brief hush fell over the room. The sidewalk on which I sprawled wasn't even as silent as the classroom now lurking in the depths of my mind. Someone was running to come to my aid.

I told myself that all I needed to do was catch up with my parents. It was too much for me. It was too much of a burden to bear. I collapsed like a puppet whose strings have been cut. You could say that I kissed the dust. As if I'd fallen from high in the sky, as if I was falling. To slow myself down, I planted the palms of my hands on the sidewalk, but, just as in the tree, that didn't stop me from getting a nasty scrape on my chin. My parents were still walking down the sidewalk, unaware that I'd fallen. I wanted to call out to them, but my voice caught in my throat.

I don't remember them turning around and helping me to my feet.

At a pharmacy, they bandaged up my chin. The palms of my hands were scraped up too. Later, when she saw me at school with my hands bandaged, Pembe would ask, "Did that happen right after you left?" I'd given up on taking notes in class. I'd sit there, looking out the window, like I'm doing now. There was a high wall covered with ivy behind the school. Just like behind our apartment.

"That girl's not right in the head."

That was how Özlem Hanım, who was also our homeroom teacher, worded the school counselor's diagnosis when she spoke with my parents. I was afraid my mother would say, "Who of us *is* right in the head!" The other faculty overheard Özlem Hanım talking on the phone. Monsieur Pierre told me that she was trying to convince everyone that I was mentally ill. He let it slip. I love it when people let things slip—it always leads to something exciting.

I thought to myself, *I'm glad that Grandma isn't here to see all this.* Because I knew she would've felt bad. She would've felt bad for me. They were saying I was sick, I was telling myself that I was sick, and so on, and so on.

15

EDIT YOUR PROFILE

My grandma was insisting that she be remembered. It was impossible for me to swat away my memories of her like a fly. I turned my attention back to the room. "You can't live in the moment because you're always thinking about tomorrow." If my grandma had risen from the grave and stood before me, that's the advice she would've offered. Don't worry, Grandma, I go through life remembering today when it becomes yesterday.

The room was clean, which pleased me. For some reason I thought it'd be messy, perhaps even a cigarette butt floating in the toilet. But there wasn't. Bits of nuts from the chocolates I'd eaten were stuck between my teeth and idling around under my tongue. I thought about filching one of the disposable toothbrushes from the bathroom. After all, I was going to be back in the treetops again soon, as they were now my home. So, what business did I have being in that hotel room? Why didn't I have the heart to let myself get filthy? Why was I so worried about brushing my teeth?

"You're running away from something, is that it?"

That was one of the first questions that Yunus asked me.

I wished that the human mind was like a bathroom faucet. That it could be shut off with the turn of a knob. That memories wouldn't rush in like a flood. Yes, I was up to my ankles in memories. My feet were now immersed in pleasantly warm water. It hadn't even been a week since I'd last taken a shower. That was what I missed: hot water, suds, steam. When I was little, my grandma always bathed me. She and I would even go to the hammam. She'd had a falling-out with the scrubber woman at Galatasaray Hammam, so we'd go to Çemberlitaş. My grandma didn't like bathing at home. She had bad memories about the tub at her place.

"I'd better finish up quickly and get out of here."

That's what my grandma said. Many, many years ago.

"The toilets and tubs in homes are breeding grounds for ghouls." That's what she'd say. But this wasn't the tub of a home. It was the tub of a fancy boutique hotel. Not only that, but I was a fugitive there. A fugitive from life. I was using the place without permission. The tree-tops, however, were mine. At last I was free.

On September 6, 1955, a disaster befell my grandma. She was just eighteen years old at the time. She'd play the oud and sing in Beyoğlu's tavernas, but only for select groups, special customers, gentlemen, ladies, connoisseurs of music. Most of the musicians were her Greek neighbors. Aside from my grandma, the only other Turkish member was the singer. They were a small, cheerful, unassuming group of musicians, ranging in age from eighteen to fifty-eight, both men and women. They mostly performed for foreigners, sometimes at two venues in a single night. And since they started late, my grandma would always sleep in. When she got up, she'd rush off to the small chocolate factory owned by her Greek neighbors, because that's where her mother worked along with Madam Eleni, the wife of the owner, and their one and only daughter, Efrosa, who played violin in the same group as my grandma. Do you remember Madam Eleni? In those years, she didn't use a cane or wear glasses—so how could you remember?

If there was a gig, Monsieur Hariapulos would call and say, "Send the girls to the taverna tonight."

They would all rush out of the chocolate factory and go to their homes in Cihangir, where they'd eat a quick dinner, get cleaned up, and put on their best clothes, adding a bit of flair. The shows would start at around nine or ten o'clock. Efrosa's fiancé, Niko, who was a music teacher, would join them as well. He could play every instrument, so if someone was sick that night, he'd take their place. Niko and Efrosa were set to get married on September 30. "That's the best time of the year for a wedding," my grandma said to one of her friends.

"The heat of Istanbul dies down, the rains haven't come yet, the weather is cool and breezy, the families who were on the islands for the summer come back, the church isn't so busy, the tailors and dressmakers have time on their hands, the fathers have saved up some money, new shipments of cacao arrive, the chocolate of the wedding cake is as fresh as can be, the engagement chocolates are exquisite, and the liqueurs have reached the peak of perfection."

"It'll be your turn next, Perihan, dear."

My grandma was in love too, with the son of a family from the neighborhood. They lived on Matara Street. To top it off, he was educated.

"Educated or not, he's a grave robber."

That's how my grandma's mother would belittle the potential groom-to-be. What she meant by "grave robber" was "archaeologist." Just like my father. Isn't it strange how fate weaves its web? His family also belittled my grandma: "Son, why don't you marry someone with a better education?"

But he was in love with my grandma: "Father's a dentist, and you're a housewife. So, Mother, why don't you tell me how *that* marriage came about?"

"It was different back in those days."

My grandma spoke of everything on her deathbed, all her memories gushing forth. Including memories of her potential mother-in-law, who didn't want her in the family.

Together with Niko and Efrosa, they secretly went to the islands, and to the cinema once. And then my grandma's sweetheart went to

France to continue his studies. She waited for him. He promised her, "As soon as I return, we'll make our relationship official. You'll breathe a sigh of relief, and so will I."

Letters shuttled back and forth between France and Istanbul. He even had a friend of his deliver a gift to my grandma: a dress made of printed fabric. My grandma was ecstatic because she'd never seen such a beautiful dress. There was a note in the box:

"My Peri, my Perihan, I wonder how this silk dress will look on you? You are silkier than silk itself. I send you embraces filled with longing. When we meet upon my return, I would like you to wear this dress. But if, out of excitement, you wear it before that time, I won't be upset, my sweet."

So there you have it, letters filled with a love, a yearning that we can't wrap our minds around. A romanticism that's always beyond our reach. Echoes from the past that emerge from the depths of my grandma's crocodile-skin purse.

My grandma was waiting for the archaeologist who went to France. Efrosa was enjoying her engagement with Niko to the utmost. They were fine; they were splendid. When my grandma's mother saw the dress from Paris, she realized how serious matters had become. She made do with lamenting, "If only he'd been a doctor, or an engineer." As for the mother of my grandma's beau, she pulled herself together when she heard the story of a young man who killed himself because his family tried to prevent him from marrying the woman he loved. She even stopped on the street to chat with the women from our family.

My grandma was happy. She was happy, not knowing that would be the first and last happiness in her life. Because if you experience something that makes you say you'd rather die than live through the likes of it again, all subsequent promises of happiness ring hollow.

When I found out about that painful memory, I wondered how my grandma had gone on living. Then I imagined her in those happy days: Overcome by excitement, Perihan put on the dress. As she looked at herself in the mirror, she said, "My love, when you come back, it will be as new as the day you sent it." One night, as she was playing onstage at the taverna, there was a customer—a famous opera singer— who declared she had the very same dress from Paris that my grandma was wearing. They got far more tips than usual that night. Monsieur Hariapulos was grinning from ear to ear: "They probably thought if one of our musicians was wearing the same dress that opera singer has, they'd better tip well to show that they're the ones with the money."

Monsieur Hariapulos, that's more than a "probably"!

Her mother warned, "She better be home by midnight. If she's not, I swear I'll never let her play at the taverna again!"

He replied, "Who, your Cinderella? Ha, just like in the fairy tales!"

Which fairy tale has a tragic end?

"The end of my fairy tale was shit!"

For years, my grandma complained bitterly. And for years, I gathered up the pearls she dropped and strung them up. It's such a shame that I was only able to piece together her story after she died.

Time passed, days at the chocolate factory and nights onstage in Beyoğlu. Each day for my grandma was even better than the one before. One day, after packaging chocolates all day, my grandma left the factory and went home. Her fingertips were covered in silvery flakes from the wrappers. That night, they were going to perform again at the taverna. She set the table, knowing her mother would be home soon, and heated a kettle full of water for washing up. Packaging was sweaty work, and she could tell that she smelled anything but pleasant. She didn't want to stink up her dress. They'd said to be at the taverna by nine o'clock. My grandma looked at the clock.

As she lay on her deathbed, my grandma slipped into murmured recollections of that night again and again. When our minds, thoughts, and spirit get stuck somewhere, that place never leaves us, and we go back there when death draws near. She didn't want to leave this world until she'd settled that account. They'd left me as her caretaker in her final days. "You're a big girl now. Stay here with your grandma." That's how my aunt justified it to herself. Her work wasn't going well. There had been a schism at the newspaper. For the first time in her life, she broke out in hives, all because of stress. In the end, she was going to get fired and be unable to find work. As for my mother, she was dealing with the fallout from her somewhat shady efforts to become a famous dietician. My father? He wasn't around. They'd separated. There was only me. And sometimes Pembe and Derin. After school they'd stop by the hospital, knock on the door, poke their heads inside, and drift toward the bedside like smoke. Loudly, so that she could hear me, I'd say, "Grandma, these are my friends." She'd moan in response. By that time, she was practically deaf. She was in another realm, waiting for death, getting closer and closer to the moment when she would settle accounts and make things right. The people at the hospital seemed to sense this, so they released her. "Let her die at home. We can't do anything else for her." That day, the day she took her last breath, she was "there," stuck in that memory she could never forget. She spoke of things she'd never told anyone:

"I stepped out of the bathroom, all freshened up, wearing the silk dress my love had sent me. I was hoping my hair would dry in time. I'd brushed my bangs into a curl so they would dry that way. My mom was supposed to be home at any moment, so I had already started cooking. The radio was on. There was news. The news always bored me. I was just about to turn off the radio when I realized that something important was going on. They reported that Atatürk's house in Thessaloniki had been bombed. In retaliation, people had started attacking the local Greeks of Istanbul. It was a little after seven o'clock. The announcer said, 'The first attack was on the Haylayf Café.' A large mob that had been rioting in Samatya and Kumkapı, looting stores, was now in Beyoğlu. I was just thinking, *We better not go out tonight with all the tumult,* when I heard the door of the apartment building bang open. A roar of voices filled the street and our building at the same time. Somehow, it was suddenly eight o'clock. When I get scared, I freeze up. Like a rabbit in a spotlight. I thought my mom had come home. She had. But with her was a gang of sinister-looking thugs.

"One of them said, 'These people are Greeks too. But they hide it. A mother and daughter. At night, the girl goes with the Greeks to the taverna.'

"'So they're Greek.'

"'I swear, we're not. We're Turkish. Muslim.'

"'Don't bother going upstairs. There's no one there.'

"'She's lying. Her daughter's up there.'

"'They told us not to mess with any Muslims.'

"'She's lying! They're not Muslim. They're Greeks pretending to be Turks.'

"'I swear. I'm Muslim, *lā ʾilāha ʾillā llāh* . . .'

"'So what, she memorized a few words from the Koran.'

"'Do you know how many Greeks have thrown themselves at my feet and said the Shahada? With men, it's easy to tell. But if your neighbor says you're Greek, then you're Greek.'

"'Please, don't bring any harm to my home.'

"'How about we bring some harm to *you*, woman?'

"'She's got a daughter, I'm telling you. A daughter.'

"'I spit on you! I thought you were a neighbor, but you're a lying snake!'

"'Ha, so you'd spit in my face? That's how these people are. Take her daughter. She's all yours. Do whatever you want with her.'"

As she lay on the floor, listening to the cataclysmic conversation going on downstairs, my grandma's eyes were wide with horror. Regret, what a harsh emotion you are! What a heavy burden to bear! She regretted that she hadn't run away and hid somewhere, that she was now stuck in a trap. She blamed herself:

"Why did I stay there, stupidly listening to the voices coming from below? It was obvious they were going to hurt me. What was I waiting

174

for? Why didn't I run away? Why didn't I try to hide somewhere? After all, I knew how to slip away like a mouse without leaving a trace. In the past I'd climbed out the window to meet up with my love. If I'd thought of escaping, I could've easily hidden in a place where that cruel mob never would've found me. But that day, at that moment, I froze up. My feet were nailed to the floor. I couldn't move."

My grandma was crying as they dragged her into the bathroom. Not just crying, but bawling, like a baby desperately begging for help. The expression on her face must've been exactly the same when she was trying to break free of the grip of those men, when she was trying to resist them. Her hands balled into fists, and she was clutching the collar of her blouse so they wouldn't pull it open, but they tore her clothes from her body. Just like what happened that day, two invisible hands pulled her arms down. She was now defenseless. My grandma was shouting. Young Peri, Perihan, was shouting.

Pleading.

Pleading.

Pleading.

In the end, she fainted, losing consciousness altogether.

"I never gave in," she said.

The men said, "Yes, you did."

"I'm not yours."

The men whispered, "You are ours now."

"Let me go. I'm begging you, let me go."

"We won't, girl. Why should we?"

As one of the men from the mob was pulling up his trousers, he whistled in the direction of the apartment across the street, where another group of men was pillaging, sending them a signal.

"My brother's going to come. He's sixteen. It'll be his first. He was going to go to a brothel, but now we've got this. Pure luck."

My grandma was squeezing her eyes shut, squeezing, squeezing. Her sobbing became a moan of agony.

"Look at her clothes. They tore them to pieces."

Her mother was showing the traces of the disaster to a neighbor who had come over to offer what consolation she could.

"The poor girl . . . So she's pregnant, but who's the father? Which one was it?"

"Ah, Perihan, ah!"

What a calamity for her.

"It was such a calamity for me," my grandma said.

The curious neighbor was asking questions, questioning, questioning. The neighborhood representative showed up. That was his job.

"Did you go to the police?"

"Even if we found the culprit, what would we do? And it wasn't just one person! Nearly all of Istanbul is at fault. How could they vandalize the city like that?"

"Are you going to pack up and leave like so many of the other Greeks?"

"We're not Greek!"

"But they thought you were, and they did the same to you as they did to them."

"We don't know any of the people who did it! We didn't recognize anyone except the ironmonger's son, who was standing at the door. That's all he did: hold the door open. Then he came in, took a look around, and left."

"So you don't think they'll come back and do the same thing again?"

"Do you think they would?"

In the depths of my grandma's mind, a balking at the unknown. The same naive optimism continued:

"The people who did this will think we've left, so they won't come back. No one could do anything worse to us here than what has already happened. We're not going to leave, because our stories follow us wherever we go and they'll find us."

Meaning?

"What if the same happens wherever we go? The people who know about the terrible things that were done to my Perihan, the people who heard about them, will die one day. Everything that happened will just be a rumor, then."

My great-grandmother was right. We shouldn't be surprised to find that the history of the country is based on hearsay; a sense of shame is passed from mob to mob, never apologized for, never accepted. So go on—write history however you want to believe it happened.

My grandma's mother wasn't able to bind her wounds. She was like a peacock of disaster, dragging her tail. The neighbor talked about the news she'd heard:

"Efrosa was locked under the stairs by her father. But she watched through the keyhole what was happening to the other women in her family, and she lost her mind. Those bastards did unspeakable things. They even threw Efrosa's mother out the window."

Screw your humanity!

It turned out that the woman we'd run into at the hairdresser's didn't use a cane because she was as old as the world but because she was thrown two stories down and broke nearly every bone in her body. She'd been using a cane ever since she was thirty-eight years old.

Efrosa was saved. But she'd seen more than she could bear.

"Niko killed himself too."

"Why did Niko kill himself?"

Hidden in the neighbor's silence was this answer:

"Either the mob hung him or he hung himself because what he'd seen was too much for him."

The peacock went on dragging her tail behind her, and the neighbor went on explaining:

"They threw Monsieur Yorgo into a huge cauldron and boiled the poor man. As soon as he arrived in Athens, they had to amputate his foot. Everything of value he had was thrown into the street. You wouldn't have believed your eyes: Pianos, armchairs, tables, silks, shoes. You sighed to yourself, looking around at all that finery underfoot. Even in a war you wouldn't see such barbarity, such savagery. Shattered mirrors, broken display cases. Young women were leaning out the windows as far as they could, crying out for help. But no one helped them. The doors of apartments and shops had all been broken down. Curtains billowed out of the windows like the sails of ships setting out for some unknown sea. I've never heard or seen such a rape of property and life. Maybe the only time there was so much destruction was when the Ottomans were taking Istanbul. The English didn't even go so far. It's a shame. A sin."

Such a shame. Such a sin.

Beautiful Perihan wasn't able to get an abortion, nor could she get herself to miscarry.

"Let's tell the neighbors that we were saved from the catastrophe. Can't we?"

That's what my great-grandmother told my grandma. And she heeded her words.

But what happened to the baby?

What happened?

One night, the baby suddenly came into the world. My great-grandmother delivered the baby. In the bathroom, nonetheless. Squatting over the toilet. The newborn splashed into the toilet bowl up to its waist. Into that filth. My great-grandmother angrily pulled the baby out with one hand, saying, *"Bismillah."* She clapped her other hand over the baby's mouth. Then she dropped the now-dead baby into a pillowcase, which she buried in a deep pit she'd dug in the backyard. The next day she had to shoo away the neighborhood's stray dogs, as they were digging at the spot. She had buried Perihan's baby so deep, however, that no one could've gotten it out.

Do you understand now why my grandma traded away her house and land?

"Why was my baby in the lap of that whore with the epitaph over her grave? Maybe he cried and cried, and unable to turn him away, that Byzantine whore took him into her arms. Maybe she even suckled him, who knows. We can't know anything about what happens in the realm of the dead."

Quietly, I stepped outside. I needed some fresh air. It was March. The year, 2013. My grandma was on her deathbed. I'd helped her drink a little water before going out, because for years she'd told me that people on the cusp of death are always thirsty and that the devil perches behind them, whispering, "Give me your faith and I'll give you some water."

I remember walking down the street, feeling distraught. The same street those thugs had walked down on September 6, 1955. The homes were different. Gone were the scattered wooden houses with pots of geraniums in front of the windows and fragrant backyards filled with wisteria and roses. In their place were apartment buildings with exteriors covered in tiles. But the street was the same. Nothing had changed. Those mobs had trod on the same soil. I turned off Kumrulu Street, which is steep but rather short, and ducked into the garden of Cihangir Mosque. The garden has benches and ancient trees, like the ones in which I live in Gülhane Park. You can sit at the foot of the wall of the mosque and face the sea. As I looked at the view, I took a few deep breaths. I was the only person there. It was a cold and gloomy day, the skies threatening rain. I shivered. Just then, something happened that changed the very essence of my life, but believe me when I say that I have no idea how I will explain that to you.

I was deeply moved by what my grandma had told me. At that moment I saw my aunt dash across the mosque courtyard, which was odd because usually at that hour she'd be at the office of the newspaper and wouldn't leave until the print run for the provinces was ready. But there she was, heading toward her home in a hurry. The courtyard of the mosque has two gates that connect the two main streets of the neighborhood. If you go down Cihangir Street to Özoğul Road and pass through the gate, you'll come out on the other side at the midpoint of Kumrulu Street, near the imam's place. The mosque and small adjoining cemetery will be on your left. There's a small garden beside the mosque, the farthest point of which offers the view I mentioned. You access the garden through a small iron gate. So that's where I was sitting, looking out over the city, which was blanketed in darkness even though it was the middle of the day. My aunt quickly went out the gate that leads to Kumrulu Street and disappeared from sight.

For a moment I turned back to the view. But a very brief moment.

That's when it happened. That thing I don't know how to describe. Sensing that someone was coming, I turned around. My grandma was coming toward me, wearing her coat. I was surprised that she'd been able to get out of bed, sick as she was. My jaw hung open, and I may have stammered. One word fell from my lips: "Grandma?" It was all I could manage to say. Just as she'd put on her ash-gray jacket, she'd put on her short boots that zip up the side. I could see that she was wearing her day clothes. What I mean by that is she hadn't just put on her jacket over her nightgown but had somehow found the strength to get dressed, even though when I'd left, she'd been muttering deliriously to herself. She was even wearing her skin-tone stockings. Needless to say, I was surprised: "Grandma, what are you doing out here?"

She acted as though she hadn't heard my question and sat down beside me. The branches over our heads were late to bud and hadn't yet sprouted any leaves. A few crows landed on the iron railing in front of us and then flew off.

"Why did you go out?" she asked. "Why did you come here?"

It had been a long time since she'd been able to formulate a question. She was being kept alive with IV drips, which my mother refreshed when they ran out. She'd whispered her biggest secret just when I thought she'd slipped into a coma. Sometimes my aunt fed her spoon-fuls of sugar water to bolster her strength. "She's going to leave us early," my aunt said. "She's only seventy-six."

Now my grandma seemed perfectly fine. As if the woman sitting beside me wasn't the woman who was lying on her deathbed.

"I was saddened by what you told me," I said.

"Don't be. That's how life goes."

"Did you see my aunt?" I asked. Then I added, "Surely you must have." In terms of the physical world and logic, that had to be the case. There's no denying that there was fear, doubt, and uneasiness in my voice. Needless to say, I was in a state of shock.

"No," she replied. "I didn't see her."

"But she just went by. If you came through the gate on the Kumrulu side . . ."

"That's the way I came."

"Then you must've seen her."

"I didn't."

We fell silent for a moment.

Getting to her feet, she said, "I'd better get going." She leaned down and kissed me on the cheeks.

"I came to see you. To tell you to not be sad." She was cupping my chin in her palm. Her hand was so cold. Then she turned around and pensively glanced at the view. She looked like she was about to say something, but then changed her mind. I watched her as she hobbled out of the small garden of that mosque that had been built for the prince who'd died of a broken heart. With her low boots she loved so much, her ash-gray jacket, and tasseled wool scarf thrown over her shoulders, she looked just like Marianne Faithfull in that film where she played a grandma who masturbates men through a glory hole in a bar so she can make enough money to save her grandson's life.

She was leaving this world.

"Goodbye, cats. I'm going to miss you very much. I'm going to miss you the most of all because your wickedness never brought me any harm. If only I'd come into the world as one of you—I wouldn't have suffered so much. Or I could've forgotten it all and not cared. Bye-bye, kitties, don't forget me."

Istanbul, don't forget my grandma either.

❦

"Istanbul, don't forget me. If you do, damn you to fucking hell!"

❦

"I may not have had that panoramic view, but when I closed my eyes, I could see it." That's what my poor grandma said. Do you call everything you went through "life"? This isn't life; it's the worst of torments. You're confused. That's all this country has to offer its women and girls, in lieu of a plaque.

Did you know that my grandma kept a "crap diary"? That's what she called her tally of days when her slow bowels actually kicked into action. Her crap diary. As for the things she despised, allow me to list them: menstrual cramps, diarrhea, vomiting, smelling sweaty, bathing with anything but old-fashioned white soap, bathing at home, house-work, smelly groins, mice, bedbugs, itching, and mosquitoes. But her obsessions and dislikes didn't stop there: bidets, bug poison, swimming pools, delivery trucks, hair in sink drains, humidity, mold, noisy motor-cycles, the sound of drawers opening and closing, and much, much more.

Her voice had been weary, melancholic, full of disappointment. That wasn't the effect of cigarettes. Life had done that to her. I'd seen her laugh on many occasions in her dimly lit apartment, but I wondered if it was because she was enjoying herself or if it was out of sorrow.

Hope never ends. In fact, the story doesn't really come to an end when death rolls around. People speak of your life and you go on existing through those stories. Like those panoramas that go on existing even after you die.

Shrugging off the mysteriousness of what had happened, I stood up and headed in the direction where I'd last seen my grandma. First I walked out of the garden and then out of the courtyard of the mosque onto our street. There was an ambulance in the middle of the road, its back doors swung wide open, which made it look like a wild, winged creature about to take flight. My aunt was standing behind the ambulance. A stretcher came rolling out of our apartment building. On it was my grandma. Her feet were bare. I could see the edge of her vervain flower-print nightgown—one of her favorites—where the blanket had been pulled up a little. But it didn't make any sense, because she'd been with me just a minute or two earlier.

I'd say that's when I lost it.

Perhaps. I'm not sure.

Everyone has experienced a moment when they were severed from life, driven hither and thither. We remember moments, not days. That's why moments are so important. I think my grandma really died that time. Even though she'd appeared to me in the small garden of Cihangir Mosque with its panoramic view and bid me farewell, she had died. But that wasn't the first time she died. True death occurs when the spirit dies, regardless of whether or not the ephemeral body goes on living.

So, how does the soul die?

Take the case of what happened to my grandma on September 6 in 1955.

But this is life, and you seek consolation. That's precisely what my grandma did. She stitched anew the tattered dress, which her mother had showed to the neighbor as if to say, "Look at what they did to the poor girl." Day and night, she sat for hours, stitching. At first her mother didn't say anything, as she thought it offered her daughter some comfort. When my grandma said that one day she was going to wear that dress when she went to Sirkeci train station to welcome back her lover, her mother planted herself in front of her and took her by the arm, prompting my grandma to scream wildly, "Let me go! I'm going to see him! I'm going to pick him up at the station! Let me go!"

We hurt the people we love the most: "Shameless! Instead of fighting with your mother, you should've fought back against those men who had their way with you!"

Grandma, if you were going to die, you would've died at that moment when you heard those daggerlike words spoken by that woman you knew as your mother. But you didn't die. Grandma, you're immortal!

But that's how it is now. Are you here among us? No. Because you're dead.

Her mother couldn't stop her. She went to the train station. He was there with his mother and father, and a distant cousin. His mother wanted to marry him off to the cousin. They all knew about it. Peri, Perihan, stood off to the side like a ghost.

"What happened to you?"

That's what he asked her. He wanted to approach her, but his mother grabbed his arm.

"Don't go to her. Now she's nothing but scrap.

"I don't want to say I told you so, but I told you so.

"Don't go to her. Now she's nothing but a trap."

He wanted to say to his lover, "You've lost so much weight." But her belly was poking out like she'd swallowed a coconut. Her cheeks were sunken, and she had bags under her eyes the color of murky water. Arm in arm, the family walked away.

"Come quick, she's fainted!"

She was in a swoon. Who could bear being left like that? Who could bear the disappointment, the pains of love, seeing your hopes and future wrenched from your grasp?

As one of the strange coincidences of life, it was a vegetable dealer who came to her aid.

"Here, sit down. You want some water, ma'am?"

He walked her all the way home. Her mother promptly made up a story to tell that steward of destiny who showed up on her doorstep, and she decided to marry my grandma off to him. After delivering and killing the baby my grandma had been carrying, her mother made up a string of lies: "Some guy tricked her, saying that they'd get married." The vegetable seller said, "I don't mind. But I've got a wife. She's sick, bedridden. I'll have to divorce her first."

And he did just that. Afterward, he and my grandma got married. But out of spite, the brothers of the woman he'd divorced reported him as being a draft dodger. He was sent off to the military, and from 1956 to 1960 he did his service, finally finishing after four grueling years. The first child they had—my father—was born in 1962. My grandma offset the pain of being with a man she didn't want to marry by putting sleeping pills in his soup and tea to keep him docile, and if she didn't have any on hand, she'd slip in some sulfate of potash. She also tried to make sure that her mother was always at home, so that he couldn't try anything. One day, however, the vegetable dealer went out, saying that he was going to the wholesale market, but he hid around the corner, and when he saw my grandma's mother go out to visit one of their neighbors, he rushed back home, and that's how my grandma unwillingly got pregnant with her second child—my aunt. She was born in 1970, eight years after my father. As for the vegetable dealer . . . One day, as he was going to Ankara, where he was born and raised, and where he did most of his business, he was killed in a car crash. My aunt was a baby at the time, just forty days old.

His business partner said, "There he was, dead, lying in a pile of cauliflower."

I don't want my grandma's husband to be parted from you in such a gentle manner. Nor do I want to give you the impression that he was a good man in his own way. My heart wouldn't allow it. He was unbearable, intolerable, even if he did only spend three days a week in Istanbul and the rest traveling back and forth to Ankara. If you ask why . . . Because he was a jackass who cut up the champagne-colored dress that my grandma kept hidden in her drawer just to look at once in a while, because he burned a pair of shoes that she'd wanted to wear when she got her picture taken at a photography studio, and because for some reason he cut off the backs of all the chairs in their home, turning them into stools.

In short? My grandma was glad to have been saved from a life with the man she'd been forced to marry.

Derin would say "in short" as if she was saying "snips" or "scalpel," like when she'd get the urge to shut up a babbler through a surgical intervention of their jabbering. Yes, so in short: being stuck for years in a forced marriage is sheer torture. Don't get the wrong idea; I'm not trying to exonerate my grandma. But at the same time, accept that I'm not going to slander her either. Back to the point: my grandma was embarrassed to be seen going around Cihangir with her vegetable-dealer husband because the man she loved still lived in the area. When you break up with your lover now, you erase their pictures from your Instagram account and you block them. They were forced to go on with their lives in the same neighborhood with lofty detachment, while now you bury each other in the virtual world. The man my grandma loved married the cousin his mother had found for him, and they ended up having twin girls, whom they would take to Cihangir Park and the garden of the mosque. My grandma wouldn't let her children play with them. It was a kind of blocking, I suppose.

My grandma's only hope for the two children she'd had with that vegetable dealer who perished in a heap of cauliflower was for them to get a good education. Still, there's more: everyone finds love in life and experiences what it's like to fall in love. The same held true for my grandma. After the death of her husband, she started working as a housekeeper at various hotels. When a hotel in Pera had to be fumigated because of an infestation of bedbugs and the customers were left in a bind, my grandma said to one of them, perhaps because he'd already caught her eye, "My place is in Cihangir. How about if you rent a room from me?"

The year was 1973. The man who settled into one of the rooms of that two-story wooden house was an American who'd been assigned to a post in Istanbul. He was in charge of a large-scale archaeological project being carried out at Hagia Sophia. That's what you call poetic justice! My grandma's mother started saying, "She just went off and married an American." As they say, a lie can travel halfway around the world before the truth can get its boots on. September 6 and 7 in 1955 were testament to that. Atatürk's house in Thessaloniki hadn't even been bombed! Getting back to the point, my grandma started falling in love with the American, and the two of them would take her kids to Cihangir Park.

My aunt would exclaim "Daddy!" in English, and throw her arms around his neck.

One day he said, "One of the archaeologists working on the Hagia Sophia project also lives in this neighborhood. He's got kids too. I told him to bring them along and meet us here."

And just who might that Turkish archaeologist be?

Who?

Who might it be, Grandma? You planned this, didn't you? Isn't it so, you imp? Isn't it so, you vindictive little thing? Isn't it so, you stubborn goat who believes that revenge is a dish best served cold? Isn't it so, woman who rose from the ashes? Isn't it so, you who are as sturdy and resilient as the dome of Hagia Sophia? Isn't it so, Perihan, our Perihan mother, who is as strong as Hagia Sophia's buttresses?

Who was it? None other than the archaeologist whom my grandma had been in love with. I suppose that's how fate weaves its web. The American was the head of the project, the lord of it all. The Turkish archaeologist worked for him, and was clinging to him in the hopes of being able to ride his coattails to America when he went back. Once upon a time, there had been a teary-eyed girl at Sirkeci Station who was left in the hands of a vegetable dealer . . . Her return was magnificent.

"You're screwed now, Mr. Archaeologist!"

I imagined that my grandma, who said that to my own father for years, whispered those same words while discreetly flipping off the man who'd left her in tears at the station.

There are so many things to experience.

So many things to say.

My grandma would've said that life is anything but short. Indeed, she would've said it is rather long. Very, very long. I agree. But don't let that frighten you. You still have a chance to grab hold of all those opportunities you let slip past and live them out to the end. There's still time for your plans to come to fruition, for you to seek vengeance, for your loved ones to return, for people to see that you were right, for justice to prevail, and for your dreams to become a reality.

In my first year of high school, we were asked to interview an elder from our families. We were allowed to do it in pairs or groups of three. A kind of oral history project. Fate had already mapped out the path for me and the others in my group. The only older person left in my family was my grandma, but since we were going to present the interview in transcription, I figured I'd need to weed out her outlandish swearing.

"She'll read our fortunes too. She's really good at doing it from the coffee grounds at the bottom of the cup."

That was the first time my friends came to my place. The apartment where Derin lived with her parents was small and basic. But very clean. The cleanest apartment in the whole country. You could hardly bring yourself to tiptoe across the floor. It was so clean that it made you feel filthy in comparison. You can probably guess what Pembe's place was like: a four-hundred-square-meter apartment in Caddebostan, a real palace. You could fit the Sea of Marmara *and* the islands in there. The furnishings were semiclassical, nice enough for people who are into that kind of thing, but the decor lacked taste. There was nothing unique about our place, however. It occupied a position somewhere between Derin's and Pembe's, and it could've been mistaken for being wannabe bohemian. There was the old sofa, the coffee table with the glass-topped inscription, my father's archaeological library, a desk in the corner, and the tiny living room, which was dominated by my mother's treadmill.

"Where do you eat?"

"We don't. My mom banned eating."

"The kitchen's bigger than a widow's cunt," my grandma said, striding through the door. "We can eat there."

We were in ninth grade at the time. Vestiges of childish behavior still clung to us. Derin and Pembe tittered with their hands over their mouths. I'd told them my grandma swore a hundred times worse than them, but they hadn't believed me. "You see?"

"Whoa!" Pembe said.

"Wow!" Derin said.

"Your grandma looks just like Marianne Faithfull!"

"Who's that?"

Thanks to the cigarettes she chain-smoked, my grandma's voice was hoarse and raspy. She dyed her own hair, insisting on Koleston's ash blond, which produced good results with her white locks. Thick black eyebrows, slightly sagging cheeks, and permanently moist eyes. "I've got eyes like a dog's. The American liked me just as I was." With her large mouth and jowls, she had all the physical characteristics of that rock-and-roll queen she'd never heard of. As she sat down, my grandma repeated her question. My friends were so polite. They'd gotten up and greeted her at the door.

"I asked you, 'Who's that?'"

"It's you, Grandma. Let me make you a cup of coffee."

Soon enough, she'd seen right through my friends. Her eyelids were being tugged downward as if weights were attached to them. For all her hawkishness, my grandma looked sad. With each passing day she looked sadder and sadder. Despite the chain of events she'd been through because of her marriage to the vegetable dealer, she was still a formidable person. She had an air of savviness about her as a woman who'd found a father for her children and a husband for herself in the American archaeologist, even if the relationship was just for show. She was a queen who'd fallen on hard times, a queen who'd been born and grew up in the heart of Istanbul, and although she'd been through so much, she persevered. Those were the things I was going to emphasize in my oral history presentation, whether my grandma actually said the words or not.

I stepped out of the kitchen, holding an Arçelik Turkish coffee maker. "Grandma, how do I use this thing? Where does the water go? Where do I put the coffee?"

The cord of the coffee maker was draped around my neck, as if it was a snake and I was a snake charmer about to perform at a circus. She replied, "You're just like a girl with no experience who doesn't know where to put a cock."

"Oh my God! We've got to get some videos of your grandma."

My grandma swelled with pride. And buoyed by that pride, she had her first and last interview in her life.

"You can't climb out till you've reached rock bottom. Everything I've been through is what every woman has been through."

That was the title. I said, "At least I think that's what she means." Derin, and therefore Pembe, didn't say a word. They weren't convinced. Truthfully, my grandma hadn't said anything like that. Not exactly. She really wasn't a Marianne Faithfull. Still, that meaning could have been extrapolated from what she said. At least, *I* thought so. With that smirk I always despised, Pembe asked, "So, girls, what's our hashtag for the interview?"

Of course, I didn't say, "Your mother's cunt!" But I wanted to. I was irritated. I was an irritable young woman. When my grandma said, "Don't think with your pussy," I wasn't about to take any advice she had

190

to give very seriously. Maybe that was the first time I swore. Granted, I was just echoing my grandma. As you know, the person who opts to swear at his enemy instead of throwing a spear has established a form of civilization. Actually, I was still clutching a spear, but my friends didn't realize it. There's more of my great sin to reveal.

Getting back to what my grandma did talk about: Cihangir, cats, how young women used to get married, her semi-second marriage, how she was always hardworking and curious about learning new things, and so on, and so on. A pack of lies, in short. True in the rough outline, pure fabrication in content. But that made sense. How's a person supposed to get over something that had such a powerful impact on their lives? My grandma was living proof that it could be done. Most of the time, there's a real image that mirrors don't reveal. Life consists of things you don't know about, things you could never predict:

"What did you do after all of your friends left Istanbul?"

"I made friends with the cats. Cihangir was wonderful in those days. The city hadn't been fucked yet. There weren't as many cats as there are now, but there were some. When my Greek friends left, I tried to keep their memory alive. I took care of the animals that had been left behind. In any case, I'd hurt my back." (My grandma fell silent at this point. I wondered innocently how she'd hurt her back. My first guess was that she'd slipped on the steep, narrow stairs of that wooden house she called a chicken coop, but now we know that wasn't the case. As her orthopedist said, "She's lucky she didn't break her back. One of her vertebrae nearly got knocked out of place." One vertebra? My grandma's entire life has been knocked out of place! But no one would ever know that.) "I couldn't get out of bed for forty days."

Yet another truth silently came to light: that illegitimate baby had been born crippled. As a result of the X-rays that were taken because of her injured back, my grandma's baby, that detritus of rape, had been born a freak of nature. I don't know if she knew she was pregnant when those X-rays were taken, or if she even cared. "Otherwise," she said,

191

tears in her eyes as she lay on her deathbed, "I never would've let my mother deliver him in the toilet."

As for what she said when she read our fortunes: Truths that cannot be uttered! Dark clouds, woes of the heart, a young woman wasting away from sadness, her mother by her side, and what is this? A train station perhaps, a wandering crowd of people filling a room. Who are these people? Your enemies?

That's how life is. Composed of things that can't be explained. A composed heart.

Yes. I feel a little bit better. Who knows, perhaps it's because I showered.

As Yunus told me to do, I put my dirty clothes in a bag. I was still in the bathroom. But, as you've seen, the mind goes where it will. My only reality just then was the bathroom filled with steam so thick I could hardly see.

The mirror fogged up. My hands were barely visible.

I like taking hot showers. "That girl liked hot water, the girl who was always bathed by her grandmother in the hammam." I had a poem with a line like that. I was going to put on the clean clothes that Yunus left for me. I thought, *Where did he get them?* All I was wearing was a hotel robe. White, soft. I was like a snowball. It was thick and fluffy.

As my grandma was breathing her last at home, how did she appear to me in the mosque garden, how was she able to talk to me? Is it possible for someone to be in two places at the same time?

"She's really starting to lose it, and she's going to get worse."

That was my aunt Hülya's prophecy about me. She whispered it, hissing like a snake. Everyone was confused, and rightly so. The nonsense in my life was piling up. The time I collapsed on the sidewalk while following after my father and mother in Nişantaşı—that was included on the list. Once a person becomes ill in the mind or spirit, doesn't everything in the world become a sign of madness, no matter how trivial or slight?

Then there were signs from the present. Dangerous signs. The door of the hotel room opened and closed. Someone came into the room. Immediately I looked at the bathroom door, hoping to find a lock. Because locks save lives. It was my grandma who taught me to be wary and watchful. The lock was on the outside of the door. *Fuck!*

16

HELP

"In the very first sentence of your novel, you state what you're going to write about."

She actually said that I "declare up front" what I'm going to write about, but I didn't want to use the word "declare" here because it strikes me as a particularly cold and colorless word.

"But are you sure that's what you're *really* writing about?"

I pondered the question of whether I could be as dispassionate as Özlem Hanım. Soon enough, Derin and Pembe would come up with a definitive solution. They paid a visit to the administration with a complaint: "Is this a writing seminar or a class on literature? If it's a class, it's not working. We need to be getting ready for university, not hearing our classmates' novels critiqued for ages."

Özlem Hanım was given a mild warning: "The follow-up evaluations of the writing competition have been going on for quite a while now, wouldn't you say?"

Özlem Hanım, a complaint has been filed against you. You really bit the dick now!

It hadn't happened yet, but I was excited at the possibility that it might.

"But wouldn't you say, teacher, that it really is hard to find those two emotions in real life?"

"Are you sure that's what your novel is about? Or are you intention-ally misleading your readers? Is this some kind of trap to lure people in to read your book?"

"No. The novel really is about those two things."

"You're wrong. It's a failed attempt at writing about the past through other people's lives. The story of a girl who talks about everyone but herself."

"Maybe by talking about others, she's actually talking about herself?"

Either Pembe or Derin—or perhaps it was both of them—jumped into the debate at that point. Pembe gave me a sly wink as Özlem Hanım was erasing the whiteboard.

"Listen up, class. Don't try to write about the past. Others before you have done a thorough job of that already."

"In that case, let's not bother writing at all."

As I made that shallow declaration out of desperation, I was chew-ing the end of my pen, trying to appear nonchalant. I was aware that I looked like a primary school student, but I didn't know what else to do. The death blow was imminent. Just wait, here it comes: "If you ask me," she said, "you shouldn't even bother trying to write."

I had the urge to say, "I have no further questions, Your Honor." That's how things should have stood; the conversation shouldn't have gone on, nor should it have started anew at any other point in time.

"I'm willing to concede that what I wrote didn't really work. The main character did something ridiculous, and it seems like she did it as a prank. But she says that she was suffering. There's a lot of repeti-tion. What I mean to say is that, yes, it's complex. Still, I thought that structuring the narrative in a way that reflects her inner world in all its vivacity might be a sign of mastery."

"Mastery?"

Özlem Hanım smirked. The light of the whiteboard was illuminat-ing that fucking sneer on her face.

I give up, Özlem Hanım, are you happy now?

"You had it coming!" That was one of Derin's outbursts of anger. She'd scribbled those words in her notebook and held it up for me to see. They were looking at me in disappointment. Not just Derin and Pembe, but the whole class, with the exception of that smart-aleck girl who wrote the winning novel. I'd held out for as long as I could, but in the end, I backed down. Like my mother who wept as the man she loved walked away, like my grandma taking one step closer to death, like my father who moved to Bodrum, like my aunt who wore herself out trying to find a job.

"Let's put an end to this conversation for good and pick up where we left off."

I burst into tears. I couldn't help it. Accepting defeat was the hardest thing in the world.

"I'd like to say just one last thing."

"Go on, we're listening."

As they say, revenge is a dish best served cold. Özlem Hanım was dragging out the process of wiping the whiteboard clean. What she was doing, in fact, was erasing the traces of Monsieur Pierre. She wiped away what he'd written about Proust. *In Search of Lost Time.* How Proust had given himself over to living in the past. Then she went on to write out the primitive contents of her lesson for the day. In the meantime, I was busy putting into words what I wanted to say with the meticulousness of trying to extract pearls from my mouth without swallowing any of them.

"Freedom and love are two of the most likely yet most improbable things in the world. They have the greatest chances of being realized, but they are experienced the least. While they are the most difficult things to experience, what could be easier than obtaining either of them? If you flee, you taste freedom. Even a stupid bird can manage that. Sorry, birds."

At that point in my monologue, I looked out the window at some birds that were taking flight with a simple flutter of their wings. So easy. In one of her blog posts, Pembe wrote, "Today's the birthday of a friend of mine who has such a big heart that she once even apologized to birds." Of course, it's open to debate who was bighearted. "She also wrote a novel with impressive care and enthusiasm that brought into being a lost world. It's a novel about us youth and our times." I'd been moved by what she'd written. Later, however, I'd come to realize that she'd only said those things because it was my birthday and she wanted to make me feel good. Yes, in those days I was still trying to offer up what I'd written to people who walked all over me.

As you saw, I was ranting in one of Özlem Hanım's fucking neverending classes, vainly trying to make a point. Ah, poor me: "While it seemed like I was writing about something else, I was actually talking about freedom and love. Precisely because, most of the time, people don't know what they're actually experiencing. They may not even be aware of the true existence of love, much less freedom. That's what I was thinking as I wrote the book."

Then I fell silent.

Özlem Hanım replied, "Believe me when I say that Proust did that long before, and he did it much better than you. So, everyone, let's say 'bonjour' to that particular giant in French and world literature, because for the next three months, you're going to be spending day and night studying the works of Proust."

As if she had the knowledge to teach us about Proust! I knew that all she'd manage to do was sound off about his influence on Turkish literature—and barely scratch the surface at that, using someone else's notes or an old thesis that had been written on the subject. Monsieur Pierre had been scheduled to teach the class before he left. No one could beat Özlem Hanım in making sweeping claims. The bitch.

If you can cry, it means you have a heart. I looked out the window of the classroom. What I saw there was like what I saw when I looked out the window of the hotel: a wall covered in ivy, trees shedding leaves one by one, and some birds.

If only someone hadn't started to come into the room, filling me with terror, I would've gone on looking out at the view as I stood there, combing my wet hair, feeling peaceful, enchanted, and in awe of the scene before me. Instead, I was hiding behind the bathroom door, as scared as a mouse. I decided that if they tried to open it, I would fight back with all my might.

Who had come into the room?

They were harmless.

Two lovers.

I could hear them talking inside.

It was a little escapade.

Tittering, the woman said, "If we get caught, you'll have hell to pay."

"No one will catch us."

No one can catch lovers.

Soon enough, I heard some moans and squeals of pleasure. I even heard the sound of them hurriedly pulling off their clothes. I surmised that both of them worked at the hotel. Maybe twenty, twenty-five years old. I wondered which of them was more in love. Which of them was willing to pay the heavier price.

Their lovemaking was quite steamy. As my grandmother would say, and so would her daughter, "Love is in the air, and so are her legs!"

Even I was starting to get wet. To tell the truth, I was imagining being in bed with Yunus. I closed my eyes and leaned against the bathroom wall, which was just as wet as me, thinking about what it would be like if we kissed. If we tumbled into bed, kissing. If his red beard stubble brushed against my cheeks, and then my breasts . . .

When cornered, the mind breaks free. Just now, mine had done the same with the sound of the couple's lovemaking, giving itself over to imaginings. And now it is trying to be saved from making embarrassing pornographic confessions. But it can't! One day, Pembe, Derin, and I were sitting together during the protests at Gezi. My aunt had brought us doner kebabs, filled with pickles, and some bottles of beer as well, of course. There was a romantic couple staying in the tent next to ours. The boyfriend was an excellent guitar player, and the girlfriend had an amazing voice. Inspired by all the sweetness around us, I asked my friends for the first and only time: "Do you read the things I write?"

I had started a blog, which is where I posted my writing. To use yet another old-time word, the postings I made were "compendious" versions of my novel. But their mouths were full at the moment, so they didn't reply. That was the moment when my heart started to crack around the edges. Derin and Pembe were always a single unit, and I was an addendum. But that's not the issue at hand here. I was stuck in a bathroom, and you know what happened to my grandma when those men dragged her off to the bathroom . . .

But let's move on. "Skip ad," as websites say.

The couple inside had wrapped up their business.

I could hear them laughing together, as happy as turtledoves.

Then the girl said, "Are you leaving already?"

"What, do you want me to do something else?"

It was clear. The girl was the one who was more in love. The guy was now grouchy, and if he was in the habit of peeing after sex, I was done for. I sensed that he had paused in front of the bathroom door. As if the door had suddenly become transparent, I felt that he was reaching for the doorknob. I'd say that I didn't just feel it, I saw it, but I know you won't believe me. Just as the blind are able to see with their emotions, I am able to see as well. I mentioned that before. You'll break my heart if you forget the things I tell you. Then you too will be among those who have broken my heart.

But he didn't open the bathroom door because, at that moment, someone knocked on the room door and then opened it. The new arrival was Yunus. Maybe he'd gotten worried about me. Naturally, he was surprised to see his co-worker in the room. But when he heard the gasp of the girl who was now hurriedly getting dressed, he realized what had happened. The guy snapped, "Is a guest coming? If so, stall them."

Yunus replied, "No, no. It's just that the air conditioner in this room is broken."

Slamming the door in Yunus's face, he said, "I know, asshole. That's why we crashed this room. Get back to work. We'll be out in a minute."

Tears in her voice, the girl asked, "Why did you give us away?"

"You moron, do you think he didn't realize that I'd brought a girl here?"

No, he wasn't in love with her.

The door of the room opened again. Maybe the guy was checking the hallway to make sure Yunus was gone. In the meantime, I imagined the girl tucking her blouse into her skirt and then putting on her shoes, and as she tossed her long, wavy hair, her mouth was half-open out of nervousness, exhaustion, and fear. She may have even tried to take hold of his hand, as if they were jumping ship as it sank beneath them. He merely asked, "Did you put everything back in its place?"

"I made the bed."

"And you're on the pill, right?"

"I told you I was."

Of course, as he would have had to pull out otherwise. And that would've meant that they would have tissues to clean up his love goo, which in turn they may have opted to throw away in the bathroom. Meaning that they would've seen me. So I was grateful to the girl who was on the pill. As for me, I hadn't used any protection and it was sheer luck I hadn't gotten pregnant. But I did tell my ex-boyfriend I was, all so that he'd come back to me. Details of a shattered love story from the past. When the time comes for me to write about myself, I'll talk about it.

The lovers left.

My imprisonment was over.

And then?

Yunus came. We laughed about what had happened. He took a package of marshmallows from the cabinet, and we ate them. Yunus had no concerns about me taking all the food and drinks I wanted, except for the alcohol.

"Otherwise, it'll go to waste."

The cola tasted terrible, which meant that within a mere week, my sense of taste had changed. The romantic moment I had envisaged with Yunus didn't happen. Why? Because Yunus was trying to help me. His behavior reflected that mission he had taken on himself. If his regular job was to lug around suitcases, his duties involving me included nothing except for looking after my well-being.

"Put your dirty clothes in the hamper. I'll have the laundry crew wash them."

It proved difficult for me to part with my dirty clothes. Among the things he'd left for me was a pair of disposable panties, the kind given to airline passengers whose luggage has been lost. My own were with my other clothes in the hamper. My size 34B bra and cotton panties with thick trim. My jeans, T-shirt, and hoodie, as well as my socks. I enjoyed smelling clean, but I was convinced that I should have already given up on any concerns about my physical cleanliness.

Like someone who has no other place on earth to hide, I was about to return to where I belonged, to the treetops. Yunus was worried. I think that he was concerned because he himself had caught a couple using the room, something that was off-limits to employees. As we left, I regretted that I hadn't used the computer to check my social media accounts and also that I hadn't called my mother. But even if I had, what would've changed? Nothing at all. I got the feeling that another girl was living out my life at home, having picked up right where I'd left off. Rather, that was how I wanted things to be.

As we quickly made our way down the corridor of the hotel, I glanced again at the old photographs on the wall, which struck me as being rather odd and reminded me of my grandma. I recalled our family photos in all their detail; I already talked about the one of my grandma using a stick to draw out the plans for the new place on the plot she'd gotten by trading with someone for her old land: "The kitchen will go here, this will be the entrance, and here is the living room." Because she hadn't been able to draw out her own destiny in that way, she'd tried to control everything and everyone around her. It wasn't for nothing that I'd said a secret can be a bomb that hits a house. Her secret had leveled her home. It was obvious why she'd traded her place for another in the neighborhood; she wanted to escape her memories, but didn't have the courage to go very far away. Otherwise, long ago she would've packed up and left without a single look back. It must have been such a torment for her to go on living year in and year out in the same house where those horrific events had taken place. The house was going to be torn down, which gave her the opportunity to leave. And she took it, preferring to give up that astounding view of the city for shrugging off those memories. When we were interviewing her for that school project, she said, "If I close my eyes, I can still see that view." That was it, nothing more.

As Yunus and I stood in front of the door that led to the fire escape, I was thinking about how I'd get back up onto the top of the wall. Perhaps I too should pop a pill to give me some courage?

Yunus was pondering it all. Just like me. He ushered his thoughts toward others as a way of avoiding thinking about his own issues.

"Ushered!" Just look at that choice of words. *Come to your senses, girl!*

"I like to use awkward words like that." My friends had decided to talk with me about my writing.

"That's how my main character prefers to speak."

They laughed. The guy playing guitar in the tent next to ours suddenly started strumming a different rhythm, as if he wanted to chime in with his own musical laughter. The couple so deeply in love smiled at us.

"You idiot, *you* are the main character, aren't you?"

They were falling into the trap so many readers fall into: thinking this or that character is actually the writer. That is the critical error of people who cannot write anything about themselves beyond a CV: the notion that, if people write, they write about themselves. Because that is simply what they do. You dream when you're asleep—right? But what if life itself, this life, is a dream . . . ? I'd made a mistake by asking Pembe and Derin if they read my writing. They didn't like it. I thought that if Yunus read some of the things I'd written, maybe he'd think the same way, but for now, he was making my life easier. He'd found a ladder leaning up against the wall along the fire escape. He took my hand as he led me there, looking back over his shoulder at me. And I kissed him. He was surprised. We gazed at each other. And he kissed me back. He even French-kissed me, holding my face with one hand.

"See you later, princess."

I was flattered that he'd addressed me in such a way, because at school, some girls had been called "princess." For example, Pembe was a "princess," but Derin and I weren't. In the past, our school had been a girls' school. Probably because of that, boys were the minority. There were girls who had permanent makeup on their lips and eyebrows, and on the way to school they would apply some Shiseido BB cream and clear mascara: "Teacher, I swear I'm not wearing any eyeliner. This is natural." The only issue that the school administration couldn't make a final decision about was permanent eyeliner. Those girls, who never failed to apply a dab of Chanel Coco Mademoiselle to their necks and wrists in the morning, would show up on the first day of school just having completed a full epilation. They were the ones who got called "princess." Not me. Pembe didn't do herself up as much as them, but she was very careful about her appearance. She even got smooth breast implants: "It's obvious that I'm completely flat. My mom and I decided on this together. I needed to get them for my spiritual well-being and to keep up my self-confidence." In spite of everything, she was the best student in the class on Proust and at the top of our class in chemistry and mathematics. Also, she was the one who had convinced Derin to go on that trip during which their bus was bombed. What I'm saying is that she was the last person on this planet who should have been blown to pieces for supposedly being a part of anarchism, separatism, or terrorism. She may have had fake boobs, but her conscience, mind, and acumen were all natural.

I thought about that while having that wet kiss with Yunus. If I was going to live in the moment, what business did I have up in the trees? Kissing him was so wonderful—even if I don't know much about the arts of pleasure . . . We pulled apart. Stopping that kiss was so hard. I felt as if there were magnets in our lips, pulling them together. Yes, so while I may have not known much about pleasure, I liked how he desired me, liked me, and showed an interest in me. As we were heading toward the ladder, I caught sight of a surveillance camera glaring at us like an inauspicious eye. I froze for a moment, but didn't let on to Yunus about what I'd seen. He was just concerned about the fact that I was sockless and shoeless.

"What size do you wear?"

"Don't worry about that. Look, you'd better get going before someone sees you."

He smiled ever so sweetly.

"Shouldn't I be the one worrying about you?"

The cute little blockhead! He hadn't noticed that I was suddenly nervous about something. He was so innocent that way.

I thought he should've known about the camera.

In fact, he had known, but he'd forgotten about it. Forgetting and being caught off guard always lead to strife and regret. Meaning? Meaning that the camera records would wind up getting Yunus into trouble. But not just him—me too.

So that was how things went the day I returned to civilization, took a shower, put on fresh clothes, bore witness to a surprising event (the couple making love), ate some chocolates, sat on a soft bed, walked on a fuzzy rug, and yet in the end it was the surveillance cameras of the world of civilization that caught the two of us sneaking in and out of the hotel through the emergency exit. It also recorded our kiss.

Back in my nest, I sniffed the new clothes that didn't belong to me and noticed that the sleeves of the new hoodie were too long. I curled up, feeling angry at myself for having snuck into the hotel and giving in to the creature comforts of life, even if just for a little while. I concluded that I was up there in the treetops because I was desperate in spirit. I was there because I wanted to create a new life without a past. I had revisited my entire past countless times, but in the end, there'd be nothing to remember after my life in the trees, which would be the same day in and day out—days without a past. Then I would be happy.

As I sat there with my head full of such silly thoughts, I suddenly realized something. I was now able to scrunch into the nest with the greatest of skill and ease. The hot shower had relaxed my body. I pulled the hood over my head and squeezed my hands between my knees. Looking around, I couldn't take my eyes from the trees and their branches. I watched them. The trees. And as I lay curled up there watching them, I fell asleep.

17

THE FLOW OF TIME

I was one of the first to set up a tent in Gezi Park. I know that it sounds funny for me to say it like that. Or maybe it just seems that way to me. In those days, I always walked to school. The graffiti that read "It is the destitute who will shake up the world!" hadn't been painted over yet. After the protests, however, the municipality itself took over that role of creating a new order. I sensed unease among the people camping out in the park. The government's plan was to cut down all the trees and reconstruct an Ottoman army barracks that had once existed there, which was the childhood dream of the prime minister. If only it had remained nothing but a flight of fancy. Look, buddy, wouldn't it be better to have a dream of bringing freedom, love, equality, camaraderie, justice, rights, and law to the country? Isn't it a shame that all your dreams are about concrete and more concrete?

It was in those days that I started asking myself, "Do I have any dreams of my own? And if I do, what are they?" My dream at the time was for the trees and park to stay just as they were. I had a dream, and it consisted of the greenery and the view. Why? Because I was walking to school, and when I stepped into that park, I felt like I was in a forest, like the children in the Chronicles of Narnia who stepped through the wardrobe into an enchanted snowy forest. I was so moved by that part, where the little girl pushes past the fur coats and suddenly finds herself in an entirely new realm. Explaining things is like that in a way.

My grandma used to take me to Gezi Park. It's like a tiny island in the center of the city. A small jungle. It didn't matter if it was summer or winter, she'd buy me ice cream. Each and every time my grandma would say, "Don't stick out your tongue like a donkey when you lick your ice cream." Apparently, I was so thickheaded that I needed the same warning over and over. We'd sit on a bench and watch the people going by. My grandma would have the same little purse that she took when she went to the shop, grocer, or butcher, and there were always tissues in there, sometimes even wet wipes—the ones she'd take from the neighborhood restaurants. When we were done with our ice cream, we'd give our mouths a thorough rubdown. "Wipe your mouth well," she'd say. "Keep it clean." Then we'd lean back and go on looking around. I never got bored. That's where I learned how to spend time like that and not get bored.

Once, my grandma told me that she'd go to the park to think to the end those things she didn't need to be thinking about. I know that sounds ridiculous, but that's exactly what she said. As if thinking is something that comes to an end, that can be concluded. Her coping strategy probably went something like this: *When I'm at the park, I'm going to think about the things that have befallen me in my life and those past days that still haunt me. But once I step out of the park, I'm going to push all those thoughts from my mind* . . . That's fine, but how did she banish those thoughts? I'm sure she had a system. She got through that which had driven Efrosa to suicide by sitting in that park. I'm not sure—have I been able to explain why Gezi Park is so important for me?

Then that politician came along, bent on laying the foundations for his childhood dream, ignoring what the people thought about the matter. Here's how it all got started: I was sitting in a small restaurant in Cihangir, having a plate of baked eggplant with a side of yogurt. The television was on. Sometimes on my way home from school, I'd stop there and get something to eat. On my way home that day, I saw that some people had pitched tents in the park and that there were some protesters. "What are they protesting?" That's what the politician on the television was asking. As one of the diners was getting up to leave, he pointed at the politician and said, "This is bullshit!"

"Shush, you," said the owner of the restaurant.

A few people laughed.

"They'll pack you off to prison for talking like that."

"Let them!" the man said rebelliously, shaking his fist at the television screen. "Screw your damn Ottoman barracks! What are you talking about?"

A kind-looking man who was chewing a mouthful of food started tapping the edge of his knife against his water glass as a form of applause.

"Right on!" said another.

After swatting at an invisible annoyance a few times, the rebel walked out.

The politician on television was still talking, stating his points one by one. As if he was settling a deal with a peddler, he said: "It's final. We've made our decision. Do whatever you want, but we're not backing down."

Those words weighed heavily on me. You might say, "Who do you think you are, at your age? Why did it bother you so much?" Because things that have been decided in the name of others are shit.

After the rebel left, I went out too. I saw him head downhill from Çukurcuma. As for me, I decided that I wasn't going home. Instead, I went straight to the park, chose a spot for myself, and sat down, leaning against a tree. Drowsy after all that eggplant and yogurt, I fell asleep. I think the deepest, most peaceful sleep I've ever had was there under that tree—and also up in my perch in the treetops. I didn't even notice how at peace I was feeling at the time, nor how long I slept.

I awoke to the sound of my phone ringing.

My family, it seemed, was worried about me. I told them something, but—and believe me when I say this—I can't remember what it was. Perhaps I told them I was at the park. I may have even said, "I'm

dreaming." Who knows. If I told them that I was at the park, they probably asked which one, because the events that led to the outbreak of the
citywide protests hadn't yet occurred.

When I awoke, I was surprised to find that evening was settling
in, so I knew I'd slept a long time. The couple sitting beside me was
concerned.

"Hey, you've been asleep since five o'clock."

"What time is it now?"

"Probably around nine."

"Seems my folks were getting worried."

"We were too. We even checked to make sure you were breathing.
Then we figured that you were just tired after a long day."

Just as my eyes were growing accustomed to the dark, the lights
in the park came on. I must have glanced questioningly at the blanket
tucked around my knees, because the couple who had taken it upon
themselves to look after me gave me a compassionate glance. Had I
awoken from a drug-induced sleep, or had it been the innocent slumber
of a weary teen who had drool running down her chin?

"It got a little cool when the sun went down, so we put the blanket
on you to make sure you wouldn't get cold."

As if it wasn't enough that I kicked off the blanket like a savage, I
didn't even deign to thank them.

"I'm Hande."

"I'm Özgür."

A feeling of brusqueness still hung over me, and I didn't tell them
my name. Then I pulled myself together a little: "I was so sound asleep
that I think I might still be trying to wake up. Now I'm not even sure
if this is a dream or reality . . ."

They smiled.

"Would you like some coffee?"

I saw that Hande had a *Shaun the Sheep* thermos, and I caught the
scent of hot coffee. Let me just say here that a beautiful, gentle spring

air hung over the park. I was trying to piece it all together and clear the cobwebs from my mind. Thinking that some coffee might help, I accepted a cup, but it didn't. Sometimes my grandma would bring a thermos like theirs along with her, filled with coffee instead of tea, which she said lost its flavor in no time at all. We had some turquoise plastic cups that my aunt had swiped on her first and last plane trip with my grandma. There were four of them. They'd flown on THY on both legs of the journey, and my aunt had tucked two of the cups into her purse on each leg. She said that four was enough to make a set with the thermos. The cup I was holding in the park was exactly the same, except that it was red. You can't help but remember things during moments like that, right?

"My grandma died two months ago," I said, and then broke down in tears. The coffee in my cup from that *Shaun the Sheep* thermos, the image of which seemed to be leering at me, rippled like a dark sea.

"She and I used to come here together. We'd sit here and look at the trees. She had a thermos filled with coffee and cups like these, which made it seem like we were kids playing house . . ."

"You poor thing," Hande said.

I know that she wasn't really sad for me, but she was compassionate. Her hand on my shoulder, she was looking at me with an expression of sadness that I knew was fake. If you ask me, Özgür was the more genuinely upset of the two. His look was one of a conscientious person worried about someone in pain. He had a mop of unruly, curly hair, which left half of his smallish face in shadow. I got the impression that he was the kind of person who made you think, "I'd put my trust in this guy," and I would have done exactly that.

As a teenager, when I'd started acting out and veering from what my aunt deemed proper, she'd admonish me, saying, "Watch your mouth. You're starting to talk like a man." And from my mother I heard, "Watch your language." In turn, I wanted to say to her, "And you stop lying!"

but I couldn't bring myself to. When a child treats its mother cruelly or a mother treats her child with wicked intent, it's all over. Life is over.

As I was wiping away my tears, Hande gave me a piece of chocolate. I guess she had the rest of the bar with her.

"Here, have some chocolate with your coffee, it will do you good. So, you used to come here with your grandma?"

I nodded and sniffled. Just then, they suddenly showed up. Speak of the devil! When I say "they," I mean my mother and my aunt. What timing! I'd just been crying, and now I'd have to be all smiles for them. You should have seen how they approached . . . Jaunty steps that set their purses swinging on their shoulders and their skirts swishing, talking with anyone and everyone who crossed their paths.

When she saw me, my mom exclaimed, "There she is!"

"What are you doing here?" my aunt asked, a hint of pride in her voice.

"They're going to raze this park . . . Completely tear it down."

My mother and my aunt looked at me affectionately. They put on expressions of gentle sympathy, nodding all the while. "Oh really . . ."

"I'm here to protest," I said.

"That's very good of you," my mother said, as if she wanted to calmly dissuade me. "But you're just a girl. You have to go to school."

Hande and Özgür were listening in on the conversation as observers.

My aunt asked, "So, you want to stay here?" There you have it. Of course she would ask the most spot-on question.

"Yes," I replied.

The truth of the matter is that I didn't know what to do. All the same, like the trees in the park that my grandma and I used to enjoy sitting under, I had a desire to stay there and send down my own roots. I wanted to protect the trees. But even more than that, I wanted to cut down to size the politicians who had taken so much from us. The trees were a symbol of life and all that was beautiful, and as such, we should never lose them. If we lost the trees, it meant we'd lost everything. My grandma, her thermos, her plastic coffee cups. Everything. What was going to be lost wasn't just the trees, but our very lives. Our freedom. I think I made my decision as I thought over those things. Clever as always, my mother immediately picked up on what I was thinking.

She shouted, "Don't be ridiculous!"

The days when she'd been reviled were behind her, but now she was leaving behind a new trail of wreckage. She'd really let herself go. Her belly bulged, as she'd put on a bit of weight, and she'd given herself over to the idea that she'd passed the point of no return. Her jowls were sagging as well. So be it. She was alive and well, which was more than enough. She'd changed her style as well, as if she didn't want to be recognized.

I fell silent, not wanting to argue with her in front of everyone. I hoped that my aunt would step in and take matters under control.

My aunt said, "I'll stay with her."

And that's what happened. My aunt stayed with me. After all, she'd worked for years as a journalist and knew about such things.

The night turned out to be unbelievably beautiful. As if it had wings of silk, as if it was a living being, alive with a spirit of its own. That kind of night. I realized that my aunt didn't know that I used to go there with my grandma. I told her about those days as I munched on the grilled cheese sandwich she bought me, wishing I'd asked for orange juice instead of *ayran*. My aunt also didn't know what had happened to her mother in her youth. Nothing at all. I watched the face of my aunt, who didn't know what I knew, as if I was watching the night. She asked, "Why are you gawking at me like that?" I replied, "I'm not." Like how I later watched the sky.

Something was drifting down from the sky. Dead leaves? They spun gently down to the ground. I was sleepy. I felt relaxed. I had seized that day, that now, the moment. I heard Yunus make his bird call, which meant that he wanted me to go down to the top of the wall, to the fire escape, but I ignored it because I was so tired. I also knew that the surveillance camera could land us in trouble. I thought it was impossible that Yunus, who knew about the cameras in the hallway and had warned me about them as he took me to an empty room, could have overlooked that detail. I had always thought. I'd thought all my life. But I hadn't lived my life because I'd thought so much. That's just how it was.

I awoke with a fever in the middle of the night. I could see the stars through the canopy of branches above me, shining like silver pins stuck into the sky. All because of the fever. My tonsils were swollen again. If my grandma had been alive, she would've said, "I told you we should get them removed." It was so painful that I couldn't even close my mouth. I felt like a powerful hand was gripping my esophagus. Esophagus, throat. Or slicing it with quick jabs. Without fail, every year I'd incur an infection throughout my body when my tonsils got inflamed. "Incur an infection"—that was a phrase we learned from reading the work of Suat Derviş, whom we'd studied the year before. Not with patriot Özlem Hanım, but in a class taught by the literature teacher who'd been fired because he'd let the students use words like "vagina" and "coochie" in the student newspaper. There you have it, a French school in Turkey. You can be sure that the fighters in the French Revolution would turn over in their graves if they heard about such censorship. Now, we were destined to be subjected to it here. But when I say "here," what do I mean? Where am I? In the treetops or in a dark sea of memories?

18

ARE YOU ONLINE?

For two days I slept, wracked by fever. Perhaps I should say that "I think" I slept, because it was Yunus who later told me that's what happened. When I didn't respond to his birdlike calls, he got worried and walked over to the tree where my nest was. But that was the next day, because the day before was his day off. He said that he'd wanted to check on me that day too, but didn't have time because at the crack of dawn his father had made him go to the hospital so he could get his yearly checkup for his kidney. Yunus said, "The lines to get a checkup are so long, I swear they're going to be the death of me." The next day he came and saw that part of my fur coat was hanging over the edge of the nest, as was one of my hands. I was unconscious, and he came to my side.

Just like that.

Let's linger on that for a moment. It was no simple feat.

Coming to my side involved a major adventure.

From the outside, he locked the door leading to the hotel's fire escape.

Then he propped the ladder up against the wall.

He climbed up to the top of the wall.

He was determined.

Using a belt he had looped through his own belt, he secured himself to a branch of the tree. Straddling the branch, he inched his way forward, not once looking down. It took him an hour to reach the nest. He hadn't even taken anything to give him courage.

My eyes were fluttering. Thankfully, I had my bottle of water. I was taking little sips, like a bird. I felt as though I'd been buried under a mountain of rubble. All the same, I felt like I was outside myself. Three squat words side by side, "all the same"! I'd tell you not to crowd around, but you already swarmed that sentence of mine. To continue: being in a dream state. It wasn't clear to me if I was sleeping or dying. I remember moaning in pain. If you've been through it, you know that tonsillitis is a horrific thing.

Then I heard Yunus whisper. At first, I wasn't sure if I was dreaming or if it was real. He seemed to understand right away that I had a fever. He placed his hand on my forehead. His hand felt as cold as ice. He later told me that I smiled. I remember that he said to me, "You're sick." I replied, "My throat hurts." Like a child that's been taken to the doctor, I even tried to open my mouth to show him what was wrong.

"I know what it's like to have a fever," he said. "When my kidney gave out, I was trembling from head to toe, burning up. It felt like it wasn't me trembling but the world."

Apparently I murmured, "Well, I'm not trembling." When I asked, "How did you get up here?" he understood that my condition wasn't life-threatening. And when I asked, "Did you get hopped up on pills again?" he knew that I wasn't delirious.

But after he left, with worry in his eyes, I became suspicious: What if he was to tell someone about my condition in order to save my life up in those trees? That fear prompted me to raise my head, which felt as heavy as a stone. I saw Yunus clumsily and apprehensively making his way toward the wall. He was straddling one of the tree's thick branches, sliding forward on his butt, holding on for dear life to the branches on each side. Even so, he lost his balance, and in a state of panic, he flailed around for something to grab on to, scratching up his arms and neck in the process. The belts he'd used to supposedly secure himself were clumsily lashed together. I called out to him. Or perhaps I moaned: "Where are you going?"

"To get some medicine and water for you."

"Don't bother. I'm fine," I said. Or perhaps I moaned.

He didn't reply. I watched him as awkwardly, always awkwardly, he clambered onto the wall using a technique that could be called "the awkward belly crawl." I curled back up in the nest. When I was in the world down below—I was actually going to say, "When I was alive"—I liked getting sick because life stopped. It ground to a halt, as though there was nothing left for you to do, as though there was nothing you could do. It was a pause.

Yunus didn't come back.

Three whole days passed. I got better, but Yunus didn't come.

I went out on a small exploratory journey.

That day, I found something that made me fall in love for the second time: a huge chestnut tree. It wasn't spring or a holiday or anything like that, but all the same, the tree had burst into pink blossoms. I gulped, thunderstruck at the power of nature to console me. I got to know about trees thanks to my grandma. Every time we went to Gezi Park, she'd tell me about them as we ate the fruit that we'd brought along.

She'd ask, "Is there anything else in the world that sends down roots?"

When I didn't reply in a flash, she'd get angry.

As I labored to chew a mouthful of orange slices, a few drops of juice dribbling down my lower lip, I'd say no, with her glowering face looming before me.

Then there was Aunt Hülya . . . She knew a lot about trees. To get her riled up, my mother would say, "The only thing that Hülya doesn't know are the five daily prayers."

Aunt Hülya would get furious with my mother. At home, once in a while she'd indulge herself in a cigarette, but she wouldn't wear a real headscarf, just a loose-fitting hood of sorts, which made her look like she'd just stepped out of Hogwarts. I told her that once. I was quite young at the time. She winked at me and said, "I went to Hogwarts. They really do have records that Harry Potter attended the school. It's a wonderful place."

She actually had a good sense of humor.

Wearing a headscarf didn't dampen her spirits in the least; it just protected her from the outside world. For her, a headscarf was a kind of shield. When she and my mother would get into squabbles, she'd say, "Your filth can't get to me! Because I wear a headscarf!"

Maybe it was like armor. Who knows what it was like to wear one? But my mother was absolutely certain that the only reason my aunt started wearing a headscarf was for the sake of her husband's political activities. Those activities weren't really going anywhere, but that's another issue. He was an unlucky man. Or the party was just stringing him along. It seemed that way because, before every election, he never made it past the stage of being short-listed as a candidate. Still, he told everyone that his name had been brought up as a candidate for district head in the local elections.

He had a faded photograph of him and the party chairman. That was the only plunder he had to show after dedicating his life to politics.

Aunt Hülya had gotten used to going through life with a headscarf.

My mother would say, "What choice did she have? She had to get used to wearing one." And she'd add, "I don't see her as being a headscarfed woman. Most of the time, she's way ahead of the rest of us anyways. Open, you know." When Aunt Hülya became irate, she'd call my other aunt a "whore" and my grandma a "slut," but in my mother's eyes, she only said such things out of anger. That vulgarity, that crassness, was just the manifestation of her pent-up rage. Grandma, I said "manifestation," which was one of your words. Can you hear your granddaughter? Do my words reach the other world?

I should confess that the pink flowers of the chestnut tree reminded me of Aunt Hülya, not my grandma. In the face of her husband's failed political ambitions, she never buckled, nor did she protest. She was skilled in the art of consolation. As for the man himself, he gave people the impression that there was always hope: "True, I haven't made much of a political career or become more than a party member, but . . ."

What that "but" meant was that, whenever a school dormitory was going to be built or an organization was going to be set up, they bought all the appliances from my uncle. As a consolation prize, he became the owner of the party's most endorsed appliance store in the entire district of Beyoğlu. Wasn't that enough? Anytime Aunt Hülya and his mother-in-law gave him a hard time, that's what he'd ask, and with tears in his eyes he'd say, "It just isn't enough, is it? Tell me, what's lacking in your lives?"

Aunt Hülya would calmly reply, "Thankfully we're not wanting for anything. We have even more than we need."

And that was the truth. Their home was jam-packed. Every year they bought new furniture and redid their kitchen. They couldn't quite settle on what to do with the bathroom. One day it was a Turkish bath; the next day it was in the French style with a bidet. The living room was another matter altogether. One year it was somber English with wallpaper, and the next it was country. Their home had a thematic style that changed more quickly than the seasons: "I think we should do something with an Ottoman touch, like gilt tulips on the walls and hand-painted ceilings."

My mother was right when she said, "Their house must be worn out."

If you were to excavate their place, who knows how many layers of culture, style, and aesthetics you'd come across!

My aunt would say, "Life is consuming us, so we may as well go through life consuming."

"Actually, Hülya is a sweet woman, a kindred spirit." Sometimes my other aunt—my father's sister—would say that. When Aunt Hülya got hooked on the idea of getting some tattoos—yes, you read that right—she asked my father's sister to do an investigative piece called "What's Under the Headscarf?" They even ran a photograph of Aunt Hülya with the story. Her face was blurred out, but you could clearly see all her tattoos. My other aunt took the pictures. Aunt Hülya's husband couldn't do a thing about it.

"Don't lecture me! You're the sniveling stooge who couldn't get a seat in parliament."

There's your answer, little man!

Aunt Hülya got her tattoos secretly done at our place, since she didn't want people to gossip. The tattoo artist was a woman, and she designed the tattoos herself. Aunt Hülya got a spiderweb on her stomach with a spider hanging from it, an ivy pattern on her arm, and a rose on her breast. She loved her tattoos. Others could only see them when the situation required it. Those "others" were the doctors who performed an operation on her gallbladder and some women at an event held at a hammam. Those women were important, however; one of them was the wife of the provincial party chairman, and the rest were her assistants. It was a pre-wedding party at a hammam, attended by important women from the capital.

"Maybe they were there, but I didn't recognize them because everyone was naked, as usual at a hammam."

Before she went, Aunt Hülya racked her brain about how she was going to be at a hammam with her tattoos. She and my mother put their heads together, trying to come up with a solution. The thing about solutions, however, is that when you seek them out, you can't find them. If there is one, it will find you. The alliance between my mother and my aunt was ongoing, which was natural because they were sisters. Despite everything. My mother suggested, "Wrap up in a hammam towel, and put a bandage on your arm. If anyone asks anything, just say you burned yourself."

As you may have guessed, my aunt had her hesitations about the plan: "What if the bandage falls off when I'm getting scrubbed?"

"Okay, so wear the Burqini you wear when you go to the beach . . . Enough already, you don't like any of our ideas!"

"That makes more sense," she replied.

In the end, it was my other aunt who came to her rescue.

"What are you so afraid of? If anyone asks, just say that you got the tattoos done before you started wearing a headscarf."

"What if they ask why I didn't get them removed?"

"Tell them it hurts too much."

Aunt Hülya's eyes gleamed. "I'll say that they remind me of my sinful past, and that I repent whenever I look at them."

"You're a sneaky one, you are! Not even a headscarf can put a damper on your greed and worship of worldly things."

"God knows best about who's going to get what and when."

There was plenty of room in my mother's and aunt's lives for Aunt Hülya. They may not have talked about their private lives or made plans together, but they had a friendship rooted in the past. Even if Aunt Hülya was launched into space and never came back, that would still be the case. Memories have their own gravity that brings people together. They weren't enemies. Nor were they friends. They just knew each other really well.

Aunt Hülya made quite an impression at the bridal hammam event that day.

"It turned out that they were really curious," she said to my mother, who asked how she pulled it off. "I said the tattoos were really old, from when I was studying at Mimar Sinan University, before I started wearing a headscarf."

The women were intrigued, and Aunt Hülya explained the situation at length, saying that my uncle had spent his life toiling away, selling appliances, so he'd never been able to launch a political career. That was the moment when the foundations for that career were laid. The women had loved Aunt Hülya to death because she wasn't dull like the other wives of party members.

Proudly, she said, "If there had been elections that day, he would've been at the top of the list of candidates."

My uncle had called Aunt Hülya and said, "Woman, you're really something!" It turned out that the provincial chairman had called him to say, "It seems that wife of yours is quite pleasant company."

Tickled, my uncle said to Aunt Hülya on the phone, "God spare me, I almost said, 'Mr. Chairman, were you there too?' He said to me, 'My wife says she wants to see her, she really must see her again, and she told me to call her husband and have her come to Ankara, where they can attend to business together. So that's why I called you. When my wife asks for something, I can't let her down. I'll do whatever she says. Don't shoot the messenger, as they say.'

"I said, 'I'm the same way, Mr. Chairman, I'm exactly the same way . . .' They're going to call you, so don't be surprised when they do."

He was ecstatic.

Whereas Aunt Hülya was put out.

She always came up with an excuse to turn down the invitations to go to Ankara. She kept finding ways to string along my uncle, promising that she would go, saying she would definitely go. One time she even said that she was going to Ankara, but in fact she went on a hot-spring spa holiday with my grandma.

Aunt Hülya was a pink flower of the chestnut tree. It's so rare to find such blossoms.

She once said to me, "If I were a tree, I'd be a Judas tree."

"Enough already," my father said.

You heard me right, Father. Shadow father, no father, father who wasn't mentioned. Did you lament to yourself, "Why doesn't she talk about her father?" What's it to you?! I'll talk about whomever I please.

As the situation calls for. As much as is needed. My father was right to be surprised when his sister-in-law said, "If I were a tree, I'd be a Judas tree," so he felt a need to tell the Judas tree's story, its place in the world. Shrugging her shoulders, my aunt ever so sweetly argued with him about everything he said.

He said, "The Judas tree was the most important symbol of the Byzantines and Istanbul."

"So? I'm in love with Istanbul."

"But, Hülya, there are the Byzantines too . . ."

"So what? Our forefathers whupped them."

"The color of the Judas inspired the Byzantine aristocrats. Purple is the rarest color. Only they were allowed to wear cloaks the color of the flowers of the Judas tree."

"Purple's my favorite color."

"There's a legend about the Judas tree; perhaps you don't know it. Because if you did, you wouldn't want to be a Judas tree . . ."

"Learning is a religious duty. Tell me, so I can know about this legend."

"Learning is a religious duty!" Ah, Aunt Hülya, how were you being molded like that?

"So: Judas, one of Jesus's disciples, betrayed Jesus after the Last Supper. Afterward, unable to bear the shame of what he'd done, he went and hung himself from a Judas tree. Even the tree couldn't bear that shame, and its white flowers turned red. That's how the tree got its name."

"Interesting. It's not just a story; it teaches us something too. Stories like that go beyond religious sects and divisions. In the end, the important thing is humanity."

My father was silent.

Queen Hülya went on: "Do you know why I like the Judas tree? Because it's a tree of light. In order to grow, all it needs is space, freedom, and light. All it wants is to open its arms to the sky and be free."

222

"So, are you free?" My father had a habit of asking pointed questions.

"For God's sake, who among us is free? Just what is freedom? Who knows, I might be freer than all of you."

My father lapsed into a silence that was like a pendulum. Either he was conceding that she was right, or he was insinuating that it would be best to drop the conversation and let her go on thinking like that. You decide.

My aunt went on as though she'd been waiting for years for the topic of the Judas tree to come up and had prepared her little speech beforehand.

"Just now I referred to the Judas tree as a tree of light . . . The blossoming of the Judas tree lasts such a short time, and then the flowers wilt and die. We mortals can only truly grasp the meaning of transience, the meaning of how everything bathed in that light comes into being and vanishes in the blink of an eye, from the Judas tree. Believe me, we mortals could learn much from it."

I'd like to say to my father, "So, did you get your answer, little man?" In the depths of my mind, my father is enveloped in a purple cloud, flickering in and out of being. You should have seen his face—it was as if it had atrophied. That is such a vile word, "atrophy." But his expression at that moment couldn't be described with a better word. Obviously, he hadn't been expecting such an outpouring.

Aunt Hülya concluded by turning to my mother and saying, "I think that, if you were a tree, you would also be a Judas tree."

That was the last thing anyone should've said to my mother, whose blossoms had so recently wilted. The story of her unrequited love, which had cooled when the doctor went to America, had been resurrected recently when she'd received a bit of news, and my mother had been shaken to her core. The doctor had gotten married! And to whom? That queen of dieticians. My mother's boss. My mother quit her job, and now she was floundering. Soon after, as she proceeded down her career path, she would say that monstrous lie that would trap her beneath it. Very soon.

My father couldn't make sense of why my mother suddenly broke down in tears. Then again, what sense could he make of anything?

"That's how men are," my grandma once said. "We women give life meaning. Men just know how to go to war and screw."

My aunt—my father's sister—replied, "Some of them speak kindly. Some of them are good hearted."

My grandma closed the issue by saying, "I'll shove my foot up the ass of the whole lot of them."

On the issue of the Judas tree, which radiates through my memories, Aunt Hülya was so inspired by the conversation that she got a tattoo of a Byzantine empress on her back, right at the base of her neck.

"It's beautiful," my mother said.

"It's exquisite," my other aunt said.

"Crazy woman," my grandma said.

I was enchanted. I have a proclivity for that. There it was, on Aunt Hülya's shapely back, kind of between her shoulders—see, I can't even really describe the spot. I'm hopeless when it comes to writing; maybe my classmates were right. In fact, that tattoo—it was temporary—wasn't actually all that exciting. I'm hammering home the point that it was temporary because in a sense it was proof that Aunt Hülya no longer had the courage to do anything. But who of us did? Who had any courage left? There was this idea of being consumed by life, and we'd all been consumed. There was only that Byzantine empress who drew your eye with all her bright colors and movement, and she was beautiful, so very beautiful—the essence of beauty. But after a while, she too was consumed. Between Aunt Hülya's shoulder blades, those shrewd eyes, that purple and green mosaic dress, that gilt crown, they all faded, until in the end they'd become nothing but a deep bruise.

That's why my aunt's question and investigation "What's Under the Headscarf?" was so important. It was published, but in truncated form.

Eventually, the parts that had been cut out were published, becoming my aunt's first journalistic book. She took it to Ünsal, that teacher of teachers, as he had promised he would read it. I was with her that day because she'd gotten stuck with me. She was the one who'd picked me up from my mountain-climbing class. When her teacher told her on the phone, "Come over. I read the book, and I have a few comments," she had no choice but to take me with her. I can't remember much of what they talked about, but I can guess. It must have been around June of 2009. I was eleven years old at the time.

Ünsal asked me, "You still reading *Don Quixote*?"

"That's a bit too much for her," my aunt said.

He turned to her and said, "You haven't understood a word of what I've taught in class or said to you. I swear, I'm going to really teach you a lesson."

I spoke up. "It's not too much for me. There are windmills and a donkey. And then there's Sancho Panza."

"Ha ha! She's a sharp one. I should've been teaching that book to her generation, not yours."

He looked like the old man in the film *Up*, which had just come out. I'd bought a pirated copy and watched it over and over. I whispered into my aunt's ear, "He looks just like that old guy."

"What did she say?" he asked.

Which meant that he placed importance on what young people had to say . . . I remember how happy that made me.

Sometimes we talk about the most trivial things in order to avoid speaking about the most important. We ramble on like we've got diarrhea of the mouth. All so that those critical things will get mixed in, and then drown.

Ünsal said, "Let's move on to what's beneath the headscarf."

With a penetrating, self-assured gaze, he went on: "I think that there is an exception beneath the headscarf you talk about in the book."

He may have said that, or I might be making it up. In any case, some of our memories are fake, crafted by our minds. Intelligence. Souls. All of them. Working together. Like a gang.

Ah, the pinks of the chestnut tree.

My father would say, "These trees live so long they get the seasons confused." But I didn't understand what he meant. In those days, he was working at the Archaeology Museum and sometimes we'd walk home together. That museum was where he'd always wanted to work, where he wanted to retire from, and where his heart was sealed in a sarcophagus. I must have been around six or seven years old. At the time, I didn't understand much of anything that he said. But now I understand him.

A chestnut tree, blooming out of season. Does this season shed flowers?

Anyways . . . I think that there's a Judas tree beneath the headscarf.

Everyone has a Judas tree within them.

Everyone has their own betrayals and feelings of shame.

A Judas tree would not conceal me nor shelter me in its branches.

They are too short to hide in, but ideal for hanging yourself.

Let's move on to something far more important . . . I had surrendered to the trees. I trusted them. That's why I gave myself over to the branches of that chestnut tree I'd fallen in love with. I stretched out on one of the branches growing off its thick trunk and let my arms hang down into the void below.

I was no longer afraid of the trees.

Nor were they of me.

We weren't afraid of each other.

Like we said at the protests, "Free and alone like a tree, yet like a forest in fraternity." But it doesn't work that way. They don't let it.

19

Yunus called out to me from the top of the wall. He parted the branches of the plane tree like it was a thick green curtain, revealing his face, which was dripping with sweat. We were bearing witness to something which, for him, was yet another miracle. He was standing fearlessly on top of the wall.

"Where have you been?" I asked. "I was getting worried."

"The real question is, How are you? You seem to be feeling better."

I got to my feet and started walking along a branch, just like I'd done all those days before on my red slackline strap. Yunus's eyes opened wide in horror.

"Be careful. Tie yourself off with your strap."

"I don't need that anymore."

"Aren't you afraid of falling?"

"'Cowards die many times before their deaths.' 'The only thing you have to fear is fear itself.' 'There is no illusion greater than fear.' Shall I go on?"

"How do you know all those sayings? I bombed the university entrance exam. They asked questions about idioms and things."

"You didn't pass?"

"Nope."

"Get back to the subject. Where were you?"

Yunus was incapable of lying.

"They saw us."

"You mean you didn't notice that there was a camera?"

"I knew there was one . . . But they never check the one on the fire escape."

"So, how did they catch us?"

"They were going through the footage looking for something else. That's when they spotted us."

"What's going to happen now?"

"Don't worry, I made a deal with them."

"With who?"

"Security."

"How did you make a deal?"

"Don't worry about it. You're the Girl in the Tree, right? Go on enjoying living up in the trees like a monkey."

"I'm not some primate! This is about me too. What if they find me?"

"I told you not to worry about it. I took care of everything."

"Fine, but how?"

"Enjoy the grapes but don't ask where they came from."

"Was that another question about expressions on the entrance exam?"

"No, it's what my older brother always says."

I was now standing on top of the ancient wall. And he was sitting atop it like he was straddling a horse. One of the rare pink flowers of the chestnut tree lay on top of the wall. He picked it up and held it out to me. Looking him in the eye, I took the flower, which must have fallen recently because it was still fresh. I put it behind my ear.

"You look beautiful like that."

It was as if we'd been whisked back to a time before the wall had been built. I felt as if such beauty and sincerity could only have existed in such ancient times. That's how it should have been.

"Come with me," I said. I held out my hand, he reached out, and I took his hand in mine.

"I'm going to take you somewhere."

When he got to his feet, his legs were shaking. There was a look of helplessness on his wan face, but he quickly put on a determined expression, which I took as a compliment, a sign of his dedication to me.

"How wonderful," he said. "You're standing there before me like a fearless princess."

"Walk as if you were walking along a path on the ground. Don't think about falling. Just imagine that you have wings."

We walked along the wall that runs between Gülhane and the palace. Taking tiny steps. Ever so slowly. As if we were walking in the dark.

"The top of the wall is like a road now. It seems wider."

"Go on thinking that way if that makes you feel better."

"Where are we going?"

"To the heart of the panorama."

I said that because it felt like we really were walking through the heart of Istanbul. Our backs to the sea, we were heading in the direction of the palace. It's not that I didn't know where I was taking Yunus. In my mind, there was a place we could go without our feet touching the ground, but I wasn't sure if we could safely get there by walking on top of that wall. Being unsure is a nasty feeling. It leaves you out of breath. It suffocates you. That's why I cast those doubts from my mind.

It was so nice to feel Yunus's hand in my own, which he was squeezing tightly. He slipped his fingers between mine and stroked them with his thumb. The place I wanted to take him appeared on the horizon. A domed roof straight out of a fairy tale.

I was taking him to the Tiled Pavilion in the gardens of the Archaeology Museum. The back of the seraglio faced Gülhane, and the entrance opened onto the gardens. The high walls surrounding Gülhane embrace from behind an elegant summer palace known as Sırça Palace, or Sırça Seraglio. My father told me about it once. We had left the museum and were walking hand in hand through Gülhane Park. He stopped and pointed it out to me. Always his mother's son—he liked explaining things. All the same, he has no place in our story. It simply wouldn't do. Ultimately, a family's story is about the women.

"We're here," I said. "This is the place."

As if entering a magical realm, we stepped onto the roof of the Tiled Pavilion with its multiple lead-sheathed domes, between which were flat areas. I tripped, as my feet were accustomed to branches and bark, not stone.

As we sat down, we leaned back against one of the domes of the building, which had been there since 1472 and seen so much: the sea, the sky, migratory birds, earthquakes, rain, storms, epidemics, weddings, holidays, explosions, coups, wars, peace, upheaval, fury, destruction, change, incrustation. That was where the Tiled Pavilion sat ever so gracefully, puckering its lips as it gazed at Istanbul, its eyes asquint.

I'd said to my father, "If the Tiled Pavilion was human, it would be a woman." He laughed.

Look, there we are still, father and daughter, looking at Sırça Palace. It made me feel good to hear my father laugh. Who doesn't like the feeling of knowing that you've made your father or your mother laugh? That's why I went on: "What's more, the Tiled Pavilion would be a girl, and she would blink her eyes as she looked out at the world. Like this . . . She would pucker her lips as if she was going to kiss the city."

Later, they would ask me to do the impression again.

"The girl's got a knack for impressions."

"She's got a strong imagination."

My father's sister, my grandma, my mother, my father, Aunt Hülya, her little husband . . . That girl is still a little girl. They never took her anywhere.

"What are you looking at?"

Yunus looked at the spot I was staring at. That void upon which my eyes were locked.

"There's no one there. You were looking at the spot as if you'd seen someone. It seemed like you were about to say something."

"No, no. Maybe it just seemed that way to you. If someone talks to themselves, people say they're crazy. That's what my grandma used to say. Then, without realizing it, she'd talk to herself."

"Who doesn't? My father says that he chats with his conscience all the time."

We were two lonely young people leaning up against the lead sheathing of a dome, and we were there to look out over the world. I wish we could've stayed forever.

"Why did you think of bringing me here?"

What was I supposed to say? "I don't know."

His expression softened and he looked around.

"But it really is beautiful here. Different."

Different. I wanted to say, "*What's* different about it? What's different?" Because we were encoding that which is beautiful as different. Different is beautiful. But different is what is fixed—*fixed* I'm telling you!

"Look, the sun is setting like a giant orange. No one could ever find us here. If the world were to go to pieces, we wouldn't be affected. That's how isolated it is here. It's like we're watching a movie."

It was nice to see how excited Yunus was getting about being there. All day long the lead dome roof had been soaking up the heat of the sun. I pressed my cheek against it, and then I spread my arms and pressed my entire body against the dome, feeling its warmth. That warmth was something like compassion. Yunus slowly approached me. I was afraid that he would ask me for permission, and my fear came true:

"Can I kiss you?"

"Well, who kissed me on top of the wall?"

"That wasn't me. It was my ghost."

"What about that girl you were seeing? On the first day we met, you said you had a girlfriend."

"She's imaginary too. A figment of a ghost's imagination."

I smiled and gave him the thumbs-up. Then I turned so he could kiss me. He leaned in. We kissed. And kissed. And kissed.

As Derin and Pembe would have said: "Kiss, kiss, kiss." Like a bird chirruping out of love.

When people kiss, it shouldn't be too quiet because then you can hear the sound of your kissing, which is funny. It makes you want to laugh. You shouldn't be thinking about other things, but then you find your mind wandering.

Derin would say, "You can't think when you're really excited."

I wrote a song with that line. Rather, I wrote the lyrics for a rap group's song. You might be thinking, "Why didn't you mention that before?" Here's my answer: "I haven't gotten to that because I've been talking about the novel." You don't stop; you just keep on going. "Okay, but why?"

Because the rap group and the poetry and lyrics I wrote for them are embedded in a love story. My story. Wreckage of love. "Warning! Hard-hat area only." I'm not saying that for nothing. That was the name of a song I wrote for the group. Being with one lover yet thinking about another . . . Who does that kind of thing? Well, it happened. You fear that which has been buried ever so deeply. That's how that love story was. So deeply buried. I mentioned it earlier but couldn't summon the courage to go on. Here goes:

He was a student at the German High School. I fell madly in love with him. He was into music. Rap. Which, of course, wasn't in line with his social standing. Rap happens in other places. Public housing. The ghetto. The farthest corners of the city, where not even the Metrobus goes. This guy and his friends—all well-fed students at the German High School—were excited about rapping. Rappers through and through, like those who break-dance. *There's no need to drag it out. These kinds of things work themselves out. All you've got to do is shout, out, shout, out, work it all out.* Those were some of the lyrics I wrote. What, did you expect something else?

He was the leader of the group. Good-looking. But spoiled. He didn't have a heart of gold like Yunus, who held me that day at sunset among the domes as he watched the reddening sky. This guy was bad. He paid a lot of attention to me at first and flirted with me, with the sole intent of seducing me in the end. We'd write to each other on WhatsApp, make love on Snapchat. Supposedly, we were writing a song. He was into obscene things. He read them to me. Wrote them. Said them. Explained them. One time he even pulled out his tool on Snapchat and showed it to me, and made me lick the screen. It was an obscene attack. On Snapchat. In that virtual world there are secret rooms just for lovers. You had to choose a time frame between one and ten seconds. I always chose ten seconds. During that time—he saw it, he saw it, he didn't see it—I felt as though I could hear the sound of the image destroying itself.

"Tell me about that Snapperchat business." My aunt asked me that. She was from that generation that would say to Superman, "Sümerbank, save me!" Okay, maybe she didn't get the bank called Sümerbank confused with Superman, but still. You get the idea.

"It's a program you put on your phone. You use it to send videos, pics, and chat and stuff. If you send a video, it erases itself after twenty-four hours. If you send it to someone you're connected to, you have to choose between one- and ten-second videos."

"And then they die?" She asked that with such emotion that I knew she'd never have the heart to send a snap.

But we were living on Snapchat. Loving there, making love there.

Single-bite loves. Get her, man. Catch her. Like an animal. It's all a bite.

"I want something harder, something more aggressive," he said to me.

"It just doesn't work. Bourgeois guys trying to act like they're from the slums. How could they ever be rappers?"

As you may have guessed, that was Pembe and Derin speaking as one.

Baby, what are you doing? Just chill at home.

But I was happy. Those promises of love made me happy, as did writing lyrics for rap songs. And he wrote to me too. Oh, did he write to me. At first—supposedly that's what we were supposed to be doing, writing—the idea was to show me the ropes.

"Has a guy ever stroked your pussy? Fingered you, going real deep? Played with your asshole?"

I was in a state of shock. No one had ever said anything so obscene to me before. I got angry. I replied, "It's a good thing we're not having this conversation face to face."

Later, we started hanging out. There wasn't any romanticism or sweetness. He had brown hair, which he meticulously worked to make it look messy, seemingly crusty eyes, and a chronically open mouth. I think his nose was always stuffed up. Actually, he had tiny skin tags around the inner part of his eyes, which is why they looked crusty. Once I tried to pluck one off, and hurt the hell out of him. He was the kind of person who is constantly irritable and speaks too loudly for no reason at all. There weren't any drugs involved in any of this. Maybe once in a while, but not often. If they did get some drugs, they'd go to this place they used as a studio. Sudden. Hard. Yes, that's how it happened. It was exciting, but I was scared at the same time. I was nervous because it was going to be my first time. I wanted to do it on a bed. That didn't happen. Then he disappeared from my life at the speed of light. The last mental image I have of him is him wiping off his schlong with a tissue. It was a little bloody, and for some reason that disgusted him. As if his schlong had been injured or something. He scowled. Yes, Grandma, I said "schlong"! *Schlong.*

For a while I tried to pursue him. He fled. Inspired by my mother, I lied to him. "I'm pregnant," I said. He called me so we could talk. "Look," he said, "that's impossible. What's your deal? What are you after?"

"You've gotten tangled up with the lowest of the low at the German High School, the worst lowlife!"

That's what people were saying when they found out that I'd been hanging out with him. And I was telling everyone, as if someone would whisper the magic formula to me that would make everything right again. I was looking for a solution. Not for my fake pregnancy, of course. I wanted to hear the perfect advice that would save me from that sickness. Derin and Pembe said to me, "You're starting to scare us. Pull yourself together."

But the harder I tried to do that, the more I fell apart.

"What you described is sexual violence, if you ask me. That guy raped you."

"But I know him, I love him . . ."

"You idiot! That doesn't give him the right to do something to you that you didn't want!"

"You still don't understand what happened to you! Look, dumbass, you're refusing to face the facts."

So I was simultaneously dealing with heartbreak and with Derin's and Pembe's attempts at trying to parent me.

It seemed best to ask him to meet me somewhere outside, because I was afraid he'd attack me again.

The park where I practiced slacklining seemed like an ideal place. I'd lost my grandma just a few weeks earlier, so I'd decided to throw myself into slacklining, day and night. Focusing and trying to keep my balance was good for me. Those were things I'd never been able to do. It was the middle of April and the spring rains had come to Istanbul. There was a Judas tree in Maçka Park. It was in bloom at the time. The air smelled of soil and rain, and sometimes the sky opened up, but I went on, fully focused on keeping my balance on the line; in fact, I was trying to stay alive. The fun times came and went. Those were the times when I was with Derin and Pembe. We wounded youths would hang out in the park. On my slackline, I'd do the surfing move. To do that, you have to tie off the line loosely and then you act as though you're riding a wave. Without falling off, of course. That move is called surfing.

He showed up at Maçka Park to talk.

He came up silently from around the back. I noticed that he was wearing rust-colored Converse. He was walking so quickly that for a moment I thought a wet dog was trotting up to me. His shoes squished in the wet grass. Squish, squish, squish. I was still on my slackline. He grabbed hold of my red raincoat and gave it a tug, sending me toppling to the ground.

I fell almost a meter.

Down on the ground, he beat me like you'd beat a man. He punched me in the face, he squeezed my throat, he headbutted me. When I got up, he kicked me in the stomach.

"If you *are* pregnant, that baby better die."

I couldn't say anything.

"If you *are* pregnant, that baby better die."

I couldn't shout.

"If you *are* pregnant, that baby better die."

I was writhing in pain. It surprised me to find I couldn't say a word out of fear. I was a sheer wreck. I was dying of pain. I'd peed myself. And I may have even crapped myself. A little. As a matter of fact, I had. Just like a baby. I'd shit myself out of fear. When I got up and the world spun around me once with all its might, I noticed that my mouth was full of blood. I spit it out. It was as if I'd spit out the world. The remnants of what I'd thought was love, the novel I wanted to write but couldn't, being humiliated, the things that weren't going well at home, the things that weren't going well at school, the things that weren't well between me and my friends, my mourning for my grandmother . . . I sat down and cried. Pulling my knees up to my chest, I closed myself off like a cosmic egg and cried. I cried until my entire body shook with my sobs. I'd been hurt. So very, very much.

What came later hurt even more.

I didn't tell anyone who had beat me up. I couldn't bring myself to. I was embarrassed. "Two guys came up to me at the park and beat me," I said. "They told me to give them all my money and my phone, but when they saw some people coming, they ran off."

Is my aunt the kind of woman to sit idly by? The first thing she did was go to the park and talk to the security guard there. He said, "She should've come straight to us."

"Why didn't you report it to the security guard?"

"I don't know. I was scared. It didn't occur to me . . ."

Then there was the footage from those security cameras that watch us all, but the two men I described didn't appear in any of it. There weren't any cameras around the area where I was beaten. All the existing footage showed was the people coming and going along the main walkway, including my guy. After all that, I couldn't believe I was still calling him "my guy." *Shit for brains! Screw this brain of mine.*

They didn't even ask, "Could it be this one?"

"If there's no footage of them, where did they enter the park, then?" The security officer was in no mood to deal with my aunt. He said, "Ma'am, if you want a more thorough investigation, go to the public prosecutor."

That was a mistake. There's nothing my aunt hates more than being called "ma'am"!

"Let's just drop it," I said. "I'm fine. I'm over it."

As if!

I didn't tell Derin or Pembe either. Whenever you keep a secret like that, it starts rotting inside you. Putrefying. Stinking.

Unable to stomach what he'd done to me, I resorted to threats: "I'll take those obscene messages you sent me and—"

"I didn't write those things, you idiot. They're from some letters that James Joyce wrote to his wife!" And then he hung up in my face.

I surmised that he couldn't close his mouth not because he always had a stuffy nose, but because he was so filled with arrogance that it had to get out somehow. That's just how it was. That and nothing more.

I told myself it was a good thing that I was remembering all those things. At least that way I drained off some of the pus within me.

Little by little, the lead dome we were leaning against started to cool off. The sun was sinking, and Yunus was silently gazing at the horizon. His silence, his innocence, his hand resting on my shoulder, his head leaning against mine—they were all so soft, so full of compassion, that I couldn't stop myself from starting to weep. It wasn't, however, the brutality of my own past that was making me cry. I was sad because I had been blind to the suffering of the person beside me.

Yunus asked, "Are you daydreaming too?"

I wiped away my tears. When he noticed that I'd been crying, he was surprised.

"You're sitting there, silently crying . . ."

He took me in his arms and hugged me tightly.

"Why are you crying? Don't cry. We come into the world alone, and we leave the world alone. Keep that in your thoughts, think about it, and don't cry. People are always alone. Even if they have someone in their lives who loves them."

20

FOLLOW

The sun slowly withdrew from the scene.

"Don't use sentences like that in your writing," my aunt said.

As I was working on my novel, I would read parts of it to my aunt. She would be lying down with her feet propped up, cigarette in hand. Silently she would listen as I read. Then she'd say, "Leave your computer here, and I'll do some editing on your memoirs."

That's about all my aunt did to help me out. But do you know what Derin said to me one day? "This novel—" She paused. I knew that she and Pembe had talked about something, because Derin mentioned her in the course of the conversation.

"We just wondered if maybe your aunt is writing the novel."

A lie.

"Since she's unemployed and all . . . To give herself something to do . . . Like, you write a sentence, and then she writes a hundred . . . Something like that?"

What a question! What slander!

Night was slowly settling over us.

Yunus had come prepared. Two cans of beer. A few packets of nuts. Snack cheese. He'd stolen all of it from the hotel, stuffing his pockets. A tiny bottle of whiskey, a tiny bottle of gin. Other drinks too. They were all in tiny bottles.

"If we drink now, how will we get back?"

"We'll fly!"

We laughed.

I didn't know his story. Everything around me, including Yunus, was always incomplete. Only half there.

We ate and drank everything he'd brought. First the stars spun, and then our heads. We were lying on our backs, laughing. The brakes had gone out, and our laughter was unstoppable.

"This is the most secret place in the world," Yunus said. "No one could ever find us. No one can see us."

"Only the birds can see us."

"And they've got no tongues to wag."

We started laughing again.

"We could stand up to the biggest disasters in the world here."

"Exactly."

"If there was an earthquake, we'd ride it out. If there was a storm, we'd fly off. If there was a flood, we'd swim."

Yunus propped himself up on his elbows. His face was as dark as the night.

"No floods. Anything else would be fine, but no floods. Because my mom was washed away by a flood. No one expected that could ever happen. It was the furthest thing from our thoughts."

Now he was openly saying what he'd only hinted at before. When we say that someone we loved "died," that person dies again. For years, Yunus had been struggling with that. That little boy who missed his mother so much that it made him tremble inside didn't know what it meant to grow up. Even though he'd grown into a man, his facial hair grew in, and he fell in love, he was still the same boy who'd lost his mother. Dead children never grow up, and the dead never age, and the same holds true for the people who are left behind. Physically, the world keeps turning. But your inner world—the realm you carry within, your internal life—stops at the moment you lose someone you love.

"Your mother . . . I thought she was still alive, just living somewhere far away."

"Her love is alive. Here. In my heart. In my mind. It's always there, even though she's gone. Dead. But it was the way she died that caused me more grief than anything. I've never gotten over it."

I stammered, "What happened?"

"She was a worker at the textile factory. She got on the service bus. It was morning. Early. It suddenly started raining. Do you remember that storm?"

I pursed my lips. There had been so many, which one could it have been?

"The highway flooded. Cars started floating like rafts. Like boats. Her service bus was stuck in the middle of it. In İkitelli. Then the flood washed them away. They couldn't get out."

"How old were you when she died?"

"I was twelve. I thought I was grown up. But I was still a little kid inside."

"Sometimes you say that you won't do certain things because your mom would be upset . . . As if she was still alive."

"That's because some feelings of love stay with us for the rest of our lives. Even if we lose that person. They will only die when we die."

Yunus lay back down. Snuggling up closer to him, I put my head on his chest. I could hear the beating of his heart. We fell silent. Some birds that had made Gülhane their home trilled. Nightingales. I heard two other birds. They seemed to be bickering, but I couldn't tell what they were by the sound of their squawks. As we embraced, our breath gently licked our skin. Like children, we stroked each other's faces. Every line of each other's features. Nose, lips, cheeks, chin, neck, earlobes, ears. One of my arms was thrown over him.

"Is this where your missing kidney used to be?"

Yunus paused for a moment. I think he was trying to figure out which side was which.

241

"No. The other side."

Then he said something that made me laugh: "You reminded me of the existence of that kidney. With your kind permission, I need to pee."

"With your kind permission . . ." I figured he'd heard that expression at the hotel. Bellboy Yunus's vocabulary had become adorned with such little courteous expressions, and he was adorable when he said those things.

He got to his feet, and as he was looking for a place to pee on the roof like a magpie, he went on talking: "Maybe the only thing we need is to be able to sing the songs we want and laugh to our heart's content in a peaceful home with the people we love."

"Yes, it's that simple," I said. Then my heart suddenly skipped a beat and I called out, "Yunus, be careful! Don't fall over the edge!"

He suddenly stopped in the darkness, right at the edge of the roof. Then he stepped behind one of the domes and started peeing. His stream of pee traced a crystalline arc in the darkness of night, tinkling against the lead and zinc alloy sheathing of the dome's roof. That night, we laughed and laughed. We were buzzed. When I laughed, Yunus would do all sorts of silly things, as if he wanted to make the whole world laugh along with us. For example, he turned the tinkling of his pee on the roof of the dome into a rhythmic patter, and that cheery concert didn't end until his bladder was drained. Tugging up his zipper, he walked back over to me and lay down. I wished that we could stay there forever. We, two afflicted youths, had found each other. I thought, *If only we could spend all our days and nights in this corner of the world that had forgotten us.*

21

SETTINGS

The winter of 1987 brought heavy snows. My aunt was seventeen years old at the time, and she was in love with the handsome developer. That winter the wooden house was going to be torn down so that the foundation could be laid for the new apartment building, winter being the season when such work was done. They had packed up the furnishings from that chicken coop and planned on staying with a neighbor, who would then stay with them in turn when their place was being built. In that way, they would all squeeze into each other's homes as they waited for their own new ones to be finished. The fact that my grandma had traded her land didn't disrupt that chain of events. The developer was helping out with the rent during the time when they didn't have a place to stay, but they were trying to spend as little as possible of that money by finding temporary solutions for their housing problem. I'm not sure why I gave that technical and financial explanation, but there you have it.

In the end, however, because of the bitter winter, which would have made it difficult for them to move, the plan was postponed. Even if they had moved, the wreckers wouldn't have been able to work anyways.

My aunt explained, "In one night, it snowed so much."

"All the way up to our waists," my grandma added.

Both of them would gaze out the window at an invisible horizon—they could each see it in their mind's eye. In the winter of 1987, my aunt, the age I am now, had bundled up and was looking out the window. "Just look! A wild snowstorm." My grandma was constantly stoking the stove so that they wouldn't have to take the remaining wood with them when they moved.

My aunt would later recall that my grandma had said, "When we move, we'll burn down the place and be done with it."

"How long is it going to keep snowing? A week, a day . . . In that case, we may as well enjoy ourselves as best we can."

When my grandma said that, they surrendered to the silence of the snow and did their best to enjoy themselves. The world was as soft as down. Daily life had curled up and gone to sleep beneath the blanket of snow, buried so deeply that not a single trace of its vulgarity or coarseness could be seen. Weighed down by the snow, the roofs of the homes started to creak and groan.

My grandma said, "It's a good thing I went to the market yesterday."

Before the snows came, the weather had been pleasant and gentle, with a mild breeze. But at one point in the night, it suddenly started snowing, and the clothes they'd hung up to dry froze. The sweaters had their arms held out, the underpants seemed to be stretched over thick thighs, the socks looked like they'd walk off on their own, and the trousers appeared to be doing the twist. All of them had come alive in the frost. My aunt went down to the garden at one point in the night to bring them in. When I say "garden," don't misunderstand; it was just a tiny outdoor area that abutted the neighbor's garden. The houses, which had been built shoulder to shoulder and back-to-back atop Byzantine ruins, ran like a stairway all the way down to Fındıklı.

Buried in snow, the garden looked so beautiful . . .

The storm eased, and now the snow was gently coming down. It didn't even seem like snow, but rather soft tufts of cotton falling from the sky. Softly. Slowly. And then? And then there was a hushed voice coming from the garden of the neighboring house: "Hey!"

My aunt looked. It was the handsome developer.

The Girl in the Tree

"What are you doing here?"

"My father asked me to come check on our properties."

My aunt was standing there, holding the frozen laundry. It looked like she was clutching an armful of arms, legs, and torsos.

"Since when is this your property? First do some construction, and then we'll see what belongs to who."

"You look so beautiful when you're angry," the developer said. Or maybe I'm making that up. But what else could he say?

My aunt glanced up at the window, wondering if her mother could see her.

The developer went on: "There's something I didn't tell you. That was just an excuse. I mean, coming to look at the houses. I was standing in the garden of your neighbor across the way, watching you. As I watched you in the darkness, you looked so beautiful, standing by the window . . . A smile of peerless beauty on your lips as you gazed out the glowing window into the distance, watching the snow fall."

Was he the one who said that?

That unforgettable developer of apartment buildings with mosaic-tiled facades, whose construction used beach sand in the concrete and swiped materials . . . Was he the one who spoke such words?

It *was* him. That's what he said. And he even kissed my aunt right there on the spot. "Tomorrow I'll be waiting for you at the bottom of the hill," he said. "Make up something to tell your mom and come."

My aunt was suddenly flushed with heat, set aflame by excitement. As the young developer walked away, his leather shoes slipping on the snow and his face tucked into the fur collar of his deerskin coat, my aunt watched him, her heart filled with love. She fanned her face with her hand. The heat was so intense that she opened her mouth in an attempt to cool down, and the snowflakes that landed on her lips melted almost with a hiss.

The next day she ran to meet her handsome beau.

245

Some kids from the neighborhood were sledding on the slope of the street. She looked around to see if there was anyone who might tell her mother that she'd been sneaking away, but they were all children. Pulling her shawl up over her mouth and nose, she thought, "No one would recognize me anyways," and she started heading down Sanatkârlar Mektebi Street.

There wasn't a single car on the streets, not even a bus. Life in Istanbul had come to a halt.

He was waiting for her.

"How did you get here?"

"I walked," he replied.

Can you imagine it? He walked all the way from Sarıyer.

"How did you get home last night?"

"The same way. I walked."

We're all screwed! There's no bigger liar in the world than a man in love.

After playing in the snow like children and having a snowball fight on the Golden Horn Bridge, which was completely empty, our sweet young man said, "Let's find somewhere to warm up! I'm freezing." Mr. Beautiful Smile. Mr. Thirty-Two Teeth.

He suggested that they take the Tunnel from Karaköy up to Beyoğlu. When they got on the single-car underground, my aunt was clutching her hands, which were freezing cold, but she couldn't take her eyes from him.

Our sly fox proposed, "Let's go to the Pera Palace Hotel."

"I'm not dressed for it," my aunt said. "It wouldn't be right."

"Why not, darling? We'll get a room, warm up a bit, and have something to eat and drink. We'll be able to sit and relax to our heart's content."

Whenever she heard the story, Aunt Hülya would ask, "But weren't you afraid?" After all, she'd grown up in the same neighborhood.

"I wasn't afraid. Why should I have been?"

They dried their socks and gloves, and then ordered two cups of *salep* to warm them up on the inside. Pulling open the sheer curtains of the hotel room, they looked out over the view of the Golden Horn, sitting opposite each other with their legs crossed. They listened to the radio, waiting for the television programming to start. Then they lay down on the bed and made out for a while. But when they both realized that they were quite hungry, they decided to order room service.

"Our food arrived on a wheeled cart just like you see in the movies, with a glimmering dome over each dish, which the waiter removed as if he was performing a magic trick. There was boiled peas, rice, and a fried chicken thigh, which hadn't been cooked all the way through."

I remember my mom and aunt asking, "That was it?"

After eating, they lay down on the bed and slept.

Again, the same question: "That was it?"

"Well, there must've at least been some kind of dry humping or something."

Only Aunt Hülya would say such a tactless thing.

No matter how hard she tried to compare that love story beneath the snow "to something that quickly melted" and revealed the bawdiness below, it wasn't going to happen.

When my father's sister said, "We thought that the time for us to be together would arise of its own accord," it wasn't a satisfactory answer, as indicated by Aunt Hülya's question: "Seriously, how long can you keep fire and gunpowder side by side?"

My father's sister knew she was going to be in trouble, as she'd left home at around noon and the evening call to prayer was already ringing out when she was on her way home. Our handsome hero accompanied her all the way to the garden of Cihangir Mosque, and along the way the two walked arm in arm.

"Are you going to Sarıyer from here?"

"No," he replied, "I'll stay at the Pera Palace."

Years later, she realized that he'd stayed at the hotel the night before and then taken her to the same room where he'd slept, which should have been obvious when the hotel attendant whispered to him, "If ya kidnapped that girl, I'll tell your father!" After all, Black Sea people always look out for each other, right?

As soon as she got home, my grandma grabbed her by the hair. That's what she always did. That's what they always did in those times. In '87 model Cihangir neighborhood life, catfights were the norm.

"Where the hell were you?"

"Well, I'm here now . . ."

"Meaning that maybe you weren't going to come back, is that it?"

"We had a snowball fight. I hung out with my friends; we walked around . . ."

"In this weather?"

So, where was my father when all this was happening? My father, who was studying archaeology at the time, had an inordinate amount of freedom concerning when he could come and go. That night, he was at the home of a French teacher from his old high school, as they often met up to talk. Many years later, that's where he would meet my mother.

Like the snow, the clamor lasted until dawn.

There was a range of events that night, spanning from my grandma throwing a slipper at her daughter, which missed and fell into the stove, to giving her a resounding slap across the face.

But my father's sister never confessed to where she'd been, so my grandma had no choice but to believe the lies she'd been told.

"If you're going to muck about the streets like that, I'm not going to send you off to university."

"What about my brother? He's studying to get his degree, and he's allowed to go out."

"He's a man."

"But I'm a person, just like him. What's the difference? I can come home when it gets dark. I'd understand if you said that you were worried. But right off you start accusing me of things."

"What's this business of spending time out walking around? How am I supposed to know what you're up to? When it snows, wolves come down into the city. But these aren't the four-legged kind! No, I'm talking about two-legged mischief and wickedness. Because snow is white. It's innocent. Beautiful. You don't dare set foot on it. All bad things happen in weather like this, when good people are having a good time with this or that."

My grandma was right.

The wife of the American archaeologist came pounding on the door on a winter's day. The city was buried in snow. That was the winter of 1975. My aunt was five years old.

When my grandma realized that the woman was her American rival, she thought, "How did the plane land in weather like this? I was afraid to go to the corner market for fear of slipping on the ice. So, how did that woman come here all the way from America?"

Crazy questions in my grandma's mind. But there was the woman, standing there with a young boy. There was another detail that caught my grandma's eye: they were both wearing nice thick coats and their feet were snugly booted. A man was standing there with them. He spoke Turkish, and was fluent in their language too.

Thankfully, my father was laid up, so he didn't see that shameful exchange transpire. At the time, the husband—the American archaeologist—was in Ankara, chasing down funds so he could keep Hagia Sophia standing.

The American woman looked my grandma up and down, while she in turn put a hand on her hip and cocked an eyebrow. Her friends said that my grandma looked like Sophia Loren, whose films they watched at the open-air summer theaters. Of course, how would they have known anything about Marianne Faithfull? So she put on airs, doing her best to impersonate Sophia, the only actress with whom she was familiar. She lamented to herself, "If only I wasn't wearing these stretched-out old socks and wool slippers." The woman's hair was done up in neat curls, her eyebrows perfectly plucked, her fingernails immaculately painted. My grandma, on the other hand, looked like a worn-out homemaker, despite the fact that a cleaning woman now came once a week and she had a wringer washing machine.

"What does it matter!" she thought. "The American loves me."

"I swear to God," she later said on her deathbed, "I didn't seduce him. Sure, I liked him, but I didn't make it obvious. Still, when he approached me, I couldn't turn him away. I wanted to raise my kids as best as I could. The American liked my kids and enjoyed spending time with them. And I had a right to be happy too . . ." No, you're not mistaken—that sentence concluded with some swearing.

"I've traveled a long ways to speak to you, woman to woman."

"As if I wouldn't have understood that without you bringing an interpreter!"

Not because she knew English, but because she was a good judge of character and immediately understood the situation.

"Out of politeness, I asked her if she would like some coffee."

"Turkish coffee?" the woman asked.

"Your husband is quite fond of it too," my grandma told her. "He wants it five times a day. I tell him that it will give him palpitations, but he doesn't listen to me."

But the interpreter didn't translate that. Or if he did, it was most likely along the lines of "Turkish coffee very good for you. Clears the mind. You like?"

In short: the interpreter played a role in making sure that that potentially explosive meeting went smoothly. And then there was the money. A large roll of it. Exchanged from dollars.

"Take this and kick my husband out. Send him away. He needs to come back to America and be with us. It's time to put an end to this double life he's leading."

Without a moment of hesitation, my grandma took the money. She sold her love.

"Rudolf"—by the way, I should mention that our adorable grandpa had European, even Russian roots—"mustn't hear anything about this. I'll talk to him myself," the woman said.

A pause.

"Thanks," she said.

"The madam says thank you."

"Screw that madam and her gratitude!" my grandma said to the interpreter. "She paid me off for her husband, and now she'll go away with him. I've got to think about my kids. That's why I'm taking the money."

My grandma didn't like how the woman flashed her a phony smile of victory. The woman must have asked, "What did she say?" because the interpreter was the last person who spoke in the conversation. Who knows what he came up with as a translation for "Screw that madam"?

When the snow melts, all the filth is laid bare. Garbage, cinders, coal ash, frozen animals, carrion, remains. The way that my grandma sold out her so-called husband, her children's sweet "father," was no different.

"The snow melted and Rudolf came back from Ankara. He called and said, 'I took the ferry from Haydarpaşa to the other side of the city, and now I'm at Hagia Sophia. Tonight I'll come back to your place.' Like a Turkish husband, he asked, 'What should I bring? Do you need anything?' I taught him that," she added proudly.

The American taught her something too. Rather, something that Turkish husbands don't say to their wives:

"I love you," he said, and hung up the phone.

"Every day he proclaimed his love like that. But what do I know of love, of passion? Am I the only one at fault here? No. Everyone is."

In any case, soon after that phone call, my grandma was standing in the middle of Hagia Sophia, holding the American's suitcase in one hand while my aunt was holding on to her skirt, facing the American. Naturally, he was surprised. *"Hayırdır?"* he said, as he'd also learned to use that Turkish expression at inauspicious moments when you're unsure of the outcome.

My grandma plonked the suitcase down in front of him. The sound echoed through Hagia Sophia, and a few tourists turned to look at them.

"Here are your things. Don't ever come to my home again."

She held out her hand, waiting for him to give her the key, but he didn't understand. She wanted him to understand without her having to say anything. It was hard for her to ask for the key, to kick the American out.

"Give me my house keys."

"I was on the verge of tears as I spoke those words," she said on her deathbed, as her consciousness was slipping away. "I was shaking like a leaf, but Rudolf thought he was being confronted by a brusque Turkish woman. Although I loved him madly, I was acting like the most heartless person you could imagine. Normally, when he came home in the evening, he'd look after the kids while I set the table. I liked that fairy tale of a cozy home. I wanted it to go on forever. Sometimes I'd secretly weep in the kitchen, saying to myself, 'What if he leaves?' I'm not stupid. Do you think I didn't know he had a family? He whispered it to me once. Fearfully. We were going to manage because we loved each other. He found me warmhearted and sincere, and I thought he was loving and affectionate."

My grandma wouldn't actually say such things, but in my mind that's how I'd have her talk. *Speak, sing like a bird! Who can hold you back?!*

On that sunny but bitterly cold winter day in 1975, she took her daughter's hand, and they walked down from Sultanahmet to Cağaloğlu and headed in the direction of Sirkeci. I imagined that my grandma bit her lip to stop herself from crying and squeezed my aunt's hand as they proceeded down the hill, and in my mind's eye I could see my aunt's small feet getting tripped up and the new coats they were wearing, coats that Rudolf had bought for them that winter.

When the American showed up at her door to ask, "There must be some reason for this," my grandma decided that the only way out was to be coarse and contemptible, so she played the role of the quarrelsome woman: "Fuck off!"

Boom.

The door closed.

The American never came back.

He went to Galatasaray High School, where my father was studying as a boarding student at the time, to bid him farewell. He gave my father some books. Then he opened a bank account for the children, into which he put a small amount of money, slipped the bankbook under the door, and left.

He left for good.

The money in the account was enough to ensure that the kids were able to go on with their studies comfortably and have everything they needed.

That's why snowy days bear such memories for my family. Whenever it snowed, my grandma would start feeling uneasy, as if at any moment someone might come knocking on the door and take away all that was dear to her. On that winter's day, my grandma beat my aunt, still bearing that grudge in her heart.

Aunt Hülya also has a particular memory about the snowy days of 1987: She lost one of her boots in the snow. As she was running around playing, somehow one of her boots slipped off her foot and they weren't able to find it, even after the snow melted. A few weeks later, she saw a street dog gnawing on it. She described the sadness she felt that day: "For me, it felt like that dog was chewing on a part of me, not on my boot."

When I opened my eyes, it was morning. But there was something strange going on. The last I could remember, I'd been on the roof of the Tiled Pavilion, among the domes, snuggled up with Yunus. I awoke, however, curled up in my nest. I had no recollection of going back there. Even more strangely, yes definitely more strangely, everything was blanketed in snow. The branches, leaves, grass, the top of the wall, the benches, everything. Some places were covered in more snow, others in less. Only the protective branches of the laurel tree had prevented me from being covered in snow too. All the same, there were gleaming snowflakes and slivers of ice on my fur coat. Things were happening that I could not wrap my mind around.

But why?

I closed my eyes again.

22

CHANGE LOCATION

When I opened my eyes, I was on the roof of the Tiled Pavilion. Where you last saw me. Yunus was asleep next to me, his mouth open, lightly snoring ever so sweetly. The packages and containers of everything we'd eaten and drunk the night before were on the roof, the empty beer cans and tiny bottles of liquor clinking against each other in the wind. A yellow plastic bag filled by the breeze fluttered, announcing its freedom, but it couldn't fly off because it was weighed down by a few empty bottles. Sometimes it's good to focus your thoughts on such silly things. The small, the mundane, have the power to heal.

Yunus opened his eyes.

"I woke up from a snowy dream," I said.

He looked at me blankly for a moment, probably thinking that he was dreaming. Then his spirit and body were reunited.

"I—I was dreaming," he said. But his voice trembled. He scowled. "I saw my mom. Maybe because I was telling you about her."

"How was she?"

"Not well. First, I dreamt about the moment she died. The service bus was filling up with water. They were trying to open the doors, but they couldn't. I remember thinking, 'So this is where she died.' There were no windows. It was like a shipping container. Like a can. When I was a kid, I'd never imagined such things. That the poor can die such deaths. That such deaths are the only fitting way for the poor to die."

Yunus's eyes were glazed over.

"Then my mom came home. Her clothes were all wet. It was night and everyone was asleep. I was pretty young. The age I was when she died. I hugged her, tears in my eyes. I thought it was my tears that were making us all wet."

I snuggled up closer to him. A single gleaming tear fell from one of his beautiful eyes and rolled down the bony features of his face.

As we kissed and held each other tightly, the sun rose a little higher in the sky. The alarm on Yunus's phone went off and the call to prayer rang out all at once from the mosques.

"Do you usually wake up so early?"

"It's the only way I can make it to work on time."

After sitting up and getting to his feet, he sniffed himself.

"If we're not freshly showered when we go to work, the manager gets upset. She even docks our paychecks."

"Let's go then, so you can take care of that."

"Did you realize that you talked all night? I've never met anyone who likes to explain things so much."

"I am the psychiatrist of youth. The psychologist of our generation."

"Don't say things like that. I don't understand what you mean. I didn't go to a good school like you."

"I don't fit the profile of the school I go to at all. At least, I try not to. School's ridiculous!"

"In what way?"

"In every way. For example, one of our literature teachers got fired because a poem about female sexuality was published in the student newspaper."

"That's silly."

"The people who fired that teacher hire male strippers for the parties they hold after the graduation ceremonies are over. Can you even imagine it? Then they boot that teacher just because a poem had the word 'vagina' in it."

We gathered up all our things and the garbage on the roof, just like a pair of lovers would do when they leave their spot on the beach . . . A couple who lounges in daily conversation, a couple who loves and is used to being around each other. But we were on the roof of a summer palace built in 1472.

As I was thinking about those things, I realized that I hadn't asked the question that had been burning in my mind since I woke up: "What did I talk about all night?"

"Beautiful stories that took place on snowy days."

I was glad to hear that. Because the things I talked about were good and pleasant, in spite of everything, and because I was still of sound mind. Also because I was in reality, not a dream, and still alive. Despite everything, I was still alive. I was in a strange place, but at least I was still among the living. I'd cut off all ties with the world, but I hadn't died. Vexed, anxious? No problem! Unfaltering perseverance! I see no issues with the fulfillment of needs. Don't ask about the outburst of self-confidence. Here I'd been searching for the love of my life on the ground, and I found him in the sky! I mean, I was about to say, what business did I have in that world where I still hadn't gotten my fill of defeats after all that time?

Those were all wonderful things, but all the same I couldn't stop myself from pausing to gaze wistfully at the city spread out before me, the city where I was born and grew up. I felt like I was sitting in the garden of Cihangir Mosque, looking at the palace of fairies, my grandma beside me. We had some sunflower seeds we picked up at the corner shop, along with some sparkling water.

"Grandma, do you know what I'm thinking about?"

"No, tell me."

"As I sit here looking at the city, I wish that everything belonging to this day and age would collapse and fall to ruin, and then everything would become overgrown by weeds. That's what I'm thinking about."

"You sound just like those anarchists your father used to hang out with in high school! Now look, they've put you into a real classy school. A school for ladies. So don't take after me and let your mouth become a hotbed of cussing—they signed you up there so you wouldn't become a foulmouthed slut. Now, come to your senses, and stop talking crazy."

The panorama that spread out before me and that I was gathering into myself—that's how it was—made me remember, feel, and think of so many things, and I told Yunus about all of them. He laughed so hard that he doubled over. He was so sweet in the morning, tired eyes and all.

"I wish that I could remember things like you," he said. "Because life isn't what we experience. It's how we remember it."

23

Now Following Your Page

Walking back along the top of the wall proved difficult. Returning to the branch upon which I had been perching proved difficult as well. Yunus froze up. I held him in my arms like a baby. We inched our way along the wall. For a while, he closed his eyes. It really was that hard.

"Think of me as a blind person," he said. "Imagine me that way. Because that's how it seems to me now."

I had to. Otherwise, we never would've made it back to the ladder leading down to the fire escape. He'd left my clothes there, the ones he'd washed. There was a package of crackers, a bottle of water, and some candy in the bag too. When we got to the ladder, I saw that the surveillance camera was now pointed in a completely different direction. Pointed at nothing, in fact. A chill went down my spine.

"Yunus, did you do that?"

"Yes."

"So, is everything solved now?"

"Thanks for walking me back."

And then he turned to leave. His eyes seemed to be dazzled by the light, squinting. Something was amiss—but what?

"Do your best to keep hidden as much as you can," he said. "Don't let anyone see you."

I didn't know Yunus's father, but I imagined that's how he would've talked. "Do your best to . . ." sounds like the kind of language a parent would use, doesn't it?

After propping the ladder up against the wall of the hotel, he locked the door leading to the fire escape and bounded down the stairs with a surprising burst of energy, unconsciously leaving behind the echoes of his steps.

I wondered what he hadn't told me.

All the same, I didn't dwell too much on his warning. Guess what I did next, as if the "I" who'd been told to keep a low profile wasn't actually me. I washed myself off.

It was still early in the morning, and the sprinklers in the park were spraying away full force. One sprinkler in particular caught my attention, because instead of watering the grass, it was squirting directly at the branch of an oak tree. I went and sat on that branch. You might even say I perched there. First, I let myself get soaked in my clothes, and then I peeled them off. The water came as a cold shock, but I was banking on the possibility that it would be a hot day—an act of sheer stubbornness in the face of the oncoming autumn. I felt a childish joy as the water rushed over me. I closed my eyes and opened my mouth. Raising my arms like a monkey, I scrubbed my armpits, and then I rinsed out my hair. That may have been the most liberated thing I'd ever done in my life until that point.

The only other time I'd been so free was during the protests. At Gezi. In the park.

Clambering back onto the wall, I wrung out my clothes and then laid them out to dry. At least now I could put on my own clothes again, now that they were clean. I pulled my hair into a dripping ponytail. Who does the sun shine upon?

It always made me laugh when my grandma would say to one of her cats, "Hey, Pussy!" Kicking out the American hadn't been as easy as she'd described it. "I could never abandon these cats," she said. "I couldn't even leave the vegetable dealer. I couldn't stab him with a bread knife. I couldn't kill him and then bury his body in the garden."

So, why did she tell me all those things on her deathbed?

When people are alive, they shouldn't hold in their anger or feelings of animosity, nor should they bite their tongues, because like a stone lashed to your foot, such things will drag you down until you drown. I stretched out on top of the wall. The rays of the sun warmed my bare feet, hands, face, and damp hair. I said to myself, "There's a way to deal with everything." But when people are alive, they cannot think that way. They poison life. Now I seemed to be dead. When people realize that there's a way to deal with everything, it's too late. They're dying.

Not moving a muscle, I lay there on top of that wall that was as old as the country itself. When I heard steps behind me, I raised my head and looked over. It was Yunus. His shift hadn't started yet. He'd washed off in the personnel shower, had breakfast, put on his uniform, and realizing that he had some time to spare, decided to stop by to see me. He'd left as shaken and scared as a child, so when I saw him strolling along the top of the wall, I wondered where he'd gotten the courage. The silver threading of his red uniform glimmered in the gentle morning light. He was even wearing that funny conical hat. I hoped I wasn't just having a bellboy dream.

"Why do you look so surprised?" he asked.

"Because not even an hour ago you were pretending to be a blind person, as that was the only way you could keep walking on top of the wall. So, what gives? Why so fearless now?"

"Don't be so surprised. Even between two moments there's always a certain amount of time."

"Well, hell! We're like a tragedy being staged as part of a school play."

"Maybe we're the heroes of our times."

"That much is true."

"I may not be able to leap from branch to branch like Tarzan like you can, but—"

"Tarzan? Do you realize that's the last thing you should ever call a girl?"

I almost added "you prick," but with great difficulty held myself back. "Tough girl" posturing is a disgusting thing. I was disgusted with myself. The truth of the matter, however, is that I wanted to be disgusted with myself. As always, Yunus replied with the utmost understanding and sweetness, perhaps because I was seeing him as a figment of my imagination, because I thought that the two of us were dreaming: "Should I have called you a monkey? It's simple, really. I overcame my fear. I've done it before. On the night of the protests."

He paused for a moment, as if he suddenly comprehended where he was. Ah, "comprehend"! Grandma, you can hear me, can't you? Even if I'm not thinking about you, your words speak through me. I wish that I could put an emoji here of a laughing face with tears squirting out of its eyes.

Yunus was unafraid. As he said, he seemed to have gotten over his fear, and he was relishing the pleasure of that victory. He was practically chirruping.

"I think that the spirit of youth is like a pendulum, swinging back and forth. But it's not that there's no power pulling them toward the middle. There is such a power. It is the joy of freedom and life that every young person has been carrying around inside since birth. But when another power comes along and rips that out in its entirety, you feel like throwing yourself in another direction. Otherwise, being young is a wonderful thing. Still, there are the storms of adolescence. Aside from hope, there's no port where you can seek refuge. But if I'm heading down a path toward a preposterous adult life, I'd rather fall from this wall to the ground and die. But that's another issue altogether."

Goodness and beauty had made him so diaphanous that it seemed as if all the light in the world were shining through him and spreading around us. Either that, or my head was still light from my cold shower in the sprinkler.

He walked over and sat down beside me.

"This is the second time I've seen you with wet hair. The first time I was quite captivated too."

Meaning that, when it came to me, he remembered things. Moments that were special for him. As he buried his hands in the dampness of my hair, the sun shone down, bathing us in its warmth.

"If you want to talk to me again like you did last night, I'm ready to listen."

Up in the trees and on that wall, a remnant of a conquest that supposedly transformed an era, I felt like a cat that was bearing witness to the fact that human history hadn't spiritually advanced a single iota despite the passage of time. And who wouldn't feel like that while lying under the sun? That's why I stretched and then, burrowing my head deeper into Yunus's lap, started talking. Or thinking. Exploring my thoughts. Remembering. Or maybe all of them at once.

The only person my grandma wouldn't let into her home was my mother's father.

Why such antagonism?

In your opinion, why?

Perhaps because he was the neighbor who had stood watch at the door and hadn't tried to stop or dissuade his friends from doing what they were doing to her?

"If he'd managed to get it up, maybe he too would've taken his turn. But he hadn't been able to. Or I was in such a wretched state that he had no desire to touch me. Maybe that fucking prick was scared. Dervish son of a bitch! Swindling blacksmith."

The last secret about our family had now been whispered. The genie was out of the bottle. That young man, who let the devil take the hindmost, had no idea at the time that he would be my mother's father and, ultimately, my grandfather. Of the looters who ravaged the city on

September 6 and 7, he was the useful idiot, the callous lout. When he came home, his father gave him a sound thrashing, saying, "What the hell were you doing with those thugs?"

Then he took his son to the Kadiri dervish lodge: "Repent and be a man!"

But we all know that you can't raise children saying, "Do this, do that." Over time, as you rail against them, they will internalize that voice of yours and make it their own. Ah, didactic education. Would you like a dose of that? "What do you have against my father?" my mother would ask, ever so naively.

Why would we want to have anything to do with your father, whose factory settings were off from the very beginning, that blacksmith grandfather of mine?

"Mind your own business. I'll never forgive him. That bigot father of yours will never set foot in this house."

"But, Perihan, Mother, it's a bit disgraceful not letting him come in."

"Don't push your Perihan, Mother, or I'll bite your damn head off!"

That was the extent of the dispute between my mother and grandmother. My grandfather would come over, but rarely, and my grandma would never be around when he did.

"In neighborhoods like this, people hold grudges all the time," my father said, without knowing what the issue was really about. Without thinking. Without even considering the possibilities. So at ease! He'd talk and talk, drink in hand, stroking his beard.

What heavy burdens my grandma carried. It should come as no surprise that it all made its way out transformed into cursing and swearing.

Was that the end of it? By no means. When those snowy days of 1987 came to an end, they moved everything out of the house. It was torn down and digging commenced for the foundation of the new apartment building. That's when it happened. Fortune smiled upon my father, who was studying archaeology at the time. The workers came upon a grave and a tablet with an inscription, as well as the skeletons of a woman and a newborn child. By reading the inscription, they wrote history. The history of lineage. It turned out that the house my grandma had blithely traded away so she could be free of it had belonged to us since time immemorial. To our family. To our lineage.

But how?

Like everything, there's a story behind it all. The history that my grandma couldn't bear to abandon and ended up seeing across the way day in and day out as the result of that childish barter is buried there. Women's history, or the tragedy of the women of these lands, was buried on that plot of land. But, of course, what had she traded it away for? And how far away could the poor woman have fled? No one can escape from the misfortune of being a woman in these lands. Don't fool yourself. So, are you ready to listen?

The woman who was buried with that inscription died in the year 1550. The houses that had been precariously perched on these hills, which are visible from the palace, were always the site of work of a less savory nature. The girls who wound up there never went of their own accord. In fact, no one *went* there—they were *taken* there. They were hunted down like birds and taken there. Some were brought from the slave market. In particular, the most down-and-out of the women were those who were left over at the slave market after the effendis of Istanbul had picked through the best ones. Some were taken there in exchange for the bribes that the bordello owners paid. Some were kidnapped from the gardens and vineyards where they worked, women who, if they'd been sold at the slave market, would have ended up in the palace because of their beauty and pedigree. The woman who had been buried beneath our land with the inscription was one of those. A young Jewish woman from Edirne. She ran and ran but was caught in the end, only to find herself in that house in Istanbul that smelled of opium and rang with laughter. What was done was done. Janissaries would come one after the other, and the house was practically shaken off its foundations.

Is there any need for an explanation of the state that the poor girl was in? Not if you ask me. There shouldn't be. The forced descent into degradation shouldn't be discussed. That girl who put up with that life, not even knowing where she was, eventually grew accustomed to it and went on living that way. My grandma described it all much better as a deterrent for me, but I think that is enough on the matter. Ultimately, the girl got sick and died. After ten years of enduring the ups and downs of working as a whore, she had an inscription carved for her while she was on her deathbed. She was buried in the garden of that house, which had its greatest days of glory and wealth as a bordello thanks to her, and the inscription was placed at the head of her grave.

That was the grave that was found on the plot of land given to the developer in 1987. As a student of archaeology, my father took the inscription into his care and spent a great deal of time translating it. Here is what it says:

Here lies a woman / She was a person just like you / Flames burn her like the rest of us / The wind buffets her / Thorns make her bleed / But she wasn't like you / If only someone had told her, "Don't be afraid" / If only she could have been given her freedom like the blowing wind / If only she could have been treated like a man by the world / Womanhood is beauty and bounty / Womanhood is that which gives life / Womanhood is misfortune in this world / This is your last breath / Here lies a woman / Who bowed to everyone's desires / In my youth I was as independent as the wind / No one could ever stop me / They grabbed me by the hair and stuck me in a cage / Youth and women and children are

more sagacious than the sages / The world
should belong to women, children, and the
youth / If only women could live as free and
beautifully as those lords and men with wicked hearts

"It's a bad translation," my father said, "but it's the best I can do."
The translation really was shitty.

Then there was a debate about whether the person buried there was
a regular woman or really a whore. My father even took the inscription
onto a television show. "In fact she was a whore, but that's beside the
point. The inscription is a eulogy for women and youth, so we prefer
to take it up as a plea related to the issue of gender."

"Let's see if the whore in the grave agrees with your preference."

That was what my grandma had to say on the matter. The woman's
remains are still on display at the Archaeology Museum as "the skeleton
of a woman dating back to 1550." It would appear that no scholars
of Byzantine history have examined the tattered remnants of cloth in
which the baby was wrapped. Otherwise, they'd be stunned by the lab
results, as they'd show that they only dated back to 1956. Anyone who
is curious should go and see for themselves, but out of respect for my
memory, they should keep their mouths shut about the story.

Of course, it doesn't end in the year 1550. As I mentioned, Sultan
Süleyman the Magnificent built a mosque in the area for his hunchbacked son. The mosque, which was completed around 1560, didn't
guide the local residents onto the true path. A woman who was my
grandma's great-great-grandma first set foot in the place in the middle of
the 1800s. She'd worked at a bordello in Galata, where all day long she
was forced to sit behind the latticed window of a dingy house that faced
the street. When a customer showed up, she'd take them inside. Like
most of the women involved in the business in the area, she was Jewish,
as was her madam. Because she was young and beautiful, they decided

to move her to Cihangir so she wouldn't go to waste in that run-down house. The house that would become the place my grandma called a chicken coop was redone and still smelled of freshly cut wood when the madam reopened it as a bordello. The lineage of the women of our family can be traced back to that girl who was taken from Galata and put to work in that bordello in Cihangir. That woman who established this royal lineage joined up with her pimp and killed the madam who'd been running the place. Supposedly, a fight had broken out. The madam got stabbed. The house caught on fire. Then they rebuilt the house, and the story goes on. Toward the end of the 1800s, the bordello was passed from mother to daughter. When it was passed down to my grandma's grandmother, things changed and it became a regular home. The stories of most of the abutting houses on the street are more or less the same.

"Are you sleeping?" I asked Yunus. "Or have you been listening to my every word?"

"If I'd fallen asleep," he said, "I probably would've rolled off the top of this wall."

He leaned down, took my head between his hands, and kissed my lips, eyes, forehead, cheeks, nose, and earlobes. And then. And then. And then he left, vanishing as if he'd never existed. If you ask me, love is a beautiful thing.

24

CHIRP

I found out later that it was the holiday of the Festival of the Sacrifice. I'd been wondering why there were more people than usual in the park. Still, the trees in which I perched were at the far edge of the park—yes, I'll repeat that a thousand times—so I remained secluded. Only people with something to hide ventured into my area, such as secret lovers. Yunus worked all through the holiday, and he came to see me whenever he got the chance. It seemed that he'd grown accustomed to being cut off from the ground below. While he may not have been as confident and nimble as me on top of the wall and in the branches of the trees, he had overcome his fear. At least, that's the impression I got.

One day, before Yunus came to visit me, I saw some other people on the fire escape for the very first time. After looking at the wall and discussing something, they readjusted the surveillance camera. Hidden in the shadows of the laurel tree, I watched them. Only my eyes were visible. If they saw anything at all, they probably thought that a bird was flitting about in the branches of the tree. That's how well hidden I was. All the same, they were looking in my direction. My best guess was that they were the security guards with whom Yunus said he'd made a deal. But I couldn't help but wonder—how had he made a deal with them? And on what issue, precisely? I think that they were trying to understand what had happened to that girl Yunus had kissed—that girl being me, of course: Where had she gone? Where had she disappeared to after lingering atop the wall?

When Yunus showed up, I explained it all to him.

"I know," he said. "I've been taking a different route when I come to see you."

"How have you been getting here?"

"There's an easier way further down the wall, past the hotel. I climb up to the top of the wall and then I walk along its length as if I were taking a stroll down a path, telling myself, 'To hell with it, if I fall, I fall.' There's a big tree on the far side of the hotel, the one with the two branches that have grown against the wall, making a kind of bridge."

"The silver birch."

"Is that what it's called?"

"Yes. The one next to it is a regular birch. And then there's a beech tree. Beside that there's an alder, and then there's my horse chestnut with its pink flowers. After passing by the thorn apple, beech, and red dogwood, you arrive at my trees. This laurel, which cradles the stork nest in its branches, and the eucalyptus, plane, and pine trees beside it."

"How do you know so much about trees? I don't know what any of them are called."

"That doesn't matter. If you want, you can look them up online. So long as you respect them, that's all that matters."

"During the Gezi protests we wrote some graffiti like that. That was my slogan. 'Respect the trees.'"

Yunus spoke those words with the utmost sincerity and excitement. I wished that I had a cigarette. Or some weed. It would've been so nice to get high together. We would've become one with the smoke and wafted up into the sky. We would've become smoke.

My thoughts drifted back to the times of the protests.

"You look distracted," Yunus said.

"What's the date today?"

"The twenty-seventh of September. Sunday."

"So I've been here for thirteen days."

"Does it seem like it's been longer?"

"It does," I said. "It was like that during the protests too. When I poked my head out of my tent one morning, I felt like I'd been there for hundreds of years. As if I'd sent down roots like a tree and been there for so many days and nights—weeks, months, years."

Yunus and I were in the embrace of the trees. After seeing those people on the fire escape and listening to their conversation, I was on full alert. I knew someone would come along the route Yunus had described, the one that led to my roost. That tree he mentioned—the silver birch—may very well have been the oldest tree in the park, and it was certainly the most respected of them all, looking over the rest. As Yunus tried to explain, its strong branches extended outward like a bridge. It really was like a bridge—I'm not exaggerating. Yunus would come to call that pathway that brought him to me so fearlessly "the bridge of love."

We were nestled in the silver birch's branches, which were so beautiful you could never get enough of stroking them, whispering to each other. As we embraced, the tree embraced us too. I mean, it seemed that way. I forgot about the security guards, who had suspicions about my existence, as well as the secret agreement they had made. Forgetting is such a wondrous thing, isn't it?

But Gezi wanted to remind me of its presence. Gezi, where I belonged. Gezi, which made me feel so deeply that I had always lived there.

"After you got wounded . . . after being at the mosque . . . did you go back?"

"My family was apprehensive. After the events of the third of June, they wouldn't let me go to the park again. But we ran away. To be more precise, first I ran away, and Derin and Pembe followed. I was so sure they'd come that I went to Decathlon and bought three sleeping bags and a tent big enough for all of us."

"I didn't have a tent. We made our own sleeping bags out of blankets. I slept outside under the trees, and all night long I watched the clouds drifting across the sky. They broke apart and merged together, only to break apart again. The night was so much like the day. I got the feeling that daytime was refusing to become night, as the sky would not darken."

"The park was like a huge open-air dormitory. Everyone was free and happy, and all the good people of the world were there. That's what my mother said. 'I don't feel the least bit afraid here.' Those were her words. Then she said, 'But I *am* afraid of the people who don't want you to stay in the park.'"

"She was right to be afraid. They tried to kill me. At first, I thought I really was dead. When I got shot in the stomach with a tear gas canister, I fell to the ground as if I'd been gunned down in a war. And when I pulled my hand away from my stomach and saw the blood—I literally started screaming my head off like a girl."

"Why do you say that? As if only girls scream! Look, things like that really piss me off. There's no need to be crass. Leave your sexism at the door along with your shoes."

Yunus laughed. That's how Gezi was. Like a smile, a grin, laughter born of pain, indescribably beautiful and powerful. I'm sorry, but I can't put it any more eloquently. Gezi can't be described because it was something different, unlike anything else that has ever happened.

Whenever they got the chance, my mother and my father's sister would stop by the park. They were happy too, and hopeful as well, as if they'd stumbled upon an unexpected consolation. There was something liberating about saying, "Enough already!" My mother compared "our movement" to a book that she'd read when she was younger in which a city was left to the youth and they lived however they pleased.

"Not so much in terms of the subject, but the way that the kids here are living so freely is a lot like that book."

My aunt said, "Like when your mom goes to visit the neighbors and you make a mess of your house?"

Although she may not have been aware of it, her eyes still welled up whenever she used the word "mom." She'd stop on the threshold of breaking into tears. Two months had passed since she'd lost her mother, and she still missed her terribly.

Yunus asked, "Where were you when you got hurt?"

Summer refused to leave the city. It went on and on, the longest summer in the history of Istanbul. Not a single leaf fell from the trees. They were making a stand. What I'm saying is that Yunus seemed to have vanished into an otherworldly green. Even his eyes looked like they were turning green, and when he smiled or grinned, his teeth looked like they were taking on a greenish hue as well.

"I," I said, unable to pry my gaze from the deep green of the leaves on the branches surrounding us, "was at the bottom of the steep road that goes to Dolmabahçe when I got hurt. In the neighborhood of Akaretler, they called us the 'Shot-Put Girls' because that's how we threw the paving stones we pried up from the sidewalks. The guys from the Çarşı group of protesters—as you know, they led a lot of the protests—cheered us on. 'But this is where things are going to heat up. You should stick around.' We went up the hill to the other side of İnönü Stadium."

"We had taken up a position behind the barricades we set up near there. I can honestly say that I made the barricade in front of the military hospital with my own two hands. I swear, it's true. I made that big old barricade all by myself."

"I believe you."

"You should."

"There was another barricade further down from the one you made."

"I know."

"That's where they got me."

"We were practically in the same place."

"Maybe. When there are concerts at the stadium, people go to that little knoll up the way to listen to the shows for free. It's right behind the stadium."

"I know where you're talking about."

"Well, that's where I was."

As one of the Shot-Put Girls, my confidence had been unbounded. Teasingly, I said to Derin, "You're the best shot-putter of all of us."

"What makes you say that?"

"Because you're the only one of us who has ankles as thick as her neck, ha ha ha!"

"The atmosphere was so strange. Or maybe it was the bombardment of tear gas. In any case, we were out of whack, that's for sure. We had been for a long time, from the very start. So there I was, dazed, incapable of looking after myself. Derin tugged at my arm a few times, and Pembe tried to shove me back. But just as I'd blindly accepted all the conditions of that stupid writing contest, I unconsciously made my way to the front lines. I went up to the front and got hit in the head with a tear gas canister."

"And then what happened?"

"For a second I thought my head had been knocked clean off my body. That's how hard it hit me. The sound of the canister meeting bone was terrifying. I really thought that my troubled head flew off like a ball."

"Huh! So it really was that brutal?"

"It was so brutal, it knocked me out. When I came around, I found myself in the mosque by the seaside that they were using as a field hospital."

"Dolmabahçe Mosque."

"Yeah, that's the place. There's a little cove next to it where some fishermen tie up their boats. When I was younger, my grandma and I used to take little trips on one of those small motorboats. She knew the owner. They were about the same age and had been friends for a long time. He lived in Cihangir too."

Then it dawned on me. He was the archaeologist whom she hadn't been able to marry. I felt something crumple inside me. As I was telling Yunus about those days from the past, I discovered yet another of my grandma's secrets. On the sly, she would spend time on the sea with her ex-lover, who had been driven from her by fate. A cordial old man from Cihangir, whose dentures didn't quite fit into his mouth: "Well, hi there," he'd say. "I've got a granddaughter the same age as you."

When her erstwhile fiancé spoke those words, she felt a need to correct him in that raspy voice of hers that grated on the ears. She did that as Marianne Faithfull, taking some fresh air on the Bosporus, puffing on a Samsun cigarette, her fingers permanently stained yellow with nicotine.

"Your granddaughter's two years older than mine."

"Yes, and she has the same name."

What was I holding, an ice cream? Was I sassily licking a Cornetto with my impudent tongue as big as a shoe?

"But I have a middle name too."

"So does she!"

"But my middle name is very rare."

"As you kids say these days . . . exactamundo."

That old archaeologist from Cihangir was surprisingly hip.

"So your granddaughter's name is also . . ."

"Yes. Exactly the same as yours. This grandma of yours copied that rare middle name that means 'beautiful view' and gave it to you. Ha ha! And then there's your aunt . . . She's the namesake of one of my twins."

Seriously, for real? It was like one of those mathematical logic problems you see on exams: How long will it take to fill a swimming pool with X number of buckets, how long will it take a car to travel from city A to city B, what percentage of money does person Y have compared with person Z, what is person C's age based on the age of person D . . . ?

Grandma, you just sit there on the stern of the boat, smoke your cigarette, and gaze into the distance. You've done as you will, so look around as if you never sinned! You haven't given up on that sweet man from the neighborhood you wanted to marry. Since fate kept you apart, you raised parallel families, giving your children and grandchildren identical names without an ounce of shame.

"The sea air is good for the kid. Her doctor said that she needed it. Last winter she came down with bronchitis."

Sure, Grandma. The sea air is wonderful. So refreshing! There I was, sitting there like a foolish cherub, Cornetto in hand, unaware that I was an excuse that legitimized your rendezvous on the sea. And you, reader, back off! I'm not going to tell you what my name is. Not my first name or my middle name. Google it if you so desire. Grandma, what you did was wrong. This isn't working at all. You didn't choose us. Instead, you opted to stay in a marriage that was only possible in another universe. You made copies of us. Are we mere clones? We are, thanks to you. But when we were packing up your things after you died . . .

"Why did my mom hide this dress?" As my father's sister held up that inauspicious dress on its hanger, it seemed to me my grandma's ghost lingered within its folds.

"Can I have it? As a memento of my grandma?"

"Sure. It's all torn up, but you can keep it if you want."

She tossed the dress in my direction, and it seemed to fly across the space between us like a bird.

"I don't remember her ever wearing that."

I remember.

Grandma, I knew the things they didn't know about, right? But I was so young! As Perihan's little companion, her one and only friend, the child of her child, we'd glide past Dolmabahçe Mosque on that small motorboat that puttered us out onto the Bosporus Strait.

"What a beautiful mosque! The one we have in Cihangir is one thing, but this is something else altogether. I wish all the mosques in this country of ours were like this . . ."

Grandma, there's no need to change the subject. My anger died down as quickly as it burst into flame. That's how it goes with you. I forgive you with a kiss to your cheek.

"Let's go under the bridge! Pretty please?"

"Sure, as you wish."

May your one desire, your happiness, your consolation, be taking in the sea air on the stern of a boat on the Bosporus. In fact, your expectations of life and your desires were indeed that simple. They thought that was too much for you, for me. It's such a shame, Grandma. Such a terrible shame.

There are so many memories, aren't there?

I could wrap up that sentence with a bit of swearing. What do you say, Grandma? Shall we put your stamp on it?

The human mind is like a dairy farm. Those things we call "memories" are like flies: try with all your might to shoo one away, but it keeps buzzing around. A dairy farm without flies would go against the very law of nature. That's why the mind cannot shake off traces of the past. That's what I was thinking about when they were stitching my head up at the mosque and I was braying like a donkey. If I didn't confess earlier that I was braying like a donkey, I'm saying it now. But don't go off and sneer or judge me. My life's screwed up enough already; show a little understanding.

Wait, where were we?

Ah yes, I was listening to Yunus.

"After I got hurt, my father started to worry. 'Don't go back there,' he said. But I couldn't think of being anywhere but the park. So I went back and started living in the park with the others, imagining that I'd spend the rest of my days there. After I got hit in the stomach with a tear gas canister, I started getting scared when the anti-riot trucks would start patrolling. I even had dreams about them."

"I know exactly how you felt. When they started burning the tents, we were terrified. That was the morning of the thirtieth of May. I remember the date so clearly because it was Pembe's birthday."

"I met so many nice people and heard so many wonderful stories. I read a lot too."

"If only the whole country was like the park in those days, because we had hope. And now? Is there still a country? Do we have a future? The horizon has been buried in darkness. We're completely lost."

"There's nothing I can say to that except 'exactly.' The situation is exactly that."

"We had hope in those times. I saw it with my own eyes. I saw things of such beauty that I'd never seen before. It was as if a circus of equality, freedom, and fraternity had been set up in the heart of the city."

"A circus?! Are you on the government's side or something?"

"I don't mean 'circus' in a bad way. But I didn't know how else to describe it. They had hung up that huge banner that read 'DON'T BACK DOWN.' And we didn't. We didn't back down."

"A guy played the trumpet at the top of the building."

"People were dancing."

"Did you see them doing the fire dance?"

"We put on a play of sorts. The story was from a children's book we found in the library that had been set up in Gezi. I suggested the story.

It was very sad. It wasn't what you'd expect of a children's book. It was called *Duck, Death and the Tulip*.

"I played Death. I had a mask, and I was wearing striped pajamas. Pembe played the main character, Duck, who went around with her neck outstretched as if she was trying to touch the sky, and by doing so, giving the impression that she really was a duck."

"What if I said that I watched the play?"

"I'd say that I don't believe you. I'd say, 'No way.' 'Get out of here.' 'You're full of it.'"

"Good. Then dish it out and move on."

"What do you remember of the play? People write, people draw, people act . . . But what do others really get out of those creations? I mean, to what extent do they truly interiorize them, trying to make sure that nothing is lost?"

"Readers are ingrates."

My father's sister said that once. I don't want to misrepresent it—I'm not sure if she was specifically referring to readers of newspapers or readers of literature. She said that to boost my confidence when I was working on my book and she was editing it. She went on to say, "But you should know that readers are finicky and meddlesome, often disliking what they read. Still, they'll die one day, while a book goes on living forever." *She said that for me, as a means of clarification.*

"Either that, or they'll like it," I said. We were in her apartment at the time, and she was stretched out on her mustard-yellow sofa. She was always so beautiful. Not at first glance, but after you gazed at her for a while. She was alluring. Charming. "I imagine that it's so nice when a reader comes to like a writer . . . Something akin to feeling a motherly, fatherly, or sisterly love."

"Don't get carried away," she said.

"I'm not. I just think that's how it would be. How it *should* be."

She didn't try to dissuade me, deciding instead to let me go on thinking that way. It was an adolescent interregnum of sorts. If you opted to be stubborn with her, matters quickly hit a dead end. I'm lucky to have had her in my life. And my grandma too, until I was fifteen years old. Without them, I'm sure that everyone in my family would've tormented each other, including that shadow of a father of mine. As matters stand, I'm a lost child up in the treetops. If it hadn't been for them, who knows what would've become of me. But wait, hang on a second! Were they the ones who lost me? Or was it our state or society, perhaps even our city planners? Weren't they guilty as well? If you ask me, they were guiltier than all the rest. May God enact his punishment on them. In any case, they will be bound to their maker soon enough. It is always better to be bound to something you can't see.

"You're lost in thought again."

I'd been picking at the skin flaking from my dry lips, thinking of bygone times, but when Yunus spoke, I found myself whisked from the past back to the present.

"I'm waiting for your answer."

"One time, in your role as Death, you weren't wearing striped pajamas. Instead, you had on a long plaid robe of sorts. And you were wearing a skull mask."

"Sorry, Yunus, but for me that doesn't count as an answer. What did you really take from the play?"

If he had visited me at my home in Cihangir, we would've sat across from each other in just the same way. The branch upon which we were perched would've been life itself—our lives. I was listening intently to what Yunus was saying. I'm always careful about listening to what others have to say.

"Death wanted to take Duck's life and then carry her off to the realm of the dead."

"Yes."

"They became friends. But the sole purpose of that friendship was the taking of Duck's life."

"Yes, but what's the point? You're just summarizing the story."

"I wept when I watched the play. But I didn't want to cry in front of all those people, so I stood there with my head bowed, acting like I'd gotten something in my eye. Everyone was watching you. I mean, they were watching you and your friend playing Duck. The narrator . . ."

"Derin."

"She was standing behind some trees. She would read from the book to fill us in on the story. As she read, her expressions were too exaggerated, and it seemed like she couldn't catch her breath the whole time."

"So tell me, why did you cry?"

"Because Duck realized that certain things would cease to exist for her when she died. She said things like, 'The word "lake" will be bereft of me.'"

"Very good."

I couldn't stop myself—I started reciting lines from that play like I'd done two years earlier for a small audience among the trees that were still standing and thriving, bringing to life the dialogues that had moved Yunus so profoundly.

I looked up. Yunus was sitting there, just like he had sat under the trees that day. I went on a while, then paused, waiting for Yunus to snap out of his reverie, but he was still sitting there among the branches, gazing off into the distance as if he was watching something. I waved my hand in front of his face.

"Hello, is anyone home? Houston, please respond! Houston, we have a problem . . ."

Yunus suddenly leaned back a little as he awoke to the world around him.

"I have no further questions, Your Honor. The witness is all yours."

I laughed. We laughed together. Even if he looked like his thoughts were elsewhere, Yunus was always fully in the present moment. No one is as they appear to be.

"Actually, Death is a really important character in both the book and the play we put on, but he has very few lines. Didn't you get that impression?"

"No . . . Death is death. In my opinion, that is. Death paved the way for the expression of some very emotional statements."

"What else? What else do you remember?"

My greed for more, which drove me to ask, "What else, what else," was making Yunus tense, and I didn't blame him. I could see with my own eyes that he was as taut as a wire.

"It's such a shame that you're so obsessive. It's a shame for the sake of living, of staying alive. You never back down. Nor do you give in, or give up for that matter. You always want more. And in trying to get more, you go to pieces."

Ah, how right he was.

Pained, I looked away. I've done that ever since I was a child, whenever I feel embarrassed, ashamed, or weighed down by sadness. I can't bring myself to look anyone in the face at times like that.

"Try to relax a little," Yunus said. "We're all going to die in the end. It's true, however, that we can't go on living with such a mindset. In that play, you had a line that went something like: 'Delicate snowflakes were flitting through the air. Something had happened. Death looked at Duck. Duck wasn't breathing. She was lying there, completely still.'"

I picked up where he left off: "'Death reached down and smoothed out Duck's ruffled feathers, and then carried her down to the large river.'"

Yunus said, "I cried a lot at that point in the play, toward the end."

His eyes were full of tears as he spoke. I also started crying, but for very different reasons.

"Yunus . . . I'm not so innocent. I did something terrible. Because of me, people have died. I'm serious."

He was taken aback. His jaw dropped, and I noticed that he gripped the branch he was holding on to even more tightly. When he did so, he seemed to take on an even greener hue, becoming immersed even more deeply in the verdancy. He was green itself. He shifted uneasily, as though what I'd told him was too much to bear. As he did so, he didn't forget for a moment that he was in the treetops, and as he clutched a branch over his head, it bent, revealing the sky above. Clouds with tattered edges drifted aimlessly. Seeing the sky and those clouds offered a ray of hope. But did I myself have any hope?

25

STALKING

My mind is being torn apart. I'm going to pieces.

If I were writing that novel now, I'd write as if I was dreaming, because that's the only time we don't lie. I know, Özlem Hanım would say, "Now, where did you hear such a thing?"

As I lay in the stork's nest, dozing off while I gazed into my mirror, I thought, *Tomorrow's Monday!* But I no longer cared about Mondays, or any of the days of the week. I had propped Calvino's *The Baron in the Trees* against the side of the nest like a painting. A decor of sorts. And I was creating a new world for myself with clouds of dust and gas. Slowly, the crowds started withdrawing from the park. All the same, few people had ventured to my side of the park. My side. The damned side. Cemetery of the nameless.

My mind is resisting.

After Yunus left, I went and took a crap. If I were an inconsiderate person, I would've just crapped on top of the wall. It would've been easier. Later, when it dried out, I could've kicked it to the ground. And, of course, I would've told Yunus so that he wouldn't step on it. I no longer felt any shame around him. There was no need—he now knew all my dirty secrets.

When people found out about the huge lie my mother had been telling, she was devastated.

I was the inspiration for that lie. Or maybe it would be better to say that I served as a conduit for a certain discovery.

The year 2013 started off with a string of disasters. My grandma fell ill. My mother was in mourning because the doctor she'd loved had gotten married. I had started writing lyrics for rap songs, and although I sensed that I would suffer in the end, I refused to stay away from my co-conspirator.

At the time, I was keener on helping my mother than myself, as I feared that she would hit rock bottom again if I didn't do something. One day, the television was on. Don't think that's an irrelevant detail, because it was something on TV that inspired me. A huge lie that would drag my mother into misery.

Britney Spears.

I can almost hear you muttering, "You've got to be kidding me."

I'm not.

Yes, I said Britney Spears. The Britney we all know who sang "Womanizer." I'm not sure what you know about her, but most likely you've never heard that she lost a lot of weight by working with a Turkish dietician. After she lost her children, came unglued, shaved her head, and was diagnosed as being bipolar, Madonna kissed her on the lips and she was reborn.

She appeared on our television singing "Scream and Shout" with will.i.am.

"She's lost a lot of weight," I said. I think I said that intentionally, as a way of getting my mother's attention. "If you'd been the one who helped her get so thin, you'd be famous in no time."

I had succeeded.

My mother was like a woeful grouper staring down the shaft of a spearfishing gun. Where did that come from? I don't know—it just popped into my mind. When I was at prep school, they had us read an article about groupers. They live as males until a certain age, and then they become female. Or maybe it's the other way around. In any case, they get to experience what it's like to be both male and female. Apparently, they can only be caught via speargun, and there was this guy who explained that in the article. It all made me so sad that I couldn't read it to the end. Since they're not accustomed to being around people, they'll often swim right up to you out of curiosity, as if they were thinking, "What is this big thing here?" The speargunner may even talk to them and stroke their heads before launching a spear straight through them. In short, groupers are easily fooled. When my mother came upon those images of Britney on the television and was taken in by what I said, she was very much like a grouper.

I needed to feel loved. I needed dialogue, conversation. I Googled Britney on my iPad to find out more about her return to society, but I couldn't find out anything about her dietician. So, I thought, why couldn't the dietician who'd worked such wonders be a woman from Istanbul?

That was just the beginning.

With my help, my mother knitted her story of success knot by knot. Here's how it proceeded: My mother had supposedly gone to Los Angeles in order to hone her skills, and while she was there, destiny led her to Britney. Or maybe it led Britney to her. Or maybe their fates collided. I don't know, but it was something along those lines.

The Turkish woman who helped Britney lose weight.

How did Britney lose weight on a diet of Turkish cuisine?

In no time at all, my mother was invited on five television shows and she was interviewed by countless newspapers. The Britney diet became a smash hit.

"This is all great," my father's sister said, "but you've never been to Los Angeles. So, what gives?" Actually, she didn't say that, she snarled it. Why? Because she knew right off where such a story would land my mother. We were in the largest room in our place, which was the kitchen, and as always, whenever we talked about important, stressful things, we were standing, not sitting. My father's sister was smoking a cigarette next to the exhaust hood, which she'd turned on (normally, no one was allowed to smoke at our place).

Matters unfolded at breakneck speed.

My mother rented an office in Cihangir and started a website, and I helped her compile some pictures of her and Britney. Ultimately, that turned out to be our undoing, as the guy who created the images of my mother and Britney side by side through the miracle of Photoshop gave us up. I was going to say that he "gave up the ghost," which would've been much better. I wish that he'd died. So in the end, it came to light that the photos were fake. In any case, there were plenty of people who wanted to see my mother's balloon of fame pop, such as her old boss, that queen of dieticians. In summary, my mother's story of stardom was short lived. She toppled down from that peak of success. Rather, she was pushed down. Shoved down. Went ass over teakettle. She enjoyed three brief months of fame and then slipped into depression as spring was approaching Istanbul. Spring is coy in this city. It seems like it's coming and suddenly backs away, only to reappear like a gift. But let's not stir the pot of that issue, as it's been stirred enough. It really became a major embarrassment, to an extent I never imagined possible.

Britney made a clear statement on the matter of whether she'd lost weight on a diet of Turkish food.

How very, very clear!

During an interview, she said, "Not once did I ever work with a Turkish dietician."

The journalist pressed her further: "So, you didn't lose weight on a Turkish-style diet?"

"No," she said, a blank expression on her face. It almost seemed as if she was being forced to make that statement. She seemed insecure, completely unsure of herself. Her self-confidence in ruins. Her self-confidence a wad of gum stuck to the sidewalk. Britney, be careful where you step. She added, "To tell the truth, I've never even met a Turkish person."

The uppity reporter said, "Really!" and then gestured toward himself. "Well, you have now!"

Britney stepped out of her SUV as if she was climbing out of an eighteen-wheeler, slammed the heavy door, and gave the cameras a phony wave and lifeless smile, saying, "Bye, see you again!" as she clomped off in her Havaianas flip-flops. She must've been in LA at the time. That hot, scorched city. The reporter turned to the camera and said, "Well, there you have it, ladies and gentlemen. That Turkish dietician who claimed to have helped Britney Spears lose weight has been exposed as a liar."

A photograph of my mother suddenly appeared on the screen. A photo that she'd never liked. But in the end, what difference did it make? She'd been shamed in front of the whole country.

"It's over," she moaned. "I'm ruined."

That was the first time I saw someone really bottom out. I watched someone—what's more, my own mother—go to pieces before my very eyes. She cried, hiccupping strangely. Or rather, she tried to cry. Her blood pressure soared and fell and soared like the dial of a bewildered scale, unsure of where to level off.

My mother fell so ill that eventually she had to be hospitalized.

My grandma said, "What else would you expect?" She hadn't yet been laid up in the hospital, even though she was convinced that her liver was little more than a firebrick, but thanks to her daughter-in-law, soon she too wound up in the hospital, not knowing that she had so little time left.

Sedatives, tranquilizers, fits of crying that couldn't be stopped.

"What happened to this poor lady?"

"My dear nurse, she screwed her life with a donkey prick—that's what happened."

You couldn't have expected anything else from my grandma, sitting by my mother's bedside.

I came across other reports about the Britney incident.

Such as when I was having some soup at Lades one day. Most likely, the denizens of Beyoğlu wouldn't have even considered the possibility that I was somehow connected to that whole business as they slurped up their soup. Life's strange, isn't it? The person who that cockmouthed reporter defamed and brought to ruin was none other than my mother, and she was now hooked up to a cocktail of sedatives at Medipol Hospital under the sponsorship of my aunt Hülya, as my mother's insurance didn't cover mental breakdowns.

And I was the one who'd given her the idea. Between news clips, the TV station served up as an appetizer the Britney video that had inspired the both of us, the one with will.i.am and Britney, bitch.

That's so Britney. Britney bitch. What harm would it have done if you'd brushed aside the Turkish journalist who was following you around? Couldn't you have just misunderstood that birdbrain's English and replied, "I really like Turkish food"? Or merely replied, Britney-style, with an "Oh yeah!"

I completely lost it. But not in public—only after I'd left Lades and met up with Derin and Pembe. I think that was the first time I cried in front of them.

Afterward, everything happened so quickly . . . I was crying nonstop. My mother got out of the hospital, whereupon my grandma was admitted, and we lost her soon after that. I threw myself into rap and then that asshole threw himself at me. After all those calamities, which happened one after the other, as I was having dinner at a small neighborhood restaurant with a levelheaded maturity far beyond my years, that tree-hating politician said on TV, "It's final. We've made our decision. Do whatever you want, but we're not backing down." You know what followed.

After Yunus had left and I was getting ready to slowly close the curtains of my mind, someone showed up at the foot of my tree like a wounded animal. It was a young man. And he really was like a wounded animal. Like a gazelle. As if he'd been shot. He sat down at the bottom of the laurel tree as if he was collapsing, falling, unable to catch his breath. I saw it all because I'd been intently peering down through the gaps in the stork's nest. What else could I do? It was impossible for me to pull my gaze away from the world below. As soon as that scrawny young man—he may have been a little older than me—leaned his back against the smooth bark of the tree, he pulled out a cheap MP3 player. When he wiped his bony, swarthy wrist across his eyes, I realized that he was crying, and then I heard the muffled sound of music.

I'd heard bits of the song, but I'd never listened to it in its entirety. The man singing the song had a deep, throaty voice. Was it Ferdi Tayfur? As if he was saying, "And you, Brutus?" he sang, "And you, Leyla?" What had Leyla done? Was everyone in the world double-crossing each other? I'd never double-crossed anyone. Just then, his phone rang and he answered, explaining where he was and how to get there. I ascertained precisely where I was in the world. Ascertaining is a matter of momentous import; is it not, Grandma :)

"What made you think it would be a good idea to put smiley faces in place of question marks?"

Ah, where were we, Özlem Hanım? I've missed you. Everyone in the classroom cringed when she asked that question. "So, a smiley face instead of a question mark . . . Do you think it bodes well that emojis are replacing punctuation?" Yet again, the text penned by the aggrieved party of the writing competition was subjected to scathing attacks with the intent to fuck it over even more thoroughly. The situation had reached the point where I could no longer bring myself to say anything in reply. I'd given up. Surrendered. At times like that, however, it is the other party who should be giving up.

Anyways, let's move on.

The friend whom he had called found the broken-down fellow at the foot of my tree. Plopping down beside him, he asked, "What's the matter, man? Why're you crying?"

At first, I assumed it was girl trouble. I suppose it was the doleful music he was listening to that made me think that way. But it turned out that wasn't the case at all. His papers had arrived, and he was being summoned for military service. That's why the poor guy was bawling his eyes out like a child.

The friend asked, "Are you scared or something?" I got the impression that he was more interested in giving his pal an earful than offering any consolation.

He scoffed. "Who's scared of going into the military?" If you ask me, he was scared.

His friend surprised me by saying, "I wouldn't blame you if you were. People die left and right doing their service." He won a place in my heart when he said in all sincerity, "I'd be scared to death if I were in your position."

Then the boy confessed what was really bothering him: "Who's going to look after my mom when I'm gone?"

His friend fell silent, making it apparent that he wasn't going to take up the responsibility. It didn't take long for me to realize that the problem came down to money—or a lack thereof.

"When you do your service, they give you a kind of salary . . . You can send that to your mom. That's what everyone does. When you're there, you'll have a place to stay and food to eat, so you won't need any money."

"Is that really how it works?"

"We can find out. Didn't you ask?"

He made a sound like the cluck of a bird, meaning no.

I'd been mistaken—the guy hadn't immediately sat down beside his crying friend. Rather, he was kneeling down in front of him, with a hand on his shoulder. Only later did he sit down.

"Don't you worry about your mom," he said. "Just make sure you make it back here in one piece. Keep your mind clear, and focus on coming home. Doing your military service is a real pain. Look, it's a bit embarrassing to say that out loud, but that's how it is . . ."

Both of them, it seemed, were local doormen. After a while they settled into conversation, talking about what they'd moved that day, from whence to where and how, who they'd met, and how much money they'd made in tips and wages. So, I mused, despite their skinny frames, they made a living through sheer muscle power. I wondered how such people could carry the weight of the world on their shoulders, and I considered my own position: I'd ended up where I was because it was too much for me to bear—high up in the treetops, I was out of reach of such burdens.

I noticed that the song "And You, Leyla?" started playing again. Maybe it had already been playing over and over, or perhaps it was just a never-ending song.

The two friends went on talking as the music played.

"Who knows, maybe you'll see one of the enemies and shoot at them."

I couldn't help but wonder: Who was that enemy he mentioned? The answer to my question was lodged in the question that followed. Wait, here it comes: "How could someone who speaks the same language be my enemy? Is the Kurd Rıza our enemy now?"

"He's different."

"Why's he different but the others are our enemy?"

"If you want my opinion, I think every Kurd is our enemy. Doesn't he say that the PKK is this or that, not doing anything wrong? Doesn't he pin the blame on others, saying the government is oppressing the Kurds?"

"Do they have to be killed?"

His friend lit a cigarette.

"Do they have to be killed?"

The smoke from his cigarette drifted up into my nostrils.

"Do they have to be killed?"

Both of them had close-cropped hair, almost shaved, and their clothes were worn thin. I could see their tattered shoes. It was obvious that they were wearing clothes that had been passed down to them. Clothes that were too big, cinched and tucked in to make them fit.

The friend apparently thought the only solution was to change the subject.

"Before you go, we'll take you to the brothel. As you know, that's the way things are done."

But the boy didn't seem to have the strength or desire to take comfort, have fun, or blow off some steam with a trip to the brothel. All his energy had been spent bearing the weight of the world, and his impoverished mother occupied his thoughts, stuck there as if with a safety pin. That was it, and nothing more. The day came to a close with their murmuring conversation. As I settled into the nest, one of them said, "I just heard a weird crackling sound," and they got up to leave, but they didn't know that the sound had come from above or that there was a person up there, the Girl in the Tree, or that the girl had given up on fighting and was now living in the treetops. How could they have known? If it had been you, would you have known?

26

AN ERROR HAS OCCURRED: APOLOGIES FOR THE INCONVENIENCE

Would you believe me if I told you that the same thing happened again? Most likely, you'd ask, "What's this about?" If you're a frank person— we might even say judgmental—you could even sneer, "But don't the same things keep happening?" So, to all those sneerers, I'd reply, "What else could happen up in the treetops?" Yes, I'd really stick it to you. As Pembe would've said, "Put a lid on it." Is the lid shut? Sealed up good, snapped tight?

People slip off into the bushes to escape their fears. Take side roads. Veer onto wildly steep paths that lead to the sea. That's exactly what I did, because dawn had broken, or it was about to break, and there was the same strangeness in the air. A stiltedness. I sensed it deep down as I opened my eyes. Still, that time, I knew as I looked out onto the world that it was a dream. Another one of the tricks my mind played on me. That sneaky mind of mine . . .

So, as I was saying, everything was buried in snow.

Again?

Yet again.

But I felt a deeper sense of peace. A sense of peace in the very marrow of my bones. I told you earlier about that morning when I poked my head out of my tent in Gezi. It was just like that. By the way, one of the girls at school had been spreading lies about me, saying that I was never actually in Gezi. Gossip is like an insect, scuttling around as fast as a cockroach. It glistens, and you feel repulsed when you happen to come across it. People who enjoy clicking their tongues are often gossipers. For them, it's as enjoyable as popping their gum. But they're sly about it, acting as though what they're doing isn't really gossiping. No, it's just that you're such a fascinating person, they simply can't get their fill of gabbing about you and your life. I knew that the biggest gossiper at our school was always going around saying things about me. Which is understandable because, after all, I was pretty interesting. As Derin once grudgingly confessed, "There's your mom, your grandma, the rapper, everything that happened at the park . . ." There's no need to go on and on, but I could also add my aunt Hülya, my father, and my other aunt, as well as much, much more to the list.

All the same, in those days I remember asking, "What happened in the end? My grandma got sick, my mother fell prey to what we could call an 'occupational accident,' the story of my relationship with the rapper was anything but exceptional, and as for the park, weren't we all there together?"

I don't have enough fingers on my hands to count all the issues, but it became clear that there was a general sense of unease about my very existence. It was chronic. One day, I stumbled upon that Gossip Queen in the school bathroom, where Pembe had once stood in front of her, unbuttoning her blouse with the audacity of Joan of Arc and saying, "I didn't get a boob job! If you don't believe me, look for yourself!" Open parenthesis, at this point, Pembe had indeed gotten silicone implants, but they looked so natural that she had no qualms about lying about the fact, close parenthesis.

When I saw the gossiper, I blurted, "What's the deal with you going around saying that I wasn't at the park?" The truth of the matter, however, is that I didn't snap at or try to corner her, much less get in her face.

As confident as could be, she replied, "Well, it's true. You weren't there."

One of her cronies flushed the toilet in another stall and stepped out, which meant I wasn't alone with her. In fact, I was the one who was alone. Unlike our group of three, there were four of them. Soon after, the other two girls emerged from adjoining stalls, but it didn't escape my attention that they didn't bother to flush.

"I *was* there," I said, flushing my own toilet with a flourish of self-confidence.

"You're lying."

She had these strangely curving lips that you couldn't get enough of looking at. Like a flower, like rose petals. And they were always glistening with lip gloss. I hadn't yet come to understand that, in some situations, the best thing to do is not to fight but rather to back down. While for a moment I did consider saying, "Yeah, whatever," and walking away, if we'd done that at the park, those trees wouldn't be there to greet us and those barracks would've been built right in the heart of our country. Because we held out, people saw what it means to resist and they found the courage to take up the cause too. They discovered the meaning of standing up for yourself, as we stood up for our way of life and the trees. At first, they had no intention of learning anything from us, but in the end, that's precisely what happened.

One of the girls in the group lunged and punched me in the eye. That was the last thing I was expecting. So there I was, reeling from the blow, even though I hadn't said anything to bring it on. The Gossip Queen didn't even bother doing it herself.

They later offered up a defense for their actions in the headmaster's office. Which, of course, was a pack of lies. Grandma, I was infirm of purpose that day. "Infirm," I said. After "desire," that is the bitterest six-letter word in the language. My eye was throbbing so badly that I thought it might pop right out of its socket. It had already started swelling up. When the nurse came rushing in, the gravity of the situation became apparent when I pulled my hand away from my eye, and her exclamation of surprise ensured that I was at least partly in the right.

That nurse had been working at the school for years, and I'm sure she'd seen all kinds of things, but even she was surprised by the sight of my face, as she'd probably never come across something of the like at such a "proper" French school.

At that moment, who should walk into the office but another one of our fabulous literature teachers, Melike Hanım. It's just like the old saying goes—right, Grandma? "The blind man asked God for an eye, and God gave him two."

The end result: thanks to Melike Hanım's confirmation of certain facts, the situation turned in my favor, which was only just. She explained that the Gossip Queen's fondness for spreading rumors had gotten her friends into no small amount of trouble. In the process, she may have stolen the limelight from the directress of the school, but justice was served. "This shouldn't be taken lightly," she added. "Just look at the poor girl's face."

"I have proof," I said proudly, "that what she's been saying about me is nothing but lies and slander."

She asked, "Sweetie, what slander are you talking about?"

Brushing aside the headmaster's exclamation "You girls carry around your phones at school?!"—in fact what I said was, "I always keep it on silent mode"—I started showing them the pictures on my phone.

Thanks to the iPhone 5 that my aunt had given to me on my birthday, everything came to light, including our performances of *Duck, Death and the Tulip*. In fact, there really wasn't a problem. What I mean to say is that, if I hadn't been punched in the eye, there wouldn't have been a problem. While there was a bit of an uproar when the mother of the girl who clobbered me showed up at the school and said, "THAT girl is the problem. My daughter didn't mean to get violent"—yeah, right!—ultimately, she was suspended and then expelled when my aunt stepped in and threw her weight around.

You see, my aunt came to the school for my sake.

I can remember it as if it was yesterday because it was New Year's Eve.

We were in the courtyard. It was snowing, and we were all rather excited about the fact that we'd enter the New Year on a snowy night. Suffice to say that my aunt was wearing a pair of her invariably pristine Isabel Marant boots, an exquisite Vivienne Westwood coat, perfectly snug Diesel jeans, and a beige Massimo Dutti sweater that gracefully accentuated the swaying of her breasts, not to mention the honey-blond highlights in her hair. A simplicity and beauty that didn't need to clamor for attention. That's the allure she possessed, which I mentioned before. She was a beautiful woman, and she was even more beautiful that day because she showed up at the school for me. Gazing at my bandaged eye with pity, she took my face in her hands—a face that, in her words, was as "gaunt as a skull"—and tried to offer me a ray of hope: "Next year is going to bring us happiness and joy."

However, starting from that sliver of 2013, the year 2014 went through with its plan of wreaking havoc: my aunt had been fired from the newspaper that very day. At the time, she seemed to take it in stride, but as I suggested earlier, I don't think that was the case at all. After knocking back two glasses of whiskey at the bar of the Divan Hotel, she calmed down to a certain extent and went to my school. The fact that she got fired, which indeed was difficult for her to accept, would have to wait until evening for further discussion. She had planned on meeting her co-workers from the evening paper at the *meyhane* Asmalı Cavit or, if not there, at Yakup. I asked, "Is it a farewell dinner?" Yet again her eyes flashed like diamonds. She stroked my face with a soft hand and replied, "Let's say it's a sending-off celebration."

Snowflakes were falling on her hair, which would never again be pampered with such natural highlights, as the hairdresser who had done them was quite expensive. Initially, she thought she'd be able to get by with her severance pay if she spent it carefully, but going to EBİL Hair & Beyond in Bebek was going to be out of the question, as was being a journalist again.

What else was there?

We stood there as the snowflakes drifted down, gently swirled by the wind. Who knows, perhaps we're still standing there on that street. Contrary to what we generally think, maybe time doesn't simply proceed forward in a linear fashion. It could even be something that is trapped within itself.

After my aunt left, Pembe and Derin showed up. They were wearing North Face jackets, as if the things were passed out for free by the Red Crescent aid society. Because it was snowing in the courtyard, we had one of those moments of adolescent joy, throwing our arms around each other and jumping up and down. Then we turned our faces skyward and opened our mouths as the thick flakes of snow kept coming down. The anti-riot trucks and tear gas hadn't been able to dampen our joy. But that was it, and nothing more. Everything was quietly changing deep down, but we were completely blind to that fact.

As a snowflake that had landed on my nose started to melt, it become one with a tear that was rolling down my cheek. Now we've moved forward in time, and I'm making it snow for you on September 28. Why didn't that dream ever come to an end? Annoyed by that sense of unease, I shifted in the stork's nest. The park really was buried in snow. I could say that a thousand times because it was true. Everyone has a memory of a moment in which they would like to remain forever. No past, no future. Just that moment. The world is nothing more than a husk out there, beyond us, and yet it acts like a husk, protecting us and embracing us with all our faults. And that world is buried in snow.

My mind is sound. I have not gone mad.

I'm not saying that I don't have any mental problems, but who of us doesn't? Can we say that one person is mentally healthier than another? I'm quite certain that the moment in which I found myself was a dream and that it was not real. As I said, I remember what reality was until that day. Then the sickness in my mind suddenly leapt into my neurons and everything became complicated. But just for a moment. At least, that's my opinion on the matter.

At one point, I heard cheerful cries coming from the direction of the park, and soon after, two girls dressed in blue appeared among the trees. They may have been as old as me, but their outfits made them look like overgrown little girls. As they went on with their snowball fight, they nearly came up to the foot of the wall. They were panting, and I could see their heaving chests, as well as the steam of their breath. As you may have guessed, it was Derin and Pembe. Before I go on to describe their matching outfits, I should mention something: just that year, they had dressed up as the twin girls in *The Shining* at a costume party and won a prize. If you haven't heard of the movie, it's a horror flick. Set in a hotel. A kid on a tricycle. Dead girls. Jack Nicholson. An ax. A bathroom door. The kid Danny, a medium who talks with his fingers.

In trying to look like the twins who confront Danny, Derin and Pembe had braided their hair and put on dresses that were tied around the waist, and they were wearing knee-high white socks. I think it was pure genius. Not the movie and the book it was based on, but their choice of costumes. For the party, I had dressed up like Amy, and as a result, I was one of twelve other Amys. But there was a difference—I had tattoos. Exactly the same as the ones that Amy had.

"How did you get those tattoos done?"

"You're not even eighteen yet!"

"Didn't the tattooist ask for a letter of permission from your mom?"

"The tattooist was a loaded addict who didn't give a damn if someone had their parents' permission or not. He was totally out of it."

In a nutshell: thanks to my tattoos, I edged close to the lead at the costume party. While it was true that my tattoos were a bit oily and hazy under a layer of Bepanthol, so be it. They were there, and they were real. Hold on to your hat, there's more: there was a photograph of the three of us, with me standing between the twins from *The Shining*, my arms over their shoulders, and it was published in the gossip supplement of the newspaper *Hürriyet* with the heading: "High School Youths Get Dressed Up."

That pair who'd been having the snowball fight were now standing under my tree asking, "Hey, what are you doing up there?"

The way they asked made it seem like they knew who I was.

"Did you forget about me?"

I wasn't hesitant at all about revealing myself up in the tree, leaning out over the edge of the nest where I'd been hiding, nor was I shy about speaking to them. All the same, they looked at me blankly, just as the twins looked at Danny as he pedaled his tricycle around inside the hotel. Just as they'd done to me at the costume party.

"We don't even know who you are."

They said that at exactly the same time. But I woke up before I had time to remind them what my name was. A beam of light that had found its way through the dense branches of the laurel tree stabbed straight into my eyes like a sword shot forth from the sun. I knew I had to believe that it was only a dream.

27

ARE YOU SURE YOU WANT TO DELETE THIS FILE?

Plane, oak, beech, poplar, silver birch, horse chestnut, alder, dog-wood, cotoneaster, cedar, pine, eucalyptus. That day I did something rather out of the ordinary: I counted all the trees in the park, one by one. For the first time since we'd stayed up until dawn on the roof of the Tiled Pavilion, I ventured far from my stork's nest, my laurel, my first love the plane tree, the eucalyptus that reached out to me with its silky branches, and the pine tree, whose cones filled my belly with their nuts. I now had full confidence in my strength. Even when doing the famous surfing move while slacklining, I didn't ever come close to plummeting to the ground. I was flexible. My sense of balance couldn't have been better. Unbalanced in mind, but balanced in body. Accepting yourself for what you are has its merits. At least, it should.

Gülhane was very different from Maçka Park. Even since Gezi, it had changed. Although it was home to some of the most splendorous trees in all of Istanbul, and in times past had been the palace's magnificent garden, it was now refuge for the lost and losers of the city. The despairing, the downcast, the flawed, and people who'd lost their aims and goals in life went there, along with the embittered, the penniless, the wretched, the lonely, and those who were waiting and those who were fleeing from something. People went there with envelopes containing X-rays from the Çapa, Cerrahpaşa, and Haseki hospitals as if the photographs were decrees of death, along with others who had found out that cancer was ripping through their bodies like wildfire. The streetcar, which passed by with a bloodcurdling screech, now deposited at the park's gates all the deadbeats of the city, even though its capacity to take them in had already long been filled. The trees were tall, yet the visitors were too weary and worn out to even raise their heads to look up at them. After a while, I came to realize that I could make my way through the trees without having to fear that I'd be spotted. One particularly destitute-looking man did, in fact, see me. He was quickly walking toward the gate that led to the street where the streetcar passed by, and he didn't even stop to marvel at the strangeness of the scene he'd witnessed. Hardly taking his eyes from his destination, he merely glanced back and then proceeded on his way. I presumed that he was a bit simpleminded, so hurt that he was blind to the world around him, or crazy. Or all three.

Aside from that, nothing happened.

Thanks to my red nylon slacklining strap and turnbuckles, I was free to roam the park as I pleased, which helped me pull myself together. I was stronger up there than I'd been in the world below, but most importantly, my expeditions drove from my thoughts—even if only a little—that snowy dream I'd had about Pembe and Derin.

But a question remained: How far could I mentally distance myself from them? It was as if they'd completely burned up and their ashes had been shoved down my throat, and, as a result, the two of them had taken over my body as their own and I couldn't cast them out. I even had a dream about that. Or should I call it a nightmare?

After the explosion, their social media accounts were trashed. I didn't tell you that story about them dressing up as the twins in *The Shining* or me going to the costume party dressed as Amy for nothing. Later, the tabloids killed me as well, but that's another story for another time. And let's not forget about the teacher who'd been fired: piss, penis, crap, vagina . . . Melike Hanım later saw me in the neighborhood of Beşiktaş and threw her arms around me, saying, "I thought that you'd gone with your friends. I thought you'd been killed too."

"No, I didn't go."

"How come?"

If you recall, my aunt had asked me the same question, since she knew I'd been planning on taking part in the trip. We met up with a group of people we'd come across during Gezi (they were the ones making posts about the trip on Facebook) at Külüstür Pub in Beşiktaş. Beforehand, we'd been exchanging messages with them, since we wanted to go along. But were the "Shot-Put Girls" of Dame de Sion just wrapped up in the excitement of it all or were their intentions sincere? I'd thought that we were going to be put to the test, but I was wrong. Anyone who wanted to join was welcome. They were worried, however, about certain "leaks" they'd heard about.

"What kind of leaks?"

"The kind made by citizen informants."

One of the guys in the group said that. He was from the town of Samsun on the Black Sea coast and was studying sociology in Istanbul.

"We want to go there and help them create a life for themselves that will give us hope."

"We want to be useful."

"After all, we were part of the Gezi protests. Sometimes we laughed, and sometimes we paid the price for our actions through suffering and loss. For example, my aunt—she's a journalist—lost her job."

A guy who was wearing a T-shirt with a picture of Ali İsmail, who had been killed during the protests, asked, "Which newspaper?" I told him. And of course, I added, "But my aunt is all about freedom and democracy. She's a really dedicated woman."

"I know, I know. Your aunt wrote some great pieces in the mainstream media."

Later, the girls told me that I grinned from ear to ear when he said that.

We ordered another round of small glasses of beer, because when you order a big glass, the beer gets warm. It was the beginning of July, and the date for the trip was drawing near. After we left the pub, we talked in detail about what we were going to take to the kids out east. There was going to be a meeting, and we talked about the day, the hour, the agenda . . .

From Beşiktaş we headed up to Akaretler along the very same street where we'd protested a few years ago. In those days, we'd Snapchatted, tweeted, and Facebooked our experiences. Was there a form of social media we hadn't used? Now we were walking up the steep road as if we were trudging along the surface of the moon. It felt as though our backpacks were trying to pull us back down the hill.

"Why are we going? For that matter, why are we going with them? Are we just high school chicks in their eyes? Did the fact that we said we wanted to go confuse them? Or is it just me who got that impression? Doing things like this is what they're all about. It's their life. Are we really like them?"

We were going to Derin's place in Nişantaşı. Her family lived in a tiny apartment on a lane below Ihlamur Street. Her mother gathered up the garbage from the neighboring apartment buildings and mopped their stairs. As for her father, you already know about him. Their only success in life was their daughter Derin, who had an older sister, but there's no need to dwell on her. For some reason, what I'd said had gotten on Derin's nerves: "What the hell are you talking about?"

"People are holding out against the government in a part of the country we hardly even knew existed. Sure, they gave us hope. We didn't want their city to fall to the state's troops. We wanted them to resist, just like we'd done in Gezi. But their situation is different. Are we like them? I mean, do we have the same profile? If we go, won't we be doing them an injustice? This isn't a costume party. It's nothing like setting up a tent in Gezi Park, and we can't think of it as something that will lighten the burden on our consciences. It's not like we can pop into H&M and pick up some green Peshmerga camouflage to wear to school. If you've got a bit of pluck, you could sport some khakis and a kaffiyeh, but you know as well as me that, in this damn country, even students wearing the Kurdish *pushi* have been arrested. It's not like that for those organizers. They're always there, wholeheartedly. It's their life. But our place is here."

"This isn't about us versus them. We're not after some idea of marginality."

"Of course not, because we're already marginalized as it is. But their issues are different, nothing like ours. Do you see what I'm saying?"

"No, because you're not making any sense!"

Derin glared at me, her eyes flashing fire. "We're not going just because we're bored and want to kill some time."

"If we hadn't joined that Facebook group, would we know anything about any of this?"

Derin was getting more and more annoyed. "But we did join it and now we know. End of story, dot.com. Why can't you see us as being part of their struggle? Can't we be an exception?"

"You're asking me?"

"No, I'm asking your mom! Weren't you saying that this is their Gezi?"

"Yeah."

"Well then, what's your problem?!"

"Did you forget that we had other plans? Then this came along."

"Now the problem is becoming clearer."

Is it, Houston? Is the problem clear now? What they were calling a "problem" was the fact that we'd made plans to go on vacation together. Yes, go on vacation. As simple as that. I was going on vacation for the first time in my life. After nearly drowning in a hotel pool when I was three years old and taking one middle-school summer trip, I was going to have a real vacation, and I'd been ecstatic about it. If that trip to the eastern part of the country had been scheduled for any other time, I would've been more than happy to go, but now it was taking the place of our holiday, for which we'd been prepared. Passports, check. Visas, check. Our plan was to go to Greece. First by a bus bound for Thessaloniki, and we would get off along the way. Chalcidice, here we come! A group of people we'd met at Gezi had made such a trip, and we planned on following the same route. We were going to be real tourists with our backpacks and tent. I'd been blown away by the pics they'd posted on Insta. They were what had given me the idea of taking such a holiday. It was as if we were going to be journeying to a piece of heaven. Deep-blue sea, umbrellas opened to the glass-like sky, worldly worries sunk beneath the waters, all kinds of people having a good time. Even though there was a note attached that read "No filter, no Photoshop!" the pics were like paintings. But in the end, that dream of a vacation had been wrenched from my grasp. In its place there was a new plan of going to a desert. I was afraid I'd be found out for thinking that way, as I really wasn't a cold or uncaring person. It was just that the clash of dates had dashed my hopes. Instead of getting on a bus bound for the most desolate place in the country, I wanted to go to heaven. I'd say to myself, "We can go another time and take those toys to the kids there ourselves. Wouldn't that work?"

"Stop being ridiculous!"

When Derin snapped at me like that, I flew into a rage. Well, that may not be entirely true. I'd already wilted under her smoldering gaze, but all the same, I was giving it my all to express myself in the clearest terms.

We arrived at her place. There was an old-fashioned tapestry hanging on the living room wall, but as I mentioned before, the place was literally spotless. In that home, not a speck of dust drifted through the air, and if such a speck dared to commit such an abuse, a broad array of precautions had been put into place to lock onto it with a radar of cleanliness and zap it into nonexistence. I resigned myself to saying, "If that's how you feel, you guys can go ahead without me." I felt like an undesired speck of dust as I spoke those words.

But after that day, everything clicked into place. No, that wasn't yet another reference to a university exam question about idioms. I wasn't going with them, and that was that.

28

Undo

Do you also get the impression that the day I sent off my friends in Kadıköy was filled with confusion? Indeed it was, because such a day had never occurred before. At least, not in my life. On that day at that hour, Derin and Pembe with their highlights in their hair got on the bus and left. I could just say we weren't on good terms at the time, but in fact we parted in anger. Perhaps I'd sensed deep down that something was amiss. In one of my dreams about my grandma, she offered such an explanation. I hadn't been able to bring myself to tell my friends about the feeling of unease that had been haunting me. That feeling that had been eating me up inside eventually morphed into regret. Why hadn't I tried harder to dissuade them from going? I became so obsessed with that idea that I even considered ratting out my friends to the police department, which has a web page for such things.

After the incident, my aunt opened two bottles of beer, one for me and one for her. I suppose she was thinking that I needed to open up and talk about my feelings. Or that I needed to let myself fall apart. I confessed to her that I felt guilty about not trying to convince Pembe and Derin not to go.

She got angry with me.

Ranting, I said, "But I didn't do it. I couldn't. I didn't tip them off. I didn't write anything on the police department's Facebook page." But it was too late.

My aunt chided me for even considering such a thing, and her rebuke weighed on me as heavily as the crime itself. Perhaps that itself *was* the crime. That's how it should have been in this country of ours, for thought is a crime. People can be hauled in by the police for believing in certain ideas. But, as with my situation, that changes according to your thoughts on certain matters.

"Even thinking about tipping off the police is as bad as doing it."

"I know, but I didn't do it!"

That's when my aunt said something that was like a slap across the face: "Since when did you become so morally corrupt?"

If my grandma had been there, she would've said, "She's not corrupt. You whore, stop trying to take out the anger you feel for other people on the poor girl!" But I didn't say anything. I bit my tongue. Falling from grace in my aunt's eyes in such an unfair way was like having a cluster bomb dropped on me. I'm ashamed to make such a comparison here, but that's how it was. I died at that moment.

I wish that I'd been with Pembe and Derin so that I could've died with them. In all honesty, I wasn't the one who identified their bodies by the highlights in their hair. But the ferry incident was real, and I really did get into an argument with that guy. We didn't scuffle or end up at the police station—I made those parts up—but we would have if that crew member hadn't pulled us apart. Everything else that followed is true.

When a heart opens up before you like a book, bursting into leaf as if it were a tree, you can stumble upon all humanity's emotions there, in its every nook and cranny. All those emotions that have been hidden away. It is human nature to try to hide our shame from others. Even from ourselves, for that matter. For people like me who openly air their grievances and confess to their wrongdoings, it's the same as saying, "Dig my grave very deep." That and nothing more.

29

SELECT A PHOTOGRAPH

There are so many things to which I should dedicate my life. All the same, for mysterious reasons, I'm ill and filled with sadness. I mean, that's how I was in the past. Now, I'm breathless. Because I've been making my way around the park branch by branch, because I've been coming to terms with my shame and the troubles I've gotten into as a result of my outspokenness, click click click. Don't be surprised that clicking has taken the place of complaining. Why? Because when you slide your finger across your timeline, it goes "click click click." It's quite natural that clicking should usurp complaining.

So, let's continue, shall we?

I may have even said to my aunt, "But I'm still just a child."

To which she possibly replied, "Yes, when it serves your purposes!"

There's this quote, but I can't remember who wrote it, forgive me: "My desires consist of nothing more than a humble village house with a tree in the yard, and six or seven of my enemies hanging from its branches." Now I remember—it was Heinrich Heine who said that. Why am I bringing this up now? Because they were unfair to me. You think they were unfair, right? I wasn't looking for support or someone to take up my cause. I'm just asking . . . As if! Dumbasses are always "just asking." So don't get me wrong: I have no intention of doing that.

When I returned, I saw that Yunus was waiting for me on the top of the wall. When I saw him like that, I was reminded of the Little

Prince sleeping on top of the planet. Before he had a chance to ask me anything, I said, "I was out counting the trees in the park."

"If you keep going out on these excursions, they'll catch on to us."

"You're saying that just as I've mustered the courage to go out into the world, like the Little Prince, who was the ruler of the world and the universe . . . Now that you can comfortably hang out on the top of this wall and in the branches of the trees."

"This isn't about me."

"I know, it's all been about me. That's exactly why I'm here. So as *not* to be the issue at hand. At least, not down in the world below."

That was perhaps the first time we got upset with each other. Rather, I was upset with him. But Yunus was so kindhearted that he merely looked at me, a gentle expression on his face. He truly could have been the Little Prince.

"Today's your birthday, right? This is no day for pouting."

"How did you know it's my birthday?"

"Because I found you."

"It would seem so. I'm standing right here, aren't I?"

"I mean, I found you on the Internet."

"How? I never told you my name."

"I know Derin's and Pembe's names. And I know that you all studied at Notre Dame de Sion."

"So, you found their accounts, and I was one of the people following them. Clever!"

"But you didn't use your real name."

"Of course not."

"You used a fake name."

"Yep. It's called a username."

"I don't know much about that kind of thing. But I was hoping that the date for your birthday was real. I'd like it to be. Whether it is or not, I'd like to celebrate your birthday with you tonight."

"The thirtieth of September. That's right."

"Happy birthday, sweetie."

We hugged. We kissed. He gave me a present. I took my present. Excitedly I opened it. He'd gotten me a red scarf. I tied it around my neck.

"Thank you."

"I hope you like it. You're blushing."

He'd also brought along dinner for us. We found a secluded spot and sat down. There was a full moon. It was so close that we could've reached out and touched it.

"Wasn't there a full moon just a few days ago?"

"Who knows? Maybe it became full again tonight for us."

"The other day it was snowing. The park was covered in snow."

"Was it a dream?"

"At first it was real, but then it turned into a dream. As if they'd suddenly decided that what I'd seen should be a dream."

"Don't let it get to you. Sometimes that happens."

"Indeed it does."

Yunus laid out the food he'd brought, and after checking to make sure that no one could see us, he lit a small candle, the crowning touch to our dinner. Let me explain exactly where we were perched so you won't find our boldness that night out of place. There was an area where the branches of the horse chestnut tree curved out over the wall, creating an arch of sorts, and the branches of the silver birch below were tightly interwoven like a net. I'm not exaggerating—they looked just like a net, after growing ever closer together over the years, interlacing. At that point along its length, the wall became one with the trees and broadened out, and the branches of the horse chestnut were like a dome over our heads. In every way it was as if the ideal of the warm, cozy home—a Hobbit home, if you will—had come into being in that very spot. As Yunus lit the candle, illuminating the small spread laid out before us, I wanted to make that place our home so much that I took the scarf off and hung it from a branch so it could be our curtain.

Yunus said, "Don't worry, no one can see us here . . ."

Then, after a pause, he turned his attention to the food. Let me list what he'd brought for my birthday dinner. There was fried chicken. Yes, that's right: fried chicken. Fried a golden brown and still warm. Roasted eggplant puree. White sandwich bread. And ginger ale. He'd gotten it all from the hotel. The chicken was from room 22, the order for its occupants having been incorrectly entered. When the bellboy writes down "chicken" instead of "roast lamb with artichoke"—that's our boon, bon appétit! As for the eggplant puree, it had already been cooked up in a big pot for the *beğendeli kebap*. There was always bread, and ginger ale was easy to get.

"The only thing I couldn't manage to get," he said, "was a cake."

Before I could say, "That's okay," I saw that he was taking some chocolate bars out of his jacket pocket. He forgot to bring plastic cutlery, but that didn't matter because we managed to get that fine cuisine down just fine using a pair of stout twigs, which I cut and pared down to chopsticks. After becoming accustomed to gripping the bark of trees, my hands had started to become rough and animal-like, or at least that's how it seemed to me.

I could tell that something was weighing heavily on Yunus's mind. At first, I tried to distract him. As I showed him how to use the chopsticks, I told him how my mother had once won some free food at the Chinese restaurant in our neighborhood by being the hundredth person to place an order with them over the phone. When the girl on the phone insisted on asking, "Would you like any dessert?" at the last moment, my mother decided against ordering some deep-fried ice cream, one of her favorites, as she would have to pay for it and she didn't have much money. But still, she would never forget that time when she was the lucky hundredth person. In those days, I was in primary school, and I remember that I was doing my math homework that night. When our order of free Chinese food was delivered, we couldn't have been happier.

Yunus was still rather quiet. Still, gazing at his face illuminated by the glow of the flickering candle brought me more joy than anything else.

Softly, I asked him, "What's bothering you?"

"I'm not going to be able to come see you for a while."

"How will I go on living without you?!"

Those words suddenly fell from my lips. Wrenched from my heart. Poured from my tongue.

"How will I go on living without you?"

"But I'll come."

He reached out and took my hand.

"Don't you worry, baby. I'm not going to leave you alone here."

This time it was my turn to lapse into silence. Plunging into the well of sorrow without a rope. Scuba diving without a tank. Call it what you will.

"Okay, but why? Why are you leaving? More importantly, *where* are you going?"

"You know that they saw us . . ."

"Yes."

"It was pointless, of course, and completely unexpected."

"You said you'd made a deal with them."

"I had. At first, I was under the impression that they believed me and were understanding about the whole situation."

"Then what happened?"

"They threatened me."

"How?"

"They said they'd tell the hotel management."

"So, what do they want?"

"My salary."

"Are you going to give it to them?"

"No. I need that money for my father. Payday is tomorrow, and then poof! I'll disappear for a while. I'm going to tell the directress that I'm sick."

"Do you think that vanishing for a few days will solve the problem?"

"I don't know. But at least I'll be able to keep my salary."

"I wish you'd told me about this after dinner was over . . ."

"Are you upset?"

I nodded. I could have even cried.

"Don't worry, it's going to be okay. Because I love you very much."

"I love you too."

We went on eating in silence. Some birds gathered in the branches above us and started chirruping. After we finished eating, I got my fur coat from the nest and we set off down our path toward Sırça Palace. When we got to our place, I laid out the coat, which, in the light of the full moon, was as luxurious as the finest of beds. We undressed and made love, under the coat, tangled in the coat, on top of the coat . . . The lead-covered domes glimmered in the moonlight, which bathed us from head to toe.

"Look," Yunus said, "it's like we're made of silver." He reached out with one hand as if he was trying to catch hold of the moon. After making love twice, we stretched out on our backs, the endless night sky spread out above us, the huge moon directly overhead. We gave ourselves over to both of them. We gave ourselves over to love. To such an extent, perhaps, that we surrendered our souls.

Yunus said again, "It's like we're made of silver." He may have been drunk on love, experiencing the dizzying pleasure of something felt for the very first time. I can say that was certainly true for me. Nothing so wonderful had ever happened to me before.

"It's like we're made of silver."

In the darkness of the space between us, his arm reaching up into the sky was as beautiful as a sculpture of silver.

"'We are such stuff as dreams are made on, and our little life is rounded with a sleep.'"

"That's beautiful!"

"It's from Shakespeare."

"I know. I mean, I didn't know those lines, but I know of Shakespeare."

"Those words are as old as Sırça Seraglio here. As they were building this palace, in another corner of the world he was writing those lines. He penned into being glass palaces, glass seraglios."

"You have such a way with words."

What is your substance, whereof are you made,
That millions of strange shadows on you tend?
Since every one hath, every one, one shade,
And you, but one, can every shadow lend.

I had Yunus memorize the lines I recited to him. His lips moved ever so slightly in the darkness as he silently repeated after me. After a while, we fell silent and listened to the hum of the city. It wasn't something noisy that grated on the ears, but rather a soothing sound. You watch the bustle of life from afar, like the trees, like me, and when you do so, the din quiets down, softens, becoming a gentle sound like that hum.

"I'd like for you to do something for me tomorrow. Call my mother. But use a pay phone, not your cell. Tell her that her daughter is fine and that she needn't worry. Naturally, don't tell her where I am. Say to her, 'She's happy and content where she is. Don't get me wrong; she's not dead. She's doing just fine. She asked me to call you and tell you this.' Tell her that."

"Sure, I can do that for you," Yunus said, slowly closing his eyes.

When I awoke in the morning, he was gone.

And I had no idea how many days it would be before I'd see him again.

My guess was that he'd slipped away so that he wouldn't have to say goodbye to me. I recalled his warning about making sure that no one saw me. Night and Yunus, his arms raised upward, us making love, me feeling so wet between my legs . . . He looked at me and said, "Be very careful while I'm away. If you can, stay here. Don't go on top of the wall, and don't go out climbing from tree to tree."

I nodded.

As I was walking back to the laurel tree, to my nest, I put on the fur coat. It was cloudy that day, and winter was rehearsing for its grand entrance. In Istanbul, winter cuts ahead of autumn to take to the stage. When I reached the place where we'd had dinner the night before, I saw that my scarf was fluttering in the breeze on the branch where I'd hung it. I stopped and watched it for a while. The remnants of our dinner were scattered around, and I figured that Yunus had pushed to the ground the remnants of the chicken, as the pack of dogs that had made off with the shoes I'd left at the foot of the tree on my first night were now gnawing the meat from the bones. Blown by the wind, the bottles of ginger ale were rolling back and forth on the top of the wall.

After taking my scarf down from the branch, I kicked the bottles off the wall. Not into the park but to the other side, where the ground was hard. They shattered. Not dizzied in the least by the height, I stood there atop the wall, looking down. At the broken bottles. I had once shattered like them too.

30

OTHER OPTIONS

There was a storm the next day, and as it blew through the city, rain hammered down and the trees swayed in the wind. I spent the entire day huddled in the nest. Every few minutes, I thanked the laurel tree, because its branches and leaves were so densely interwoven that they protected me from the wind and rain. It had grown strong over the years. I wondered how old it could be—two hundred years, maybe? I too needed time to grow strong. But I hoped it wouldn't take two centuries for me to do so.

Sometimes the rain blew in from the other direction.

When that happened, it would spatter my coat. I hadn't been so immobile in a really long time. It reminded me of the adventure of a man who crossed the ocean in something like a barrel he'd made himself. My father and I had watched the documentary together on the National Geographic Channel. And then there was the man who explored the poles of the earth. In order to avoid freezing to death, he'd squeezed into the corpse of a dead animal and remained there for days. While watching both documentaries, I remember that I kept thinking about immobility and how hard it must be to remain still. But now, it was doing me good. It felt nice to stop moving. I felt as though I could hibernate through the winter in the stork's nest, wrapped up in my soft, warm coat. I even thought that perhaps I really had drifted off into hibernation. A feeling of peace swelled within me. When Yunus left, he'd hung a bag filled with water, crackers, cookies, and apples on a branch. But I knew that soon my period was going to start—what would I do then? Make do with leaves? Or be civilized and make use of one of the pads he had brought me? Based on the amount of food he'd left, I tried to estimate how long he'd planned on staying away, and I wondered why I hadn't directly asked him the night before. Probably I didn't want to make him feel like I was scared of being alone, and I certainly didn't want to be a burden on him, especially since he was already in so much trouble already.

After all, they were trying to force him to hand over his salary.

As I got more and more irritated with those men I didn't even know, I started getting worked up, but it didn't bother me in the least to have to sit still.

I lay there curled up, as if I'd slipped into depression and didn't want to get out of bed. It wasn't the least bit uncomfortable. Once in a while I'd wiggle my toes and flex my fingers, and give my wrists and ankles a few turns to keep my blood circulating.

There's something else I said that wasn't quite true. During their trip, Derin and Pembe didn't send me a single text or video. You ask, Why am I bringing that up now? Because they'd posted on Twitter that the long journey was wreaking havoc on their joints. I stalked their tweets the whole while. "But it's all worth it," they wrote. At the time I wished like crazy that I'd gone with them. I knew that it would've done me good and helped me get a grip on myself and my feelings. They knew it as well.

"You need this trip more than either of us," Pembe said. "To come with us, to go there. And, to be honest, out of the three of us, at heart you're the kindest hearted, the most conscientious, and the most sensitive."

Unable to hold back her feelings on the matter, she texted that to me three days before they left.

"Out of the three of us, at heart you're the kindest hearted, the most conscientious, and the most sensitive."

I think we can agree that "at heart" was pretty out of place in that sentence and should have been cut. Its presence said, "Actually, you're *not* those things, but we're trying to put the squeeze on you."

I'd bought a bunch of notebooks and markers for the kids, as well as some coloring books.

In that sense, I was ready for the trip.

But then my mother had those breakdowns, the window frame came loose and slid down, and we had the worst of our traditional mother/daughter arguments. Those things had nothing to do with my plans to take part in the trip and arose in parallel with it:

"Sure, you're so sensitive to the needs of people you don't even know. You love kids, so much so that you want to help them. Wonderful. Good for you. What a generous child I've raised. But at the same time, I've brought up this little demon who's blind to her own mother's suffering!"

She compared herself to the mothers of classic tragedies, who, in the middle of the play, would fall prey to fits of shouting:

"Just look at this child! She doesn't see that her mother has died. She doesn't see that she's living with the corpse of her mother. She can't smell the stench of rotting flesh. And now she's leaving that corpse behind to go off on a trip. My child has such a good heart! She's a real angel. See how she tries to make herself look like a good person in the face of tragedy."

With that last sentence of her monologue, my mother lit the fuse of the bomb nestled in the core of our argument. The longer I stayed silent, the hotter the fire roared. But, as always happened during our fights, I yelled back at her, yet I was unable to break free and run out the door. I didn't make it to the ferry. I didn't cross to the other side of the city. I didn't get on the bus. I didn't join Pembe and Derin. I was stuck there.

We would've gone on vacation when we got back. Really, we would have. Or we would've been together in heaven and perhaps taken a short jaunt down to hell to give that suicide bomber a thorough thrashing. Well, I'd like to say that we'd beat the fuck out of her, but the fact of the matter is that because we hold solidarity with our fellow women in such high regard, we wouldn't have done anything to her. Because women, youth, and children are blameless. The reason we put life jackets on them and shuffle them into lifeboats first is not because they're weak, but because they're blameless. They're going to heaven anyways, so they are the first to be sent off to safety by the powerful who can't seem to make enough room for themselves to squeeze into the world . . .

Have a good trip. When I said to that cock-mouth Özlem Hanım, "I wrote a novel about a country that despises its children and youth," she leered at me through her ass. Let me tell you, if the women, children, and youth in a given geography are suffering, that's a shitty place. If I were you, I'd flee without looking back, but then again, the ghost of this place will track you down and find you no matter where you go. No one can escape their own reality. The realities of our countries become our personal realities, infecting our private lives, our loves, and our friendships. It's a terrible, terrible thing!

A gust of wind shook the laurel tree violently. I had nothing to worry about, however, because I'd lashed myself to a branch with my slackline strap, so even if the nest were to topple to the ground, I'd be fine. And it's a good thing I did so, because it wasn't the wind I needed to be concerned about but what seemed to be the forty thieves gathered at the foot of my tree.

They were saying, "Hey, there's something up there! In the stork's nest. Something's covering it. It moved! I can see it moving!"

I was so scared that my breath caught in my throat. Out of fear I couldn't bring myself to pry an opening in the branches and peer down. I lay there as still as possible, listening to them. One must have picked up a rock and thrown it at the nest, because it lurched to the side.

"Go get some more rocks! It's her, the girl! Stone her!"

They started to stone me.

I couldn't figure out where they were finding such big rocks. Were they prying up paving stones like we'd done during the protests? Each one they threw hit its mark. After a while, I couldn't help but make a sound.

"Hey! Did you hear that?"

In the end, they managed to knock the nest loose and it started to slide downward. Horrified, I realized that the turnbuckle on my strap suddenly popped open and the strap let go, zipping around my body once, and then the nest and I were falling to the ground. I fell.

When I hit the ground, there was a sudden silence. There was the sound of the rain, the sound of the crows, and the hum of the city, but the men who had knocked me out of the tree with stones were eerily silent. Perhaps they didn't believe it could be true, that there was a girl hiding in a stork's nest up in a tree. But there she was. And right in front of them! The pain I felt at first quickly died away. It felt as though I was bleeding from my mouth and ears.

Now it was the bullies' turn to be scared.

"Her mouth and nose are bleeding."

For a moment I caught sight of their bodies as they leaned in to take a closer look. Dirty jeans. They were all wearing fake Nike Airs, as if they'd been handed out for free. As my eyes started to close, I thought, *Is this how it all ends? It's so unjust.* I revolted with all my might. But I was pleased that I was going to be with Pembe, Derin, my aunt, and my grandma. That is, of course, if there was a place where we could meet up.

I woke up filled with that feeling of doubt, which made no sense.

It had been a dream.

The effects of that dream clung to me for a long time. Eventually the rain slowed to a patter, but the feeling that dream instilled in me refused to dwindle. It was a dream. A dream.

31

Your Preferences

When my grandma got home, she came across some things that the American archaeologist hadn't taken with him. Things he couldn't pack into his suitcase. His İzzet Ziya paintings.

The American really loved those paintings. He hung one of them up over the dining table and the other one in the living room. My grandma told me that he could hardly take his eyes from them when they were eating or when he was sitting in the living room, waiting for his Turkish coffee.

"Looking at them makes me feel at peace." That's what he would say.

My grandma knew that if she took the paintings back, she might wind up getting back together with the American again, not unlike a bird caught in a snare, so she refused to do so. And because she knew that they were precious, the works of a palace painter created for a sultan, she refused to turn them over to the guard at Hagia Sophia. She'd gotten angry at the American when he'd bought them because they'd cost a fortune—in her mind, at least as much as a new refrigerator would cost.

In the end, she kept them as a memento of the American. I was told that, when she was a little girl, my aunt would look at them and say, "Mom, when's my American daddy coming back?"

When my father would come home for the weekends from the lice-ridden boardinghouse at Galatasaray High School, he'd sit and gaze sadly at the painting over the dining table as he ate the meatballs and potatoes that his mother had prepared in honor of his visit. And when he'd sit in the living room, waiting for his coffee to be brought to him—a sign of prestige, as he was now the man of the house—he'd do the same there as well. Over time, the paintings became part of the home and family. When the family moved, the paintings found their places on the walls of the new apartment, but the traces they'd left on the walls of the old wood house, where they'd hung for years, left my grandma with a heavy heart. The passing of time leaves similar traces on the human spirit. Fools and saps like us realize that time has been passing when we see the outlines on the walls left behind by such paintings. Walls yellow and fade, just as time takes its toll on us. How are we to bear it? If you ask me, we can't.

Thankfully the paintings were cheerful. One of them depicted a young boy standing naked on a beach, and the other some women enjoying a day at the sea as they lounged under a canopy held up by four sticks, their legs stretched out. Beautiful, right? Heartwarming.

My grandma had been put off by the naked boy, but when my aunt looked at the painting and took her pacifier out of her mouth and said, "Pretty willy," everyone laughed, and thereby the painting was saved from a life of being stashed away behind a wardrobe. Many years later, my grandma and I took that "pretty willy" to the neighborhood of Çukurcuma and sold it for a fraction of its real value. That was in 2007. So all that was left was *Seaside Leisure* with its cheerful women. My grandma said, "That one is your birthday present. It'll be part of your dowry." Knowing they were valuable, she had asked her son-in-law how much the most expensive refrigerator cost and pinned the price of *Pretty Willy* to that. When the antiques dealer asked, "How much do you want for the painting?" that was the price she gave. Without saying a word, he handed over the money in full. Two days later, my aunt noticed that the painting was missing. "Mom," she screamed, "what have you done?!"

My grandma replied, "I really loved that painting. But what else *could* I do?"

She was right. Deep love brings about equally deep hatred.

"Water carries hatred to the mill of being deeply loved."

Ah, Grandma, you put it so beautifully!

In the end, my aunt took me with her to the antique shop and got the painting back.

My aunt.

Our story starts with our names. While it starts there, it also ends, like all things that have a beginning. Which is precisely why I didn't mention her name—I didn't want her story to end. My story is unimportant. But she should have lived. You know that desire to "live on in name," right? Well, it's something along those lines.

I told you about my grandfather—the vegetable dealer—who wasn't allowed to be part of my father's side of the family. The one who died. When my aunt was born, he picked her up in her swaddling clothes with his large, calloused hands and said, "She's beautiful, just like a rose."

My grandma scowled at him when he said "like a rose." It was a glare that said, "You, seller of vegetables, what the hell would you know about roses?!" Mother and daughter, of like mind, would go on to forge the most powerful alliance in the world. Deserving of men and evil!

"Just like a flower," he added. "She should be named Rose."

Appalled, my grandma said, "What kind of a name is that?!" She proposed the names of the twin girls she often saw at the park with their parents and whom she was quite fond of. That way, there wouldn't be any room for the name that the vegetable seller wanted to give her. The name entry on her birth certificate would be too full.

The vegetable seller wasn't able to say, "Is this some kind of joke?"

But that didn't mean it was the end of the struggle over how she would be named. Like me, she wound up with two names.

Not far back, I mentioned something when I was describing my dream. In fact, long before that, I said something as well. But first I'm going to tell you about something else. Another memory that flashes through my mind like tiny strikes of lightning: as my aunt was trying to console me with insipid statements like "What's done is done" and "The dead can't help us get through what's happened," I said, "I've started working on my novel again."

"What?!" she exclaimed.

In those days, she was staying with us. She'd become fed up with rural life and the municipality's so-called press and human relations department, so she moved back to Istanbul, and since her tenant couldn't pay the rent, she wasn't able to get a place of her own. So there we were, us three women, living together. For those of you who like timelines, my grandma's place had been sold long before then. If you're wondering what happened to the money, suffice to say that my father bought a boat and was trying his hand at a ridiculous venture: underwater archaeological tours. What happened next was nothing short of a "speak of the devil" moment, as just that morning she'd been having a bitter argument on the phone with my father.

"That son of a bitch is out on a boat! He's hustled some rich tourists into taking a tour of some underwater ruins or something."

I think it was my father who hung up, thereby concluding the conversation, because when my aunt tried to call back, he wouldn't answer. The operator continued to try getting through to him, but eventually his number was closed to all incoming calls.

It had been a month since Pembe and Derin had been killed. I wondered if I'd managed to pull myself together a little, and concluded that I had. At the very least, I wanted to talk. I wanted to talk without listening to what the other person had to say. Because of the "golden shot" confession I'd made to my aunt not long before, I was feeling ashamed. Like a complete loser. I wanted my relationship with my aunt to be as it had been before.

"Perhaps," I said, "instead of messing around with the novel, I should go on that trip I'd been dreaming about." I brought it up in the hope that it would reopen the lines of communication.

We were sitting at the kitchen table, which bore the remnants of the breakfast we'd just had. No longer did my aunt smoke her cigarettes huddled up by the exhaust hood—now she puffed away everywhere.

I could tell she wanted to lash out at me: "Forget about that book. You have to be a good person in order to write. Honest, conscientious."

"Really? Are we going to write a new constitution?" That was how I wanted to respond, but I opted to remain silent.

"There's no substance in your writing. That teacher of yours—Özlem Hanım—she was right. The other night I couldn't sleep, but since there wasn't anything else to read, I took a look over the copy of your book you'd given me. It's complete crap. I'd even say drivel. You may have thought that you were toying with the reader, but what you wound up doing was bullshit."

"For example?"

I had to force the question out of my mouth. And it burned my lips on the way out.

"For example . . . you describe something as if it were real, but then you say it was a dream. That's the cheapest trick you can use. It's like when stupid kids do something wrong and then say it was a joke. I despise writers who do that in their work."

"Özlem Hanım said the same thing."

"Meaning that she understands how things really operate."

Who *doesn't* understand—right, Grandma? Who doesn't understand . . . True, the ending deserved a sound volley of verbal abuse, but who cares. We'll keep womanhood for ourselves.

I wanted to say to my aunt, "Please don't hate me too." But I couldn't. Sometimes our silences express so much more than the things we say. At the very least, I hope that is the case.

My aunt didn't have to commit suicide.

Okay, so she did it, but I wish that her body hadn't been found so soon. I know that may sound strange, but try to curb your indignant anger. There's a certain amount of legitimacy to what I said. If her body had never been found, we could've gone on hoping that perhaps she was still alive somewhere and would reappear in our lives one day. Like the daughter of Muhterem Hanım, who swapped properties with my grandma. Muhterem Hanım's daughter was a flight attendant. Her plane crashed in the Sea of Marmara, but her body never was found. Every time someone knocked on Muhterem Hanım's door, her heart would fill with hope. She even wrote a letter to Sarah Jessica Parker, who looked a lot like her daughter, because she thought that maybe she'd washed up on the shores of America, having lost her memory.

It is good to hope.

It is good to have desires.

I wish that I had hope and desires. I'm here because I don't have either.

When I found out that my aunt was dead, the first emotion I felt was anger, not sadness.

At the time, I'd recently lost my two best friends, had one foot in the grave already, and hadn't recovered at all; on the contrary, I'd been multiplied and divided, even pared back to my square root, so how could she set off another bomb in my life? What was the point of committing suicide just then? Not long before, we'd found the building developer on Facebook. His pics revealed a man of impressive horizontal girth.

She cried, "What's become of him?!"

"Oh wow," I said. "And look at you, fit as ever. If he saw you, he'd crap his pants."

"Judging by this picture, it looks like he already has." And she was right.

He was now married with three kids, and appeared to have a bale of hay sagging in the rear of his trousers.

"I wonder what it would've been like if he and I had gotten married?"

I wondered: When you were seventeen years old, why couldn't you leave him out there in the snow? In that way, how are you any different from my aunt Hülya? Right, she wears a headscarf, and you don't. But the raw materials are the same. If only your tenant's TV series had caught on, if only the ratings had been better. Then he would've paid the rent and the three of us wouldn't have been living together in a shoebox like broke students. In those days, we weren't on speaking terms with my aunt Hülya. If we had been, we could've at least asked for some logistical support. There was that time my mother ate at a café in Cihangir and sent the bill to Aunt Hülya. She didn't pay the bill, so we were never able to go back there again. The café happened to be on our street, which didn't really make any difference; there were now more cafés than roads in Cihangir. The neighborhood had changed a lot. My mother once saw someone famous in one of those cafés and, after running up to her table, introduced herself as a dietician, then said, "If you'd like, I can help you lose weight." She placed her business card on the table. The star gagged for a moment on the piece of cheesecake she was eating and then proceeded to ignore my mother, which the others in the café took to mean, "Get this woman away from me." Within seconds, the waiters showed up and frog-marched my mother straight out the door. She lost it for a few seconds: "Whose damn neighborhood do you think this is? I was here a long time before you! Instead of going to the bathroom at home, we used to use this place. It was always empty. And now you're throwing me out of this place where I'd come to take a shit?"

The topic at hand, however, is not my mother. It's my aunt. So, Mother, would you please step aside? Please take a seat right over here.

So, to continue:

My aunt slowly approached the threshold of suicide in the same way that Yunus and I walked atop the wall: tiny, tiny steps. Be that as it may, there were other options aside from death. In my opinion, it happened suddenly. I decided that I did the right thing by not telling her about my grandma's secrets, the stories that she told me while lying on her deathbed . . .

Secrets are bombs that slam into our homes. One had blasted the hell out of our place already.

That night my aunt would disappear from our lives forever, she came and kissed me on the cheek, which may have meant that she didn't want to part on bad terms. She left her phone. I answered it whenever it rang. Just the day before, she'd applied for the position of editor at a newspaper and they were calling her in for an interview.

After twenty-four hours had passed, the news editor and police reporter who worked for the paper that had fired my aunt offered to help find her. But there was no need for help. No need to search. There was no need for me to mumble that I thought I saw her jump into the crevasse between the two retaining walls, nor any need for anyone to probe that chasm between the apartment buildings, which purportedly led all the way out to sea, a story she herself had reported on years earlier. No, my aunt would be found of her own accord.

Her fate was to be caught in a fisherman's net like a beautiful fish.

The fisherman would say, "I thought I'd snared a really nice fish. Forty years ago, I used to be able to catch cod. I thought that's what had found its way into my net."

The fact that the fisherman was familiar with cod, could properly identify a cod when he saw a cod, was a miracle of sorts—it reflected a touch of elegance, a certain refinement. Even my aunt's death had an air of sophistication to it.

"Or a swordfish. I thought it could be a swordfish as the net churned through the sea toward me."

We were at the police station in Istanbul's Hisar district. From there, they took us to the Sarıyer Public Hospital. "Are you going to identify her body?" My mother had fainted at the hospital. My father, deeply tanned from being out at sea all the time, simply stood there, staring at one of the hospital walls as if it were the Wall of Shame, becoming an inseparable part of it in the process. It was left in my hands. The fisherman explained how he pulled her from the Bosporus so poetically: "I took her in my arms, just as I had taken my beautiful bride into my arms years and years ago. I held her and pulled that beautiful woman out of the water."

That's why I wasn't scared of seeing the body of my aunt. To the contrary, I was glad I was going to have a chance to see her one last time.

My aunt was lying stretched out on the table. The fisherman had been right; the water had not caused her to swell nor inflicted any harm on her. Even down beneath the waves, she'd remained untouched. A swift current had swept her along and protected her. It was a shame that the goodness she'd deserved in life had only found her in death. Quickly she'd traversed a safe path from life to death. The current had pulled one of her boots from her feet, but the other Isabel Marant remained . . . My aunt . . . Beauty. Courage.

When the seller of lottery tickets, who also sold iced almonds, said to her, "Ma'am, you're an extremely beautiful woman," he couldn't have been more right.

"I'm a woman. A lady, if you prefer. But a 'ma'am' is something I'm not and will never be."

My grandma, aunt, mother, and I were at a restaurant. A spontaneous night out together for drinks.

As she popped a few almonds into her mouth, my grandma said, "So, you're not a 'ma'am,' eh? Well, don't be so hard on the guy."

I disagree, Aunt. Let them go on being what they are. And you stay just as you are. In all your beauty.

I wrote to the developer on Facebook to tell him that my aunt was dead.

"Had she been sick?"

"She committed suicide."

"What happened?"

What I'm giving you here is the corrected version, as his messages had a lot of spelling mistakes.

"She jumped into the sea."

"I'm so sorry to hear that. May God give her peace. She was such a good person."

Who knows what thoughts were running through the mind of Mr. Smile, Mr. Beautiful Thirty-Two Teeth, what memories he was dwelling on.

That beauty sitting up in bed in the room at the Pera Palace Hotel with a view of the snowstorm. That beauty's squeals of pleasure as they played in the snow at Fındıklı Park. That delicious thing, like a burst grape, in the back seat of the Mercedes on Lovers' Hill. That beauty, love itself.

I got straight to the point: "You're a moron!"

"What gives you the right to say that?!"

"It would've been better if you'd taken my aunt as your wife and moved in with us. All of Cihangir would've been yours for the taking. You could've torn the entire neighborhood down and rebuilt it as you wanted."

He said, "I was too scared of that witchy grandmother of yours."

There was no way I was going to let him go on with what he was saying—I couldn't bear yet another bomb slamming into our home.

What would I do if he started to say something like, "I bought the flowers and the chocolates, and I was on my way to ask for your aunt's hand in marriage, but that Perihan witch, ah, that hag!"?

So I blocked him on the spot. But that wasn't enough, so I deleted him and filed a complaint. But then I couldn't stop myself, so I went to his excavation business on the other side of the city in Ümraniye, where he sells sand and gravel. It turned out just as I expected it would.

"What did your aunt tell you about me?" he asked with the smug confidence of someone who believes themselves to be unforgettable.

Adjusting that "heartthrob," thirty-two-toothed smile beneath his mustache to creepy leer mode, he stirred his glass of tea, the tassel of the prayer beads around his wrist constantly threatening to dip into the glass.

"Nothing," I said, and started heading toward the door.

As I was stepping out, he asked, "By the way, how old are you?" I think the nitwit was considering the possibility that I might be the illegitimate fruit of his affair with my aunt.

"Things like that only happen in the movies. I'm not your daughter, dumbass." With that, I walked away.

Some things are best left alone. You shouldn't dwell on them because, if you do, you'll end up being scooped up in the briny deep by a sand excavator and dumped into a construction site to be mixed into concrete. And as a result, you'll be the death of that building when the concrete crumbles, eaten away by the salt. That's just how it is.

At the end of it all, I said farewell to everyone. I did it up here in the treetops. I said farewell to all the people in my life. Every single one of them.

32

FOLLOWERS

When I opened my eyes on October 4, 2015, I was happy.

Yunus had come. He'd made his way all the way to the stork's nest. That was the second time he displayed such courage. While he may have started getting used to being up in the treetops, as you know, he usually waited somewhere where it was safe. Since the day when he found me in the grip of a fever, this was the first time he'd dared come all the way out to my nestside.

I lay there for a while, looking at him, thinking, *Is this a dream too?* I was like a baby in her cradle, looking up at the faces of the people dotingly hovering over her. Yunus gently stroked my hair.

That's when I realized that his face was battered and bruised.

Even though I had strong suspicions that I was dreaming, I still bolted upright.

"What happened to you?"

"A little tussle."

"With who?"

"Who do you think?"

He nodded in the direction of the hotel.

"They really did a number on you."

"This is what happens to you when you learn how to fight by watching movies."

"Didn't you grow up on the streets?"

"Yeah, but we didn't fight each other much. Turns out I don't know what to do when you're getting beaten. I didn't get in a single punch!"

"That's a shame. But what started it all?"

"That's why I'm here, to tell you all about it . . ."

Yunus spoke for the most part, and I listened. He was still wound up and nervous. He said they could come after us at any minute, maybe try to track us down. I decided it would be best not to tell him about the nightmare I had.

He said that he'd managed to pass his entire salary along to his father.

"But why did you do that?"

"He needs it. He's got a lot of debts."

"Because?"

"The banks don't like to give people like us loans. No social security, no guarantees. We can't document the money we make by the sweat of our brow. Even when we tell them that a debt is a debt and we'll pay it back, they don't believe us."

"They don't pay your social security at the hotel?"

Yunus shook his head.

"Look at what this country's coming to!"

I wanted to shut down that dull, dry talk about social security. Still, isn't it strange that people have to live in such a state of uncertainty? Is that any way to live? But people do it.

"Because he couldn't get a loan from a bank, my dad went to a loan shark. He didn't have any other choice. We make payment after payment, but we can't pay off the debt. We're stuck."

"I see . . . So, what happened at the hotel?"

"Those pricks working security came pounding on our door, thinking they could force me to hand over the money. But there wasn't a single *kuruş* left. So they beat me instead."

Here's an inventory of the external damage that had been inflicted on Yunus: he had a split lip, a swollen eye, and a busted eyebrow that was held shut with one stitch. Completely at ease, as though he was unaware of the damage, he quickly went on: "I thought a lot about the situation. I said, 'Come on, Yunus, don't be afraid of those guys. Go to the head manager and explain what happened.' And that's exactly what I did. After listening to what I had to say, he watched the security camera footage."

"The footage of us?"

"Yes."

Which meant that they had all seen us kissing on the fire escape. Yunus seemed embarrassed.

"They watched up until you went into the room and then as you left the room, noting the times and date. They even started watching the other employees who were going into rooms and using them. Now they're screwed too. My guess is that they were thinking, 'You guys were having orgies and didn't invite us?' Or something like, 'You're planning to rob us.' That's how their minds work. It's always dirty business with them. Then they asked me where you went after you returned to the wall. I said that I didn't know."

He pursed his lips as if he really didn't know and shrugged his shoulders.

"Then they asked me why you used the fire escape to get into the hotel."

"What did you say?"

"Because you were sneaking in."

Not a very illuminating answer.

"After that, they tried to figure out where you could have gone from the top of the wall. Since they would never think that a girl like you would want to live in the trees, they decided that the only possibility was that you used the steps—if they can be called steps—that lead down into the tea garden. They think that's how you came and went."

"So I escaped."

"Right. I used those steps to get up onto the top of the wall today. I won't be able to get to the top of the wall using the fire escape anymore, because they fired me."

"I'm sorry to hear that."

"There's more," Yunus went on to say. "They're going to tear down those steps I used today and put up a barrier between the fire escape and the wall. They were surprised, because they thought you'd somehow climbed up the wall. 'That's quite a girl. Good on her.' That's what the manager said."

"We'll find a way to meet," I said.

"Of course." Still, his expression was full of despair.

"I'm sure there's a way onto the roof from Sırça Palace or somewhere else. If not, you'll learn how to climb the trees. I could pull you up using a rope. There must be a way."

The weak smile he offered made it obvious that all my suggestions sounded impossible. As was my habit, I pressed him: "Well, couldn't you do it? You'll find a way to get up into the trees, just as I did."

"Couldn't you find a way to come *down* from the trees?"

After a pause, he said what was really on his mind: "What good is it doing you to be here? Okay, I know that you have emotional reasons for wanting to be up in the trees. I believe you, and you have every right to be here, but . . ."

"Then what's the problem?"

"The problem is that I love you. That I'm so in love with you."

"I'm in love too. I'm in love with *you*. I fell more deeply in love with you than I ever expected."

"Then come with me and let's make this work."

"It doesn't work that way. I'm the Girl in the Tree. Did you forget that?"

Like all people who are desperate, Yunus lashed out with a meaningless question, almost bellowing, "Fine, but why?!"

"Why, why, Grandpa's in the rye!" He didn't even grin when I said that. In fact, he frowned, as though calling on me to be serious. "Yunus, because—life gets in the way of being able to speak of life. Here, I'm far from life, so I'm able to do that."

If I'd been in his position, I would've asked, "Is it really necessary to do that up here?"

Instead, he said, tears in his eyes, "Life exists so that it can be *lived*, not explained. Otherwise, it's not life at all."

He reached out and stroked my cheek.

"Love, remember the good days. Come down with me from the trees. Live with me. So many wonderful days await us, and there will always be more to come. Let's go through life together, in love, in happiness."

How could I not want to live with him? If my grandma hadn't sold *Pretty Willy* and my father hadn't made off with *Seaside Leisure*, what more could I want than to hang those paintings on the wall of our home and life a live of joy?

Even the birds stopped chirruping for a moment. They roosted and flew in silence.

Reaching into his pocket, Yunus pulled out a small bag, which he held out to me. "I brought these for you. I called your mother as well. But she didn't answer. Another woman picked up the phone. She said her name's Hülya and that she's your other aunt."

After my uncle-in-law played the song "And You, Leyla?" for my aunt Hülya, he played her another romantic track, this one a number about the silences between lovers titled "Hülya." I forgot to mention that detail. Or did I? In either case, my mind skipped back and forward, like the cheap MP3 player that the doorman who was afraid of going to the military carried in his pocket. And then it stopped.

If my aunt Hülya answered my mother's phone, that meant she had probably gone through her messages and so on. Which, in turn, might mean that she was staying with my mother, looking after her. Truth be told, both my grandma and Aunt Hülya tried to take care of us. Don't be misled by the way Aunt Hülya refused to pay the café bill my mother palmed off on her. She just didn't like that it was an imposition after the fact. It actually marked the starting point of the "secret" assistance that began to come in. Envelopes of money slipped under the door, packages of meat delivered by the butcher's apprentice. Although I should note that the second time such a delivery of meat arrived, my aunt—the other one, my father's sister—happened to be at our place, and she sent the apprentice away, saying, "We don't need their charity." So away went the cutlets, lamb chops, steaks, and ground meat. In fact, we were hardly getting any protein at all in those days and we *did* need it. Just a week or two earlier, my aunt had happily devoured one of those steaks, not knowing where it had come from. She had a strange naivete, as do many good-hearted people. My mother was like that too, as was Yunus.

As I took the bag from Yunus, I asked, unable to conceal the sadness in my voice, "So, this is it? Now we go our separate ways?"

At first, he refused to say yes or no.

Just as I was thinking, *Fine, let's put our separation in there between the dried nuts and sanitary pads,* Yunus said firmly, "No. We could never be strangers to each other . . ."

I was unsure of how I should interpret his wording, when he could've simply said, "We'll never be apart."

Getting to know one another is more important than falling in love. I have no doubt about that. And I wasn't blind to the possibility that, in our case, the fact that Yunus and I had met was more important than the burning love I felt for him. As my grandma was fond of saying, "Passionate love is like perfume. In no time at all it wafts away. What really matters is that when two people come together, they grow accustomed to one another, build up a feeling of mutual love, share their secrets, and spend time together."

That was one of those rare proclamations of hers that didn't include any swearing.

Yunus and I were sitting on a thick branch high up in that tree, facing each other. We were a miracle. I thought that if I tried to put that moment into words, I might get excited, lose my balance, and fall to the ground, so I held my tongue. Love and passion have the power to dispel all your fears. That came out sounding like an advertisement for a reliable brand of medicine you'd find at a pharmacy, but all the same it's true.

And people never forget those they love. Take the case of my grandma. She never forgot. Not the American or the archaeologist. Especially not the American. One day, when I was at her place, she told me to turn up the volume on the television. At that moment, her parrot started squawking shrilly, and she silenced it with a well-aimed house slipper. There was an old film on, in which Ajda Pekkan was singing and dancing. She seemed immortal, untouched by the passing years, but of course her extraordinary ability to resist aging has nothing to do with the topic at hand, so let's move on to the song she was singing as if for my grandma. It was a song about lovers who'd grown apart, about wanting to go back to the way things were.

My grandma was listening intently to the song, enveloped in a sentimentality that I'd never seen in her before. Afterward, she'd gone into the kitchen and started chopping some onions as a way to hide the fact that she'd been crying. Grandma, don't you know that kids notice everything?

One day, as we were passing through the garden of Cihangir Mosque as a shortcut to Kumrulu, we saw a man sitting on a bench who seemed like he was dressed up as Clint Eastwood. It didn't take long for me to figure out who he was (by the way, if you ask me, Clint Eastwood and Marianne Faithfull would be a great love combo). He turned in our direction, looking at us long and hard, at which point my grandma tightened her grip on my arm and rushed home, practically dragging me behind her. Soon after, the doorbell rang.

"Grandma, someone's at the door. Don't you hear it?"

"Oh, I hear it all right. Son of a whore's pimp. I'm not going to open it."

We could see the weary Clint on the cheap plastic screen of the video camera system. When he narrowed his eyes in what appeared to be pain, the wrinkles on his forehead deepened. He didn't persist for an inordinate amount of time, but he did pause and linger in the entryway for a bit longer. Clint had played out the role of his life, but when I say "role," don't get the wrong idea. The American really was in pain, and he'd come to see my grandma one last time.

And what did she do?

She ran away.

And what did he do?

He left a letter at the informal outdoor cat shelter my grandma ran. It was a kind of cat neighborhood with bowls of water and food and cardboard cat houses (soon after, the municipal police would get an earful from my grandma as they tore the place down). So anyways, as I was saying, the American left a letter for her there.

"Peri Hanım, I think this is for you?"

One of the local cat lovers had come upon the letter and was now holding it out to my grandma. Perihan Hanım snatched the letter from her hand like a cat lashing out with its claws. Her reading glasses happened to be hanging around her neck, so she read the letter on the spot. If she hadn't had them with her, she would've had no recourse but to ask for my help. Naturally, whether she'd let anyone else read the letter would've depended on what she thought it might say and in how much detail. But that's beside the point, because she read it herself, and was ready to reply at once.

"Do you have a pen?"

Those cat lovers carry around all sorts of things. After rummaging through her purse, producing, among other things, a flashlight, a lighter, a phone, cigarettes, keys, and chewing gum, at last she pulled out a pen.

"Here you are, Perihan Hanım."

She laid out the letter and wrote at the bottom, "Farewell, my love." I was thinking, *For God's sake, is that really the right thing to say to your lover from days of yore who now has cancer, your erstwhile common-law husband?* But she deemed it appropriate, because deep down she was still thinking about how easily the American had given up on her. If only he'd come to the apartment again. If only he hadn't slid his bankbook under the door all those years ago. In those days, my grandma had often wept as she lingered in the kitchen, the one place she could be alone, and the hem of her apron was always damp from wiping away her tears. My aunt could snap, "Mom, stop blowing your nose on your apron!" till she was blue in the face. But she wasn't blowing her nose; she was wiping away her tears. If the American had divorced his wife and come back to her, saying, "Peri, even if you try to kill me, I won't go. Look at the state I'm in, Perihan!" would she have sent him away? Cold composure is an illness that afflicts many Westerners. The American had been infected as well, as the result of accepting everything that happened in his life with cool equanimity.

My grandma placed the letter back where it had been found, not even thinking about whether the woman who'd discovered it would get curious and have a peek for herself. Don't ever be afraid of people who love cats. Cat lovers will never bring you any harm. Being an animal lover is one thing, but being a cat lover involves an entirely different range of factors. Cat lovers are honest. They don't do people wrong. Isn't it true that someone who would try to save the life of a cat would do just about anything for the sake of this thing we call life? There's not an ounce of wicked intent in such efforts. It's 100 percent organic.

That's it.

That's it, and nothing more.

Grandma, would you believe that I was afraid Yunus would speak those words?

"Farewell, my love."

Yunus sensed that I was scared. He sensed that I'd stopped talking because I was upset. Now it was time for him to say something that would cast off my sorrow.

"I won't ever leave you. I'm going to come back. Don't you worry, okay? I'll be back here before you know it."

"Come back. What would I do without you?" I broke down in tears. We hugged each other and kissed. Before leaving, he warned me again: "Those security guards got fired too. Out of curiosity they might come here and search the park, so be careful. One of them has a BB gun. On the holidays, he takes it down to the seaside so people can pay to shoot at the balloons he sets up."

That explained why I kept seeing leaves full of holes. Had I told you about that? No, I don't think so.

In that case, maybe what I'd thought were dreams weren't really dreams at all. Maybe I'd picked up on some external forces that gave me visions of those bullies throwing rocks at me when I was up in my perch. They may not have spotted me, but still they threw rocks up into the branches, fired random shots into the leaves, snooped around, stood under the trees talking, pissed on the wall, and then left.

Could all that have really happened?

Yunus said, and said, and said, "I'm going to come back, don't worry," and I watched him moving along the branches through the leaves and then clambering onto the wall. At one point I caught sight of his blue DeFacto jacket in the distance, but soon enough that vanished from sight too. He was gone. I wondered if he really would come back, as he'd said he would.

33

EXIT

I stopped caring about my personal hygiene. I didn't clean my ass, no longer using laurel leaves to wipe up after taking a crap. Only once when it seemed to be hurting from being so filthy did I sprinkle on a little water, and after a few swipes with a leaf, it was fine. But I stank. Badly. All I had to do was scratch at my skin and the stench would burst forth. Mind you, none of that had anything to do with being scared—I was malodorous, pure and simple, not maladapted to my environment. Much to the contrary. Smile, friends. Smile. But was I really finding the solution to everything? I wondered if I would be able to go on living in the treetops if Yunus didn't come. But when I first found myself there, in the middle of the night on September 14, 2015, I didn't have anything and I didn't have Yunus in my life. All I had was the belief that I could cling to life despite everything that had happened.

But I have to admit that Yunus saved my life. If it hadn't been for him, would I have been able to stay up there for so long? Did I ever truly ask myself that question? Or was I too scared? Maybe I could've eaten leaves and twigs, or the leftovers of crows. I could've filched food from the hotel. By stalking the people who came to the park, I could've found just the right moment to leap down, wrench the doner kebabs from their hands, and run off. Would I have done that? Yes, I would have.

My arms and legs had become surprisingly powerful. But my fingernails and toenails were stuffed with grime, and my hands were as black as those of a coal seller's apprentice. Once in a while I'd catch myself looking at my hands with concern. The visible traces of the transformation I was undergoing . . . Maybe my mirror was lying to me, but my face seemed to be changing too. I was becoming a wild animal. My legs, armpits, groin, and eyebrows were all forests in their own right. I considered the possibility that I would never bathe again. Never *be able* to bathe again. I wasn't about to go leaping from rooftop to rooftop in the direction of the bathhouse. I hadn't gone to the park to become filthy, but rather to cleanse myself. Even though I was physically dirty, spiritually I was purer than ever.

I had remained quite well hidden for a very long time, but I wasn't sure how long I'd be able to keep it up. The managers at the hotel were on high alert. Since it was inconceivable to them that a young woman could be living in the treetops in the park, they were on the lookout for your run-of-the-mill type of robbery. That suspicion drove them to cut off all access to the top of the wall. But hadn't anyone ever run the risk of trying to clamber up the trees? Why the lack of allure? Why had only I and the baron with his perch seriously entertained the notion, going so far as to put it into practice? Were we the strange ones, or were you? Had the world been unable to come to terms with us, or had we been unable to come to terms with it?

Neither my telephone nor my social media accounts held any attraction for me anymore. I'd grown accustomed to a life of being on my own, waiting, tarrying, looking around, sleeping, waking up, doing nothing, and scratching myself—yes, even scratching had become a pastime. I didn't dream of food or fancy drinks. It had been easy to turn my back on the world. But I knew that if Yunus didn't come back, it could prove to be difficult. At least for a while. But then I would get used to his absence too.

I asked myself if I would weep and grieve if Yunus didn't come back.

The only activity into which I threw myself wholeheartedly was keeping track of the days. Whether ten years had passed or a hundred,

I wanted to be able to tell Yunus precisely how much time had gone by. I knew I could do it. Time seemed to be the key. It seemed that through time I could assimilate to the trees. I would become one of them, and for hundreds of years I would stand rooted among their ranks. Who knows—perhaps when we die, that is the fate awaiting us! We become soil and, driven by the wind, go where we ultimately are destined to be.

One day, I hung upside down from one of the trees like a bat. The next day, I ate some rather strange-looking fruit growing on another tree, but I didn't get sick, not even a stomachache. I frequented the chestnut trees. Thanks to them, I could stuff myself to the gills. I knew that over time I'd be saved from a life of hiding myself away in that corner of the park. Just as I'd struck upon the idea of gathering up chestnuts for later, I'd figure out how to bind the whole park to myself so that its entirety would become my domain. Since I had no intention whatsoever of descending from the trees, they could call in the fire department anytime they wanted, but it wouldn't make any difference. What ladder could reach me? Would a fireman even dare approach? If they shot me with a tranquilizer dart like they do to animals, I'd probably fall to my death, and they'd be responsible. What would they say to my mother then? "Well, she shouldn't have been up there at the top of that tree"? I wasn't alone. At least not yet.

Of course, I was trying to console myself by saying such things.

In these lands, only evil and tyranny are embraced, while goodness and beauty are buried the instant they arise, and all the while, intolerance flourishes.

I began to wonder if, over time, people would start coming to the park to see me, just as they would flock to see a strange bird. Would they respect my presence in the park and my desire to stay there? Could the equality, fraternity, and freedom you can't find in the world below exist up in the treetops?

I focused my gaze on the branches and leaves, and I think I stayed that way for a fairly long time.

Yunus finally showed up.

I whispered the date to myself: "On October 9, 2015, a Friday, Yunus came back."

But this time, he didn't come along the branches of the trees.

They had blocked off all the access points to the top of the wall.

I reached out for my red rope.

He motioned for me to stop. "I can't go up there," he said. "But you can come down here."

The red strap dangled and coiled in the gap between us like a snake.

If I could choose a time in which to be stuck for the rest of my life, it would have to be one of my birthday parties, when we celebrated with karaoke. Even my mother had fun that night. As if she wanted to create the crowning moment of the night, she sang Britney's "(Hit Me) Baby One More Time." That's it! We could pursue our desires, forget, and live—if we were given a second chance.

But it was my aunt whose performance set the party on fire. In tribute to my grandma, she sang, "You Wanna Be Americano," shaking her hips and narrowing her eyes like Sophia Loren.

While speaking American, how do you know if someone loves you? While making love in the moonlight . . .

My aunt, who had graduated from the Italian High School, then went on to sing Nina Zilli's "50 Mila." I've never really understood how such melancholy lyrics can be rendered in such an upbeat way. Perhaps it's the nature of the Italian language. A bit like ours in that sense. Even its sorrow is sanguine. And just like one of the lines from the song, I didn't want Yunus to see me fall.

While the red of that strap swinging in the empty space between me and Yunus may have reminded me of the red cable of the microphone that no one wanted to share at that unforgettably wild karaoke party, I wasn't even really there.

I was here.

34

It's Over

As usual, Yunus was wearing his blue jacket and a pair of jeans. Under his jacket he had on a bright-green T-shirt. His shoes looked new, and his backpack, which was nice but obviously a knockoff, was slung over his shoulder. He looked more clean-cut and healthier compared with the days when he was wearing his hotel uniform. Maybe that was because he wasn't in the tree but beneath it, on the ground where he belonged. I don't know. I'd seen him wearing his regular clothes before, but somehow this time was different.

He was clean shaven, which made the scars on his face stand out more, and his hair seemed a bit shorter than before. Wondrous scents were rising from him all the way up to my nostrils: lavender, cinnamon, lemon, tea. Even though he was insisting yet again that I descend from my tree, it was so good to see him that I couldn't help but smile. And not just any smile—a huge grin spread across my face. Like that developer of ours, I may have been flashing all thirty-two of my teeth.

"I'm not joking around. All of the paths that once led me to you have been blocked off."

As I looked down at him, my hair came undone and part of it fell over my face.

"You look so beautiful from here . . ." It was Yunus who said that.

"And you from here."

"That's just how it seems to you."

He pulled a long envelope out of his jacket pocket.

"What do you think I've got in here?"

As he answered his own question, he waved the envelope in my direction. "Train tickets."

"To where?"

"You're coming with me."

He held up a plastic bag I hadn't noticed in his other hand.

"Look, I even got you some new shoes."

"Why?"

"Because you're coming with me, that's why."

"Where are we going?"

"We're going to get on the train and go."

"If we're going by train, why did you buy shoes? It's not like we'll be walking . . ."

This time it was Yunus's turn to grin.

The day's last rays of light were skimming across the ground. The day was dying. A few of those weakening beams of light were shining directly into his eyes, which was why one of them was squinted shut. And when he did that, his jaw also went slightly askew. As he stood there under the tree, he tried to escape from the sun's last light, but his efforts were in vain, so he gave up trying to resist. His face, illuminated by the setting sun, looked even more beautiful and handsome, awry as he looked up at me against the incoming light. Handsome: that was how I'd always thought of him. Can someone be so beautiful at heart and so physically attractive as well?

"What are you thinking about?"

"You."

Was it a lie? As you are my witness, all my thoughts were of him.

"Come. It's time to come down now."

"Yunus, why don't you believe me when I say that I'm not going to come down? Do you think I'm doing this out of sheer obstinacy and nothing else? Is that how it looks from down there? Can't you see that, like a corpse, I've shed all my desires?"

Sullenly, he turned his face away, and now the side of his head and his ear were the target of the cinnamon-red light. He quickly glanced around, afraid that we'd get caught. Afraid that I'd get caught, that someone would realize I was up there . . .

"Have you solved those problems you were dealing with?"

"Those things don't matter anymore. As soon as you solve one problem, another one comes along. No one's looking out for us. We're all alone."

"True, but what makes you say that just now?"

"On my way here, a TV reporter was stopping young men to ask them about the kinds of problems they're facing in their lives. A few young guys—obviously addicted to huffing paint thinner—grabbed the microphone, and they said those things. They explained it all better than anyone else. They got straight to the point."

"Did the reporter ask you any questions?"

"He came running up to me."

"What did you do?"

"Basically told him to fuck off."

"Why?"

"Because, before the paint-thinner guys got hold of the microphone, a decent-looking young man was angrily saying things like, 'What we want is freedom, to be treated with respect, and for this tyranny to come to an end.' The reporter pulled away the microphone and said, 'Look, if you've got something nice to say, we'll air it.'"

Yunus acted out the reporter cutting off the young man dedicated to freedom, being very even-tempered and cool. He even pretended he was holding a microphone: "'Look, I'm warning you. Otherwise, what you say will just get cut out during editing anyways.' I don't get it . . . Is this a land of giants or a land of dwarves?"

Suddenly he stopped, seeming to realize that it would be best to change the subject, as he was on the tipping point.

"But that's not what I came here to talk to you about. That shouldn't be what we're talking about at all. Look, I brought some shoes for you. Come down from there, and go with me. Our tickets are ready."

"Where's the train going?"

"To Ankara. There's going to be a march for peace."

"You go."

He may not have even heard me. Hoping I could somehow flee from his insistence, I'd already stood up and started pacing from branch to branch. I heard Yunus heave a sigh of dismay. Even from high up in the tree, I could see from the corner of my eye his sadness and disappointment as his dream crumbled. He put the train tickets back in his pocket, but he seemed unsure of what to do with the bag containing the shoes.

"The train will arrive in Ankara on Saturday morning," he said, "and the march will start in front of the train station." After a pause, he added, "Lower the rope a bit more, and I'll tie the bag to the end so you can pull it up."

"I don't need shoes. But thanks."

He sighed again. After setting the bag down, he turned and started walking away. He was leaving. I thought about the possibility that I would never see him again. The last rays of light were following his lean silhouette, or maybe it just seemed like that to me. If there was light, it existed through our desire. I hadn't died yet. I wasn't as passionless as a corpse. That had been a lie.

I stopped on the strongest branch of the tree, my toes practically digging into the bark, and stood there, watching my lover walk away. My love was leaving.

I called out to him, "Hey, young man!"

He turned around and looked at me, probably buoyed by the hope that I would go with him after all. But I said, "You don't even know my name!"

"The Girl in the Tree," he said. "You are the Girl in the Tree . . . That girl I love so much. That girl whose story I know better than my own."

He raised one hand and waved goodbye.

Goodbye, Girl in the Tree. Goodbye.

Goodbye, trees, wall, stork's nest.

You might be thinking, "Well, you didn't even tell *us* your name." Very well, so that there aren't any hurt feelings and no one is wronged: sit tight. I'm calling out to you, just as I called out to Yunus.

"My name is Deniz!"

There, is that better? For whatever it's worth, if that's anything at all.

"My name is Deniz!"

The more brazen who have slipped into your ranks, the finicky and fussy, the naysayers, the rapacious, may ask, "What about that middle name your grandma gave you, the rare one? Are you going to tell us what that one is?"

To them I'd say, "But now you're breaking my heart." As you can see, I'm sad and tears are welling up in my eyes.

When I called out to Yunus for the second time, telling him my name, he turned around again, holding up his hand as if a bird had landed on it but was still flapping its wings.

"Don't ever forget me," I said as I watched him walk away.

But in fact he was the one who mustn't be forgotten, and he was leaving. He was about to disappear from sight.

In the last light of the dying day, he was about to disappear from sight.

Goodbye, my friend.

Farewell, my love.

I will never forget you.

Because people never forget those they love.

September 2015–August 2016
Istanbul

ABOUT THE AUTHOR

Photo © Manuel Citak

Şebnem İşigüzel was born in 1973. Her first book, *Hanene ay doğacak* (*The Future Looks Bright*), won the prestigious Yunus Nadi Literature Award for published collections of short stories in 1993. She has gone on to write eight novels and two more short story collections. *The Girl in the Tree*, published in Turkey in 2016, is her first novel to be translated into English.

ABOUT THE TRANSLATOR

Photo © Berker Berki

Mark David Wyers completed his BA in literature at the University of Tampa and his MA in Turkish studies at the University of Arizona. From 2008 to 2013 he was the director of the academic writing center at Kadir Has University in Istanbul, during which time he drew upon his master's thesis to write a historical book-length study titled *"Wicked" Istanbul: The Regulation of Prostitution in the Early Turkish Republic*. He has since dedicated himself to working on translations of Turkish novels, published examples of which include *Boundless Solitude* by Selim İleri, *The King of Taksim Square* by Emrah Serbes, *The Pasha of Cuisine* by Saygın Ersin, and *The Peace Machine* by Özgür Mumcu. His translations of Turkish short stories have been published in a number of anthologies and journals.